More Praise for *The Persistence of Memory*

"*The Persistence of Memory* is a richly imagined novel of growing up, its political revelations leavened by absurdist humor and social satire. . . . Like *Candide*, this novel records the natural shocks of a good-hearted youth as he learns the way of the world. . . . *The Persistence of Memory* is a magnanimous introduction to a South Africa we haven't quite encountered before. It's not a long novel, but it's a big one."

—Frances Taliaferro, *Washington Post Book World*

"*The Persistence of Memory* is a mixture of indictment, therapy and confession . . . this is a humane, rich and very personal book. . . . Eprile, himself a South African now living in the United States, has written a novel that is not just clever but also a passionate fictional attempt to wake from a nightmare of historical complicity." —Theo Tait, *New York Times*

"Charged with a shining imagination, *The Persistence of Memory* is reflective of everything it meets up with, at once capacious and finely honed. Think Laurence Sterne meets Proust meets the antic, dissembling spirit of Stanley Elkin. It's part bricolage, part lyric paean to the passage of childhood, part bitter yet nonmoralistic indictment of a country—South Africa—steeped in horror and exploitation yet also a country like any other. . . . This is an unforgettable book."

—Daphne Merkin, *Los Angeles Times Book Review*

"With the end of apartheid in South Africa, many in the West have forgotten the abuses of the former regimes. In *The Persistence of Memory*, Tony Eprile eloquently asserts the necessity of remembering."

—Victoria Brownworth, *Baltimore Sun*

"A stunning bit of writing: its prose is at once lyrical, haunted and yet sturdy enough to carry a world on its back. . . . *The Persistence of Mem-*

ory makes a singular contribution to the Jewish literature of memory, for it is the memory not of oppression, but of moral ambiguity, of being on the white side of a system of racial contempt and exclusion and finding opportunity in a police state. It is, if you like, one man's personal Truth and Reconciliation Commission." —Mark Shechner, *Forward*

"*The Persistence of Memory* . . . adds an intelligent voice to the chorus of young writers wanting to contribute their memory to the developing South African reality. . . . [*The Persistence of Memory*] has an arresting beauty and naivete which will accord it a place in the new generation of literature about the rainbow nation." —Jackie Stein, *Jerusalem Post*

"A testament to the assured performance of a skilful writer, who is appreciably aware of the fallacies behind any narrated history and, more importantly, of their creative possibilities." —*Times Literary Supplement*

"A South African novel of tremendous emotion and accomplishment, *The Persistence of Memory* is haunting, elegant, utterly memorable. Rarely are the psychological incidents of life brought to readers with such cinematic vividness. . . . Tony Eprile is a treasure." —Howard Norman, author of *The Bird Artist* and *My Famous Evening*

"In *The Persistence of Memory*, Tony Eprile turns the recent vexed history of his native South Africa into a novel of scintillating power. From first page to last, I was enthralled by his gorgeous prose, his genius for transforming pain into art, and, not least, by the fiercely comic gifts of his unforgettable, and unforgetting, narrator. This is an important novel and an immensely pleasurable one."
—Margot Livesey, author of *Eva Moves the Furniture*

"Eerie, biting, fabulistic, this unusual novel conveys as few others have done the sheer strangeness of apartheid and its endlessly corrosive effects." —Andrea Barrett

Also by Tony Eprile

Temporary Sojourner & Other South African Stories

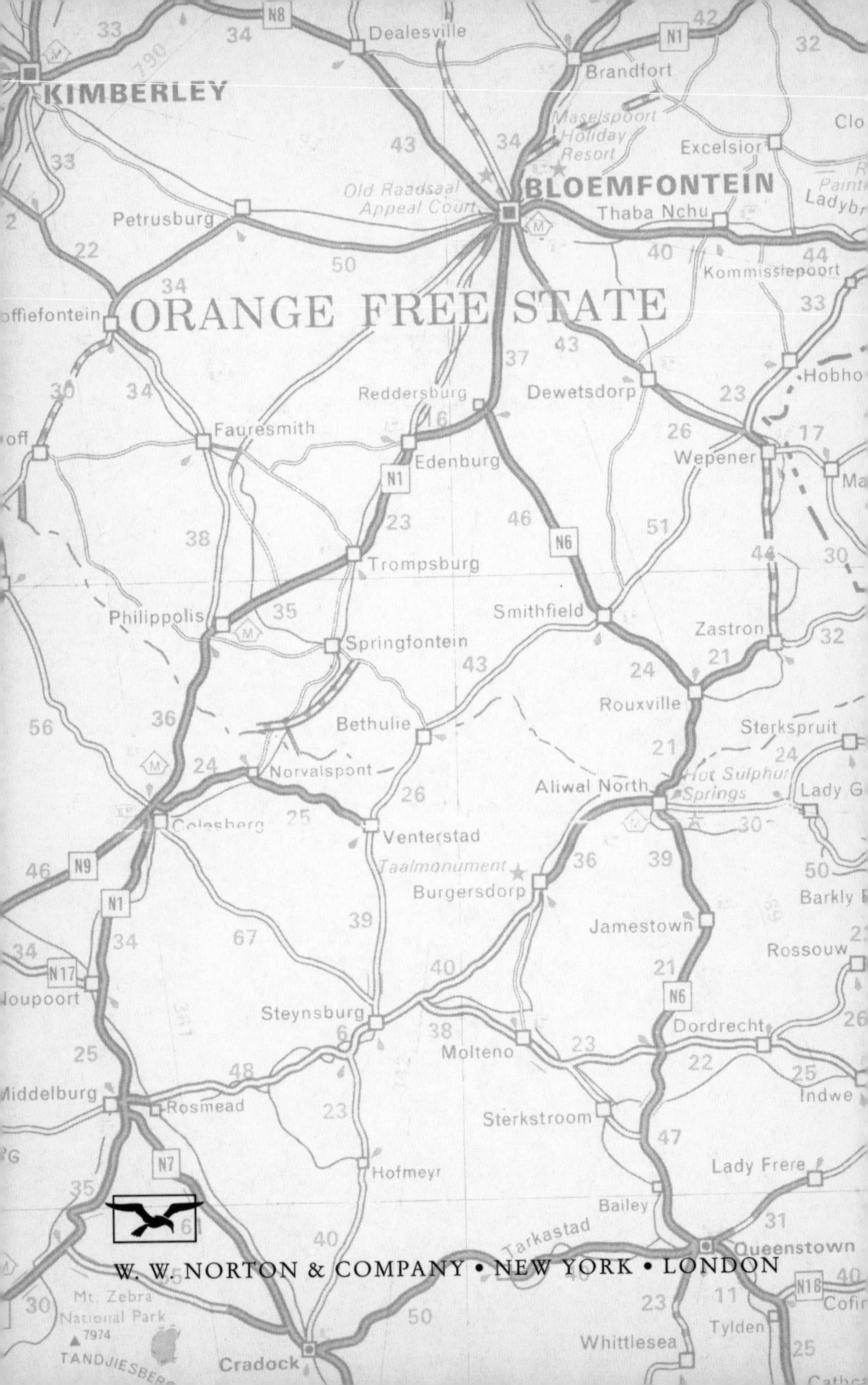

W. W. NORTON & COMPANY • NEW YORK • LONDON

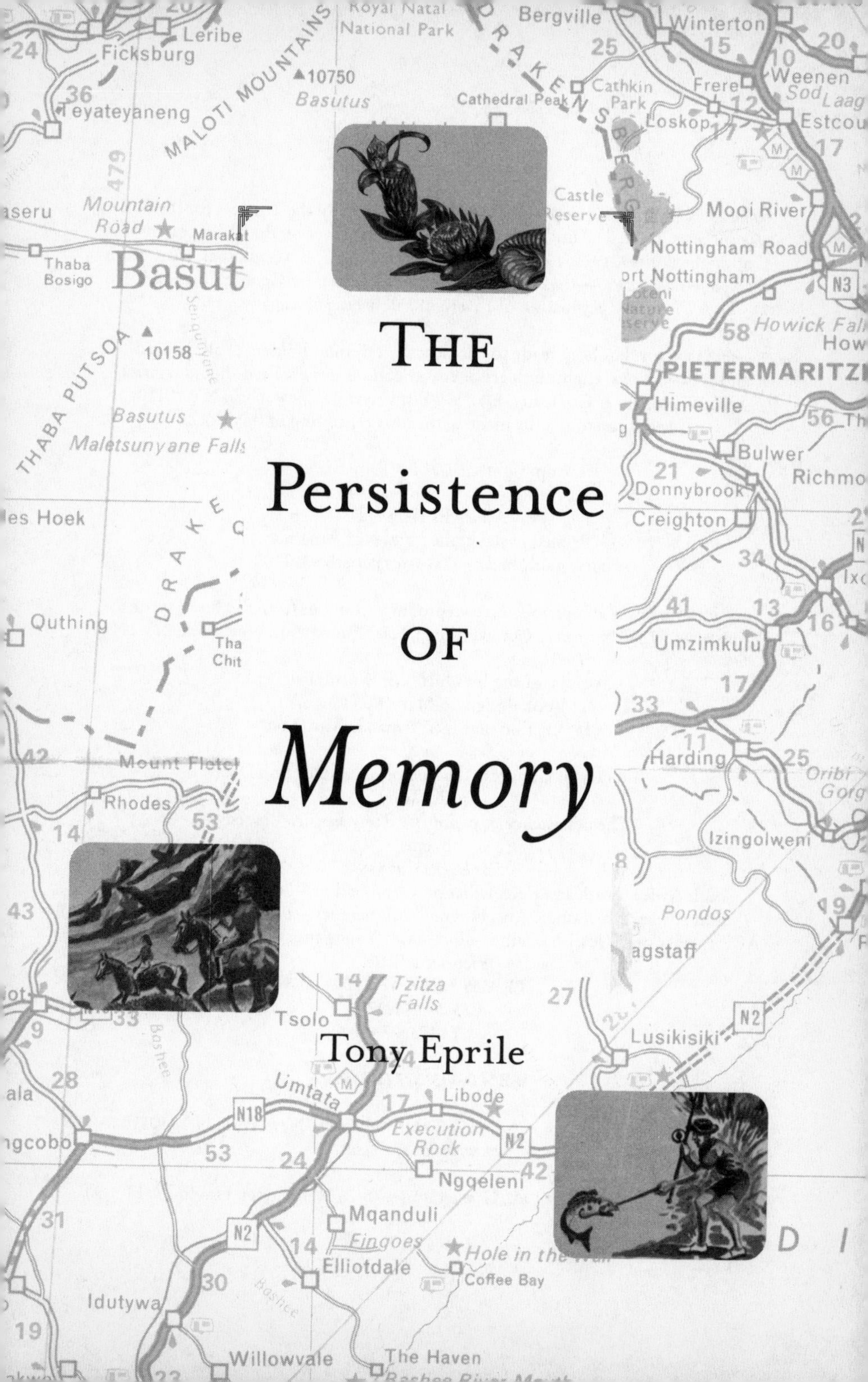
THE
Persistence
OF
Memory
Tony Eprile

Printed in the United States of America
First published as a Norton paperback 2005

Manufacturing by Quebecor World, Fairfield
Book design by Mary McDonnell
Production manager: Amanda Morrison

Library of Congress Cataloging-in-Publication Data
Eprile, Tony.
The persistence of memory / Tony Eprile.—1st ed
p. cm.
ISBN 0-393-05888-3
1. South Africa. Truth and Reconciliation Commission—Fiction. 2. Johannesburg (South Africa)—Fiction. 3. Autobiographical memory—Fiction. 4. Jews—South Africa—Fiction. 5. Jewish families—Fiction. 6. Young men—Fiction. 7. Memory—Fiction. I. Title.
PR9369.3.E67P47 2004
823'.94—dc22
200403627

ISBN 0-393-32722-1 pbk.

W. W. Norton & Company, Inc., 500 Fifth Avenue, New York, N.Y. 10110
www.wwnorton.com

W. W. Norton & Company Ltd., Castle House, 75/76 Wells Street, London W1T 3QT

1 2 3 4 5 6 7 8 9 0

For Cecil Lionel Eprile (1914–1993)

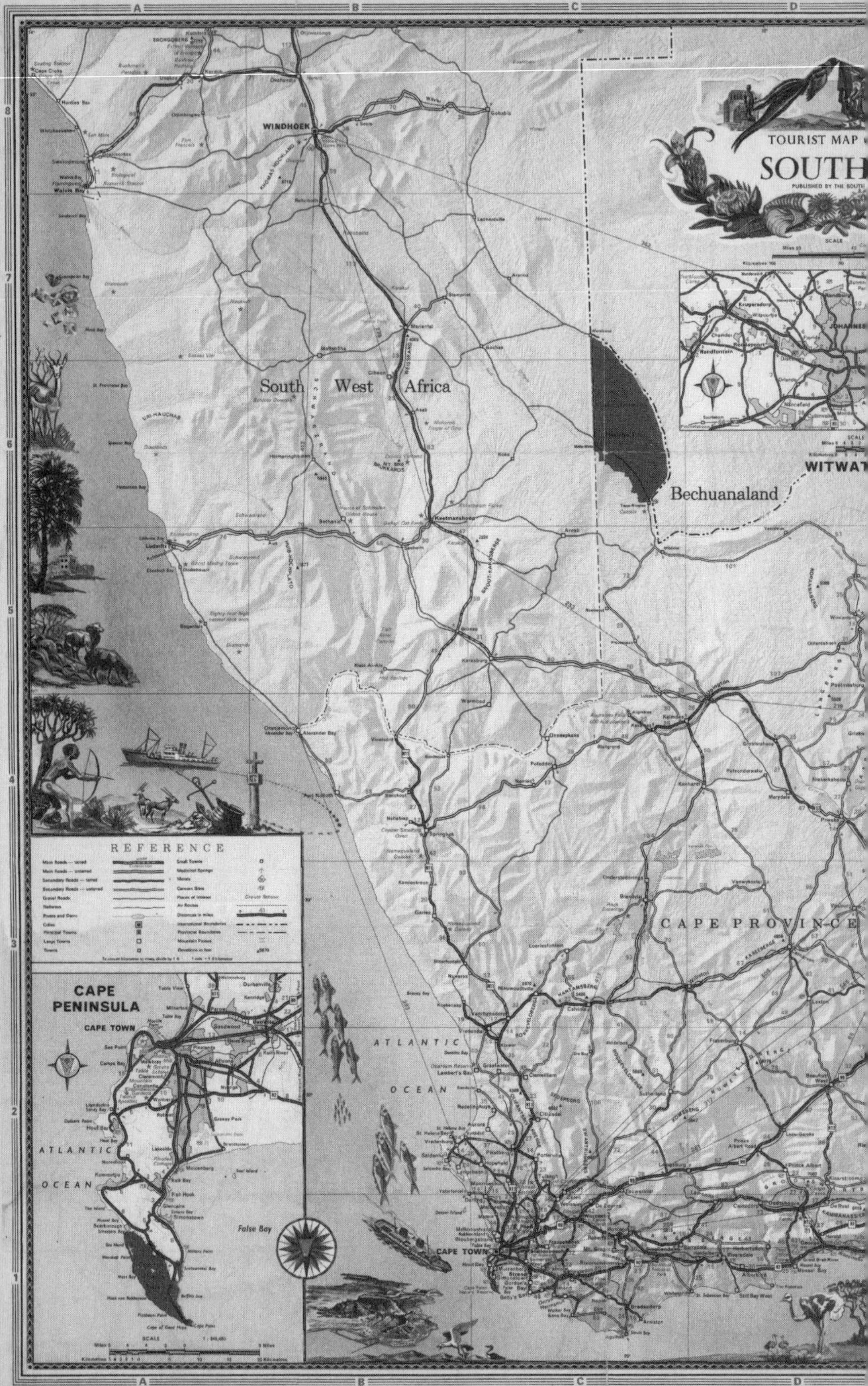

TOURIST MAP
SOUTH
South West Africa
WINDHOEK
Walvis Bay
Keetmanshoop
Bechuanaland
WITWAT
CAPE PROVINCE
Alexander Bay
ATLANTIC
OCEAN
CAPE TOWN
REFERENCE
Main Roads — tarred
Main Roads — untarred
Secondary Roads — tarred
Secondary Roads — untarred
Gravel Roads
Railways
Pools and Dams
Cities
Principal Towns
Large Towns
Towns
Small Towns
Medicinal Springs
Mines
Caravan Sites
Places of Interest
Air Routes
Distances in miles
International Boundaries
Provincial Boundaries
Mountain Passes
Elevations in feet
CAPE
PENINSULA
CAPE TOWN
ATLANTIC
OCEAN
False Bay

Bechuanaland
Rhodesia
Moçambique
TRANSVAAL
PRETORIA
JOHANNESBURG
GERMISTON
LOURENCO MARQUES
Swaziland
KIMBERLEY
BLOEMFONTEIN
ORANGE FREE STATE
Basutoland
NATAL
PIETERMARITZBURG
DURBAN
EAST LONDON
GRAHAMSTOWN
PORT ELIZABETH
INDIAN
OCEAN
NATAL
SOUTH COAST

BOOK ONE

The Present

1968 – 1987

how fortunate are you and i, whose home
is timelessness:

E. E. Cummings

It was Miss Tompkins who helped me put a name to the toxin lurking in my being. "After the war," Miss Tompkins told our class, her precise English voice nipping off each word like a milliner biting the ends of stray cotton thread, "the Red Cross, to whom I was attached, sent packages of food and small household items to the German D.P.s—displaced persons, Helen. Don't look so ignorant, girl, we discussed this last week.

"The problem was that the packages were labeled 'Gift,' and no one in England bothered to realize that in the German language, *Gift* means poison . . . that's right, it is similar in Afrikaans. So there were these poor, starving people . . . European women and children with bloated bellies like malnourished Africans in Pondoland . . . and rotting away in unopened packages were good British sausages, and scones, and biscuits."

Miss Tompkins—who had a habit of repeating herself, as well as of digressing to chide an inattentive child here and there—told us this story at least once every term. Sometimes the gift packages contained sides of beef or smoked hams or squares of Cheshire cheese, Devonshire clotted cream and Yorkshire pudding, the Red Cross's largesse metamorphosing into longed-for British fare not readily available to Miss Tompkins in benighted South Africa. Her lament seemed directed more at the wasted food than at the sad fate of the Deepies, hollow-eyed specters who pursued me unceasingly on those nights I could not sleep.

Miss Tompkins spoke to us often of World War II, heralding the start of her reminiscence with one of two phrases: "During the Blitz . . ." or "Before the war . . ." For a time, Nigel Bloomstein and I would amuse ourselves by keeping tally of these talismanic opening gambits, comparing our scores after class. And once, Jeremy Goldberg, the class play-the-fool, piped up: "Was this the Boer War, miss?" earning himself one hundred lines to be written after school. Having etched in the assigned sentence—"I would not have survived the Blitz, due to the fact that I lack moral fibre"—over and over again one long afternoon, he must have come to believe it expressed a fundamental truth about himself, for afterward he lost his characteristic shine of humor and developed into a serious, somewhat melancholy scholar.

Miss Tompkins never had to resort to such drastic means to garner my rapt attention, for I knew from early on just how much I owed her for whatever ability I had to make my way through a perplexing and hostile world. It was not, as you might think, simply that she provided me with the revelation that my God- or gene-given natural endowment, a picture-perfect memory, was really itself a poisoned gift—botulin puffing out the sides of baked bean tins, salmonella swarming in the bangers and mash. As early as nursery school, I had sensed the danger of drawing attention to oneself as an oddity. There can be no more horrifying sight than a crowd of four-year-olds jeering at their fellow cherub who has just soiled his trousers (Lucas Escott, midmorning break, May 12, 1972). A nervous boy with army-style short-back-and-sides haircut, nystagmic eyes that did not visibly have a point of focus . . . he became known as "Estcourt Sausages" following this incident, the name a reference to a pork-processing town on the main road to Durban famous for its sausages and penetrating reek of the abattoir. This is precisely the problem with having a power of recall that is not only accurate but empathetic, for at the mere mention of the word "Estcourt," a lumpy stickiness invades the base of my legs, a brown sewer smell rises over the characteristic milk-and-rodent odor of the "Little Green School." Although the hushed giggles and behind-the-palm whispers of my gentle schoolmates were directed elsewhere at the time, in retrospection they are for my benefit. This is the only distortion my memory allows: I have become their freak.

That I have a somatic response to such images can have its uses, though. This in spite of years of being plagued by sympathetic responses to thoughts I would have preferred to avoid. You know the mind-control game: Don't think of a white bear! Of course, it's hard not to do so. Now try it this way: Don't think of a white bear. Don't think of being torn to shreds by a white bear. Don't feel its savage claws raking deep welts in your thighs and back. Don't feel yourself being devoured piecemeal by a twelve-foot white bear—hand, wrist, radius, ulna.

But every cloud has its lining . . . or, as Fanie du Preez, who was determined to uphold his Afrikaner honor in a classful of Jewish boys, liked to declare: even the blackest kaffir has white teeth. When the time comes for me to stand in for my army physical, which will not be too long from now, I have the perfect reminiscence in store. That is, if I decide not to go ahead and "show what sort of stuff I'm really made of." I'm thinking of the day that Mr. Coetzee's Standard III class discussed *Lord of the Flies*— dangerous reading material for such a tender impressionable age, and more than a few parents blamed Mr. C's poor judgment for what followed next. Had you happened to be driving by my primary school on a certain morning in the year 1976, you would have witnessed Cameron Kramer fleeing in terror from a bloodlusting mob armed with orange-wood stakes pulled up from the headmaster's prize rose garden. Roll down your windows and you can hear the gleeful yelling: "Kill the Pig! Drink his blood. Kill the Pig! Drink his blood."

It was only a matter of chance that I had ducked a moment or two earlier into a toilet stall to savor a chocolate-covered Turkish delight undisturbed. Cammie was the other fat boy, outclassing me by several layers of adipose tissue. I had seen him eat, as part of his lunch, not only the edible caseinate portion of a small wheel of sweetmilk cheese but its waxy rind as well. I had told myself that this was what made him fat, that I could keep my own corporeal self within normal bounds if I did not eat the rinds of cheeses. I was mistaken, of course. Such fine distinctions were quite beyond the rude boys from Standard III; one fatty was as good as another when it came to the exuberant joy of poking with sticks, the pleasures of righteous violence (it was surely a *mitzvah* to destroy Beelzebub's representative, no matter how weak and vulnerable he might be), and the hypnotic cadences—"Kill the Pig! Drink his blood!"—wiping away any stray thought of mercy.

It should have been me that day who was reduced to a blubbery mass rolling on the red dirt playground, howling in terror as the mob grew increasingly clamorous—"Kill the Pig! Drink his blood!"—rescued finally by Assistant Headmaster Duncan ("Old Mister Drunken") and walked hiccoughing tears to the school nurse's office. I felt Cammie Kramer's pain that day, witnessed from the barred windows of the boys' bathroom as I clutched and moaned inside the stall, and when I undressed at home after school, there were sympathy welts all over my body. I need only reenter that stall on that distant sunny spring day in primary school to cause my AV node to misfire all over the place and have my heart go pronking in my chest like an alarmed springbok, while patches of hives appear on my skin in eidetic verisimilitude. Even as I write this, it is happening. It is just as well that I now know how to interrupt the process by envisioning Dr. Vishinski's magic slate erasing each horrific picture. Thank you, my analyst and friend.

I am chasing the butterflies of memory, as the good Dr. Vish would say. See him now, his jet-black eyebrows like curved scimitars quivering in thought, his square chin resting on fingertips unconsciously joined to make a steeple—open it up, and here's the people. How like me to get sidetracked from telling the story of Miss Tompkins and why two years under her tutelage seem one pleasant passing day. Perhaps I have come to imitate her own art of the looping digression in my thinking, a way of bypassing the linear certitudes that have turned my schoolmates into either bigoted automatons or strident Trotskyists. Actually, I think it's her undisguised contempt for this country that tickled me: a freak always recognizes a freak.

In truth, she was disdainful of all things not English; Americans were a favorite subject of scorn. South Africa, closer to hand, received the sort of offhand drubbing with which an epicure would respond to Colonel Sanders' finest dinner offering. I enjoyed, particularly, her deflating estimation of such peculiarities as our national holidays. Let us consider Dingaan's Day, the annual celebration of the Battle of Blood River, which underwent a name change to the Day of the Covenant (appositely mispronounced the "Day of the Government" by much of the country's population). The Zulus, Miss Tompkins would point out, were really quite civilized in their way of conducting warfare. You stood around, drummed your feet on the earth, beat on your rawhide shield with your spear, and let out bloodcurdling shrieks. After a while, any sensible enemy would lose their nerve and run home, sending you propitiatory gifts in the hope you would not keep on scaring the living daylights out of them. Far, far better than the worldwide slaughter of this terrible century, wouldn't you say? Unfortunately for the innocent and incorruptibly orthodox natives, the stupid settlers ignored the rules and barricaded themselves behind their ox wagons, to fire shot after accurate shot into the performers of what must have been one of the great "mine-dances" of all time.

"If we must celebrate the slaughter of inadequately armed Africans, I suppose we must," Miss Tompkins would sigh. "Although I should think that we could find more seemly occasions to commemorate."

What pleasure I took in her clipped tones and precise language! The way she tried to stamp out Transvaalisms from our English—*niks ops*, for when we didn't want to share a treat (the devil's definition of greed was saying *niks ops* while eating your own snot); *lekker'sit*, for things we really liked; *alies*, for marbles. "*Kaffir*," she would say, "is nothing more than the Arab word for someone not of the Muslim faith. That makes all of us in this room 'kaffirs.'" This was further cause for complaints at PTA meetings: not only is Miss Tompkins' teaching unorthodox, she insults the children.

I like to picture her saying these very words, striding in front of the blackboard on her long bony legs, smoke curling upward from the Rothman's King Size clutched with finishing-school finesse between her middle and third fingers. She looked like nothing so much as one of the cancer sticks she chain-smoked, with her bluish black and silver-streaked hair like strands of combed-out steel wool smoldering on top of her head in a bouffant upsweep; a straight, slim figure favoring white slacks, a slash of bright red lipstick constantly reinventing her almost lipless mouth. It's a truism that we in this country come to resemble our vices: Uncle Yitzhak, that self-avowed rarity the Jewish drunkard, a *schicker*, with his round jolly figure like a bottle of Van der Hum; Miss Tompkins burning to ash in front of a class of nine-year-olds; Mother and me feasting on *vetkoeke* and *koeksisters*, as we grow side by side more larded and doughlike.

We resemble our vices and our pets, but never our servants. If the mistress of the house is lean, then in the kitchen you will be sure to find an *ousie* of mammoth girth. It is like Dorian Gray in protoplasm; when I was an infant, Mother was slim and fair and played tennis daily, leaving me to be rocked in the arms of vast, dark Miriam, an infinite expanse of warm flesh for a baby to love. Then, when I was three, Mother fell pregnant again, ballooning out as if she daily inhaled helium but did not expel it, her mood bungee-jumping from joy to fury. Placid Miriam soon moved on to other pastures, displacing an equal volume of absence in my childish heart. She was replaced by Corinthia, with a figure like Zola Budd's. Although she remained with us for six years, Corinthia invariably treated me with polite distance spilling, when her guard was down, into open contempt, and I developed no love for her. *My* feelings were not the issue here.

The embers of Miss Tompkins' cigarettes glow yet in my memory, unerased. Her husky voice . . . the smoker's rusty larynx lending a breathy, bedroom quality to the utterances of this spinster. The way she valiantly attempted two or three times a year to discourage us from taking up her own weakness: She would puff a cloud of cigarette smoke through a white linen handkerchief (embroidered "L.R.T." in red on the right corner), then proudly display the resulting ashen smudge like some Rorschach blot from the rachitic land of the hopelessly addicted. Did she know that I catalogued each variance in her tales? How six months before, the American soldier who had rudely told her to "Step on it!" (by which he meant she should get a move on) when she volunteered at the Red Cross canteen was long and thin like James Stewart, and in this latest telling he is overfed with a belly hanging over his belt, in stark contrast to the wiry British soldiers who slogged through Burmese jungles on a diet of roots, grubs, and rancid bully beef? But she always got the ending right: "More fool you," the American replied when she told him she was not *paid* to serve him sandwiches but *volunteered* for the benefit of her country. Did she know I loved her for her quixotic enterprise, this sere, thorny woman trying to instill a sense of history into ignorant South African schoolchildren who wanted no part of it?

I am sitting at my desk two down from the door; the name "Anne" has been etched into the yellow wood with the point of a compass, but not by me. Miss Tompkins' high heels click on the wood floor, in her left hand the usual Rothman's King Size, in her right a bamboo pointer. "Those who cannot remember history are doomed to repeat it," she rasps. I look around at my peers . . . at Colin Goldberg's freckled face, Sedgewick Schwartz's fresh-scrubbed one, at Ophelia Birnbaum's blank gaze. *So what?* all the faces say. They have no objection to repeating their parents' histories: to be a lawyer or chartered financial accountant like Dad, to play tennis and attend afternoon teas like Mum. History, memory, is plastic here in the R.S.A. You remember it the way you would have wanted it to be, not the way it was.

...

I was in Miss Tompkins' class for Standards I and II, or from the ages of seven to nine. I had hoped that my next teacher would be Mr. Coetzee, who was known for quoting the Romantic poets and for his remarkably loud sneezes. A tall, white-haired, white-bearded man, Mr. Coetzee loved cricket and on practice days he wore his cricket whites throughout the school day—a vision of whiteness strolling across our retinas as if he had already been translated to the Elysian Cricket Fields. When the jacarandas bloomed all along King Arthur Street, competing with the headmaster's beloved ivy geraniums, mimosas, Zimbabwe creeper, and exotic bunchgrasses to scent and pollinate the air, our afternoon quiet would be shattered by Mr. Coetzee's allergic detonations, followed moments later by a foghorn honk as he blew his nose on a clean white handkerchief the size, so the children who were his pupils claimed, of a small tablecloth.

Alas, I was assigned instead to red-haired Mrs. Sanders, a widow in her forties with sun-baked, leathery skin and a cat's green eyes beneath slanted eyebrows. She was as russet as Mr. Coetzee was white, with her lacquered hair piled on top of her head like a Zulu hut aflame, her heavily rouged cheeks, and her favored red-leather boots. The boys from the Hebrew Orphanage called her "Rooibos," not after the redbush herbal tea (*Aspalathus linearis*) that she drank at eleven o'clock break, but because they meant something rude by it. For two years she made my life a misery. In part, it's because she suspected me of cheating. (I had grown careless of revealing my talents with Miss Tompkins, who was silently pleased by them.) Mrs. Sanders liked to give surprise exams: Describe Jan van Riebeeck's arrival at the Cape, children.

Easy enough . . . in my mind, I flipped back to the week before when, sitting on the brick wall at playtime, I read that page. I could feel the warmth of the rough bricks through my thin shorts, and all I had to do was read off the page exactly as I saw it. "On April 7, 1652, a small party of Dutchmen led by Jan van Riebeeck came ashore at Table Bay. Their purpose: to set up a refreshment station for the ships of the great Dutch East India Company. . . ."

After I had scored one hundred marks on the first exam, Mrs. Sanders came and stood behind me the next time she gave us a surprise test. It was harder to recall what I needed (mainly because I hate people reading over my shoulder), but as soon as she moved away I was able to do so and quickly fill in the missing part. When I got only sixty percent on this test although all my answers matched what she had written on the blackboard, I went up to her to point out the discrepancy. She raised one auburn, painted eyebrow sarcastically and purred: "How do *you* know where I get my marks?"

...

It is midsummer, a warm night. I am outside in our enclosed garden reading our first national poet, Pringle—"The freeborn Kosa still doth hold/ The fields his fathers held of old;/ With club and spear, in jocund ranks . . ."—with the remaining quarter of a deep-dish lemon curd pie resting at my elbow, when he appears. I have borrowed a tall standing lamp from the living room and powered it with an extension cord thrown carelessly atop the slasto still damp from watered houseplants. He is perched halfway up the wooden newel that decorates the brass stem of the standing lamp, his pale yellow body visibly contrasting with the dark wood. I reach under the sheet of muslin that protects the pie from marauding insects and take a comforting nibble of crust.

"Dad?" I say, my voice croaking in the stillness.

The praying mantis turns its triangular head in my direction, eyes me inquisitively. Well, it sounds stupid now, but it could have been him. It had the same angular face and elongated limbs, the same skeptical expression, though Dad always wore glasses. I had never seen a mantis like this one, and have not seen one like it since. About twelve inches long, pale yellow instead of the usual green, it moved with deliberation up the lamp stem, only turning occasionally to nod in my direction in that familiar vaguely friendly way. I eat more lemon curd pie, turn back to Pringle, try to forget the apparition. There is a buzzing sound, one of those beetles we called "brown bombers" as kids (I have never bothered to look up its real name). Mother has long since given up going outside on warm nights because of the brown bombers, which careen around in clangorous flight crashing into any hapless object in their path. The last time Mother stepped out-of-doors in the evening, it was right into the erratic flight path of a beetle that became noisily enmeshed in her sprayed, bouffant hairdo. She tripped and stumbled across the slasto on her six-inch heels, slapping at her head in horror, until finally collapsing in fear and exhaustion on the chaise-longue, which creaked in an ominous fashion but did not give way under her bulk. This gave me the chance to use the tweezers from my trusty Swiss army knife to extricate the vigorously protesting creature from the jungle reaches of her lacquered thatch.

Now one of the bombers is living up to its name, repeatedly crashing into the standing lamp's glowing bulb. It settles finally in a state of mild concussion on the lamp stem to regain energy for a new assault. Its thorny back legs dangle like the limbs of a drunken swimmer, and a bit of cellophane underwing protrudes sloppily from beneath the shiny carapace. In its woebegone preoccupation, the unfortunate brute does not see the mantis swivel its long body elegantly and raise hooked forearms in a boxer's stance. I am expecting the strike, but it comes so swiftly I barely see it. The mantis turns back in my direction, raises the burring, protesting snack to its mouth in a friendly toast, and begins to feed with a loud rustling. I break off more pie and watch him eat. Crumbs drop onto my lap; a detached brown wing spirals downward. *Why, Dad? Why did you do it?* I want to ask, but self-consciousness stops me. What am I doing here, the voice of reason asks, talking to an insect in the middle of the night? The mantis's pale yellow abdomen pulses in near-sexual pleasure at its meal. I cram lemon curd into my mouth. We absorb what we can catch; we wax, and grow fat.

...

Where do I get my marks? I am soon in trouble again with old Rooibos. It is a couple of weeks after our history lesson on Van Riebeeck's landing, and the refreshment station comes up again as a topic. We are now doing the Hottentots; Rooibos tells us they're called that because everything they say sounds like "hot en tot" to the arriving Dutch. Miss

Tompkins told us last year that this term was racialistic and prejudiced, that we should talk instead about the *Khoikhoi*, a term that simply meant "the people," *die Volk*, in their language. Rooibos tells us that the Hottentot language had seventeen clicks, the present-day Xhosa only five,* and then she tries to click the word Hottentot, spraying Danny Mainzer with saliva and starting up a near-riot of spitting and galloping horse noises in the classroom. I am reading ahead in our textbook and soon have my hand up. "Yes, Gogga?" she sighs. (She has her nicknames for most of the kids in the class, nicknames based on our parents' professions. Sedgewick Schwartz's father owns a chain of liquor stores, so he is known as Mister Bottle. Larry Snipworth is Judge, Deon Jones is Bricks, Nigel Capeland is Settee, Fanie DuPreez, whose dad works at the post office, is Parcel, Anne Greensward is Flute (more obscure, her mother caters weddings), and I, horribly, am Gogga.

"Miss, it says in the book that three years after Van Riebeeck's arrival the Hottentots attacked the seventy families, killing a baby and running off with a herd of fat-tailed sheep."

"Yes, I can read too. So what is your question?"

"How did the baby get there?"

There is general laughter at this. Rooibos plays it to the hilt: "The usual way, of course."

"No, no. What I mean is . . . the families, the baby. How is that possible? There were ninety men set on shore, and the book says that the Dutch East India Company didn't allow anyone else to land, that they didn't want to build a colony, just to have a temporary refreshment station. So how did these babies get there?"

There is a silence while this question sinks in. Rooibos chews her lip, then she tears a sheet of paper out of the nearest child's notebook and walks off to her desk, where she sits writing something down. She folds

* Like every South African "fact," this figure is subject to dispute. *Rosenthal's Encyclopedia* agrees with Rooibos, but contemporary linguists recognize as many as eighteen Xhosa clicks. An African-languages lecturer at Wits tells me that older, rural Xhosa-speakers use more elaborate clicks than do the young and the city-dwellers.

the paper in half, then in half again. We are all used to these deliberate gestures of hers; they spell no good for whatever child has attracted her ire. She looks at me kindly—always a scary sign—and says, "Now, Gogga, you can do me a little favor and deliver this message to Mr. Duncan. The rest of you, open your history books to page seventy-four and answer the questions you will find at the bottom of the page."

I go to take the note, but when I grasp it she does not let go and we stand in this intimate way for a moment, as if we are indulging in a secret handshake. "I suggest you make up those same questions for your homework tonight. Study them well. They will help you know what is the right sort of thing to ask."

I have already looked at these questions; the first one asks: "Why was a refreshment station needed at the Cape of Good Hope?" I might have asked, needed by whom? Not the Hottentots, that's for sure. But I am in trouble enough already.

I walk as slowly as I can past the other Standard III classrooms, down the flower-bordered pathway to the separate building where the headmaster and the assistant headmaster hold court. I know that dragging my feet only delays the inevitable. Long before any of us meet Rosencrantz and Guildenstern, every colonial schoolboy knows that the note you are asked to bear contains within it the seeds of your own doom. I am tempted to unfold the piece of paper and read it; unlike some of the other teachers, Mrs. Sanders does not tape her notes closed . . . but there is a rumor that she folds them in some intricate way that will reveal if any foolish child has breached protocol and read a message not intended for him. Danny Mainzer claims that he had taken a quick peek at the note he was carrying, and old Burnside the headmaster knew immediately and doubled his punishment.

Mr. Duncan's door is closed. It is an enormous door, its surface unbroken except by a small plaque way above my head. I crane my neck and read its notice: "Jhs. Duncan, Assistant Headmaster." Jesus? Johannesburgs? I can't think what the abbreviation could be, perhaps a title of some kind. Your Highness? And there it is, reminding me of Dad's joke about why the Taiwanese like us (the Chinese don't, and in the R.S.A. the Chinese are considered Asian and the Taiwanese white). You see, our ambassador to Taiwan was named Johannes Prinsloo, and members of his entourage referred to him either as Johannes—pronounced in the Afrikaans way as Yo-*high*-ness—or Prinsloo. The Taiwanese were very happy that we'd sent them a member of our nobility to serve as consul.

Ah, well. No more putting it off. I knock timidly. A gruff voice bids me "Come in" in Afrikaans. I enter a dark office which smells of instant coffee and stale cigarette smoke, my feet falling softly on a thick russet carpet. Mr. Duncan sits writing something at an enormous oak desk, not bothering to look at me. (It's possible he does not see me, dwarfed as I am by the expanse of his broad desk.) Behind him is a bookshelf with leather volumes in orderly procession on the wooden shelves, flanked by a watercolor painting. It is one of Burnside's pieces: a white vase filled with pink and blue hydrangeas. Perfectly rendered, and perfectly lifeless.

After a while, Mr. Duncan extends his hand, still not looking up from his papers. I place Rooibos Sanders' message in his plump palm and step back again. He scrutinizes the note and then looks at me in silent inspection. He is a very large, jowly man with thinning brown hair. In shaving, he has nicked the tops off pimples on either side of his jaw, each one denoting its presence by a dot of darkened dried blood. I feel the pain of each lopped-off whitehead. And then a voice rumbles from the middle of the large man: "I see. You have been rude and impertinent to your teacher. A *lady* teacher, no less. How do you explain yourself?"

"I only asked a question," I say, half in tears.

"A *rrrude* and impertinent question, I understand," Mr. Duncan growls.

"No, *meneer*. I asked about the refreshment station—"

He is holding up his thick index finger in warning. "No. I will not interfere. If Mrs. Sanders, a respected teacher, says you have been rude, then that is good enough for me. Anything else you have to say?"

"No, sir."

"Good. Turn around. You know the drill."

I have not hitherto been sent before either the head or his assistant, but I have heard from others what the procedure is. Girls must flip the back of their uniform skirts up but keep on their underpants, boys must take down both pants and underwear once their backs are turned. In the moment before I turn around, my eyes are drawn to the corner where several different sticks lean against the wall: a stout walking stick, a standard flat wooden ruler, several lengths of bamboo. The story is that Mr. Duncan has never hit someone with the walking stick, that if he did it would surely break that person's back. "You would be a cripple for life," Danny Mainzer had relayed to a rapt audience. "And you'd have to have a special servant to collect your pee in a bottle."

I hear Mr. Duncan shuffling around in the corner, then start trudging toward me. I hope it is not the cudgel; surely my offense is not so bad that I should spend my life in a wheelchair for it? "Hands on your knees," Mr. Duncan says quietly. His plump, soft hand touches me gently on the back of my head, pushing me an inch or two lower. There is an airy swish, and I have the briefest of moments to rejoice that it is not the cudgel before the bamboo cane lays a line of fire across my buttocks. I clutch my knees tightly, trying to breathe while tears pour unbidden from my clenched eyelids.

"Don't move," the voice says. There is no anger in it. "You will get a total of three, since this is your first offense."

Another swish. The pain is worse this time, and I find myself hopping around, roaring in agony. The hand touches me on the back of my head again, and, like an automaton or some primitive bowing to an idol, I bend myself down again. The cane rattles in the air and the last blow seems to hit me simultaneously in three different places. There is a piercing shriek ringing in my ears. Not mine, surely? Strangely, breathing is what hurts the most, my breaths coming in ragged sobs. The shadowed room seems filled with flashes of light. In one of them, I see Mr. Duncan examining a length of bamboo that has split into three and hear him muttering, "That's funny. Never happened before." I pull up my undies and gray short trousers and thread the belt. Such simple gestures, I've done them a thousand times before, 486 times, to be precise, but how different they seem now.

"All right, off you go, Sweetbread. Try to behave more politely around your elders," Mr. Duncan grumbles, looking at me strangely through his thick glasses, the left lens of which bears a thumbprint visible from where I stand. He resembles a large, poisonous toad that has just gulped down a slender mayfly, a meal that was not to its satisfaction. Everything is very sharp to me right now, and I wonder what does he see, this large man who has just been so calmly and deliberately violent to me? A small, plump boy struggling with a belt buckle? His duty discharged?

I am hyperventilating by the time I return to the classroom, and with each step my trousers stick to my buttocks. I knock and am bade to come in. Rooibos smiles sarcastically at me, then bites her lip and motions me toward my seat. The lesson is on geography, the origins of sugar cane in Natal. "The Indians were brought in by the British, as they were excellent cane cutters." She unrolls a map that shows the four provinces, says no not that map, then unrolls another of the Natal coast and the Indian Ocean. There is a picture on the left-hand side of a Zulu rickshaw driver in fancy feathered headdress, on the right of an Indian "coolie" bending low with a panga in his hand, the other hand clutching a stalk of cane. He bends low and slashes the cane, bends and slashes the cane. I hear a voice telling Missy Hoffman, our class prefect, that Paul looks unwell and should be helped to the nurse's office. Missy, a tall freckled girl whose favorite activity is netball, offers me her hand, which is surprisingly rough and callused. I say thank you, miss, to the teacher and my schoolmate leads me out of the room and back along the corridor, past the girls' bathrooms to the building that holds the library and the nurse's office. The headmaster's bright red poppies bow mockingly to me from their bordered flower bed. My body goes along obediently, my mind sees the Indian slashing his way through a jungle of cane stalks, his arms scratched by the sharp edges of the leaves, his sandaled feet and bare legs vulnerable to the brown mambas and large-fanged spiders that lurk amid the cane. "Backbreaking work," the book called it; backbreaking work.

Mrs. Worthington, the nurse, is in her early sixties, a round woman with white wool straying from under her kerchief. Her hands smell of Dettol, and she has a pleasant voice like a meadowlark. She helps me to lie down on the cot, then gently lowers my trousers, easing away the cotton underpants that pull at my slashes, reawakening them. "I've seen worse," she says cheerfully. "I'll put a little zinc ointment on them, Paul, and you'll be much happier."

Mrs. W. was a WAAF nurse during the war, and Miss Tompkins had invited her to talk about her experiences to our class. "Burns were the worst thing," she had told us. She notices my rapid breathing and comes back from her cabinet of supplies with both the ointment tube and a balloon that she tells me to slowly inflate. Doing this brings my breathing back to normal, and occupies my attention while she smoothes the cream professionally over my backside.

"Would you like to go home early? I'll call your mommy and see if she's able to pick you up."

After a while I hear Mother's heels along the corridor and then her gentle voice. "How are you, my love?" The usually cloying smell of her scented powder is comforting. A pause, and then she tells me she'll be right back and afterward we'll go home for a nice rest. I can tell she's hopping mad.

"Where is the brute who did this?" she demands of Mrs. Worthington before storming off to Mr. Duncan's office. Soon I hear her high-pitched shouts drifting through the window with the morning sunshine. Mother is in good voice, and the whole school can hear her reproving the assistant headmaster for his viciousness. When she returns, she tells the nurse: "I said he should come and take a good look at his handiwork but he declined, the coward. Said that discipline has to be kept. I told him I'd show him discipline if he ever dared to touch my child again, a great ox like him hitting a small boy. Imagine!"

That afternoon I enjoyed my mother's pampering, the special tea she made for me with ladyfingers topped with whipped cream and strawberry jam. The treat was ostensibly to take away the bitter taste of the

Aspro she gave me for the pain, but she had already ground up the little white tablets with sugar and dissolved them in a tablespoon of water. I started to worry that her actions would further enhance my reputation as a namby-pamby, the weak impala in the herd.

Physical punishment was a common feature of our lives . . . nothing Dickensian, just the odd clout here, the smack with the ruler there. Some of the teachers had their own signature methods: Headmaster Burnside would make a chap put his head under the wooden desk when he smacked him on the behind with a ruler. If the boy jerked at being hit (we were supposed to be tough), he would get a lump on the head as well as a sore bum. Rooibos Sanders added humiliation to her blows: she would draw a red line for each smack on a square of paper and pin that to the child's shirt. You had to wear your "stripes" all day, or be corrected again.

Sometimes the punishment fitted the crime, as happened with an otherwise mild-mannered substitute teacher during the height of our peashooter wars. These took place between two other fads—"spud" guns, which used compressed air to fire pieces of potato, and yo-yos. We had all recently gotten new banana-yellow Bic pens, and it hadn't taken long for one of the boys to discover that the ballpoint and ink reservoir could be quickly yanked out with one's teeth and you had a made-to-order blowgun. We also inadvertently discovered that if you sucked on the back of the pen, the ink would slide upward, so it was a time of blue lips as well. We all became adept at biting off a corner of paper, chewing it into a tight wad, then a quick chomp down, pull, shoot, slide the ballpoint back in place, and you're once more an innocent writing notes in your notebook.

The substitute, a slim and pretty young woman with smooth, unblemished skin and blond hair, Miss Lyons, caught on that if you turned quickly after the telltale *pffft*! you could catch the perpetrator, who usually had the evidence of his guilt in the form of torn notebook corners. But there was one brilliant sniper who could not be caught. His shooting was silent and deadly accurate—even Danny Mainzer, the reigning champion, was unmercifully stung at unpredictable moments, finally going off to the nurse after he got hit in the corner of the eye while turning to whisper something to his friend Roger ("Dodger") Stone. None of us knew the shooter's identity, and we took to calling him "The Phantom," amid hot debate that it might even be a girl, one or two of whom had joined in the sport. I eventually figured out that it was Cammie Kramer, for the angle of shooting suggested that the sniper sat among the swots, and I couldn't imagine it being the ever-perfect Missy Hoffman or demure Anne Greensward. Cammie had burned his hand soldering parts of his model train set, and the burn had gotten infected. He had his left hand in a bandage and a sling to protect the injury. I saw him raise this bandage-wrapped hand slowly to his lips and then Dodger Stone did a little jump in his seat, rubbing his neck ruefully afterward. (The Phantom, like one or two others, had taken to shooting barley seeds . . . which stung more than chewed paper). And, of course, no one would notice Cammie Kramer putting something in his mouth, as he was always eating, whether in class or not. He'd gotten very bold, though. Each time Miss Lyons turned her back on us to write on the blackboard, there would be the audible ping of tiny missiles bouncing inches away from her hand. Her normally placid and amiable face began to look strained, her eyes darting anxiously around the room, and her right cheek developed a nervous twitch.

The barley was his downfall. One morning, Miss Lyons was distributing our previous day's arithmetic test around the room when she stopped next to him and he sneezed, unexpectedly. Perhaps it was her perfume; she wore a lot of it, and Cammie was allergic to all kinds of things that were not food. When he sneezed, a couple of tiny seeds of barley landed on the back of Missy's dark gray jersey, a background that made them clearly visible.

"What's in your hand?" Miss Lyons demanded icily.

Cammie opened his right hand—a regular, click-type ballpoint with the name of his father's motorcar company emblazoned on the side. Clever. He began to explain that he liked to eat barley, and he might have gotten away with it if Missy had not drawn attention to the tip of a Bic protruding from beneath his bandage. Miss Lyons had reminded me of one of the heroines in *How the West Was Won*, but now her face was pinched and spiteful with anger, a ferret about to bite off the head of a fat rat. She grabbed Cammie by the ear and hauled him to the front of the class, though he weighed easily as much as she did. She told him to hold out his hands, both of them.

"But my left hand is infected, miss," Cammie whined. "It hasn't healed yet."

"You should have thought of that earlier! Both hands, now!"

Three sharp raps on the right palm, then three sharp raps on the bandaged left, and the sniveling Cammie was sent back to his seat. The peashooting wars stopped, and Miss Lyons went back to the business of being the likable, attractive young substitute.

I need not have worried about the consequences of my mother's visit to the assistant headmaster's office. My schoolfellows were impressed that anyone had stood up to the intimidating Mr. Duncan. That my mother's voice had carried to every ear in the school redounded to my credit. When I walked by some Standard IV boys during lunch break, one of them (Jannie Smit, our school's second-best fast bowler) said to me: "Yirrah. Your ma really told off that fat bugger, hey?"

Mother eventually comes around to being angry with me too. It takes about a week before she asks me what I had done to get punished. When I tell her, she responds: "Well, you shouldn't ask stupid questions. Really. You sometimes behave just like your father."

This seems a serious offense, as she rarely mentions the existence of any paternal progenitor for me . . . the unspoken myth being that I spontaneously generated inside her uterus. Her comment does give me an idea, for there is a blue book on Father's shelves with the words *Jan Van Riebeeck*, *Leipoldt*, and *Longmans* written in gold on its spine.

It had not occurred to me that someone would have written a biography of Van Riebeeck, although that does seem foolish in retrospect: after all, he was in charge of the first white enterprise on the southern tip of the African continent, the Dutch East India Company's refreshment station for their ships bound for the spice islands. He was in that pantheon of great white forefathers, including Vasco da Gama and Oom Paul Kruger. More surprising is that the biography of the great man is written by my favorite cookbook author.

I find it makes for somewhat tedious reading, although the opening line is not bad: *When William the Silent, wounded to death by the bullets of Belthasar Gerard, fell back in to the arms of his sister, he had ample reason for his passionate supplication, "Lord, take pity on this poor people."* There is much tiresome detail about the Lords Seventeen and the provisioning of the ships *Dromedary*, *Heron*, and *Good Hope*, although I'm intrigued by the later description of the tenderness of rock-conies (the little hyraxes we now call *dassies*) when prepared in the correct manner. I do find what I want, though: confirmation that our schoolbook's numbers are haphazard at best. It's a little hard to tell how many men originally came ashore, since some left with the ships that sailed on, but at one point there were 116 men, 6 women, and 12 children. There is also the curious mention of the nuptials in May 1655 "between Jan Wouters and Catherine of Bengal, the first marriage between a white man and a coloured woman." The book explains that the first settlers followed the custom of other Dutch colonies—like that in Batavia—where intermarriage was perfectly fine and the children of such marriages were considered European. The same children were non-European if the parents did not "solemnise" the union.

...

Corinthia had high Eurasian cheekbones and skin the color of planed cedar, and I wondered if this was what Catherine of Bengal or her daughters had looked like. Her attractive features were marred by a hardened and resentful expression. In a different time and place, she might have been a clothing model or the glamorous owner of her own catering company; here she was just another coloured servant in the Jewish northern suburbs of Johannesburg. She truly was an excellent cook; that was the one thing I did like about her. She had worked for a caterer at one time, I think, and she made pastries that were unsurpassable.

"My girl makes the most marvelous pastries," Mother told Mrs. Wissle, offering her another petits fours, while I dragged my jeep on a string between the legs of the furniture. She also made mille-feuilles—a laborious process of separating layers of thin dough—and more traditional offerings like *melkterte* and *vetkoeke*. I used to sit on the kitchen chair—it folded to form a stepladder—and watch her intently, memorizing every move, the number of teaspoonfuls of sugar added to the flour, the way she sliced the lemon zest into thin slivers. Even then I knew that she would not be with us forever, that sometime she would be going away, taking her wonderful desserts with her and whatever other precious goods she could lay her hands on.

"What you want, you cockroach?" she would suddenly turn on me in fury, catching me observing her. "Go outside and play like a real boy." I think she disliked me as much as I disliked her. Or perhaps I just made her uncomfortable.

"I'll tell on my dad that you called me a bad word."

She smiled at this poor excuse for a threat. "Yebo, you tell your dad." She knew better than me. While she was with us, the kitchen smelled of wonderful baking odors, underlain by a subtler, sweet-scented perfume . . . some kin to essence of sandalwood. It was a captivating odor, and when my father came home he would find some excuse to step into the kitchen, where he would stand still, inhaling deeply, the surprisingly wide nostrils in his aquiline nose flaring in appreciation. Mother's reaction was in stark contrast; walking into the kitchen in search of a praedormitory snack, she would fling open the corrugated window behind the sink, muttering: "My whole house smells like Sophiatown."

...

IT IS MY VERY first visit to Dr. Vishinski and already I know that his steeple-making gesture will become horribly familiar to me. In an effort to fight against this knowledge—which has the inexorable quality of gravity's pull as you release your handgrip on a water slide—I act stubborn and obtuse. "So, what am I supposed to talk to you about?"

"Anything you want."

"Anything? Like shoes? Shall I just talk to you about shoes?" I ask sarcastically. But already my mind is producing images of all the shoes I have known, from my earliest baby slippers that hang now from the ornate finial atop the dresser mirror in my mother's room, to Mother's pink stiletto high heels, the source, I suspect, of her continuing lower-back pain.

"Is there a particular pair of shoes you would like to talk about?" Dr. Vishinski inquires in a friendly, neutral voice. Damn him. He has, I find out in the course of successive sessions like this one, an uncanny knack of focusing on just what I want obliterated. For there, hovering like foxfire at the outermost corners of my vision, are the pale leather soles of an expensive pair of hand-stitched brogans glimpsed dangling luminously in the crepuscular recesses of the maid's quarters by a frightened child who is doing his best to hide behind his mother's ample hips. There are suddenly men in uniform everywhere, and I am swept away by strong arms to the comforting familiarity of the kitchen chair, while somewhere a woman's voice screeches horribly without cease. Conspicuous by its abrupt cessation is the mechanical thumping of one of Dad's company's power compressors. That was why the van was backed up in the driveway in place of the Mercedes. I should have immediately recognized the choking-termite logo, the peppery odor of industrial-grade pesticide.

...

ALTHOUGH MOST OF THE traces of Father's presence began to disappear from the Sweetbread house soon after his demise, Mother had a superstitious reverence for books, and his extensive library remained for years virtually untouched except for the occasional caress with a large yellow feather duster. On hot and sultry days when Mother was usually upstairs lying on her bed with a "megrim" headache, I liked to stand in the cool hush of the library, taking out here and there a cloth- or leather-covered volume and examining its contents, then putting it back and taking another. I often returned to that red, leatherbound Juta edition of *Pringle's Life and Poems*—the one that had brought about Mantis Dad's visitation. (I'm now quite sure it was a real visit from the other side, and not a delusion or what our new G.P., an adenoidal fellow whose own adolescence was still vivid and recent, liked to call "sugar intoxication.") I was attracted by its well-handled surface buffed by the natural oils in Father's fingers and by the overly ornate fleur-de-lis escutcheon on the front cover.

It's funny, all those books from earlier in the century are emblazoned with fascia: Everyman, whose pictograph has acquired new life telling pedestrians when it is safe to cross the street; Warne's *Illustrated Encyclopedia of Southern Africa* with its leaping springbok, as if an encyclopedia that opens with a page of Voortrekker flags (Natalia, Stellaland, Goshen, *die Vierkleur*) and a line drawing of *abaKweta* dancers could be mistaken by anyone for the *Britannica*; Kipling's *Stalky and Co.*, whose swastika is the right way around; and the first edition of Paton's *Phalarope* with its miscegenating doves in flight. Readers of the time added their own *ex libris* labels, spreading the horse-hoof mucilage with a boar's-hair brush onto the backs of the labels and then carefully gumming them into the inside cover, little thinking that fifty years later the glue will have dried into varnish where it has not added variety to the diet of the ancient little arthropods (*Lepisma saccharina*) we call silverfish. Father, an expert in all things insect, knew better than to paint an attractant onto something you wished to preserve . . . so I can easily tell his books apart from his mother's in the dark.

Pringle—*Thos.* Pringle, as Dad liked to call him—had been favorite reading of my father's, mostly, I suspect, because his mother had read aloud to him from this transplanted nineteenth-century Scottish bard in the few years that she survived her own uprooting and relocation. She had been seasick from the moment their boat left port at Harwich and she had spent most of the voyage in the tiny dank cabin in the lower tier of the ship. Strangely enough, her inability to keep food down continued for months after her first footfall on South Africa's red, dusty earth. Once, when Mother got food poisoning after a fish dinner at Anthony's Seafood Grotto, Dad said the sound of retching recalled his early childhood. My grandmother had begun to enjoy six months of more robust health when she suddenly succumbed to the bite of a banana spider that had stolen a ride on a bunch of fruit she had bought to celebrate Father's sixth birthday. I suspect that Corinthia immediately won Dad's heart when the first sweet she served us was flaming bananas in a butter-rum sauce, the very dish that his mother had not gotten around to completing, having taken to her bed with chills, fever, and a hand swollen up like a rugby ball.

It was at her funeral that Father, to his surprise, had discovered that he knew how to read: "'Come Awa, Come Awa'!" he intoned in a trembling voice at his mother's burial, holding the volume close to his chest with the veneration usually reserved for the Bible, deeply aware that this was a sad travesty of their quotidian nighttime ritual. ("Come awa, come awa/ An' o'er the march wi' me, lassie . . .") He liked to claim that his reading had such an effect on the mourners that a lush bed of Kikuyu grass surrounded his mother's grave for months afterward, the ground having been well soaked that dry afternoon. Before that day, he had always been read *to*, an eclectic fare from Pringle's songs and sonnets to Kipling's *Light That Failed*. When he wandered into a room where Mother and I were each engaged in some business of our own in companionable silence, he would invariably murmur (to our mutual annoyance): "My mother read aloud to me every chance she got." I, personally, have never liked the sentimental side of Pringle, and after the first wonderful chapter Kipling's novel seems to me unreadable.

Dad's parents had the same last names before they married—in fact, their match was arranged by someone with the same surname who may or may not have been related. Although his mother was first-generation Scottish, her father had come from the small Polish/Lithuanian village that my grandfather lived in, a village where the Jewish population all seemed to be named Schwartzbart. Grandfather had traveled to Scotland, a bride waiting for him, although his heart was set on going to South Africa, where another Schwartzbart was said to have struck untold riches selling the feathers of some strange bird. Father, the punning Mantis, liked to say that his parents had a good marriage but otherwise were Poles apart. His mother loved poetry and had ambitions of being a radio announcer ("She had a beautiful voice, like a bell"); she had a refined manner and a delicate constitution. His father was short, broad-shouldered, strong as an Afrikander bull; he never learned English properly, his speech the kind music-hall comedians delight in imitating.

Even Mother, who rarely displays signs of humor—although she insists that she appreciates my jokes—likes to tell Mrs. Wissle about the day the old man said to her: "Cousin Izzy, he got da Voss." "He got the wash? He fetched the washing?" "No, no, no. He gotted da Voss!" "He got the Voss? What is the Voss?" "A *get*! From the rebbe, he gotted a *get*. Gott!"

There is something cruel in this anecdote—not just in making fun of the educational disability of a man I know she never liked,* a man she described as obdurate, hard as nails—but in telling this story of divorce to Mrs. Wissle, whose own husband had abruptly decamped to Durban with his secretary, a woman , it was generally agreed, of consummate ugliness. And sure enough, Mrs. Wissle would sigh: "What he sees in her I cannot imagine. Such an ugly stick of a woman, flat as a board and with that hideous mole on her face!" Mother, having opened the wound, could now set about salving it, offering soothing comments regarding the unfathomable tastes of men in general and furniture salesmen in particular.

Grandfather's rich cousin helped set him up in business by unloading on him a barely functioning ten-year-old Ford and some thirty typewriters, all to be paid back at usurious interest. Fortunately, Grandfather

* Since Grandfather also spoke Russian and Polish fluently, he, in fact, knew more languages than did Mother. I've never understood her pride in not speaking Yiddish . . . although so many people are smug about their monolingualism. For the English, it has always been a mark of higher civilization that they understood neither Afrikaans nor any of the indigenous African languages.

could fix just about any piece of machinery, murmuring the Hebrew prayers thanking G*d for our tubes and orifices while his hands got covered in grease and motor oil. And fortunately Grandmother insisted that farm women did not want typewriters but sharp scissors and pretty gewgaws to brighten the relentless bleakness of their lives. She accordingly packed a box full of buttons and silver thimbles, fancy gold-covered thread, tiny handheld mirrors, and a dozen or so lacquered fans she had somehow acquired from a Chinaman on Fox Street. Grandfather had packed them indulgently in a corner of the back seat and winked at his two-year-old son—his wedding advice, years later, was, *Der Vife is alvays right, even vhen she's wrong*—and set off on a four-month journey deep into the Platteland. Except for his carriage being drawn by a malodorous exhaust-spewing engine and not a broken-down pair of horses, he was the perfect cliché of the *smous*, the itinerant Jewish salesmen of the nineteenth century. You can see photographs of his like in the South African Museum: small broad men in black gabardine, swart, with sharp bony features and aquiline nostrils.

He did not succeed in selling any typewriters, although he did repair one for free that his predecessor had sold, a whole afternoon spent cleaning the gears and springs with petrol, straightening out the long narrow bars of the *t*, the *h*, and the *j*. The knickknacks were a considerable success, and Grandfather survived on their sale and by sharpening all the kitchen knives on the whetstone that he had almost not brought along with him. He came back thinner and with a ferocious addiction to coffee, the only sustenance besides bread that he would accept from his Afrikaner hosts, reasoning that they were not likely to have put pork in the drinking mugs.

Back in Johannesburg, Grandmother indulged her small son, letting him cuddle up to her beneath the soft, goose-down comforter that had been a wedding present from her parents; the Highveld nights were cold and long and there would be plenty of time to get the boy used to sleeping on his own when her husband returned. She read to him from her favorites: Pringle, Burns, Kipling, Dickens, Mad King Lear. I've never read *David Copperfield*, but I know all about Jip, and Mister Murdstone, and Mrs. Gummidge, who is a lone lorn woman and feels it all more than others do, the latter announced in the same gentle brogue that always infected my father's voice when he recited from the memory of his own mother's narration. They struggled financially for years, living in a one-room cinderblock house only a little bigger than our maid's quarters now. Grandmother was thought snooty by her neighbors—at first Litvak Jews, then Afrikaners, then Indians. She did washing (*da voss*) on occasion for her Indian neighbors but did not tell her husband, lest he be ashamed that she was doing kaffir work to make ends meet. She advertised in *Arthur Barlow's Weekly*, offering elocution lessons. Only one person answered, an Afrikaans woman who was marrying an Englishman. She came once, but not again. ("She was hopeless," Dad would say in his mother's voice. "I could not unrrrroll her *r*'s.")

When his father returned, infant Dad was moved back to the cot that took up half the kitchen and which was folded away in the morning so the breakfast table could be put up. It left him with an abiding fury, one his father immediately noticed. "You vant Mummy to yourself? Kom, vee fight for her." He spoke only English to his child, not wanting him to be handicapped with Yiddish. The resulting communication was satisfactory to neither of them. He rolled back his sleeve to bare his corded, muscular forearm and grinned wickedly at his child.

Dad had been in only one "fight" in his life: at the park, when another child took his wheeled duckie away and he'd grabbed back the string. The other boy had bitten him on the hand, holding on until his chuckling nanny forced open his jaws.The little crop-headed boy's tiny pearllike teeth had hurt like hell. His father had wide square teeth set like blocks in his powerful jaws; he liked to tell the story of the Scotsman in an Edinburgh bar who called him a "wee spalpeen" and demanded a fight: ("I trank my schnapps, zen I ate da glass. Vhen I turn around again, he is not dere anymore.") He shook his small head, no. Resentfully, he toddled off to the kitchen, pursued by his father's merry laughter.

My father watched his mother die, wheezing, grossly edemic as if someone had given her an extra epidermis and filled it with a hose. His father had gone off to fetch the doctor, and so was away when the distorted figure on the bed gave a loud snort and then was still. He went back to playing with his duckie, gazing on dispassionately when his father returned with *der Artzt* and flung himself full-length on the corpse, howling, tugging furiously at his long dark sidelocks. Later, the women from the burial society came to spend the night with what had once been his mother. His father would not allow him into the room again, though he caught a glimpse through the slightly open doorway of the women washing his mother's naked body with a cloth and a basin of water. He tried to sleep on his little cot in the kitchen (in exile again!) despite the Hebrew songs and murmured conversations of the Hevreh Kadisher, sallow-skinned women of indeterminate age who smelled as if they had been removed from an airless cupboard for the occasion. Then there was the funeral, his recital of Pringle, and his father's mournful kaddish in a surprisingly mellifluous, deep voice that he had not heard before. Then his father rented out their little house—the Indians next door were happy to uncrowd themselves of the cousins who had taken up lodging in their small house—and he found himself in the passenger seat of the Ford, pressed against a cardboard samples case. The roads were corrugated and pitted with holes, his father drove too fast, bouncing the car over the ruts so it felt to the child as if he were riding in a giant cement mixer, and a steady blast of exhaust fumes leaked into the car from the rusted and road-damaged tailpipes. When singing nursery rhymes and Hebrew songs didn't keep the resultant nausea from erupting, he quickly rolled down the window and hung his head over the side, a spume of vomit trailing the car like Isadora Duncan's scarf. His father grasped the back of his shirt firmly with his left hand and kept on driving, only muttering: "Goot. You didn't mess on de semples."

They slept out on the veld that night—as they would every night for the next three months. His father made dinner by boiling kasha over a little camp stove that ran on methylated spirits. Then he took all the cardboard cases out, forming a barrier around the car, and ran a stout rope through their handles so no wandering herdsman would sneak up and run away with the precious samples during the night. He spread a rough blanket on the ground, rolled up his jacket as a pillow, and bade the boy do the same. The child thought, momentarily, of asking his father to read to him, then thought better of it. He began reciting Pringle's "Autumnal Excursion" in a low voice to lull himself to sleep, then stopped when his father blew his nose noisily into his checked handkerchief and said in a choked voice: "Pleese. You're killink me. . . ."

Father remembered best the enormous dome of the anthracite night sky with its brilliant pinhole stars, the constant flutter and squawk of nightbirds, and the yipping chatter of a jackal. They were up at the first graying of the dawn, well before the giant orange ball of morning, stared at with dull bovine curiosity by a stray cow as his father performed his morning prayers and careful ablutions from a jerrican of water. Their first stop was a rickety farmhouse in the middle of a lonely plain, where two enormous black dogs a full hand higher than the child's head threatened them until called off by the Boerevrou, who served him milky coffee and rusks so hard and dry they hurt your teeth even after being dipped for several minutes in the coffee. His father sharpened scissors, a scythe, several vicious-looking hunting knives, and hammered straight a number of bent forks and spoons. He haggled with the farm mistress over the price of some buttons and thread and a small tarnished mirror in which she could admire her sharp chin with its protuberant wen that bore three long hairs. Together with her enormous now-silent brutes, she watched them leave with eyes filled with suspicion; she had heard those stories of the stranger who came with a smile and wound up owning your farm, banishing you into the wilderness, the Afrikaans farmers' habitual nightmare that so closely echoes what they themselves had done to the indigenous inhabitants of the land.

Next, they drove around to the kraal surrounding the farm, where they bargained over more goods while drinking sour newly malted beer—he noted the oddity that his father would not eat off the plates proffered by the Afrikaans farmers, but he would drink from the communal tin cup passed around by the Bantu headman, wiping his mouth on his sleeve in the local manner. He had no fear of germs, being gifted with a robust constitution, but there was a far worse pollution about in the land: *treyf*! He doubtless recognized that the Bantu were cattle people, not swine owners, for nowhere in evidence were the fat shoats, sows, and boars rooting in the mud of wooden pens, their stink offending his nostrils, that he encountered in the white farms. ("My pa always parked upwind of the pigpen," Father used to say. "Much in life can be borne if you're upwind.")

The bargaining with the African elders was interrupted by a scrawny half-grown rooster exploding into their midst, pursued by a gaggle of laughing children. They left the kraal with some grubby coins unloaded from a grubbier cloth purse and with the rooster dangling upside down, its legs now firmly tied with string made from dried elephant grass. Before putting the bird in the back seat of the car, his father tied a handkerchief over its eyes, an action that calmed it down so it sat quietly in the back like a condemned prisoner resigned to his fate. That evening, his father hung the chicken upside down from a withered kaffir boom near which they had parked, pulled out a small clasp knife from his pants pocket, and cut its throat in the ritual manner. In the gradually darkening dusk, its blood created a black circle in the bare sand beneath the tree. When the bird had finally ceased to fertilize the dusty earth, his father plucked it with brutal swiftness and boiled it for hours over the camp stove, their meals for days to come.

He had not realized how much of their income derived from the African kraals. These were sometimes makeshift huts on the edge of the white farmhouses, rickety structures with rusty corrugated tin roofs. Sometimes they were well-made beehive rondavels, decorated with colored mud and covered with beautifully woven thatch. They visited the kraal of an important chief one day, a man who—his father informed him—had forty wives and over a hundred and fifty children. The kraal did, indeed, seem to be teeming with children. They stood around him, giggling, noses leaking mucus, right ankles hooked around their left legs or squatting on their heels. A tallish, handsome fellow of about eight peered intently at him, smiled, and pronounced his judgment, which sounded something like "*iBunghane*." The other children shrilled with laughter, pointed at him, and called out, "*iBunghane! iBunghane.*" It was all most unpleasant, although later the handsome young leader showed him a prized possession: a bicycle rim that he whipped along with a stick, running as fleet as a gazelle in his bare feet across rocky and thorny ground, never letting the flashing silver hoop fall on its side. The young aristocrat generously offered Father a turn, but he lacked the herd boys' knowledge of applied physics and the hoop was soon inscribing narrower and narrower circles before wobbling over onto its side. The others had laughed, but the chief's son touched him gently, sympathetically, on the arm (the first time he'd been touched by a native!), then this superior being raced off, pursued by his entourage. Father had been left behind, idly scratching his foot in the dust and feeling both ashamed and resentful, until his own dad's business was completed and they departed again.

"I think about that fine chappie sometimes," Father would always say when he came to the end of this story. "I bet you he's someone's garden boy now."

On May 29, 1948, the two of them drove into the sleepy Northern Transvaal town of Louis Trichardt only to find the dorp bustling with activity. The narrow streets were jammed with donkey carts, as well as cars. Burly men walked around in their Sunday-best waistcoats and starched white shirts, their faces beaming beneath their broad-brimmed hats. They smoked pipes and talked in loud, confident voices. The women wore long dresses usually reserved for weddings; they sat on the veranda of the main hotel drinking tea and chattering spiritedly, or strolled on the street holding up their long skirts against the dust. The Afrikaners were mostly, in my grandfather's experience, a dour folk, tempered by Calvinism and suspicion, so he sought to find out what had occasioned this mood of vibrant celebration. The day before, it turned out, the Afrikaner Nationalist Party had won the general election (*general* being a relative term in South Africa). My grandfather's face clouded over: Smuts, the Boer war general, the visionary international statesman, the only human being to be a signatory to the treaties that ended both world wars, had been defeated by a Nazi sympathizer! Those ox-wagon torch-wavers—the pro-Nazi Ossewabrandwag—who had tried to sabotage the war effort were now the government. He insisted that the two of them get out of town as soon as they could, although Father was eager to go and explore the cattle warehouse from which sounds of accordions and fiddles could be heard.

"No," his father had declared. "This place is not for us. Zis is not for us a celebration."

As he drove out of town and up into the hills, he continuously muttered the words, "Terrible, terrible." After a while, he began to talk, explaining first that the small town—but as many people as Louis Trichardt, yes, even more—where he had grown up no longer existed. Nor did his three brothers and five sisters, his cousins, his aunts and uncles, his mother, two grandmothers and one grandfather, all his neighbors, and every one of the Jewish children who had gone to school with him . . . all had perished. Killed by "Gitler," with the help of the Polski, their other neighbors. Beaten with shovels and hoes, shot, stabbed, hanged, "gessed." And this Daniel François Malan, "For him, dat vas just fine. He did not vant South Effrica to fight Gitler. He vould have liked for Gitler to vin!" Things were going to be bad, very bad. For the Jews, who knows how bad? For the kaffirs, terrible!

His predictions were borne out, for in the coming months they could see new prosperity in the dorps and small towns they passed through, as the Nationalist government put into place its policy of providing state jobs for the Afrikaner population. They also saw more shabby and downtrodden rural blacks making their way toward the towns for work, or wandering itinerantly hither and yon after being forced off their smallholdings, treated ever more brutally by farmers whose arrogance had grown with their electoral victory. A glimmer of an idea began to stir in a little boy's mind, how they could share in the pie of prosperity that was now being served in oversized steaming slices to the white population.

Over the next year, he kept track of his idea, noting those observations that fit in with it. First there was the farmwife who told of her cousin who had gotten a job of issuing the natives' passes, the little slips of official paper that determined where they could or could not be, whether they could or could not have a job. It's very hard work, she had said. So much to write down, all those difficult forms! Then, on one of the rare occasions they had stayed in a small lodge in town, he had watched one of the new khaki-wearing bureaucrats struggling with a mess of papers. Finally, he shared his idea with his father.

"Yes," my grandfather said, stroking his chin. "They do need typewriters in all those offices. But vhy vould they buy them from me?"

"Because you will fix them when they break, Papa," his clever eight-year-old son answered. "You don't sell them a typewriter. You let them borrow it, and every so often you come by and fix it or give them another."

The typewriter-leasing program was a success. The government had bought typewriters for the newly installed Native Affairs offices and the various levels of municipal bureaucracy, but the keys had quickly gotten bent, the platen dented, the carriages knocked off kilter, the ribbons overused and rended to tatters that clogged the wheels. The office clerks were eager to sell the government's broken and cast-off machinery to this itinerant Jew for whatever he was willing to pay for the useless objects. These canny country folk delighted in profiting from a stranger's foolishness.

Grandfather oiled and repaired the machines he leased, straightening bent keys, even changing ribbons when he came through. It made his and Father's lives more regulated, since he needed to return to the towns and *stoepdorps* at scheduled intervals to make sure that the bureaucracy was functioning smoothly, typing triplicate forms that "endorsed" the natives with tighter chains, creating marriage certificates and driver's licenses, writing its reports to be sent to Pretoria. He very quickly went through the supply of machines he had for several years been forced to store in a small brick shed attached to the Indians' courtyard at his old house, and he both bought new ones and went around purchasing the damaged and used ones that were gathering dust in people's houses, stores, or government warehouses. He began to prosper, to employ others to fulfill the extra demand for his service contracts. He trained African handymen to dismantle, fix, and put typewriters back together, and he hired Afrikaans-speaking white men to do the chatting while the Africans did the skilled labor.

Although his new vocation kept him more and more to the built-up areas, there was a particular farmhouse that Grandfather went out of his way to continue visiting. It stood on top of a hill overlooking a rolling plain and a broad expanse of *mielies* growing in the sun, a vision of tranquillity that held dominion over its environment. There he liked to sit in companionable silence with the family patriarch, a giant old man with white hair and beard and the glazed near-blind eyes of an old dog. The old man had been a leader of a commando group in the Anglo-Boer War, and his physical power was still palpable despite his crippling arthritis. On one of the visits to the farmhouse, the old man had come outside slowly onto the stoep, his arm supported by his middle-aged granddaughter, who led him to his favorite rocking chair, a massive piece of furniture he had put together himself out of hand-carved stinkwood in his young days. He had positioned himself over the chair and sat down heavily, only to disappear from view with a hoarse shout as the floor beneath the chair collapsed under his considerable weight. Father, now almost eleven, noticed some small pale-bodied insects hurrying about the disintegrated edges of the hole in the stoep. They were termites, carrying their larvae out of harm's way. The seemingly solid floor had been eaten from within.

When their rounds again brought them near the farmhouse a few months later, the granddaughter informed them that the old commando officer had died in his bed a week or two after his fall, never getting over the shock. "This whole house has been white-anted," she declared. "We're building another over there; may the Heavenly Father keep this one from falling on our heads first."

White ants were the scourge of any wooden construction in South Africa: not only the native termites who build those wonderful tall mounds that give character to the landscape, mounds that are their version of high-rise buildings complete with air-conditioning, but the Formosa ants and other imports that came in with the wood the British brought to Southern Africa for their railways along with the Indians when they decided that African trees didn't grow straight enough, South African natives didn't work hard enough. When Grandfather came across a wooden bridge built over the dry sloots that would turn into rushing watercourses at the first rains, he would stop the car and walk all over the bridge, pounding it with a stout stick he kept for that purpose and perhaps for protection as well. If he noticed any faint sprinkling of sawdust drifting down after he pounded the timbers, he would drive however far was needed to find a better crossing. Of course, if the sloot was dry, he would just drive across it at a flatter spot before returning to the roadway. Once, they arrived at such a bridge to find another car suspended midway along the bridge by a supporting spar of wood, its front end having crashed through planks whose hearts had been eaten out, their surfaces still pristine but undermined.

In the mornings too, when they slept out on the veld, Grandfather would carefully shake out their boots before they put them on again. Once in a while, out would tumble a pale yellow or brown scorpion, pretty as a lady's brooch. The little ones with the small pincers in front and the large tails were the dangerous ones; the more menacing larger scorpions with big clawlike pincers gave a sting no worse than a bee, but the *kleintjies* could kill a child.

Father was struck by the number and variety of insects he encountered in his travels through the countryside. He did not yet know the saying of J. B. Haldane, the English evolutionary biologist, that if in fact a heavenly Creator exists, He clearly has "an inordinate fondness for beetles," but Father came to much the same conclusion. There were huge spiders with yellow-striped bodies like inflated cobra heads, giant rhinoceros beetles, tiger beetles with mandibles powerful enough to penetrate human skin, flying ants whispering out of the ground after the rains, fierce red ants that would climb your leg, seize a piece of skin in their jaws, and simultaneously use their tail stingers to inject you with muric acid. There were brown ticks that would climb your bare legs and secrete themselves in the folds of your testicles, where they would happily feed on your blood while injecting bacteria that gave you a high fever. (Yes, these are arachnids like the spiders, and not truly insects, but they're still *nunus*, *goggas*, bugs, or *shekhetsim* . . . the same Yiddish word, interestingly enough, that *shikse* comes from. If you marry out of the faith, you are marrying a bug.) There were myriads of grasshoppers, singing happily from every grassy patch of earth, but these would occasionally congregate for no clear reason and darken the skies, lay waste to the *mielie* fields, and provide a tasty treat for the African children. There were the good insects—good because they ate their harmful fellows—such as the mantids and the giant dragonflies like World War I biplanes, or the tachinid flies that laid their eggs on caterpillars. There were mosquitoes and biting flies, flies that didn't bite but whose larvae did, ferocious bees and aggressive wasps, and twelve-inch stick insects that imitated the smaller branches of trees. There were more varieties of beetle than any one man could catalogue.

It was after the demise of the old commando, the floor pulled out from under him by six-legged prestidigitators, that Father realized his life's work. There was no doubt that people would be glad to pay to be rid of this new land's inexhaustible cornucopia of stinging and chewing creatures. Today the business he started in his early twenties is owned by a corporation, but you can still see the yellow vans skittering around Johannesburg with their motto—"No More Goggas!"—and the rendering of a very human myrmid lying belly-up, one black leg clutching at its throat.

. . .

"Do you think it likely," I ask Dr. Vish during one of our last sessions, "that—assuming for the sake of argument transmigration of souls really is possible—someone who spent his entire adult life killing insects would come back a creepy-crawly himself, a *gogga*?"

"What do you think?"

"I don't know. The only thing I can say is: If there's that kind of justice in the world, we're all in a hell of a lot of trouble."

"Dr. Vish, why do psychiatrists always answer a question with a question?"

"Why do you want to know?"

All right, all right, I'll admit that I never asked that question. (It's actually a joke we used to tell in school about Jews, but psychiatrists will do just as well—they're sort of super-Jews anyway, a mix of science and angst taken to the *n*th degree.) But you get a sense of the frustrating nature of the process, made worse by my being the sort of patient who can replay the whole session over and over again at will. I'm not trying to make out that the treatment was a waste. Once in a while, Dr. Vish would step in and ask a helpful question, and one day he advised me of a surprisingly simple and effective means to get rid of unwanted memories. That morning, he brought in one of those children's erasable slates, the kind where you lift up the wax paper and the impression disappears. With unexpected skill and speed, he drew a representation of a house viewed from the front, with a little pathway leading to its entrance. "Picture this innocent house as being one of those images that trouble you," he told me, then snapped the waxy paper up smartly and handed me what was now a tabula rasa. "You can use your imagination to imprint whatever it is you want to forget on the slate; then just lift up the wax paper. It's as easy as that."

But it was rare for him to answer a question directly. When I pressed him further, he told me he didn't want me to think I could get someone else to find my answers for me.

...

"HE WAS SUCH A considerate man, my Max," Mother is saying to Mrs. Wissle and Auntie Brenda who have come over for tea. "He worried about others' comfort so, much more than his own, and it killed him in the end." She is relating her version of Father's demise to her visitors for the umpteenth time, a story of altruism gone awry that grows more tragic with each telling. Killed while fumigating the maid's desolate quarters, a man so deeply concerned about the comfort of future domestics that he would put his own life in jeopardy to keep a bunch of unwashed natives safe from bedbugs.

It quite gives me hope, Mother's remarkable ability to re-remember the past in a positive light. Oh, sure, the court findings back her up. "Death by misadventure" was the official verdict. What then of the screaming fight a few months before, in the presence of that dour private detective in his shabby safari suit? Phrases float down to me heard from behind bolted doors: "How could you? And with a bloody kaffir. . . ." Even when I write them on the slate and snap the wax paper, they persist like the afterglow on a defeated computer screen. And there was Father's beaten, hangdog expression for months after Corinthia's departure, the icy silence at dinner . . . which Mother served up now at the kitchen table instead of in the dining room, moving around with agonizing slowness while refusing every offer of help, her back problems making of every meal a martyrdom.

"He was so good to the blacks," Mother is saying now, "the boys who worked for Terminex used to come to him with their troubles. Whatever advice he gave, they took it. Of course, they took advantage too . . . borrowing money, asking to be let off to go to funerals for aunts and uncles who'd already been buried a couple of times before. He was too good to them, in fact. But what can you do? It was his nature."

Actually, the funny thing is my father didn't much care for Africans. He spoke to them with that same sense of anticipatory irritation—you just know they're going to make some mistake—that edges into Mother's voice whenever we go shopping. And of course there was Johannes, the butt of everybody's jokes at work. "Johannes fell off the van today,"

Dad would announce at dinner. "Don't worry, he's all right. He landed on his head."

I'd already heard this one at school, so it's probable that Johannes—a rheumy-eyed elderly man with an arthritic posture and an apprehensive grin—did not really fall off the van. On the other hand, there's no need to doubt the story of how Johannes was sent into the sealed house to check the position of the outlet hose and Piet Erasmus turned on the compressor. "The hose it is working too good, Baas Piet, *uuggh-huh-uugghh*." I couldn't help but laugh at Dad's imitation of the coughing and wheezing worker, an odd shameful heat creeping through my insides like the beginnings of an enteric disorder. Somehow Dad caught exactly the look of an enraged man trying to show deferential good humor. My father did not much like the Baas Piets and the other Afrikaans foremen, but for them, at least, he had a fearful respect. Erasmus was a tall, squarely built man with wide shoulders, a roll of fat around his neck, and a Lion lager paunch. Once, when I was waiting for Dad at the warehouse while he picked up some paperwork, Piet Erasmus came in and looked at me coldly, muttering under his breath: "*Daardie gogga het te groot geword*," not aware or not caring that schoolchildren were required to learn Afrikaans even if his Jewish boss was not and might not like to be referred to as a bug that's gotten too big. Father often said, "If I didn't hire those johnnies I wouldn't have a single municipal contract."

So what *was* he doing in the empty maid's quarters that November afternoon? Perhaps I have misinterpreted things and he was merely trying to get rid of the haunting odor of his mistress, to shake off the succubus that had slipped through the door of his orderly white man's world hidden in her invisible magic cloak of sandalwood and musk. I will never know. I try to take the portrait of him fumigating the bedbugs and superimpose it over that other image, my father weeping in an abandonment of thwarted passion while arsenious hydrochloride, kept in tall canisters marked with a skull and crossbones and the label "giftig," billows into the cell-like enclosure, but I cannot do it. I can make the image fade a little, like a photograph left in the sunlight, but I cannot change or falsify it. I must have missed something in my schooling, daydreamed through the elementary lessons on manipulating recall, since even the most obtuse of my schoolfellows wouldn't have the slightest problem performing this simple task.

...

It was Miss Tompkins who counseled Mother to send me to Dr. Vish. Perhaps she had seen me sitting apart from my fellow students at lunch break, wadding a huge sandwich roll filled with cold meats, mayonnaise, and coleslaw into my mouth, my shirt pocket still damp from the core of the apple I had surreptitiously scarfed during class. I learned to overcome this nuisance by consuming all fruit whole, reasoning that the little bit of cyanide in the seeds would do me no harm. Or perhaps she wondered why my marks had fallen, my blue cardboard report sheet filled with red-ink comments about a disappointing term. I was in Mrs. Sanders' class at the time, who merely assumed that my loss had affected my conscience and I had abandoned whatever recondite method of cheating I had hit upon. But Miss Tompkins may well have known more about what had happened in my family and felt sorry for me, for there was a heart in that desiccated, spindly frame and she liked to say that we would all always be her pupils no matter how old we got.

I should say here that my poor performance in class had nothing to do with my being overcome with grief, as preferably romantic as that would appear. No, the real difficulty was not that my memory was getting worse or being blocked by emotion, but that it was getting better . . . to the point that I could let nothing go and every word in the present suggested something from before, time melting into a series of continually running screens in which the present moment was indistinguishable from recollections of the past. "Discuss the causes of the Great Trek," Rooibos Sanders would prescribe, during one of her spot quizzes. And there I would be flooded with thoughts and recollections. *Causes* sounds a lot like Xhosas, the indigenous tribe of the Cape, and I would find myself meandering along the beach where Nonqawuse had her vision, the one that led to her people destroying their crops and cattle. The Great Trek. Father referred to it as "the "Great Dreck," and I could feel myself sitting outside with him in the chill evening air, the scent of rum-soaked Dutch mariner's tobacco rising from his pipe, his surprisingly high-pitched and sustained chuckle at his own humor. My recollection will be barely begun when it is just as suddenly interrupted by the command, "Pencils down," and there is old Rooibos already going around the room to collect the narrow, pale blue examination booklets.

...

I AM SITTING IN the plush red armchair in Dr. Vish's office; no clichéd couch for him, although he does sit behind me and to my right so he's almost completely hidden unless I crane my neck, and the soft, enfolding chair—which I recognize as one of the more expensive items from my friend Nigel Capeland's father's furniture shop—has a distinctly womb-like feel which can only be intentional. Dr. Vish has asked me to talk about my earliest memories, and I have been telling, not for the first time, about my anguish over my first nanny, Miriam.

"But you're an only child?" Dr. Vish says, making the statement a question.

"Yes?" Two can play that game.

"And you say that your mother's bad moods, the ones that drove away the servant who was also like a mother to you, were the result of pregnancy? So, perhaps you would tell me what happened?"

"I was an only child and a lonely child," I once wrote for my high school history master, Mr. Brenner, when he had asked us to create our own "personal, written oral history." I was plagiarizing Arthur Koestler, but Mr. Brenner did not catch the reference and instead told me to try to avoid feeling sorry for myself. So what did happen to the baby, who would have made the vaunted mnemonist into a sibling rather than a singleton? What about the blessed event that gave Mother permission to eat all she wanted—after all, each bite was feeding two, and therefore she was really eating only half of whatever was passing into her open maw . . . less, even, for don't growing children eat more, after all, and what child grows faster than a fetus?

And what about Mother's hormonal rages, stemming from the joyous occurrence? Rages that had bewildered me, used as I was to the monarchic luxury of being a Jewish child, *male* child, only child (hear the fanfare of trumpets when I walk into the room); that led to my beloved Miriam's tears when falsely accused of purloining a silver bracelet that was later found in its usual place in the bedside table drawer, found, I should add, without apology or mention. That led, in turn, to a Saturday morning after the month's wages had been paid, when there was no clatter of dishes in the kitchen shortly after dawn, no morning tea served to the mistress of the house in her double bed, no warmed-up bottle of milk for the small child in his crib: I can still see that tender testing of temperature, the white spurt from the plastic teat onto the delicate dusky skin of Miriam's inner arm. Out the kitchen door and past the small vegetable garden that grew mostly beets, the leaves used for *botsvinne* (think of it as borscht without the blood), the servant's quarters stand empty, the wooden door swinging in the breeze like a scene from the Last Chance Saloon. The iron bedstand is cold and hard, the horsehair mattress devoid of the blue and yellow rough wool blankets that I loved to bury my face in despite the resulting rash, only the faint lingering scent of kerosene from the night lamp and a distant memory of buchu tea, of sweet herbs burnt to keep away the *tokoloshe*, a malicious, sexually rapacious gnome said to haunt the backyards of South Africa's suburbs. The bare concrete pillbox has been swept utterly clean by the ever-conscientious and dearly departed Miriam, who has been goaded beyond endurance into fleeing during the night, for I know I did not imagine the love she lavished on the fat pink baby, the tubby toddler, that was me. And Mother's words: "Bloody typical. Gone on the weekend, and what am I going to do about the guests coming for dinner tonight?"

There is no dark secret here, no off-hours abortion in some back room of a doctor's quiet suburban house (illegal, but still available if you really cared and had the money), no—God forbid—café au lait infant clandestinely dropped off at the coloured orphanage. Mother took me with her on her visit to Dr. Harschleit when, at six months, she was yet to feel the child kick (although I'm told I regularly played soccer with her internal organs from the fourth month). She is an imposing figure, fortified by the additional seventy pounds distributed around her frame, as she apologizes for missing the last two visits. "I felt so good, you see, and I had no trouble with the first pregnancy. But now I'm worried, Doctor." He's our regular G.P., with his offices in the back of a large house in Houghton. I am sitting in the waiting room, close enough to the door that I can hear every word of mother's, though the doctor's murmur is a little too low for me to follow all but the gist. I hear him murmuring as he examines her, then his voice: "So you've had no periods at all for six months?"

"Of course not. What are you talking about?"

There is some murmuring about a negative frog test, an assumed mistake, then something mumbled that causes Mother to yell in outrage: "What do you mean, 'hysterical' pregnancy? I should know what a pregnancy feels like. My body remembers, or are you going to tell me that child sitting outside is an illusion? I have been pregnant before. *You*, excuse my saying so, Doctor, have never experienced that!"

"I'm sorry to tell you, Mrs. Sweetbread, there is no heartbeat because there is no baby." By this time, the inner-office door has been flung open as Mother is leaving, pulling on her clothes as she goes. "The body and the mind are closely connected, and sometimes we trick ourselves to avoid disappointment. I'm afraid all that's happened is you've put on a lot of weight."

The latter sentence stops Mother in her tracks. She pulls herself up to her full, half-dressed height and looks the doctor squarely in the eye. "Good day, you quack. I am off to see a real doctor. One with a South African degree."

"You're velcome to seek a second opinion," Dr. Harschleit says in a trembling voice, his accent more pronounced. Although he had received his medical education in Berlin, he had also gone back to university and qualified at Wits. Then, sadly, "But it von't make any difference. Perhaps you should ask why it is so important to be pregnant?"

Mother has a tight hold on my hand, practically wrenching my arm out of its socket. "Quack," she yells again, tears running down her fat cheeks as she slams the door hard behind her.

Mother is ill for several months after the visit to Dr. H. She keeps to herself in a darkened room, or lies like some grotesque odalisque on the living room sofa, daintily eating from a box marked "Rahat Loukoum." I try one of the little powdered-sugar-covered squares: it is cloyingly sweet with a strong odor of rosewater and the annoying stickiness of bird lime. Still, they seem to make Mother happy. Dad drives me to school at this time, and usually picks me up too. "It's good we have this chance to get to know each other," he says on our first journey, though I am silent, disapproving , in the back seat. I know that somehow this is all his fault.

Father seems not to notice my silences on our daily drives. Perhaps he does not expect a reply. Certainly he is more conversational, more friendly than he ever has been . . . or is he just seeking an ally in a house of gloom? He tells me tales of his early days traveling with his own father; he informs me in detail of the life histories of a range of insects that are a nuisance to humankind: army worms, boll weevils, the lice that carried bubonic plague. Often, he shares with me the latest joke that he has heard—a joke hardly suitable for a child my age. Van der Merwe (the archetype of the dim-witted Afrikaner) is being interviewed on the radio: Do you consider sex with your wife work or pleasure? "Well," says Van after some thought, "it must be pleasure or I'd have a kaffir do it for me."

...

It is Sedgewick Schwartz who comes up with the idea that we should pay a visit to Triomf. Our new history teacher, Mr. Brenner, has spent the last two weeks telling us about the forced removals that began in the mid-'50s, the so-called black spots and white spots, the millions of displaced persons in consequence of the mad Dutchman, Hendrik Frensch Verwoerd's "Grand Apartheid." Mr. Brenner was until recently a graduate student at Wits, studying under the redoubtable Charles van Onselen. The rumor is that he took up teaching to avoid being conscripted. I have my doubts, though, as a job at an elite Jewish high school like the Sons of Abraham hardly qualifies as alternative government service. Brenner seems determined to have us do what he calls *real history*, and not just learn to parrot our official textbooks. "Just listen to this rubbish," he says, reading to us from the story of "Martha," a former dweller in the slums of Sophiatown. "'Martha looked around at her government-issued house. There were no vermin crawling up the clean new walls. The bright morning sun fell upon her sleeping baby and she quickly moved to cover it up. Soon little Thembi would be going to the nice new school the government had built nearby. Tears ran down Martha's face while she thought about how all her dreams had come true.'

"I mean, for Pete's sake, this is an insult to anyone's intelligence. Do you really think this woman was going to be happy about having a long commute to work, because I can assure you that's what the move meant for her. And how come they don't give her a last name? Africans have last names, you know. In fact, they have a whole bunch of names, each one telling you something of the proud history of their clan. How many of you even know the last names of the maids and nannies who brought you up?"

This is hitting a little closer to home. He does warn us that we will need to know what's in these books for the Matric but that there's so much else to learn. The more conservative kids mutter ominously that he is a Communist; the children of liberals and dissidents nod at every word he utters and look around at the rest of us. *You see*?

We have just spent our day's lesson on Sophiatown, the multiracial neighborhood that had grown up organically with the expansion of Johannesburg and its labor needs. This thriving, vibrant, crime-ridden place was then declared a "black spot" in 1955, razed to the ground, and renamed the Afrikaans word for Triumph. Mr. Brenner plays for us some tapes of the musicians who came out of Kofifi: Kippie Moeketsi's fabulous sax; Todd Matshikiza's *King Kong*, a jazzy musical—"Boxing, boxing. Boxing makes men strong"—that is a distant cousin to *Carmen*; Miriam Makeba singing about the legendary shebeen "Back of the Moon." Some of the students nod delightedly, a few furrow their eyebrows. (Sure, we know the kaffirs can sing. Doesn't mean we have to live next door to them.) None are bored, even the lacquer-haired premature housewives who normally file their nails in class or look blankly out of the window. Mr. Brenner is handsome, in a blocky sort of way—square-framed glasses, squarish head, square chin—and there's no denying his energy.

As we file out of the classroom, Sedgewick says in his drama-trained voice: "Hey, everybody. Come over here, I have an idea." Those who are not urgently rushing to games or for their rides gather around him. Sedgewick is a popular fellow, and his wealthy family has donated generously to the school. "Why don't we go see it?" he asks, beaming around at his audience.

"See what?" asks Dodger, always a little slow.

"You know, what happened to Sophiatown. Triomf."

"Ag, man, that's no fun. A bunch of *rocks* live there.* They'll kill us . . . and anyway, who wants to wander around some crunchy neighborhood." You can see that Dodger is disappointed. He was hoping that Sedgewick was going to suggest everyone drive down to his father's game farm or come see a banned film.

"Don't be so prejudiced, Dodge. Afrikaners are people too, like us, and this is a chance to see living history firsthand. Maybe we'll hear the ghost of Kippie playing his horn." He looks around at us, smiling, and it's

* English South Africans seem to regard Afrikaners as close kin to the arachnids, especially the large, hairy spiders found underneath rocks on the veld. Hence the epithets: rockspiders, hairybacks, crunchies.

agreed that we will meet on Friday afternoon, when Sedgewick has had a chance to organize a *bakkie* and a couple of other cars.

By the time Friday comes, there are only six of us other than the initiator of the plan who do not have some other engagement or have changed our minds. We are able to all fit in one vehicle, Sedgewick's gleaming new bakkie lovingly polished by hand that morning to prepare it for its journey into the very belly of Separate Development. We drive west along the Roodepoort road, Sedgewick blasting a banned song on the state-of-the-art sound system: "Hey, teachers, leave us kids alone."

"How will we know when we get there?" Dodger asks glumly. In his loyal earnestness, he is more profound than he can know.

"I'll know, don't worry. I wonder if they'll let us into Father Huddleston's church. Brenner says it's still there, the paintings all whitewashed over, sterilized for Dr. Verwoerd's grand plan."

"They have to let us in," Dodger says with conviction. "It's a church. I'll tell them I have to confess my sins or something. Forgive me, Father, I have lust in my heart."

"You're getting your organs all mixed up again," Danny Mainzer chaffs, and I am crushed against the door handle in the ensuing wrestling match.

"Did you know that Sophiatown was named after a Jewish lady, Sophia Tobiansky?" I say when calm has been restored. "And that the streets are named after her children: Bertha and Gerty and Toby and—"

"Oh, do shut up, Sweetbread," Danny grumbles.

"Oy veh, who brought the *Encyclopedia Judaica*?" comes a voice from the back. Nigel's, I think.

"No, you miss my point. When the Nats kicked all the blacks and coloureds out of Sophiatown and changed its name, they also erased Mrs. Tobiansky. How many other places can you think of in the Republic that are named after Jewish women?"

"Ladysmith," says Danny, quick as a jack-in-the-box. "Or how about Vrededorp? I think it's named after my Aunt Frieda." He and Dodger start wrestling again.

"Calm down, children, I think we're here." For the first time, Sedgewick's voice betrays a hint of uncertainty. We're in a typical little *stoepdorp*, the kind our families might drive through on the way to Pilanesberg. It's hillier than I had expected, but there's a barren sameness to the buildings, a shabbiness that suggests some magic dust has been sprinkled here to make everything sag a little and begin to fall apart. There is no trouble finding parking, and we pull up behind a battered red *kombi.*

"You're not worried about the car getting stolen?" Danny asks. Sedgewick opens his palm to reveal an odd plastic object, with copper wires gleaming inside its socketlike interior. Ignition-killer, he tells us. No way to move the car without it.

"Just don't drop the blerry thing," says Danny. "I'd hate to be stuck in this dorp come nightfall."

We walk down strangely deserted streets, then ahead of us, leaning in a doorway, is our first sign of human life. He is a chunky individual in his early twenties with stringy long hair and bad skin, his eyes narrow as he looks at us through smoke from the unfiltered cigarette in his mouth. His T-shirt reads: "Parabats! Death from Above."

"Do you know where the Huddleston church is?" Sedgewick asks him. The fellow's eyes light up, suspicion lifted. He tells us there's a whole bunch of churches around here but he's never heard of that one. It is obvious that he has mistaken us for a religious group. He has not been told of the church where Yehudi Menuhin played to an all-African audience and Hugh Masakela learned the trumpet, though he has no doubt lived here all his life. The door behind him opens, emitting a cloud of smoke and the smell of sour hops soaking into vinyl. A voice tells him it's his turn on the billiards table, and our sole cultural informant wishes us luck before disappearing inside. There is a sign on the glass pane of the door, shakily hand-painted by someone with a bad hangover: "*die Ark.*"

"That's really funny," says Danny. "The rockspiders have a sense of humor. I can't wait to see it in the tourist guidebooks: Visit *die Ark van Triomf.*"

We continue past some boarded doorways, a closed repair shop, and a garage from which come loud male voices and the clang of dropped metal. As we turn a corner onto Ray Street, we see walking toward us a tall woman with a face that would be young and pretty were it not so tired. She is holding a sack of cans and milk bottles in one hand, her other hand clutching tightly that of a squalling nine-year-old who stops mid-howl when he catches sight of us. The mother looks at us through red-rimmed eyes, too fatigued to register any surprise. "*Kom, Fanie, ons moet huis toe*," she says softly, tugging at the child, who has now dug his heels in. Behind them, carrying in one hand a nylon-net bag filled with bottles of wine and cans of beer with no evident strain on his long arm muscles, comes a man who is astonishingly, frighteningly tall. He is acromegalic, his head longer than any normal head, his arms as long as my legs. His nose is about twice the length of my index finger, yet proportional to his bony face. In one or two quick strides he is right before us, looking down on us in furious amazement, an angry tree.

"What . . . ? What . . . fff?" he sputters, a teakettle newly placed on the hob. "What are you fucking doing here?"

"Just looking for— " Sedgewick begins.

"Looking? Looking *die fok*," the man interrupts. He glances around in surprise, as if there may be more of us. "This isn't the Johannesburg Zoo, you bastards. You better . . . you better fucking get away from here, hey." He moves threateningly toward us. "*Voetsek*! Come on, just *voetsek*."

We beat a hasty retreat, watched by this Goliath all the way. Even the unflappable Sedgewick seems scared as he fumbles for his ignition-killer electronic key. Most unnerving of all is that this is not a gang of teenagers rousting us from their turf but a man in his thirties, a *paterfamilias*.

"Did you see how big he was?" Dodger murmurs. "What on earth do they put in the water around here?"

"Not just big, but *kwaai*. Like a hornet when you've brushed against its nest," Danny says in awe. "He could have *dondered* the lot of us."

As we drive back to the comfort of the northern suburbs, the excursion takes on new dimensions of glamour and adventure with each retelling. "Just loo . . . loo . . . looking," says Nigel Capeland, and we explode with mirth. So we didn't find the Church of Christ the King with its desecrated murals and ghost memories of the saintly Father. We have experienced our own eviction, encountered the beast in his lair, and lived to tell the tale.

...

There is a practice among the BaPedi muti-men of the Northern Transvaal that the last arcana taught to an apprentice are the incantations, herbs, and knuckle-bone tossings needed to bind his teacher forever into immobility. Rather, I should say, this ritual was claimed to exist by my high school textbook: *Customs and Superstitions of the South African Natives*, a gaudily illustrated tome that has since shown itself to be a work of vivid imagination by an expert who never left his front stoep. Still, I confess to having always liked the flashy illustration depicting a hapless, grizzled witch doctor draped in the coils of a huge serpent and surrounded by howling skeletons, while his successfully trained former student stands grinning with evil pride nearby.

This colorful drawing floats into my mind during my final session with Dr. Vish, he of the pointed goatee and folded hands, when I choose to call him a hypocrite. "What is your duty?" I rail at him, quite enjoying the melodrama of it all. "To restore me to my full, rather my *fullest*, mental faculties? Or to make me fit into this insane society?" I hadn't read R. D. Laing then; I am drawing entirely on my own coarse ruminations on the purpose of our therapy. "How can anyone honestly practice psychiatry in this police state? If you really cured your patients, what choice would they have but to bomb Pretoria Central at the first opportunity?"

"Come now, do you really see the purpose of psychiatry as inciting revolution? Wouldn't you see the goal as allowing you to make your own choices?"

"Always the question without the answer, Dr. Vish. What if my choice was to put an end to this farce, to just walk out that door and never come back?"

"I would wish you godspeed, my friend, *hamba kahle*, as our African brothers say. If nothing else, you have some new tools to deal with your memory's excesses, so you should do all right. Just remember that there are many doors in this world. And that this one is always open to you."

So I leave Dr. Vishinski on a note of anger, which he of course opts to turn into part of the therapeutic process. In this, he may be right. By acquiring some, even if imperfect, control over the veracity and verisimilitude of my memory, I had reached a rubicon of sorts. It is finally becoming up to me whether I am going to continue to chronicle the vicissitudes of myself, my family, and my country. The key is there for me at long last to learn the national dysmnesia, the art of rose-colored recall.

...

I am narrowing down the focus of the vast lens of memory. Here is our green planet with its trailing wisps of smoke from burning fields and forests. Here is my country, shaped like a laughing clown face (or a Swiss cheese, if you accept the government's definition of the homelands). Here is my house, in this city of blue pools with its wart of townships larger than its own head. Here, in the kitchen, Corinthia is making her marvelous pastries. I zoom in until there are only her hands, sifting flour into the batter, kneading dough, laying out preserved fruit. As if in a trance, I follow the movements of her hands, bear down on the temperature setting of the oven. Getting just the right length of baking time is a little trickier, but I manage by a combination of guesstimation and following every movement between the moment she puts the pie, cake, or tart into the oven and when she takes it out again.

Mother does not appear to notice that the delicacies I unload onto our receptive table are the same as those prepared in the past by her nemesis. She is too busy eating to notice that I have stopped attending the university to devote myself full-time to baking and helping her consume the results. Together we absorb it all and grow vast.

I have also not told her about the standard-issue light brown envelope calling me to report for my army induction which arrived by the post a week ago. I am contemplating the possibilities it offers me to raise the wax cover on the slate over and over again. The opportunity to forget, to finally become a good son, a good South African.

Book Two

Time to Serve

1987 – 1989

To make a Bobootie, one must have clean hands. . . .

Anonymous
seventeenth-century cookbook,
quoted in *Leipoldt's Cape Cookery*

Man is the only animal that . . . ?

Feel free to fill in the blanks, to come up with your own version of just what it is that makes us the beauty of the world, the paragon of animals. After all, we have been asserting our specialness for centuries, determined to convince ourselves that people are set apart from the rest of the animal kingdom in some profound way.

Man is the only animal that goes to war? A popular notion, if a negative one: the idea is that we are the only creature that kills its own species. This philosophy has been used to explain—if not justify—the gruesome slaughter of our world wars. Place a group of us on a deserted island, and we will begin to fight and to murder each other, especially the weakest among us. Such is the plot of *Lord of the Flies*, and the philosophy underpinning our renowned anthropologist Raymond Dart's theory, his explanation for why one of the earliest hominid skulls found at Taung had a hole in its head. We go to war because it's our particular and unique nature. But any entomologist will tell you that ants regularly war with each other, and indeed the Argentine ant, an immigrant settler accidentally introduced by Europeans, has virtually wiped out the country's native ants.

Man is the only animal to cultivate crops and use tools? Sorry, once again the ants got there first, raising crops of fungi and herds of aphids, and wasps use sticks and small pebbles to tamp down mud. Finches and nuthatches use twigs or pieces of bark to get at juicy bugs in crevices, and some songbirds even pick up live ants and put them in their plumage to act as personal grooming devices. And, of course, Jane Goodall has filmed chimpanzees using bones, stones, and sticks to dig for food or kill their fellows. (War, again.)

The one use for a simple tool that no other animal has conceived of is to write things down. (Ignore, for the moment, the Muslim belief that water striders are inscribing the name of the Prophet over and over again on the blank slate of a pond's surface.) We have found a way to transcend the limitations of our individual minds and brief life spans through our scribbles and inscriptions, our runes and hieroglyphs, our palimpsests, holographs, and multiple printings, our *furor scribendi*. The greatest of human inventions is the library, a vast repository of collective memory far larger than any single mind can hold. Written memory becomes fixed in time, regardless of the distortions it contains, and the adventures we recount on paper are there to be reexperienced by those who are not oneself, the writer. So long as one's narrative survives, one's ideas and versions of history are passed along, like genetic code, to ensuing generations. Control what goes into the library, what becomes the available record, and you control what the future thinks.

I think there is a certain hubris in trying to determine which memories get saved, and that is no doubt why libraries have brought little good fortune to their creators. The Mughal Emperor Humāyūn died falling down the steps of the magnificent library he had built. One of his descendants, Dārā Shikōh, was on the way to becoming as famous for the library he put together as his own father, Shāh Jāhān, was for building the Taj Mahal. Then his warrior brother, Aurangzeb, beheaded him and destroyed his collection of manuscripts. Throughout time, this has been the response of fighting men to those who dare lay claim to the recording of the era's events, and the first act of despotic regimes is to burn books, as anyone who recalls the early days of the Nazis knows, and banish anyone whose outlook is different from their own. And perhaps because it is so strongly opposed, the urge to provide a faithful transcription of one's times comes to feel like a sacred trust.

Fear not, reader, I have no intention of subjecting you to every minute recollection that adheres to the flypaper of my memory. I will be faithful in my transcription, but selective, for otherwise I would be like Borges' mapmaker who tried to reproduce every feature of the landscape and wound up with a map the size of the world.

My adolescence is the first thing I would like to relocate to the homelands of amnesia. Bad enough that you have to remember your own version of that time of messy and unruly emotions, the absurdity of acne, the aching tedium of high school. Bad enough that in my white nights I have to relive each of those moments—the long, dread hours of the schoolmaster's drivel: South African history, or rather the government's contemptuous rehashing of the tales told behind the thorn-covered walls of the laager. (Here's the swill, swallow it.) There was the steady dull reminding of the white man's superiority and the burden of brutality required to civilize the savage. One aspect of adolescence I do need to face up to, however, is an initiation as enormous as that the military visited on men of my generation . . . I'm talking, of course, of falling in love, its joys and attendant humiliations. I hope you will forgive me as I stipple my narrative with these interludes. They have made me who I am, these brief rites of passage, tragic and silly though they might have been.

Patience. We will come to this by and by.

...

THE BLIGHTED LANDSCAPE FOR which our army camp served as some sort of apex or fingerpost at the crossroads was the first real encounter that many of us conscripts—especially those from the city suburbs—had with the realities of rural Southern Africa. We had all, of course, spent time at the Kruger Park or holidayed at one of the platteland farms, selectively not noticing the impoverished huts we drove by—cardboard and corrugated tin put to imaginative use, the landscape seared by years of drought and yet inhabited by people. That tattered man walking with the aid of a bent stick from nowhere to nowhere, is he just an ornament to the eye or do his bunions hurt? But we would have returned to the green gardens of our suburban homes, the fantail sprinklers and abundance of tropical fruits, the blue pools, the happy decorous servants laboring with the assiduous good humor of weaver birds.

Here in the Kaokoland in the northwest section of "the Nam,"* we dwell amid absence: absence of color; absence of water other than that which gets pumped from deep in the ground by the generator-assisted windmill, a tall metal insect constantly chirring in the center of the camp; absence of birdsong except just before dawn, a strange silence during the day other than the wind. The local population, a village of Himba tribesmen (an offshoot of the Owambo) some fifteen miles away, are lethargic, depressed by malnutrition and the constant passing of the vehicles of war. We were told in school that the African is like the grasshopper in the fable, thinking only of today with no plan for the future, but it is plain to see why no one would want to plant crops that would be stolen by one set of warring forces or burnt in reprisal by the other, crops that require constant coaxing and attention and yet still wither beneath an unrelenting sun.

It was easy enough to believe, having grown up in the Northern Suburbs, that Africans were happy with their lot, that they were being gently raised by the kind paternal hands of their white employers so as to be

* Namibia. We are quick to recognize the affinity we have with young Americans in Vietnam, a generation ago, and our language reflects this: when we leave South-West Africa for the Republic, we are going "back to the States." Distances aren't referred to as miles or kilometers but "klicks."

ready for the responsibilities and demands of advanced civilization some hazy time in the future. Morose, unsmiling black people were rarely hired as household servants, and it was the wise employee who flattered his master's and missis's elevated sense of benevolence. God knows, most white householders knew little to nothing about their servants' lives beyond the confines of the dining room, kitchen, or garden.

I had my own vivid demonstration of this sociological verity when Nigel Capeland (Kaplan in the original) had asked me a few months ago if I would like to house-sit for his family while they were on holiday—a visit to a game farm and health spa near the Kruger Park. It was just a few weeks before I was due to enter the army, and Mother could not have been less pleased that I was abandoning her "when there is so little time to still enjoy you."

"Ag, Ma, most of the other blokes go on a nice holiday before they *klaar in* for their two years' state servitude. You know we can't afford that, so this will be my little vacation." I felt a little bad about reminding her of our financial straits; she had sold Terminex at a fraction of its financial worth, refusing to believe that the offspring of Father's obsessions could be of any real value. Seeing a shadow cross her face, I continued, "Besides, I'll be coming home every day. I'm just supposed to sleep there at night, so the place looks occupied. I'll get to use the pool—"

"A pool? Oh, that makes all the difference. What chance does a mother have against a pool?"

"Come on, Mother. It'll be good for us both to start getting used to being on our own, even in a small way. And, in addition, I'll be well paid."

This latter claim was not backed up by specific knowledge. There was no exact agreed-on remuneration, but Nigel had told me that his parents were "quite generous," and Mr. Capeland had several times hinted at the fact that a young man my age and in my situation should have the wherewithal to enjoy his last days of freedom. "The army takes care of you," he said. "But do they give you any choice? No. You eat what they tell you when they tell you. In fact, you don't do anything except what you're ordered to do. But you'll come out better for the discipline."

I had wondered whether this was directed at Nigel, who had wangled a course of study in England and deferred his call-up. I had gone to their house for dinner the night before they left, part send-off for the holidaymakers and part opportunity to show me around so that I would know my "duties" as a house-sitter. I was informed, in great detail, as to the care of Fluffy, Mrs. Capeland's toy poodle. Fluffy is a trembly little white dog, kept carefully clipped like some miniature baroque shrubbery. She looks at me suspiciously from her small dark eyes and gives an irritable yip in my direction before cuddling up to Mrs. Capeland. I had somehow thought the dog would be accompanying them, or be sent to some luxurious health kennel. Instead, Fluffy was to be my responsibility, a veritable privilege, they thought, and I was introduced to the arcane rites of mixing the dry and tinned dog foods in the correct proportions, the necessity to take her for a walk twice a day, and the whereabouts of her favorite rubber toys.

"You'll find her an absolute joy . . . yessss, aren't you, my little sweetie-pie," Mrs. Capeland said, kissing the little beast's nose while it squirmed in her tight grasp. It was hard to tell when she was addressing me, when the dog. "Give her tons of hugs and cuddles, otherwise she'll just pine away without her mommy to look after her."

We had a fine meal of roast beef and Yorkshire pudding, prepared and served by Alini, the cook and nanny who had taken care of Nigel since he was five. Nigel and I weren't close friends, although I had gone to birthday parties at his house and occasionally played with him when we were small. I had always liked Alini, though; she and Nigel had a funny ritual going on, much like Kato and Inspector Clouseau. Nigel would be reading quietly on a chair or doing his homework at the dining table, when Alini would dart out from a corner and deliver a quick slap or pinch. Other times it would be Alini who was ironing or drying the dishes and in stockinged feet Nigel would sneak up close to her and yell, "Boo!" in her ear or give her a quick pinch on her ample rear. "Ag, you gave me a helluva *skrik*, Master Nigel," she would say, wiping tears of laughter from the corners of her eyes, her bosom heaving with startled fright and hilarity. Nigel had confessed to me that he so enjoyed her chuckling "hee-hee-hee" laugh when she had successfully surprised him, that he quite often pretended not to notice when she stalked him.

Now that he is grown up, Nigel towers over the five-foot-one Alini. He is as large as me, although more athletic in a langorous way. In fact, all of us seated at the dinner table this night are large—Brobdingnags to the tiny Gulliver voyaging from the kitchen with steaming plates of food. Mrs. Capeland is herself a homely six-footer made taller by the lacquered hairdo of women of her and Mother's generation. She has a high, chirruping, little girl's voice and a habit of singing her speech—"Ohhh, Ni-gellllll. I have something for yoooou."—when she's any distance from her audience.

At dinner, Mr. Capeland amuses himself telling us stories of his days as a baboon guard in the cornfields surrounding his parents' farm in Zambia when he was our age, and how this hard and thankless, hot and dusty work led him to go into business—"clean, indoor work"—a decision he'd never regretted. Mr. Capeland is a tall, heavyset man with thinning light brown hair and a blond mustache streaked with gray and red bristles (the 'stache of many colors, Nigel calls it). He is tennis-tanned, with dry skin that is turning into leather. For all his city-earned wealth, he still looks like a farmer on a jaunt to the provincial capital. He talks of his early days in Johannesburg, whence he came with a song in his heart, "the Jewish lullaby: *Buy low, sell high*. First I sold other people's furniture, then I cut out the middleman and manufactured and sold my own. I've done what I want in life, and I have no regrets. I'm a happy man, and that's something few can say without telling a lie. My advice, my boys, is look for an opportunity for yourselves and then go after it until you get it. Then you'll be happy in work and happy in life."

"Sure, Pa," Nigel responds. "But Jo'burg was expanding then, more people moving in all the time. Back then, any halfway decent business was bound to grow like a mushroom after rain. Now the whites are leaving as fast as they can book their tickets, and the Africans can't afford luxury items."

"No, no, no, my boy. If you make a good product, people will buy it. People are proud to own a Capeland chair"—he gestures expansively at an example of the latter standing in the corner of the room—"and do you know why? Because they are built to *last*." The latter statement is a precise echo of the advertisements appearing in every edition of the *Sunday Express*.

"I thought shoes were built to last." Nigel winks at me; it is clear that this is an argument they had frequently, and he knows just how to rile the old man.

"Very funny, Nigel, I'm sure. Now do eat up, all of you, because we've still got lots and lots of packing," Mrs. Capeland trills. Turning to me, she adds: "You must remind me to show you the food for Alini and Jethro." The former quietly removes our plates that are now empty except for daubings of brown gravy. "One package for each night."

I am puzzled. Watching Alini's broad blue-uniformed back retreat into the corridor to the kitchen, I ask, "Aren't you giving them time off? I don't need any servants while I'm here." Mother didn't keep servants after the fall of Corinthia; even our gardening was done by a succession of itinerants, some of whom made it bloom, while others—in the throes of hangovers or mental disorder—would weed so ferociously and indiscriminately that the flowers grew only in haphazard patches. The thought of sharing a house with a constantly present unknown other is disturbing to me.

"No, no, no. They do need the wages," Mrs. C. replies, her voice clearly indicating her indulgence of an innocent's thoughtless question. "And besides, Alini's family are way off in remote Zululand or some such place. She wouldn't be able to visit them and still be back in time to prepare for our return. You know, they think they're losing their jobs and they get *very* upset if you give them time off when it's not their scheduled holiday."

She pays little attention to Alini, who is placing small plates with pound cake covered in canned fruit topped with whipped cream in front of each of us. Mr. C. notices her, though, and hails her loudly: "You're happy to stay here, hey?" She giggles and inclines her head, and he gives me a triumphant look.

The large freezer compartment in the kitchen has one shelf stacked high with wrapped individual square packages, each containing a mutton chop. Mrs. C. explains that I should take out two plastic bags and put six slices of buttered white bread and one chop in each of them by nine o'clock at night, then hang them on the outside handle of the kitchen door and double-bolt the lock. "Very important to lock all the doors at night."

I nod. I am to unlock the door and leave out twelve slices of buttered white bread by eight each morning, except for Sunday, when the servants attend church and aren't due in until four, unless of course the Capelands are having a big Sunday dinner.

"There's just the right number of chops for the time we're away," Mrs. C. says meaningfully, in a voice loud enough to be heard above the running water where Alini is washing the dishes. "So if anyone does any stealing, they'll have to do without."

"Do they always get chops? What about a piece of chicken sometime? or a steak? And can't Alini take her rations with her when she leaves in the evening?" Mr. Brenner liked to use the phrase "intimate tyranny" to describe the master-servant relationship, and I'm beginning to see what he meant.

"No, no, no. Routine is very important to them. And we can't just let her take her own food. Do you know, scientists have shown that Africans will eat their own weight in meat in ten days if left to themselves?"

I consider asking her if she really believes that Alini could consume seven kilos of meat a day, but decide better of it. I doubt Mrs. C. has ever troubled to do the arithmetic. I acquiesce quietly to the notion that I am to be, for the next ten days, a servant of the servants, doomed to hurry home before nine in the evening and to rise long before my usual waking time to prepare their handouts.

And indeed, house-sitting ("The Jew squats on the windowsill") proves more arduous than I would ever have suspected, a career (like so many others, alas) that I am ill-suited for. The beloved Fluffy dislikes me by day—fleeing into a corner and nipping at me with her tiny needle-sharp teeth when I approach her with a sequined leash for her walk (if she didn't get her regulated promenade, there would be a little gift left for my delectation in the corner of the guest bedroom where I've taken up residence, an object that Alini, for all that there is little cleaning to do with the householders away, ostentatiously ignores)—and seeks me by night, following me around whimpering and sleeping in a surprisingly weighty ball on my feet when I go to bed.

Like her owners, Fluffy is neurotic about intruders: two or three times a night, usually when I have just entered REM sleep, she flings herself viciously against the gated bedroom door—every room has its locked and barred gate, thus did the wealthy of Johannesburg make common cause with the inmates of John Vorster Square and Pretoria Central. Still asleep, the venerable Fluffy hurls herself forward, barking and bouncing off the unyielding reinforced steel bars. These sounds inevitably set off the neighbor's two Alsatians—a pair of killers each the size of a wild boar—who commence a rising crescendo of thunderous barks and high-pitched yips. This cacophony subsides after half an hour or so, leaving me wide awake, my dreams having irretrievably fled. Call me Macumazahn. Although, unlike Rider Haggard's Alan Quatermain, I spend my nights not with one eye open but with both, my Umslopogaas not a magnificent six-foot-three-inch black warrior but a pathetic, trembling white cur.

I wake from troubled dreams earlier than my usual wont, so that I might stumble into the kitchen, make a quick cup of instant coffee, sleepily butter the thick slices of white bread I purchased later and later each day at the nearby Greek *caf.* For some reason, what Americans call general stores—a name that to me suggests some dilapidated officer from the Great War: "General Stores has ordered the company to advance five hundred yards"—we South Africans refer to as cafés. Then there are *bazaars*, our word, with its tinge of Eastern exoticism, for what Americans call "the mall." (You've seen one, you've seen the mall, Mantis-man would have said.) I know, I know, I'm chasing butterflies again, but lately the alternative English-language weekly has run a column called "Let's Speak South

Effrican," as if even the language we speak can best be appreciated as a quaint antique soon to disappear from memory forever, our familiar phrases eccentric verbal artifacts that not-so-distant generations will scratch their heads over and wonder what possible purpose they could have served. And of course, what the paper's enlightened editors are joking about is white South African English, for gone are the days when the malapropisms of the servants can safely be mocked. No more radio shows where Sixpence mangles the language to the bewilderment and fury of his white interlocutors. The exasperated shopkeeper complains: "You say you don't want black pepper, you don't want white pepper, you don't want cayenne pepper. Just what kind of pepper do you want?"

"*Lavatory pepper,* pliss, baas," Sixpence earnestly responds.

Mother having primary use of our sole car, I find myself returning home only when she bestirs herself to fetch me. Most days, I walk to the Pick 'n Pay some two miles hence and take the bus back after I have picked out my dinner items and paid for them. Knowing that I am soon to eat what the army dishes out—both literally and figuratively—and anticipating some glorious paycheck from the Capelands, I spend my savings to indulge my palate. I buy smoked snoek for lunch or breakfast, a variety of condiments (Mrs. Ball's *blatjang* , as well as Crosse and Blackwell's Major Grey's Chutney), and more steak than is good for my overwrought ticker. In the afternoons, I sit by the pool drinking iced tea, chewing on biltong and macadamia nuts or on the ripe figs that otherwise fall with a soft plop on the slasto, the bushes filled with flocks of riotous birds toward evening. I close my eyes and listen to the slow swishing of the pool-skimmer as Jethro lifts out the fallen bluegum leaves, enjoy the noisy gabble of the hadedah ibises who have a nest in the bluegums, and revel in the warmth of sunlight on my closed eyelids while I contemplate what I might treat myself to for dinner. I have, in other words, become a *madam*.

Unlike most of the other madams, I don't take up Alini on her offer to cook for me. I'm not sure she regards this as a kindness, as she is restless and bored without her usual tasks. I could have sworn she had ironed that same sheet half an hour ago. I tell her that I will gladly have her cook for me if she will cook me something that she'd make for her own family. "*Hayikona*," she says, giggling and shaking her head.

"No, I'm serious. You can give me boerewors and pap. I love boerie and pap."

At the Pic 'n Pay the next morning, I buy a large piece of boerewors, the fresh sausage like some ropy dog turd in appearance, and a box of *mielie* meal. Even if Alini declines, I can cook it for myself. However, that evening, when I come in from a shower following a late afternoon wallow in the pool, I am greeted with the delicious smell of boerewors frying on a griddle, that mingled odor of smoking fat and heated fennel seeds. When it is ready, Alini asks if I want to eat in the dining room, but I tell her the kitchen table will do. Does she want to join me for dinner? She makes no response other than a barely audible *mmm*. Some questions are too mad to acknowledge. At least do stay in the kitchen, I tell her as she is making a move to go to some other part of the house. I tell her I hate to eat alone, a little white lie.

"I will do my work," she says emphatically. She takes out some of the Capeland silver and some polish, and begins to energetically rub the knives and forks with a soft cloth. She has the radio on, but so softly I have trouble telling what language it is in.

"Is that the Zulu radio?" I ask.

"Sotho." She expertly spins the dial and there is a rapid Bantu language patter in which the only words I can make out are Life cigarettes. "This one is Zulu."

"Do you understand them both? And the boerewors is really *lekker*, by the way."

"Mmmm. You welcome."

I take this *mmm* for an affirmative and ask her what other languages she speaks. Zulu. Sotho. Tswana, Afrikaans. English. I tell her the only languages I know are English and Afrikaans, and a smattering of Hebrew.

"Ag, shame."

It is the first time I have really conversed with a domestic servant—I have not had reason or opportunity to in the past—and I find myself asking questions as if I were an interviewer on Radio 702. How much schooling did she have? Standard V. Where did she learn all those languages? You just learn, you have to. Does she have kids? Ag, sure. Yvonne is a nursing sister. There is a son, fifteen, Bheki. He is still in school, but he's a naughty boy. She clucks fondly, this naughtiness a clear sign of character. There are grandchildren. Does she get to Zululand often to see them? What is this *Zululand*? Why would she go that side? She is Sotho, and her daughter lives in Potch so she sees her and the kids every other weekend. Often they meet at church, if Yvonne doesn't have to work. She pointedly does not mention her own employers' occasional habit of keeping her around when there are brunch visitors.

She quickly clears away my dishes and washes them, then asks if it is all right if she goes off now. Tomorrow is church day, and she won't be in until dinnertime. I tell her that I am eating dinner with my mother and she needn't come in until the following morning. That is nice, she says, though I have the feeling she's commending my filiality more than the bestowal of free time. And if I want to sleep late, she tells me, I can put out the morning bread this night. This is welcome news. I have made no plans for Saturday night—which is hardly unusual—but I still wouldn't mind a morning lie-in.

Sunday is pleasant, with no one but Fluffy to witness my doings. I have trouble getting used to being subject to the constant scrutiny of someone most white South Africans had trained themselves to regard as invisible. I feel oddly disapproved-of by Alini: here am I, a master without portfolio, the stranger brought in to watch over her familiar world, and, Mother has pointed out, to keep the neighborhood *tsotsis* from pressuring her to let them into the house. I don't see her that day, but looking out of the kitchen window in the late afternoon I catch a glimpse of her blue and gold church robes and hat waving merrily on a clothesline in the servant quarters yard.

The week passes quickly and I grow used to my routine, enjoying the comfort of a large house and a well-tended pool. I discuss soccer with Jethro: he's hoping to try out for the Orlando Pirates, his favorite team.

Are you that good? I ask him. Smiling shyly, he inclines his head in assent. Sometimes I talk to him, but Alini often contrives to pass by when he and I are outside at the same time, favoring him with a ferocious scowl. Jethro stops work to talk to me, unlike Alini, who keeps up her bustling routine and whom I have to follow from room to room to complete a thought. Sometimes I read—I have picked up a couple of books on Namibia, figuring the knowledge might be of use if I'm sent there—and I find the sound of Jethro's working (the swish-swish of the pool cleaner, his quiet but tuneful whistling) fades into the background like that of the *mossies* and weavers darting around the garden. The book that I had hoped would give me a feel for my likely destination in the SADF*— a solid enough tome called simply *South West Africa* and written by an American college professor—proves disappointing. Less a guide than the kind of self-congratulatory diatribe I've been hearing all my life—"The district commissioner's task is to lift the Bushmen out of the Neolithic, tend hundreds of cases of disease, teach primitive natives the art of rational cultivation far above the ingrained habits of subsistence farming . . ."—this is a political work in favor of benign paternalism rather than a travelogue. There is a brief but dismissive mention of the "White Lady," the famous cave painting in the Brandberg, containing the curious statement that "Bushmen are not known to have painted on the walls of caves or on rocks." Since every South African schoolchild is told of how the bushmen spent much of their time drawing on rocks instead of doing useful work, this comment made so authoritatively makes me doubt his sanity. I should have been warned by the statement on the back cover that describes the itinerant professor as a traveler who carries few prejudices with him.

* South African Defence Force. This is the land of the acronym. Even our nearest township, with its African-sounding name of Soweto, is an acronym for South West Township. Then there's Cosatu and Fosatu, not two children in an African fairy tale but the Congress of South African Trade Unions and the Federation of et cetera. There's the ANC and the CNA (one a political party, the other a chain of bookshops); the IDP, HNP, and CODESA; UNISA and UNITA, and so on, or, as the Germans would write it, u.s.w.

Still, I am intrigued, and not a little amused, at the mention of a mineworkers' compound in Walvis Bay, a seaport in the middle of Namibia that strangely enough is officially part of our own Cape Province, where such care is taken of the laborers' appetites that "there are fourteen menus worked out so that the same dish cannot appear on the table more than twice a month." The small guide to the birds of South-West is more pleasurable, and I can look forward to seeing violet woodhoepoes, Cinderella waxbills, and rosyface lovebirds while practicing leopard crawls and bayonet thrusts or however one passes one's time as a member of an occupying army.

I am, at this point in my life, woefully ignorant of the vast and arid land that I would likely soon be defending. I know it to have been settled by the Germans—including Field Marshal Goering's father, Heinrich, who became the territory's first Reich commissioner—and that it is the size of Western Europe but with a population not much more than Johannesburg's. The colonial Germans had systematically eradicated most of the Herero people when the latter rebelled against being kicked off their land. Mr. Brenner told us that the concentration camp was invented by the British in South Africa for use against Boer women and children,* and that twentieth-century genocide was first practiced by the Germans against South-West Africa's Herero and Damara peoples. I know that South Africa took over the territory following the end of the First World War in Europe (the German troops in Africa were winning *their* part of the war, having been the first to take the unusual tack of using trained black African troops against their European enemy.) We were now "administering" the country, and protecting it and its peoples from the Communist "Total Onslaught" that required our "Total Response." Like everyone else, I had been subjected to the photographs of Cuban and East German troops in Angola that regularly appeared on television or in the papers.

* Another of South African history's false facts: archaeologists have recently established that concentration camps were first used by the Romans against the Picts of Scotland. The invading Roman army was commanded by Gnaeus Julius Agricola, whose surname would translate to *Boer* in Afrikaans.

When Sedgewick Schwartz—who is better informed than the rest of us, thanks to his father's low-key political activism—asks Mr. Brenner about our "illegal" occupation of South-West Africa, our usually fiery teacher is quite reticent. Sedgewick later tells me that it is because you can get arrested merely for repeating information about the armed forces that is widely known and that might appear without incident in overseas newspapers. You were not allowed to take photographs of members of the army or police, although this edict was not usually enforced if you were a family member or taking pictures of your army buddies. One of our classmates' fathers was detained for several hours when he took snapshots of a handsome old building in a small town he was passing through, and it turned out to be a military barracks. So Brenner's uncharacteristic caginess was understandable, although he couldn't resist infoming us that there had been only a handful of Cubans in Angola until the American CIA and our military joined forces with that champion of democracy, Jonas Savimbi. "The funny thing is," he had told us, unable to let an irony pass by unheralded, "the Cubans wound up defending British and French oil companies against us and the Americans. But of course, diamonds and oil really have nothing to do with this war, right?"

One morning the gardener asks if he might go and "buy a cooldrink by the Greek's," and I say of course. I realize that he would certainly take advantage of my laxity if the watchful Alini were not around, but I do not care. He has a sweet, sunny nature even if he is inclined, as Mrs. Capeland warned me, to be lazy. A grasshopper, not an ant. I tell him he should ask *Alini* if she wants anything and let her know I've given him permission to leave the grounds. He smiles and waves cheerily as he passes the pool on his way down the driveway to the gate. About twenty minutes later, I jump up from my deck chair, startled by a shrill scream coming from the road below. The scream tapers to a high-pitched wailing, the sound of a jackal at night or a child in pain. I run down the driveway, draping a towel over my shoulders, my sandals flopping awkwardly. The thong breaks on my right sandal, causing me to twist my ankle, and I hobble the rest of the way to the road. I see the neighbor from the house with the dogs charging toward a figure sitting on the ground, near which Jethro stands, his head turned resentfully aside. The neighbor is an elegantly dressed middle-aged woman, and I am aware of my ill-fitting swimming costume over whose elastic my flabby belly protrudes. She is wiping blood off the forehead of a young African woman whose pretty face is contorted with crying.

"For shame, Jethro. With a bottle! Did you have to hit her with the bottle? What's wrong with you people?"

He makes no reply, but gives us both a sour look. I tell him to go back to work, we'll take care of his girlfriend. He turns on his heel and dawdles his way back to the house. I have made an offer I have no means to follow through on, not having a car at my disposal and not knowing anything about first aid. She's not so badly hurt that she'd need an ambulance—would one even come for an injured African?—and I wonder if our young family doctor would make a housecall for a domestic. Fortunately the neighbor intervenes. "Ag, I'm late for my meeting anyway. But you come with me, my girl, and I'll drop you off at the clinic. And you." She turns to me. "Why don't you get her a towel or something so she doesn't bleed all over my car? Put some ice in it too."

I can't say I'm sorry to have a reason to get away from the keening girl, who sits rocking from side to side, one shapely brown leg on display where her skirt has ridden up when she fell. (I'll dream of that leg later, I know already.) I hurry to the house, hesitate over the luxuriant expensive bath towels and the threadbare rags that are used for drying the floors after they have been damp-mopped, and choose something in between, a solid enough swimming towel but one unlikely to be missed. I run hot water over the bottom of the metal ice tray (remember those!) and pull hard enough on the release lever that the cubes all crack before I dump them into the towel. The neighbor's mini is outside our driveway when I get back down, and I hand the towel to the young injured woman. "Thank you, Mrs. . . . ?"

"Van Tonder," says the neighbor. "And I know, you're the house-sitter. I hope you're keeping a better eye on the house than you are on Jethro." She speedily pulls off before I can reply.

I return to the Capelands' home chastened, try to read by the pool for a while, but the madam's life has lost its appeal and I have little desire to chat with Jethro about football. (Do you practice your header on that tender girl's face, free kick your darling's rear end?) He is sullen now and avoids my glance, like a child who has done something wrong and resents your pointing it out. (How quickly one falls into the thinking habits of paternalism!) Inside the house, things are worse. I can see that Alini is angry with me, as if my indulging Jethro in his desire for a nice cold Fanta led to the violence that seems so out of place on this sunny gorgeous day. I gather my things, walk down to the corner, and take the bus to the university, glad to get away from this house of ill humors. Wandering around the campus, I find myself questioning my decision to defer my studies and go straight into the army. I have that feeling you get when you have leaped off the diving board and the icy water is rushing upward toward you: you're committed to a course that may prove exhilarating but wish you could grow wings.

You may well wonder why I chose the army over the university, when so many of my coevals were desperately trying to extend their study deferments. The fact is, I was in danger of being gated, of failing my course of studies. It wasn't that swotting had become any more difficult for me, or that rote repetition of one's reading or lecture notes was an ineffective means to success at the university, but that I just couldn't be bothered. I had become like that little boy in the Afrikaans story who does things "just because." I'd always had a problem of being easily distracted, of dreaming, and now I didn't care any longer to hold myself back from the paths of endless association that a particular word or name might offer. I had chosen my classes indifferently and had landed some of the duller, least popular lecturers. I simply failed to show up for some exams; for others I answered only one or two questions, daydreaming my allotted time away as I followed ever more attenuated paths of memory. I needed a good shake-up; I was tired of being the glum fat boy, the lonely outsider watching as if through glass while my peers enjoyed themselves or got on with their lives. I lived from minute to minute, from day to day—a state some young people foolishly associate with nirvana but that is really the apathy of despair.

Now I walk past the university pool, currently occupied by the water polo team, young South African men of such vigor in their water-churning repetitive strokes that they might as well be a different species from me. I look enviously at the cheerful couples that seem to be everywhere paired off today, some simply chatting, others walking hand in hand, some ostentatiously snogging under the trees or in doorways. I am like some lungfish that has crawled up onto land only to discover that the age of mammals is already in full swing, my bold move an anachronistic late development. I must be careful not to become food or sport for these more developed creatures, as I gasp and crawl my way up the grassy hills and past the crisp buildings.

In my perambulations, I notice that a door to an old building near the medical college is open. I haven't taken notice of this place before, and I enter curiously. It is the Adler Museum of Medical History, a collection of ancient rusty implements that look much like farm tools, some beautifully weighted apothecary scales, leeching cups, a floppy skeleton. "We're not really open," a voice says from behind an open file cabinet. "I just came over to look up some information, but feel free to wander around while I'm here." A short man in a white coat emerges from behind the cabinet that is the same height as he. He notices me looking at some saws in a glass cabinet and says: "How would you like to be operated on with that and no anesthetic?" He stands close to me, reeking of disinfectant, his voice humorous as if we're sharing a good joke. "The poor souls having a limb amputated were given a rag soaked in brandy to bite down on. I suppose that's where the phrase 'biting the bullet comes from.' Of course, you wouldn't want to bite a bullet, certainly not at the cartridge end, but it sounds better than biting the rag."

"Thank God for anesthetics," I say in a rush, feeling foolish as the inane words tumble out. "I mean, there's times you have to dull your feelings. That is, if you don't want to kill the patient."

"Yes, better not to kill the patient. The family always asks such awkward questions. Of course, shock is a great anesthetic. Livingstone didn't even feel the lion biting and clawing him, at the time. You better believe he felt it later, though. You're a medical student, I presume."

"No, I'm not. I'm not anything."

"Oh, dear. That is serious."

"I mean I'm not a student. Not now. When I get out of the army I want to be."

"Well, you come back and see me after the army. I'm Dr. Snyman. The endocrine system, you know, but now I lecture on medical anthropology. And I was never a surgeon. I couldn't stand to be a surgical doctor, with my name. Too many jokes."

In school we used to ask each other the name of our mohel—Pipi Snyman being the correct answer. Even though the name probably refers to a tailor, I could understand why someone called "he who cuts" would seek some other specialty.

"As I was saying, shock can be a great anesthetic if it doesn't kill you. It's like the army. By the way, did you know that Paul Kruger used to take a pinch of gold dust every night? He believed it would make him immortal." Dr. Snyman points out a small quantity of yellowish metal in one of the cabinets, then proceeds to call attention to some of the other exhibits, the potassium permanganate for serious wounds, the "*Engelse Sout*" or Epsom Salts that the British used to settle their disquieted stomachs and which were valued as an all-purpose medicine by both the early Boers and the African tribesmen. The African chiefs traded hectares of land for a few ounces of the laxative; the Boers bought it from the Jewish smous or the Indian shopkeeper. Snyman is an odd, fascinating little man, a mine of facts and digressions, and he quite cheers me up.

My good mood leaves me at dusk as I am coming up to the gate of the Capelands' house. An African maid is waiting demurely by the gate, and it takes me a moment to recognize the injured girl of this morning. She now sports an inch-long zipper of blue stitches above her eyebrow and her cheek is swollen as if she has lopsided mumps, but otherwise she is still pretty.

"Do you need to be let in?" I ask, my voice gruffer than I intend.

"Please, baas," she murmurs. I unlock the gate and hold it courteously open for her, before locking it again. We walk up the drive in silence, and I notice that Fluffy does not bark as with strangers. It makes me wonder how many people live in those back rooms beyond the kitchen.

I sit in the dark after dinner, resting my elbows at the kitchen table. The museum visit has left me strangely placated, and I can once again enjoy time to myself being quietly dull. I am reminded of a school visit we once made to the Police Museum in Pretoria: the coffee flask murderess who flavored her husband's and son's coffee with strychnine, the sewing machine used to beat someone to death (its frame still flecked with real dried blood), Dingaka the African muti man who traded in human parts, and who was luridly represented in molded plastic in an ill-lit diorama. Perhaps that can be my vocation someday, to guide schoolkids around an obscure museum or showplace. I would cultivate the manner of a lovable eccentric. Perhaps the snake park? . . . but I'm afraid of snakes and would probably get bitten the first time I tried to milk a mamba or rouse a puff adder from its torpor. I imagine that one day in the distant future (you can see I have trouble contemplating the esoteric notion of employment in the near future), there will be a museum of Apartheid, for who would have believed the degree of absurdity attained by the mad Dutchman's philosophy? Who could have invented the idea of toilets destined only for bottoms of a particular hue, primarily "European" women? (Africans, for all Rooibos Sanders telling us they are closer to nature, apparently do not experience the usual bodily functions with the same urgency or frequency . . . at least judging by the dearth of toilets available for them.) Or the butcher's window offering cheap cuts of "boy's meat"? And the multiplicity of our official terms for *them*: natives, plurals (that one didn't last long), Bantu, Africans . . . as if we are not all the latter.

My thoughts are interrupted by the sounds of shouting from the servants' quarters: a woman's shrill voice yelling rapidly in Sotho, the deep basso of a man's voice that is at once low and angry. Not again. I open the kitchen door and step out into the night. There is no moon and the outdoor light for the kitchen door has its switch stupidly placed on the far wall and I have neglected to turn it on. The neighboring hounds lend their guttural barks to the argument that is still raging in the dark, but Fluffy is silent, cowering under a bed somewhere. I feel vulnerable with only the brilliant stars in the dark canopy of night to light my way; perhaps this is a ruse, and a gang of *tsotsis* is quietly sneaking up on me, knives drawn, waiting for me to step away from the safety of the house.

"Stop it," I yell, my voice cracking. "Stop that fighting and noise at once!"

I do not have the gift of authority, for there is no letup in the argument that seems, at least so far, to be verbal only. I wait, irresolute. "If you don't stop that, I'm going to call the police," I shout, and the words have a magic effect, silencing the stream of mellifluous Sotho immediately. A few minutes later, Alini appears. She is not wearing her characteristic *doekie* and I see that her hair is gray and cut short. "No police, young baas. I will get them to behave. Sorry to disturb."

"Thank you, Alini." She turns her back and disappears into the *ombrage*, and I feel ashamed of myself. She has never called me baas before, but in this moment of crisis I've reverted to type by invoking the hated apartheid authorities. No doubt the police would soon sort out this problem, arresting whatever family and friends are living in the back rooms without properly signed passes. I hear Alini's voice, soft but commanding, and then there is quiet again. Even the dogs stop braying.

Later, just when I am brushing my teeth, I hear a harsh and persistent coughing coming from the back quarters. It keeps up for some fifteen minutes before I feel compelled to go outside and call out: "What on earth is going on over there?" Nothing. No sound, but for a car engine idling somewhere down the street. The coughing is as absent as if I had imagined it. "Is everything all right?" I ask, but the night makes no reply.

~

The days pass. For a while, Alini seems suspicious of me, and my attempts to return to our old conversations are met with polite rebuff, but then she relents and we talk again. I even get her to try the kedgeree I have cooked for my breakfast, and she tells me that it is very good but she does not like fish. Africans do not eat fish, she informs me with authority. (Mrs. Capeland is clearly not the only anthropologist in the house.) Coloured people, yes. Indians. But Africans like meat. I try her again with a roast lamb marinated with white wine and olive oil and rosemary and thyme I have picked from where it grows abundantly in the rock garden. I hope Jethro has not sprayed the herbs with the flit gun that he so generously uses to attack the aphids on the rosebushes, perhaps imagining that he is carrying an AK47 and each of the diminutive white bugs is a settler. This meat dish she likes "too much," but she eats only a polite mouthful; I take as the mark of her favor that she requests the recipe so she can make it for the master and madam when they return. I ask her about her church, and she tells me that it is a good church, for hardworking people. If more people went to church, things would be better. The Capelands, she tells me, are good people: they only go to the shul church on the holidays, but they pray every Friday night and light candles for God.

The Capelands return on Friday afternoon in plenty of time for Shabbat, driving up in the late afternoon in their bottle-green Mercedes, which boasts a holiday coat of red dust. "I'll tell Jethro to wash it first thing," Mr. Capeland states as I come out to greet them and help carry in their bags. Alini stands in the doorway, grinning and wringing a dish towel in her hands.

"The house is still standing, at least," Mr. Capeland says jovially. They invite me to stay and welcome in the Sabbath with them, and I accept, not the least because the lovely aroma of Alini's oxtail bredie has permeated the house all afternoon. At dinner, they tell me about the trip: "We stayed in rondavels, but nice and clean with comfortable beds. Luxury rondavels, not like at Kruger. At night we went driving to see the game." "That lion kill was incredible." "Ja, the driver took us a few yards away but the lions were so busy eating they ignored us . . . or maybe they're used to people gawking at them." "And the food! Fantastic. Real gourmet stuff. Rack of impala one night, guinea fowl the next, bushpig bacon for breakfast. It's kosher if it's wild, you know. Read your Leviticus and you'll see."

I feel it is my duty to tell them about Jethro, especially as they will probably hear about it from the neighbor. It has worried me for a few days that they might fire him, but they seem incurious about the details. Mr. Capeland seems amused, if anything. "It's a good thing he didn't have an assegai with him. Just you see, that will be next. He'll get cross with her one of these days and . . ." He makes a stabbing motion at my chest with his dinner fork. "First it's fists, then it's a bottle, then the knife or a good sharp spear."

After dinner, I give Mrs. Capeland the pad where I've written down telephone messages for her, and Nigel shows me the new Swiss watch he found on his pillow the first night of the trip. It has a setting that will allow him to instantly know the time in South Africa when he is in England. I am admiring the watch, when I notice Mr. Capeland at the edge of the doorway, crooking his finger at me. He invites me into his study and hands me a bulky packet wrapped in tissue paper. "Open it when you get home," he says. "I think you'll be pleasantly surprised."

I can crinkle the package beneath my fingers, and it feels as if there are several sheafs of paper inside. Lately it has been the habit among the Lower Houghton set to give small birthday gifts that are elaborately wrapped. I had gone along with Mother and Mrs. Wissle to the latter's sister's sixtieth birthday. She had married a wealthy art collector, and lost no opportunity to favorably compare her circumstances with those of the abandoned Mrs. Wissle, who, I am sure, had brought us along to the celebration as some kind of buffer, or perhaps as an example that one could do even worse than she herself had. The sister greeted us at the door with kisses to the cheek in the European style, marveling at how only yesterday I had been a toddler but that is only a silly thing adults say and perhaps I had not really grown at all but she had shrunk. We wished her happy birthday, but she said no no this was just a party let us keep all talk of passing years out of it. There had been a gorgeous Raoul Dufy over the lintel to the entrance foyer, and I remarked on what a luminous painting it was. *Quatsch*, she told me, it's all right but I must come and see this other one, this one is much more valuable, a *Picasso*. Later, there was a small present-opening ceremony, the word *birthday* not permitted. Her husband had brought in a tinsel-wrapped box the size and shape of a small pony. As successive layers of cardboard, crepe, and wrapping paper were torn off to litter the floor, the present shrank until there was a velvet case the size of a box of household matches, and inside that a smoky topaz ring surrounded by diamonds. No doubt this packet given to me now by Mr. Capeland would contain a nice bundle of fifty-rand notes wrapped in butcher paper or parchment.

After I have been dropped off, spent some time chatting with Mother over tea and Marie biscuits, and unpacked my suitcase with all my clothes nicely washed and folded by Alini (who I realize, to my everlasting shame, had not gotten any goodbye present from me), I set to unwrapping *my* reward for watching the house, dog, and servants. Sure enough, there is a second layer of coarser paper beneath the gift-wrap, which I eagerly tear open. Inside that is a rolled animal-hide painting of a giraffe, still smelling of its curing. It's the sort of thing you buy on the roadside near the game parks for a couple of rand. There is a smudgy signature in the bottom right corner, the artist being named Moses Ngwenya, as well as I can determine. Crocodile, the surname means. I shake the painting several times, feel along its edges to see whether nothing is folded in there, double-check the pile of wrapping paper on my bed, but that is all there is. No gold-clipped sheaf of rand notes like that Mr. Capeland had removed from his trouser pocket when he called over the young boy selling the *Star* evening edition at a red light, no smoky topaz. I am reminded of Fluffy's habit after she has gobbled down her rations. She would meticulously lick the edges of the bowl, stare closely at the cleanly laved porcelain, then march out of the room. A moment later, she would come running back in at full gallop and screech to a halt in front of her bowl, her claws scrabbling at the linoleum. She would stare at the empty vessel in mingled hope and disbelief, clearly not understanding why it had not by some miracle refilled itself. I had thought this an endearing sign of the faith that accompanies limited intelligence, her doggy optimism in the matter of food a pleasant change from her usual petulant personality. Now I understand her better.

I am standing guard late at night, looking out into the blighted landscape of the Nam, the only other sentinel the windmill creaking as it draws water for our morning ablutions. This is one of the pleasures of being a thrall in the South African army; you can come back to base after a day spent running with rifle and gear in the hot sun, or practicing leopard crawls on a blazing desert floor, and after a brief and cursory meal be told by the sergeant: "You're on sentinel duty tonight, Sweetbread. Perimeter guard, stat!"

It is very quiet out here, standing too far from the tents of sleeping fellow soldiers to hear their mutters and snores, their restless turnings, with only the rare rasping squawk of a nightjar for company. Still, I dare not fall asleep, tempting though it might be, as heavy as my eyelids are. I fell asleep once on night guard duty. The staff sergeant, a man called Fynbos who never seems to need any kind of rest, so invigorating is the imposition of army discipline for him, showed up on silent feet very late in the night. Receiving no challenge to his movements, he tossed a thunder flash in my direction. If you have ever been jolted out of a sweet doze by a blinding, apocalyptic explosion, and later gotten punched and kicked by your comrades for being the cause of *their* disturbed night, then you will have no desire to repeat the experience.

I try to keep myself awake by reviewing, bitterly, the way I passed my last days of freedom, tethered like a donkey to the luxuries of the Capelands' house. Our English master at Sons of Abraham, Mr. Fawkes—known to the students as "Guy," though none would have dared call him that to his face—delighted in poems that spoke of the joys of youth . . . although he would invariably add that youth was wasted on the young. He was forever mentioning Housman's rose-lipt maidens and lightfoot lads, or telling us about Dylan Thomas being young and easy under the apple boughs, while we, of course, couldn't wait to escape from the very condition he extolled. Sometimes, on night duty, I took solace in reexamining in minutest detail each meal I had cooked in the Capelands' kitchen, or dwelling on the cool shock of the swimming pool on a hot day, followed by the sensual delight of flopping my wet body onto the sun-baked tiles. But often, as the gray light of dawn invaded the harsh landscape, and my body ached with an exhaustion beyond limits, I asked myself if I had not wasted the green days of my untrammeled youth by spending them as a substitute madam, a grampus wallowing in a blue suburban pool oblivious to its impending extinction.

...

"I have only learnt to get the better of words
For the thing one no longer has to say."

If Thomas Stearns Eliot had trouble finding the right words, then how am I going to do so for those things I want to say but cannot? I feel so strongly the urge to make sense of that unruly juncture between childhood and adulthood, that time when hormones stalk through our veins like *tsotsis* let loose into the city after Influx Control was lifted. Adolescent love is so messy, silly, and sentimental that there are only a handful of writers in English capable of re-creating the intensity of feelings, the noble shock of one's own fallible humanness, that comes with first falling in love. And even they don't get it quite right, the best work bordering on the maudlin and sentimental while simultaneously waking in the reader that quiescent, long-suppressed memory. I'm thinking here of Nabokov (more the perfect moments in the rose arbor in *Speak, Memory* than the lubricious quiverings of *Ada*). Silly

Dorothy in *David Copperfield* is hard to take, though Dickens gets his eponymous hero's feelings down just right. Then there are the works in translation: Thomas Mann's *Tonio Kröger*, parts of Turgenev's *First Love*, but not the all-too-predictable ending. Stendhal is better, perhaps because he is so unabashedly puerile (the root word being boy, and what we're talking about are boys' feelings, regardless of age).

What I'm trying to get at here (keep swimming, keep swimming) is that every sensible person reaches that moment in pubescence when he is plunged into the tumultuous lava flow of bliss, shame, soaring ecstasy, and icy freefall. And it's all roiled with hormonal lust, those unexpected bouts of tented trousers at inopportune moments—in physics class, for God's sake, in the middle of a discussion of how velocity is a function of distance over time! And how much harder it all is when you are physically unprepossessing, unresemblant to the hard-bodied males of noble mien in the women's journal stories and advertisements. Even those writers I've talked about take the easy way out—the same route as the authors of less literary romances—for their heroes are incurably good-looking, their sensitivity writ for all to see in their delicate features. What kind of bildungsroman is it, though, when the focal point is a shapeless blob?

Do you glance aside in shame and irritation, your eyes perusing this page, forced to glance at the wet-sheet evidence of vile adolescent imaginings? Who wants to remember again this silly stuff? Yet mine is a story of growing up, of a white South African rearing, and the mess of adolescence is part of it. Living through it once was enough, and so I disassociate myself from that foolish *he* whose interludes—like Prince Albert intruding on Mr. Dick's memoirs—elbow their way into my narrative.

Our hero is sixteen years old. It is December 16, 1984, Dingaan's Day, the Day of the Covenant, a national holiday of remembrance and celebration when South Africans of different hues and political stripes remember something different and only some celebrate. The scene is Clifton Beach, on the Atlantic Ocean, close to Cape Town but away from the parades celebrating a Boer victory and even farther from the restive, angry townships. Everyone here is beautiful, an illustration for the medieval architects' belief that the perfect arrangement of proportion is the human form. Everyone, that is, but for a gnarled and ancient African desperately trying to sell his singularly ugly driftwood carvings, and yours truly, our hero thus far.

"Best wood carvings, baas?" the African asks.

Flexing muscles as articulated as any gracing the sculptures outside Pretoria's Provincial Museum, a bronzed young Afrikaner Adonis chases the strandloper away with the words: "You're disgusting, man. Get your stink away from me."

"Ag, shame," says the exquisite young thing lying beside him, her impossibly smooth skin glistening like oiled Knysna yellow-wood. She has no awareness whatsoever that the great beached whale lying flaccid in the sand two body lengths away from her is near swooning at the curved lengths of her thigh and calf, the faint dimpling at the navel, the delicate dusting of hair in the shadows of her axillae. Once, after she turns the page of her magazine, an impetuous raspberry peaks out from beneath the skimpy bikini top, to be tucked back in with a petulant frown of indescribable loveliness. The beached whale dies a thousand exquisite deaths at this glimpse of nirvana. He is sixteen and exploding with hooligan hormones, sixteen and never been touched by the light fingertips of such a sweet enchantress. His skin aches for the experience, instantly producing a few more pimples out of sheer pique. But sensual pleasure eludes him—aside from the solace of edible goods—hence the profile that he tries to diminish by surreptitiously digging deeper into the declivity in the sand in which he lies.

Adonis sprinkles sand on his luscious companion's newly oiled back, and with a shriek she leaps up and trips on dainty metatarsals to the blue water's edge, diving in with barely a splash, her wet otter head reappearing moments later beyond the breaking waves. Adonis himself stands ponderously, overdeveloped hamstrings bulging; he rolls his gargantuan head in an elliptical arc on an eighteen-inch neck, and stretches muscle-corded arms, flexes Olympic weightlifter's biceps. "See something you like, Vaalie?" he says menacingly to our narrator, who cannot stop himself from gazing after the smoothly swimming unattainable object of his unstoppable daydreams. The pale cetacean pretends not to hear, fakes engrossment in his book—S. H. Scaife's *Memoirs of a Naturalist*, he was hoping some member of the fairer sex would ask about it and he could dazzle her with his extensive knowledge of the phylum *Arthropoda*. He is insulted that he has been equated with the groups of noisy students from the Transvaal who descend on the Cape at this time of the year laughing too loudly at their own jokes, shoving each other into female passersby on the pavements of Sea Point, and haggling furiously with the sellers of soapstone statues and Ndebele dolls at Greenmarket Square before walking off without buying anything.

"Deon. Where've you been? I was looking for you all over the place. For an hour at least."

The muscular blond turns his limited attention to the hefty and unbeautiful girl who has just arrived. (His sister?) She has brought a small vinyl bag, from which he extracts a can of Castle lager misty-hued with condensation. He pops the top and drinks it all in one draught. Burps loudly and melodiously. "Ag, don't be a pig," says the homely girl, who spreads her towel on the golden sand with an air of prim concentration. He follows suit again, proving that the bountiful lord has blessed him with the ability to produce eructations at will. "Did you save me a sip, hey?" asks a dripping nereid just emerged from the ocean, her graceful form silhouetted by the afternoon sun.

Our hero can take no more. He stands, feeling a moment of plunging dizziness, a positional hypotension that quickly passes, then lumbers toward the ocean. He notes with shame the white lines—

three of them—crossing his abdomen where the creases of his belly have preserved a thin rule of pale skin from sunburn. He launches himself into the water, which is a shock of ice-fed Antarctic currents, and there is a moment when a black ceiling closes down in his mind. Snorting salt water, he rises to coruscating brightness and quickly submerges again to avoid being dumped by the curling wave that thunders down onto the beach. He opens his eyes underwater to a world of green, his head aching with a metal-band tightness as if he had seized a full scoop of ice cream in his mouth. He breeches, takes a big gulp of air, and swims out a short distance to revel in his buoyancy. There are forces that he has no control of pulling him this way and that. He panics and tries to make his way back to the strand, striking out heroically toward a patch of white foam created by wavelets folding together like the wings of a dove. This is a mistake: the foam is the apex of alternate currents clashing in the light. The smallish wave upon which he tries to ride elegantly to the beach bubbles and froths in the sudden shallows, tumbling him extravagantly. He is upside down in the grip of a superior power that gleefully rubs his face in the fine sand with the meticulous cruelty of a schoolyard bully. Interminable moments later, he is allowed to reenter the daylit world, a comic sight with sand in his nostrils, mouth, and ears, reddish furze in his hair, strange bits of grit in every cranny of his swim shorts. Oh, the agony of suppressing that urge to scratch publicly at his crotch! He struggles onto the beach, puffing and blustering ("Thar she blows, the white whale!"), wiping away a snail's trail of mucus with his upper arm. He rumbles back toward his towel, where further humiliation awaits him. The callipygian object of his lustful imaginings is perched on top of Adonis's shoulders, who trots up and down like a game bull. The girl spies our brave swimmer and calls over to Adonis's blowsy sibling: "Hey, Viv. Why don't you get on the Vaalie's shoulders and we'll have chicken fights in the water." This suggestion is met with a moue of disgust by unlovely Viv. Atop her consort's shoulders, the beauty laughs hysterically. . . .

As if I wanted your fat thighs around my neck. As if my contempt were no less than your contempt. How would you know where I get my marks?

...

VACATIONS ARE SUPPOSED TO provide pleasant memories. Mine, however, seem fated to have the opposite effect. There is a tranquil town some sixty kilometers outside of Johannesburg on the Durban road, a place of rest camps and tearooms. When I was small, Mother and I had occasionally gone to one such resort, run by a devout Christian couple. Our last visit occurred when I was twelve, and was something of a disaster. I had first slipped on a wet rock beside the lily pond and plunged my foot into the burbling runoff canal leading into the smaller pond below. My shoes were new, and Mother was quite annoyed that one of them was now sodden and smeared with green slime.

"What on earth were you doing over there, Paul?" she snapped at me.

"Looking to see if I could find the baboons, Ma. I heard the owner say they get real baboons here."

"Oh, darling, honestly!" A fleeting smile appeared on her lips. "He was talking about how hard it is to get decent help around here. The natives are much more raw in this part of the country than in Jo'burg."

We sat in the shade of a willow and were brought a tray of tea and freshly baked scones by a shy, soft-spoken African maid who gave a little dip of a curtsy as she placed the tea things on our table. Mother thanked her, and she cast her eyes down in acknowledgment. I knew the homemade orange marmalade to be uncommonly good—just the right tartness of the fruit rind to go with the preserving sugar—and I broke one of the scones in half before applying a generous amount of the conserve to its steaming interior. I was watching the owners at their tea—the man had a tight clasp of his wife's hand, his eyes were shut, and he was murmuring a silent but fervent prayer—and so I did not notice that a bee had landed on my scone, attracted by the sweetness spread there. When I went to take a bite, the little worker stung me on the upper lip, which promptly swelled to several times its own size so I came to resemble one of those primitive tribesmen who has stretched his lips with wooden plugs in homage to some fat-mouthed god. Mother had to abandon her own tea, pack me up, and drive me to the nearest doctor recommended by our Christian host. The doctor proved to be an elderly man with violently trembling hands and a miasma of alcohol emanating from his pores. He gave me a shot of Benadryl and a bag of ice, redolent of stale freezer smells, to hold against my swollen mouth.

When we learn that my basic training will take place at the army camp in Heidelberg, Mother sees this as a bad omen.

"Of course, I worry about you up there," she tells me. "You could die if you get stung on the face again."

"Mother, they're not going to be serving scones and jam in the camps. And anyway, the army does have doctors, so it's not like I'm going off on my own into the wilderness."

"Well, I still wish you had found a way to postpone this whole awful business and finish your education. I really don't think you were trying, Paul."

On arrival at the army camp in Heidelberg, we were not given time to admire the surrounding veld, nor were there shady oases with ponds and willow trees, or panoramic views of the Suikerbosrand to enjoy with our tea. Instead, we were made to run laps in the hot sun for a while, then sent at double-speed to exchange our "civvies" for "kit." Kit included an R4 rifle, overalls, two pairs of boots and two pairs of sneakers, canvas webbing and tin-pot helmet, and of course the well-known *kakbruine* (the shit-brown nutria uniforms), not to mention underwear (four pairs), socks, etc. These were packed into heavy metal trunks, with blankets and a sleeping bag adding to the weight, and we had to run back to barracks with the trunks on our shoulders, again at double-time. We were "*roofies*," neophytes, chrysalids in the process of transformation, and it was the army's aim and delight to beat hell out of whatever personalities we had arrived with and turn us into soldiering automata instinctively responding to the bellowed order. We had to be destroyed in order to be saved, and it was not a pleasant process.

My seven months of basic training can be described in a word and in a phrase:

The word is *opfok*. When you fail to bring back the right leaf from the distant thorn tree, the one that your staff sergeant wanted immediately, then you got an *opfok*: fifty push-ups and then run back to the tree for another leaf, "not that one, you fokken idiot, but the other leaf. Over there!" Slow or incompetent individuals—like me—got our own *opfoks*, but sections got group *opfoks* because of those same slow or incompetent individuals. Smart groups learned to ease their pace or help the weakest links, since the *opfok* was coming anyway. Less smart sections—avid believers in the army way—took revenge on their feeble and lame on the assumption that a good *klap* to the head at shower or bedtime would transform less-enduring flesh and muscles the next day. Mine was not a group likely to win any prizes for intelligence.

The one good thing that could be said about the military training and the *opfoks* is that they gave me a hitherto unsuspected awareness of the ability of the flesh to eclipse the mind. Imagine, two three-centimeter patches of skin on your chafed heels become your entire focus, your sun and moon, obliterating even the trembling of your lactic-acid-filled muscles as you march with a full pack through stubbly veld and over rocky hills. Blisters! Blisters! Burning bright, in the forests of the night!

I also learned to be wary of my habit of daydreaming, taught myself new vigilance and self-monitoring no matter how tedious the activity. It came about this way: We were practicing a night raid on an unsuspecting terrorist camp (actually, a group of plywood huts dropped off by truck earlier on that day). I was in the rear group and found myself inexplicably ambling forward, my thoughts filled with the breakfast I had prepared for Mother and myself a few weeks before I arrived at camp (eggs baked in a hollowed-out orange, a Louis Leipoldt recipe; bread fried in chicken fat; chicken livers browned on the outside and just the right shade of pink inside). Perhaps it was the gray, rough exterior of the plywood shacks, resembling the texture of the fried bread, that drew me forward. Suddenly I was rugby-tackled from behind, hitting the ground hard with my torso and forearms. Moments later there was a tremendous series of explosions, and dirt clods and small rocks rained down on my back as each of the claymore mines that our commanding officer had strung in a line near the huts detonated. I stood up, my ears ringing from the thunderous noise, only to be knocked to the ground again by the staff sergeant, who screamed at me how it would have been a blessing for the army if he'd just had the sense to let me blow myself up. "You sleepwalk here," he yelled, "and we'll send you home in a box."

The phrase that best describes my basic training? It is drawn from South Africa's one claim to film history: *The Gods Must Be Crazy*. You remember, whenever hapless Steyn (who at least had Sandra Prinsloo to gladden his eye when he was not examining beetle maggots in elephant dung) returned from some disaster, his response to questions was quite simple: *I don't want to talk about it.*

I don't want to talk about it.

...

We fly out at night in a Hercules C-130 transport plane, where we sit uncomfortably on canvas benches with our duffel bags at our feet. Staff Sergeant Fynbos insists on our staying awake despite the hours of inactivity and near-darkness, a darkness relieved only once for me when I go to the toilet and the pilot motions me into the cockpit. Below us there is an empty blackboard, its slate expanse broken only by pinpricks of light indicating a farmhouse or a military outpost. "Looks like a lot of fun down there, hey?" the friendly pilot says, before I hear the sergeant's voice yelling at me to finish my business and get back to my place. My weight makes the canvas sag and grip my thighs, cutting off the circulation, and I sit in darkness, knowing that there is only blackness below, blackness above, and a deepening void in our hearts. It is not yet morning when we eventually arrive at a military landing strip outside of a small, ramshackle town. We know that it is far from anything, for when we look out of the open cargo door we see a few pale yellow lights illuminating windblown tin-roofed huts as if we have landed beside some tombstone town in a western film, the dusty army vehicles substituting for the bad guys' horses.

None of the officers bothers to tell us where we are, but one of the Permanent Force recces* has spent time here before. "Welcome to Opuwo," he says, "and if you've never heard of this shit little dorp before, that's no surprise." He tells us there's nothing here worth speaking about, but at least there are whores. They're the kind you want to wear two French letters with, he explains, unless you care to contract one of the more interesting venereal diseases. "You don't listen to me," he says, "and you'll wind up with your *piesang* covered with sores. Plus, it's a disciplinary infraction on top of that." I remember from my reading that the town's name, Opuwo, means "the end," a term that is either descriptive of its charms or refers to the fact that it's the last outpost of civilization before the Angola border.

The plane sits on the ground in the gathering dawn for about two hours, the cargo door opened only long enough for our duffels to be thrown unceremoniously to the ground. The air grows more stale and sour from the exhalations of unbreakfasted men, and I try to distract myself by interpreting the sounds coming from outside: mostly revving engines and the occasional shouted conversation in an unfamiliar African language. The tedious waiting is interrupted by sudden frenetic bustling as the cargo doors are again flung open and Sergeant Fynbos begins bellowing at us to hurry up, get the fok off the plane, grab our things, and get moving. "*Vat jou goed en trek.*" This was the same age-old command given to black farmers following the Native Land Act of 1913. (Thank you, Mr. Brenner.)

We are loaded onto Samil 50 transport lorries, which pull off in clouds of fine red dust. Jockeying to peer out the back, we catch glimpses of dilap-

* Reconnaissance Command. In my childhood I would have thought the spelling to be "wreckies," which is appropriate enough. The recces were the South African bush commando, often spending months at a time living off the land and going on secret missions. They were a well-trained and very effective elite unit.

idated buildings and flyblown shops, giving way to a shantytown of corrugated tin huts as the sun rapidly appears on the horizon. Outside a hut that is no more than several boxes of cardboard and some tarpaper, a small boy with a stomach protruding out from under his jersey and his forefinger deeply embedded in his right nostril watches us with astonished eyes. We cheer loudly at him, waving and laughing and cracking jokes about him digging for Namibia's fabled diamonds until he is hidden by our dusty wake and Fynbos' stentorian voice rises above the din to order us to shut our beaks. Then, for several hours, there is only that dry and rocky nondescript landscape of Southern Africa in the dry season, the only refreshment to the eye being the misshapen hills that our lorry judders over or circumvents. Our sole sustenance has been the thermoses of hot sweet tea in a box in the back of the truck, and we all grow more morose and depressed. My head aches with the hum of the motor, and my nose, mouth, and eyes feel as if the moisture has been suctioned out of them.

Finally, the lorries stop. Our destination—nowhere, it seems—has been reached. "This is Gemsbok Camp," Fynbos informs us, "or that's what it will be when you've set it up. After it's been put together, then you sorry and bloody useless lot might be lucky enough to get lunch." It's midmorning and the sun has already had time to heat up several inches of the red gravelly soil. Now the land on which we walk feels like a broiling pan that has been preheated before the steak is thrown onto it. We sizzle on top and bottom until we are universally charred. We engage in all the usual busy activity of an army troop, setting up tents, clearing brush, distributing cots and bedding, digging holes for the mortars, posting sentries at the perimeter. I am assigned to dig holes and afterward to sweep away lingering debris from the brush-clearing, so that this patch of bushveld may resemble a military parade ground. There is a girdle of pain around my lower back from the digging, and my right arm aches with the shock of ramming the shovel into earth that has been baked hard like a giant brick of terra-cotta. I console myself with the thought that the "softer" job of setting up the cots in the tents is probably worse—the canvas-surrounded interiors heating up like giant ovens—but at least there one would find companionship in the misery, and here I am sent off in solitary separation, put in coventry so I should not infect the others with my slovenly ways.

The bones of my wrist feel shattered from my futile blows against the stubborn earth, and my brainpan is entirely filled by the ferocious white orb that hangs suspended in the sky above me. And this is late winter! A few hundred kilometers to the west of us is the Skeleton Coast, so named because those unfortunate enough to be shipwrecked here could expect their remaining life span to be very brief. I can see myself being discovered later in the morning, a pile of bleached bones identifiable only by the shovel still tightly clasped in my fleshless fingers. Thus begins my first day of defending our sacred borders—though the border really belongs to someone else, and my endeavors most resemble those of prisoners in Robben Island, set to tasks chosen for their arduousness and futility.

My routine remains the same for the first week, with me being sent each day to the perimeter of the expanding camp to clear the scraggy but tenacious brush and grasses, to dig foxholes in the rain-starved soil, to tie barbed wire or inspect the barbed wire that has already been put in place, to move away rocks and pebbles and keep the ground as smooth as a ballroom dance floor. Being slow-moving and clumsy, I had been isolated often enough in basic training in the camp at Heidelberg. Here it is that much worse. Fynbos has told me he can't stand the sight of me, and he seems determined to remove me from my fellow troepies, to send me out into the bush like some young bull elephant kicked out of the herd. I suffer from loneliness, I even scratch into the dirt for my brief amusement E. E. Cummings's

l . . .
one
l

iness

. . . but I suffer most from the heat.

My bulk would be an advantage if I were posted to Antarctica. It nicely serves the same purpose as seal's blubber and does a fine job of insulating the vital inner core from any outside chill. I see its advantages only when we rise very early, before sunrise, and the *bosveld* is cold enough that the other soldiers blow on their hands and stamp up and down to keep their blood circulating. Except for the downward pressure on my weary head and droopy eyelids (has any physicist studied the fact that the pull of gravity is magnified early in the morning?), I am quite happy on such occasions. Little work is required of us, and most of the men spend their time stamping and blowing and warming their hands on the dullish coals of the breakfast fires.

It is a week, exactly, from the day of our first arrival at Gemsbok Camp (where no self-respecting gemsbok would set hoof). I have cleared and polished a surprising amount of obdurate rock-hard rocky soil, and am out of earshot of the activities of the rest of the camp, where some of my peers have even found time to engage in pickup games of soccer, their tasks in the inner circle being accomplished. The officers are relaxing in the shade of the *lapa*—an open stick-and-thatch structure—that *die ouens* have built for them. The morning cool is a memory even I have trouble holding on to, and now my body pours sweat, wringing me out like a bathroom sponge.

I am plagued also by small, moisture-seeking flies that like to insert themselves into any available orifice or get stuck in the crevices of my several chins. The flies crawl along my hairline and do buzzing battle with the stubby stalks that remain after the army barber's massacre of my finest feature. I wave my hat at them, which seems to cool down my head somewhat, though it has little effect on the persistent creatures. Some find their way into the corners of my eyes, where they drown and release an acrid final micturition in their death throes. I catch one in my hand, where it buzzes around until it gets used to captivity and does not fly away again when I open my closed fist. It sits in my palm, this winged myrmidon that was around to torment the first land mammals scurrying to avoid the attention of the giant saurians, rubbing its hands together like a surgeon scrubbing up. Then it wiggles its antennae rakishly at me and is airborne again, no doubt to renew its attack on my unprotected and tender surfaces, the wretched ingrate. It would like nothing so much as to have me expire on the spot so it could crawl up my nose and lay its eggs.

I understand much better Father's urge to eradicate these minuscule tormentors, and I find myself wishing he were here with his arsenal of flit guns and compressed-air sprayers, his tanks of noxious chemicals deadly to the *diptera* and the *hymenoptera*. Our mortars and repeating rifles, our grenades and rocket launchers, are all useless against this tiny winged enemy.

Another fly lands on my arm; carefully using its forelegs to move aside the golden hairs that stand straight up in a vestigial attempt to cool me down, the fly begins to scythe my tender flesh between its mandibles. I push down on it with my index finger, and the fly struggles for a moment before literally going belly-up, lying on its back in the abandoned plain of my broad arm, one leg kicking in its final palsied movements. Almost instantly, one of its kinsmen is on top of it, busy, its head bobbing up and down, its legs smoothing over any last remaining resistance. Two others are buzzing around my forefinger, obviously drawn to some delectable sanguine scent from the squashed muscid. I meditate on the odd fact that there must be some genetic survival value for these flying pests in giving off an attractant when crushed to death. Kill one, and you are sending out a signal to hundreds of others . . . at least one of which will successfully make you its blood meal, the nutriment for its thousands of offspring. There is a lesson in here somewhere. Maybe I will write it up and send it to Jannie Geldenhuys* and he can stick it in a poem or somewhere else.

After a while even the flies disappear, driven to the shade of some desiccated bush by the blasting heat. Or it may be that I have stopped sweating. My khaki shirt that was sopping wet on my back has dried out, leaving it

* Commander-in-chief of the SADF. His poems were given to us at training camp to provide inspiration.

stiff as a salted hide and chafing my sensitive skin at my every slightest motion. My brow is no longer a waterfall ledge over which a cascade of brine pours into my eyes; instead it is dry and my temple seems to give off its own inner heat to match that bearing down on me from the sky. Even my armpits no longer are moist.

This is all most unusual, for I have to confess that under normal circumstances I am a prodigious perspirer, a miraculous font of saline, a copious condenser. I've seen passengers on public buses wipe down the hard plastic seats with their hankies (even, once, a swimming towel!) after I get up, or sometimes they refuse to sit down at all on my relinquished seat. It is worst when I eat, for in the abandonment of my principal physical pleasure I labor and sweat, breathing stertorously as a man hauling rocks up a steep hill. The Sisyphus metaphor is apt, for the hard work of eating often as not makes me hungry again. I think now of the lunch I treated myself to in the short break between basic training and being sent to Namibia.

This was a new American-style Indian restaurant called Gandhi South. I don't mean that we were served pemmican or elk steaks, but that all was shiny and new and the food was not brought to you by a waiter but itself sat buffet-style in beautiful gleaming galvanized pans over spirit burners. It was an all-you-can-eat luncheon for a mere fifteen rand. Perhaps the proprietor had assumed that his customers would eat no more than they might order à la carte, but he certainly hadn't figured on me. I'm not sure where he'd gotten the idea, or why the banner outside proclaimed this an "American-style luncheonette." Perhaps Naidoo in Forest Hills, New York, had written to Naidoo in Rosebank, P.W.V., and told him this was the way to achieve success as a restaurateur. I soon stopped speculating about the whys and wherefores, my eyes lost in contemplation of the gleaming trays filled with fragrant delectable stews in different hues of yellow—the chef had a heavy hand with the turmeric. There were also several different birianis, the rice somehow managing to be both dry and glutinous, and there were platters of puffed-up oily pooris. Relieving the color monotony was a plate of sad henna-colored tandoori chicken carcasses.

I loaded my plate with saag paneer, mutton korma, bindhi saag, peas pillau, and a Kiplingesque biriani, topping the morass with fried onion and a few chunks of the chicken. I could have done a much better job of cooking any of these dishes—the chicken had been cooked at too low a temperature and for too long; the stale spices had been added all at once, muddying their flavor; the mutton was dead as England, drowned in a bath of ghee. But still it was plentiful, and the mixed pickle and green coriander chutney on the table could be poured over everything to give it flavor. I ate. When I was done, I went back for more. I ate that too. When I was returning to the buffet cart after my third plateful, I noticed that the owner's entire family had come out of the kitchen and back rooms and were watching me in speechless astonishment.

I ignored them and set to my task again, for it was hard work, this eating, and it required my total absorption. I was dimly aware of my own deep athletic breathing and the pools of perspiration that made my shirt cling to my back and armpits. I was Hercules at his labors, sweating, straining mightily, accomplishing the impossible. The Indian family watched me with awe and horror. The pretty, dark-eyed eight-year-old girl tugged at an older woman's sari and asked: "Is he going to eat it *all*, Auntie?"

Midway through my fourth plate, I unwrapped the serviette from the cutlery setting next to me and used it to wipe away the honest sweat from my brow. (The cloth napkin on my lap was dotted with yellow rosettes of oleaginous glop, as was my formerly white shirt.) I was the only customer in the restaurant besides an older Indian couple in the corner. Every now and then the woman would get up and place some delicacies from the buffet onto a plate, which she would then set before her husband. She left behind her a pleasant trail of sandalwood and patchouli oil. As far as I could tell, she ate nothing at all herself.

I had just finished the food and was sopping up the last vestiges of orange-colored oil on my plate with a folded piece of naan, when the proprietor sidled up to me as deftly and gracefully as a ballet dancer and whisked the plate out of my grasp.

"Please, sir, that is enough. You must leave something for the other guests." He looked at me through the bottom of his spectacles, and recited: "For sweets there is Jalebi—it is a kind of Indian doughnut—rice pudding, or vanilla ice cream. One sweet only. You must choose."

I forbore from telling him that I had not, in fact, eaten all I could eat, and that the sign outside was thus false advertising. It was not my fault that his business plan did not include the possibility that one day a black hole—or rather, a white giant—would enter his restaurant and steadily, inexorably, engulf all consumables. I ordered the rice pudding, which proved to be creamy and lightly flavored with rose water, cinnamon, and a hint of cardamom. It earned higher marks than everything else, and I wondered whether it was not what the family themselves ate, prepared by the old grandmother rather than the indifferent chef. It was gone all too soon, and that this was the one item that was not readily available for repeated helpings is surely a further sign—as if one is needed—that life is unfair.

I return to myself leaning stock-still against my broom, no trays of food in sight but only a few scraggly ironwood trees, the baking red earth, the harsh glare of the pitiless sun. I am glad that Sergeant Fynbos has not caught me in my moment of reverie; he would have delighted in setting me to some ridiculous and strenuous task beginning with a quick fifty push-ups. Nothing seems to give him greater refreshment than to bellow orders directly into my face. He has no sense of the boundaries of personal space—ironic, given that we are here to defend "borders"—and since we are exactly the same height I would feel his halitotic breath and spittle on my own lips in some awful travesty of a lover's intimacy. If you dare glance away from his mad blue glare, you're a shifty-eyed bastard, a lying thief. If you gaze at him boldly, he will snarl: "*Moenie so vir my loer nie, ek is nie jou hoer nie.*"* No one would mistake you for his lover, my dear sergeant.

Someone seems to be popping flashbulbs in my face, so I stagger over to the one stunted tree that offers something resembling shade.

* "Don't leer at me that way. I'm not your whore." There were many variations on the leering theme, the most creative being followed with the threat "or I'll suck out your eyeball and spit it in backwards so you can see what shit you have for brains." This cheerful phrase was invariably delivered in Afrikaans at high speed and great volume.

Each time I blink, the paparazzi flash another candid shot, and my retina registers alternately black Rorschach blot, then white flash, then black blot again. Shutting my eyes helps a little, and I sit with my back leaning against the ancient tree, waiting for the thrumming of blood in my ears and phosphene explosions in my eyes to settle down. I move forward suddenly, remembering that each of these stunted desert trees harbors a colony of biting ants, souls toiling in hell to gather a mouthful of turpentinelike sap from the scarred ridges of the sere bark. A slim lizard skitters along and stops a few yards in front of me. It is sand-colored, with a bright blue throat, and it dances from foot to foot in slow motion, keeping any one limb from having extended contact with the burning ground.

I stare at the dancing lizard and think of the fellow we used to call the "mad African." Dressed in discarded army khaki shorts and shirt, his muscular legs streaked with old dirt, he would park his bicycle cart outside the school playground and thumb the bell. He had a device like an organ-grinder's crank, and when he turned it, shaved ice would slide down a chute into the little paper cup held in his gnarled left hand. We would point to one of the bottles of colored syrup—cherry, grape, granadilla—and he would pour a dash over the shaved ice, all the time keeping up a crazy litany: "You go to school. You fight. Breaka da umm. You play foo'ball, breaka da leg. You cross da road, heet by car, you die." He too would dance from foot to foot like a shovel-snouted lizard (*Meroles anchietae*) while chanting his litany.

The teachers warned us against him: his food was unhygienic, he did not have a license, we would get amoebic dysentery or tuberculosis from his ice cream. (He spat often, but always to one side of his ice cart.) We told stories about him too: a Standard III boy had made fun of him, imitating his liturgy, and had been chased screaming down the street inches in advance of a wicked-looking knife. But still we bought his ices: they were so good, so sweet, so cold.

The lizard has disappeared, and in its place is a size-thirteen army boot, laces tied in perfect symmetry. I find myself being hauled suddenly vertical, Sergeant Fynbos screaming in my face: "Do you think you're at the fokking beach? Maybe you'd like me to massage you with suntan oil, hey."

I try to answer but my voice croaks from between parched lips. Water is dashed in my face from the sergeant's canteen, delicious and humiliating. I am pushed along stumbling back to camp, the sergeant grumbling about a fokking English *soutie*, five minutes in the sun and he's getting sunstroke. Then I'm lying down inside a tent, waking briefly in the night, then in the day, then in the night again. All the while my head throbs as if my brain is trying to push its way out from too-tight a cranium. I am visited one morning by Captain Lyddie, who looks at me hard with his cold gray eyes, his mouth fixed in his habitual sardonic grin, and says: "Are you feeling a little better now? Because my good friend Sergeant Fynbos wants to court-martial you."

"For coming down with sunstroke?"

"No, man. For direct contravention of an order. In other words, for not wearing your hat when you had been specifically told to keep your hat on. Do you remember that order?"

I do. It was when we were aboard the Hercules droning through the African night. I had glanced at my watch a few minutes before the sergeant began his harangue of orders to do with setting up camp: 10:45 P.M., or 22:45 military time, and most of the men were half asleep, including myself, lulled into somnolence by the dull steady roar of the engines despite Fynbos' exhortations to keep our wits about us. Some of the men even managed to sleep bent over despite the discomfort of the canvas benches, elbows on knees to brace the weight of their upper bodies. "Your bush hat is your friend, your shelter; keep it on at all times," Fynbos intoned at the same pitch as the engines' drone, stopping to tap Trooper Halcket awake as his head lolled toward a neighbor.

"So why weren't you wearing your hat? Did you think we'd send you back home to Mommy if you got your tender little scalp sunburned?" Lyddie demands.

"I was hot. I took it off to scare away the flies, and then I was just hot. It seemed to help, having it off."

"What you should do," Lyddie says, "is pour a little water over your hat. Then it will act like an air conditioner. It's the Principle of Evaporation, or don't they teach you physics in the Northern Suburbs?"

There is little I can do but apologize. Lyddie laughs, having made his point, and says, "Don't you know the motto of the British Foreign Service in World War II? *Never complain, never explain*. Think about it."

"I'm sorry— " I begin, but he holds up a cautionary finger and mock growls, "*Pasop, jong,*" with almost the same expression and phrasing as Rooibos warning a schoolboy to watch himself.

"No. I want you back in the field tomorrow," he admonishes me. "No excuses. You have today and tonight to rest and recuperate, to dream your dreams of courtly love and virgin maidens, for tomorrow you're going to be a soldier."

...

HE IS SIXTEEN AND a half, attending a birthday party for Sedgewick Schwartz, who has grown into a lean-limbed, long-lashed youth tanned the color of caramel, with long flaxen hair cut into a fringe over his eyes. Sedgewick would not be out of place in the Prince Valiant cartoons that adorn the back of the Sunday papers, and is still several years away from openly revealing his true sexual inclinations. Already Ruthie Mann's mother has embarrassed them all by seizing Sedgewick's cheek—the fleshy part, below his sculpted maxilla—and pinching him hard, singsonging: "Ag, you beau-tee. If I were ten years younger, you'd be in trouble, hey?"

He has known Ruthie Mann, the family dentist Dr. Poenskop's daughter, since primary school. She has also "shot up," as the pre-heroin generation would say, inheriting her father's height and angularity, her mother's full figure and lubricious pout. He nods to her, two shy people relegated to the corner of the room while the other teenagers—male and female alike—dance attendance on the resplendent Sedgewick. She reminds him disconcertingly of a ring-tailed cat (South Africa's "raccoon"), having overassiduously covered both her top and lower eyelashes with jet-black eyeliner. (Cleopatra is back in fashion.) "How's old—" he almost says it, the Afrikaans slang for baldie. . . . (Her father would not have minded: he's an avid collector of desert tortoises but likes to tell his patients that he always wears a hat when he's out in the Karroo, "so I don't wind up like poor old Aeschylus.")

"How's your pa?" he amends. "I have not been to him in over a year. Thirteen months and four days, to be exact."

"You're due a visit."

"Ja. I suppose."

What an ass he's been, reminding her of her father's profession, which had been enough to make her an outcast in primary school. He might as well have talked about the perils of plaque! The kids who had to suffer under old Poenskop's whistling drill and his inevitable admonition that they should remember this moment the next time they were inclined to eat sweeties could at least avenge themselves on the daughter. Her best friend, Jenny de Groot, had coined a cruel song that the others liked to sing, their open mouths glinting silver amalgam from the good dentist's ministrations: "Ruthie Mann. Ruthie Mann. You think you're a girl, but you're really a Mann."

In a sudden nervous gesture, he tugs at the curtain they are standing beside, and now they are enveloped by it. "Why did you do that?" she asks softly, leaning closer, her perfect white teeth glistening behind her parted lips. She is a big, horsey girl, the beauty she is to become still hidden behind a coltish edginess. (Just a few years later she is to become famous for a dazzling nude scene at the Market Theatre, a politicized Maid Marian whose discarding of her jerkin is as scandalous to the Censorship Board as the allusions to P. W. Botha in the theater company's portrayal of the Sheriff of Nottingham.)

"*Sommer*," he says.

"I remember that book," she says with a laugh. "It was the only one of those bloody Afrikaans assigned books that I liked, that little boy who's always answering *sommer* when he's asked why he put the cat in the dustbin or set fire to his grandfather's beard. You remind me a little of him."

He shrugs, the gestural equivalent of the word *sommer*. He feels extraordinarily dull, loutish, numbed as if her father had overdosed him with novocaine. He feels this way more so when she steps closer to him, her pneumatically firm bosom resting against his crooked arm.

"I wonder what the others think we're doing behind the curtain," she whispers. Her breath smells cloyingly of the small pink sweets called cachous, a bowl of which had been on the side table; a scent too sweet and blending nauseatingly with the faint odor of ammonia cleanser from the window.

"I don't know. Do you think they even noticed?"

He is behind the curtain with a *girl*, a pretty girl even if her face is a bit long, the wings of her nostrils a touch too broad. A girl who is hinting that she wants to be kissed. So why does he feel so leaden? Is it the vividly present memory of her father's hands smelling of Dettol, the shrill whine of the drill enlarging a cavity only to fill it? Or is that just an excuse for his gutlessness?

Probably no one has noticed, she agrees, the implication being that nothing the two of them could do would be worthy of the others' attention. The moment having passed, she reverts to being a shy girl again. "It must look silly, just our feet sticking out, I mean."

Yes. He pulls the curtain open again and they step back into the party, where they eat Black Forest chocolate cake with vanilla ice cream and sing happy birthday. He remarks to Ruthie that he used to think the maker of the ice cream was a company called Roomys, and she laughs and says that she used to think so too, that she was never much good at Afrikaans anyway and had completely forgotten that *room* is cream and *ys* is ice. No one seems to have taken note of the interlude, but when he is calling out his goodbyes Sedgewick wags a finger at him: naughty! naughty!

That night, alone in his room, he curses his torpid passivity. Faint heart never won fair lady, you fool, he torments himself. Almost asleep, his mind frees itself to let him be a demon lover, Valmont in *Les Liaisons Dangereuses*, who uses the curtain like a cloak behind which he brings the flushed and now-beautiful Ruthie to ever higher pinnacles of delight. He cups her round chin in his strong, firm hand and gently sips on the sweet nectar of her lips. Waking in the dark reaches of the night, he turns on the light and sees that he has soaked his pillow, a round patch of drool. He would not have been surprised to see his head in the bathroom mirror sporting a pair of donkey's ears, but it is the same overlarge round head as always, the same grumpy quizzical expression. "Tonight you looked a gift horse in the mouth, my boy," he murmurs . . . and is immediately assailed by a hideous image. There, puckering equine lips for a disgusting kiss, is a creature with old Poenskop's broad teeth and weathered face, Ruthie's hair and sorrowful brown eyes. What Puck has transformed his adolescence into this nightmare? He brays, and the neighbor's dog answers with a mournful howl. His mother's voice calls out in alarm from down the hall: "What is it? What's going on? Is someone breaking in?"

"Don't worry, Ma. It's only me, coughing. Go back to sleep."

"Okay, lovie. Feel better."

"Feeling is not the problem," he says quietly to himself.

...

I don't hear any more about a court-martial, so I assume that he has told Fynbos to drop it. Fynbos worships the captain, his ideal man. He wishes he could make us into the captain's like, but his way of encouraging this transformation is to tell us we're a bunch of *moffies* not fit to lick the captain's boots. Sergeant Fynbos' rhetoric largely consists of unflattering comparisons between the conscripts and members of the fairer sex or those men who engage in what Fynbos calls "unnatural practices." "Come on, *moffies*," he yells during training as we run in our heavy boots, rifles held above our heads. "Move it, ladies. Afraid a little sweat will ruin your makeup?" When a conscript balks at crossing a narrow log suspended over a donga, he is told not to wet his panties. "I've seen the girls' netball team do better," Fynbos tells us when we return from a twenty-four-hour march. And always it's, "*Maak gou, julle moffies.* I'm going to make men out of you pansies if it's the last thing I do."

He is right about Captain Lyddie, though. The captain is a perfect specimen of South African manhood: tall, muscular, with well-shaped thoroughbred muscles that come from good genetic material and an active outdoor life, not the overdeveloped protuberances of the Nautilus-and-steroid addict. He is the glass of fashion and the mold of form. His short-cut hair is thick though receding a little at the temples, and there are crinkling laugh lines around his eyes. He could have been the illustration for a reissue of *Teddy Lester, Captain of Cricket*, if Teddy Lester had grown up to become an efficient killer. The soldiers are all more than half in love with him. Looking at him strolling gracefully through the camp, his well-developed calf muscles coiling and retracting as he bounces on the soles of his feet while exchanging a laugh with some troepies who had been assigned to retie the tent guylines, I can see why he is someone men would be prepared to die for. There is a communicable brightness to him, and the men stand a little straighter, work a little harder and more willingly, when he is nearby. Even Fynbos responds to his presence, puffing out his pigeon chest and raising his voice beyond normal human limits as he cajoles us, a veritable Joshua, he, as imaginary Jerichos crumble at each bellow. His language even improves slightly, as if he does not want the captain to think him unrefined.

I owe a particular debt to Captain Lyddie, for not only has he saved me from prosecution for getting sunstroke (just because it was a ridiculous idea doesn't mean the army would not have pursued it), but he is responsible for my new, and more appropriate, employment.

"What the hell are we going to do with that sack of shit?" Fynbos remarks aloud as I toddle on unsteady legs toward the lunch pot my first day out of bed.

"This stew is truly disgusting," Lyddie replies, putting aside his bowl with a wry expression. He has a habit of circuitous replies. "It's burnt, for one thing. It's cold, for another. And I just ate a vile lump of congealed curry powder. Now, listen, I have seen that fat bastard eat, so why don't we see if he can cook too."

It hurts to have Lyddie call me fat bastard, though I daily hear much worse from Fynbos and my fellow troepies. I don't dare print what they called me when I delayed my group in the relay races in basic training. But Fynbos reluctantly agrees to the idea, growling that I would probably poison them all. At first, I am assigned to the task of peeling potatoes and turnips, while the de facto head cook, a slovenly, squint-eyed Durbanite whose brains have been addled by smoking the eponymous "Poison" his city is famous for, continues to turn perfectly good if uninspired ingredients into the foulest concoctions imaginable. He has been trained at the army chef's training base at Okahandja, where he learned to boil beef and cabbage for the army's nutritious if flatus-inducing dinner staple. To this simple food he likes to add large quantities of Worcestershire sauce "for flavor"—this dark concoction is delivered in the same two-and-a-half-liter plastic bottles as the cleaning fluid, so it is only a matter of time before Durbs pours the wrong liquid into the night's stew, and I am determined to keep a sharp eye on him. He had probably started out as a reasonably competent cook but has gotten steadily worse as Klipdrift and dagga engage in a successful blitzkrieg against his cerebral cortex. One afternoon, Durbs is in such a state of hallucinatory paranoia, the result of hastily swallowing his stash during a surprise bunk inspection that morning, that even Fynbos notices his mental confusion. Durbs is hauled off to the medic's tent, railing about invisible giant birds flying overhead.*

* Years later, I read about how the Himba elders assume the form of gigantic birds called *omazila* and take to the skies during their circumcision rituals, so maybe Durbs wasn't so bosbefok after all.

At any rate, I am allowed to take full charge of the huge iron pots suspended over paraffin burners or wood fires, and the results so noticeably please the hungry men and officers that there is soon no question who should be the Gemsbok Camp head chef. This proves a boon for me, as well as all the soldiers during my reign, as I also use some of my pay to send away to my preferred spice supplier, Mr. Mahalingam Soonaswamy on Fox Street, for bulky packets of cumin, bird's-eye pepper, and fenugreek.* I take the precaution of letting Lyddie know what I'm up to: following Durbs' breakdown there has been a renewed vigilance about checking for drugs coming in with our post.

My generous initiative backfires on me with my cooking the worst meal I've ever made: I decide to replicate one of my beloved Cape Malay curries. I had last made this dish—a mutton and potato curry with plenty of garlic—for Mother's forty-ninth birthday . . . although she had ceased to add years at age thirty-nine, celebrating the same pre-fortieth anniversary year after year. I can smell mingled odors of the kitchen now—the onions frying in clarified butter, each of the bowls of *sambals* (we liked a lot of condiments) as I set them out: lemon *atjar*; homemade *dhunia* (cilantro) chutney; pineapple with green chilies, cumin, and *dhunia*; braised Malay cabbage with spices—each individual note coming together to form a single glorious chorus. Mother kept popping her head into the kitchen to ask if she should fetch the recipe book (I'd already read it) or to chop onions for me (I was much faster and didn't want to interrupt my activities to bandage her fingers) or find a spice for me (not necessary, I always know where I left it the last time), but really to savor the progress of her birthday dinner.

The problem with the same meal at Gemsbok Camp is not that I lack fresh *dhunia*, which can be done without, but that I am used to cooking for two people rather than sixty-five and so I foolishly increase the spices

* Perhaps realizing from the army address that I am far from home, he sends me some inferior-grade *borrie*—turmeric—with tiny beetles wandering around inside the closed package. I think of Jan Smuts, our last pre-apartheid prime minister, and his fear of the Eastern subcontinent. "Beware the Indian," he liked to say.

in the same ratio as the other ingredients. The final product is so fiery from my liberties with the cayenne pepper that no one can take more than a mouthful without blistering their lips, and one soldier presents a melted army boot to me with the claim that he'd spilled a little of his dinner on it. Fortunately for me, Lyddie finds the whole mishap exceedingly funny. When Fynbos threatens to beat the *kak* out of me, Lyddie laughs and says: "Chaka toughened his warriors by making them dance barefoot on thorns. After one of Sweetbread's curries, who's going to worry about fucking Swapo lobbing a few mortar shells in our direction?"

The camp kitchen seemed to attract or be the dumping ground for a pool of miscreants and ne'er-do-wells. Along with dagga-crazed Durbs, there is Reggie Plimsoll, who surreptitiously scarfs little white Mandrax pills that slow his motions to that of a chameleon or some elderly practitioner of tai chi. There are the Marie brothers (generally known as the "biscuits"), whose IQs are appreciably lower than their body temperature but who do a hell of a job scrubbing pots. Then there is a real anomaly, Roelof de Wet, a tall, gangly Afrikaner who peels the potatoes on Sundays. He has been transferred to our camp from Oshakati; though no one voices the sentiment, we all know this is a comedown in the world.

I ask Roelof why he doesn't have time off like everyone else, whether there is no Sunday religious service for him to attend. This question opens the tap for a flood of words: "Ag, *boetie*, you're sounding just like Sergeant Fynbos. 'Don't I want to go to church?' he says. 'No, man. I would rather peel potatoes.' Jesus, you should have seen his face when I told him that, and that was *before* I explained that I don't believe in God. What an idea! 'You're an Afrikaner, aren't you?' Ja, and my grandfather was a *dominee* and my great-great-uncle was you-know-who. 'So how's it possible you don't believe in God?' 'She doesn't exist,' I explained. I thought for sure his head was going to blow right off and I'd be up for the murder of a superior. 'S*he*!' he says. 'Go and peel potatoes and don't make blerry jokes.'"

I see him every Sunday after that, both of us spending our day of relaxation preparing the large meals that leisure seems to bring out a demand for in our soldiers. DeWet is always cheerful. He actually does seem to enjoy peeling potatoes—a brutal job, I know because I've done it: the potatoes are rough-skinned and hard as stones, peeling them inevitably leads to scraped knuckles and hands that are red, raw, and cracked from friction and cold water. He sings traditional songs while he peels, "Suikerbossie," "Daar Kom die Alibama," "Sarie Marais." Roelof's is one of the most celebrated Boer names, his ancestor being the renowned Boer War general Christiaan R. de Wet* (no doubts about God there!), who brilliantly led the Orange Free State commandos in successful raids against the British. The general was a bitter-ender, with contempt for the Boers who sued for peace (the *hensoppers*, or hands-uppers) after the British fenced off the veld, burned all the farms, and put the women and children in concentration camps. Like Roelof, Christiaan R. was a born dissenter . . . but on the opposite side: for his opposition to British imperialism during WWI, he was charged with treason and this time did land in prison.

Unlike me, Roelof is athletic and a crack shot, and the officers and men treat him with respect and puzzlement. Roelof is proud of being an Afrikaner, and our friendship is cemented when I tell him I've read Eugene Marais' *Soul of the White Ant* (*Die Siel van die Mier*), a book sent in manuscript to the great biologist Maurice Maeterlinck, who wrote it off as bad scholarship and then published it under his own name, breaking the old Afrikaner's heart.

"His poetry is beautiful, you know," Roelof says reverently. "Would someone like Fynbos have ever read it? Hell, no. But he won't lose a chance to *kreg* about how you English *soutpiele*† don't bother to learn

* Another of Dad's jokes: Why did the Boer commandos sleep with their boots on? Answer: "To keep de Wet from defeat."

† English-speaking South Africans are thought of by the Afrikaners as having one foot in England and one in South Africa, hence their *piele* dangle into the ocean and are covered with salt.

Afrikaans. Now, Fynbos, he doesn't speak real Afrikaans; he speaks that Germanic ostrich shit the government has instilled in his head. Real Afrikaans, street Afrikaans . . . *Here*!* that's a language!"

Roelof has a gangly, wiry strength, handling the large tubs of food as easily as I do despite our considerable weight difference. He is the model ectomorph, and I think back to when Rooibos Sanders explained these terms in class to us one day. She had begun by telling us about how early physiognomists had elaborate theories as to how our faces reflected our personalities, and she showed us some illustrations of the facial types that indicate criminal tendencies. Then she moved on to physical types, calling out tall, skinny Roger Stone to be the ectomorph; husky, well-built Danny Mainzer to represent the mesomorph; and me, of course—though Cammie Kramer would have served better—as the endomorph.

"What makes people one type or another?" Jenny de Groot asked. She was the kind of swot who was happy to play the inquiring straight man for the explanations teachers would have given anyway.

"A very good question, Jennifer. Mostly it's genes that are the culprit," Rooibos replied. "I think in Paul's case he represents the fatter body type because he eats all the time."

Perhaps because I was annoyed by the word *fat* being applied to me, however accurately, I misunderstood the cadence and syntax of her words: according to Rooibos, I was an eater of time, the whole of it. For a moment I felt pleased; so she did understand my memory's excesses after all! I could not help but take in time and contain it, my past and present moments butting against each other like cattle in a chute.

My ectomorph friend, DeWet, is a good soldier and a didactic patriot, who believes in the defense of the borders more than most of us here do. But there is that same streak of rebellion and independence in him as in his illustrious forebear. He won't go and spend an hour listening to the predikant or sit in silence with his head bowed over the Holy Book, just

* For those of you who don't speak Afrikaans—and why should you?—this is pronounced Yirrah, is often misspelled that way, and it means "Lord."

because it will please someone else. Often, he tells me of his latest conversation with Sergeant Fynbos, how our superior has to keep gnawing at this particular bone. "It really bothers him that I don't believe in God. You know, he asked me why don't I just pretend, go through the motions? I pointed out that would make me a hypocrite. 'Do you really want to be a pagan?' he says. So I pointed out that the word *pagan* is Latin for a country dweller . . . in other words, a *boer*. Then he told me that if I just prayed to God, I would start believing in God. It's funny, but there's a sentimental side to old Fynbos. There often is with brutal people, don't you find that?"

Yes, I had found that. But how had he answered Fynbos' question? After all, there were plenty of atheists and agnostics willing to sit quietly for an hour so they could have the rest of the day unhampered by orders or chores.

"I tried to explain that false prayers would be more offensive to God—if she or it should really exist—than true rejection, but Fynbos is not much for theological argument. When I told him that I'm actually serving God by peeling potatoes *mindfully*, he told me to have it my way and walked off."

"Really. He told you to have it your way?"

"Welll . . ." Roelof laughs. "Actually, he said *gaan kak!*, but I'm sure that's what he meant."

...

"I'M GOING TO BE spending less time cooking with you," Roelof tells me as we watch the satiated, still-greasy faces of the soldiers who have just feasted on garlic-crusted pork chops. Although I enjoy all variety of foods, there is some genetic memory inside me that doesn't particularly like cooking or eating pork—though I'll happily make other *treyf*, like shrimp, or crayfish, or *dum gosht*, which mixes meat and milk—and so Roelof did much of the frying tonight. It's disturbing how much pork or pork fat goes into our army food; the metal *varkpanne* at our base camp were more than aptly named: "pig troughs" to serve pig meat to pigs.

"I'm a reformed character," Roelof tells me. "We Afrikaners like that word: reformed. Just like our church, *die Nederduits Gereformeerde Kerk*. It underlies our whole philosophy. And me, I'm going to church on Sunday, where I will pray with great fervor. I'm not going to cheek old Fynbos anymore, but will treat him with the respect he deserves."

"'God's bodykins, man, much better: use every man after his desert, and who should 'scape whipping? Use them after your own honor and dignity: the less they deserve, the more merit is in your bounty.'" I quote at him. "So, what's your plan . . . other than giving Fynbos the whipping he deserves?" He has told me that he is always scheming (*'n Boer maak 'n plan*), and the happy look in his eyes confirms my guess.

"The army is going to send me to school." He grins. "Ask not what you can do for your SADF, but what your SADF can do for you. I want to further my education and get posted to one of the video units. Perhaps I'll come back and make a film about you."

"*Hero of the Iron Pot*," I suggest.

"*Memorable Order of the Aluminium Frypan*," he says. "Sort of like the MOTHs* from the Great War."

"If Fynbos has anything to do with it, that name will be changed to Mothies. Perhaps you could film him giving instructions, then ask the question: How would you like to spend a year in the desert with this man? That should swell the ranks of the End Conscription Campaign."

Despite our lighthearted tone, I know that I am going to sorely miss Roelof, who has broken past my isolation and proven to be one of the rare human beings I can share my thoughts with. Prior to this time, the only Afrikaners I had met had been people I was afraid of. They were the shaven-headed, hard-eyed teenagers standing outside cafés on the street corners, tough kids who liked to fight. Once, at one of our away games that the rugby coach insisted I go to, although—as he said himself—there wasn't a chance in hell I would be sent out with the team, I was followed

* Memorable Order of the Tin Hat, a politically conservative ex-serviceman's organization.

into the bathroom by two such youths. They had probably planned to beat up this "sissy Jew," but they found it much funnier to give me a hard push as I was standing at the urinal so that I wet my socks and shoes and spent a humiliating afternoon with my own fellow Jews laughing at me. We all had to learn Afrikaans, but we didn't have to like it. Part of the government's determined effort to make the country "bilingual" showed itself in the evening news being in English one night, in Afrikaans (*die Nuus*) the next . . . and in neither case was it *news* but rather an assault of images and comments designed to make us aware of the "Total Onslaught" being waged against us.

Roelof is both proud of being an Afrikaner and mocking of his race's pretensions. He loses no opportunity to rail against the bowdlerization of the language by *Die Genootskap Van Regte Afrikaners* (the Society of Real Afrikaners). "An Englishman like you cannot possibly imagine how fulfilling it is to be a member of one of the *original* Afrikaans families," he tells me. "You see, the government wanted to show the purity and nobility of our great names, so they asked the director of the National Library to do a genealogical study. The poor man did as he was asked, but made the mistake of being truthful about what he found. Every one of us *pure* Afrikaners—the Cilliers, the Duplessis, the DeVilliers, the DeWets—has somewhere in the past a Malay great-great-grandmother or a *vrijgelaten swarte,* a "free black," grandpa. The poor old director got in such trouble; even after he apologized, I think someone shot at him. But who wants to remember that little girl who was taken away from her white family because she came out too dark? Mark my words, a few years from now the pure Afrikaners are going to fall over themselves claiming that free black ancestor."

. . .

I AM STIRRING A large pot of mutton bredie over the camp fire one late afternoon when Captain Lyddie appears suddenly at my side and dunks a heel of bread into the pot. He winks at me, wiping the back of his arm across his mouth. "*Potjiekos*, like the trekboers ate. The sergeant may say you're not up to much, but this place is like a five-star restaurant since you got to be cook. Keep it up, laddie."

"Thank you, sir," I say, pleased out of all proportion at this simple compliment. It is a reminder of how few kind words I've heard since being inducted into the army, how rare it is for an officer to speak at a normal decibel level. For Sergeant Fynbos, even my culinary skills are a sign that I should be wearing petticoats and an apron like some *meid* in the kitchen, not tripping up a fighting unit. The congealed mess of half-frozen mutton and tinned tomatoes looks like gourmet fare after these words, and the hard work of stirring it around with a heavy ladle while erupting bubbles of hot tomato gravy painfully splash my bare arms is rendered easier, almost pleasant. Briefly, cooking is not just a means of escape from the daily bleakness of army life, but *my* contribution to the war effort. In my state of gratitude, I keep an eye out for Lyddie when it is my turn to eat. I see him, already finished dinner, joking with some of the soldiers. He puts a fresh cigarette in his mouth, and half a dozen hands are suddenly outstretched with lit matches or butane lighters, and he laughs with real pleasure, eyes crinkling up like the leading man in a western.

I come to realize after a while that I am not the only one watching the captain so intently. Resting his considerable bulk against the wall of the kitchen hut, and obscured by the shadow of its roof, is Sergeant Fynbos. I start at first, guiltily, at the thought that he has noticed my attention to Lyddie's doings, but I can see I am too insignificant to merit Fynbos' consideration. The sinking sun's long rays pass down the side of the hut, and still he watches the captain joshing with his inferiors. Now the red beam lights up Fynbos' own features, his eyes are near-wet with awe and admiration. And suddenly he makes sense to me, his bullying swagger accentuated by his curved muscular buttocks, his assiduously waxed mustaches, his bellowing stentorian voice. Coming to himself, he is aware of my noticing and growls, "What're you looking at, *moffie*?" but his heart is not in it, the enchantment is still on him. I nod sympathetically to him, and a look of confusion crosses his face.

"Better stop drooling and go scrub those pots," he says.

"Ja, *meneer.*"

He searches my face for traces of sarcasm, but there is none. I too prefer our usual roles, am discomfited at what I now know. I rise to my feet and shuffle off to where the pots and dishes wait for me, not too slow and not too fast, maintaining the illusion that I am behaving with my usual indolence.

...

"LITTLE" GIDDING IS FOLLOWING me around the camp, aping my every move. He is not subtle, for when his lumbering, knuckle-dragging walk fails to attract my attention, he purses his lips and utters *hoo-hoo haa-haa* sounds. He may have chosen me as his victim simply because he is small and slight, his nondescript features dotted with adolescent acne and his upper lip barely covered by his little pubic mustache, which he checks every morning in the mirror on the off chance that a luxuriant growth has sprung up during the night. Without me, he would be the camp scapegoat, the runt who has trouble keeping up and is soft and vulnerable besides. Or perhaps he really does hate me, for I absentmindedly noted the name on his breastplate and, saying what it brought to mind, uttered aloud the nickname that stuck.

There is also a Norton here, Charlie Norton, who later is helicopter casevacced to Oshakati with third-degree burns, the only survivor of a Samil 50 whose petrol tank got hit by tracers. The middle two of the *Four Quartets* are yet to manifest themselves, but I'm sure there's a Coker somewhere in the army. Whether he's been sent East to the Mozambique border, is interred somewhere in Southern Africa's parched eviscerate earth ("every poem an epitaph"), or is marching around somewhere in Owamboland, I have no idea. The symbolism of *The Wasteland* would be simply too obvious, so I'm glad to see the old word-hewing anti-Semite's spirit is more subtly immanent here in this dry and sere country, this death of earth.

Gidding's Christian name is Leo, and I think he was hoping to be called Lion or Cub or something like that, but *I* had to be the one to pass remark on his diminutive stature, and for that he is going to make me pay.

"Knock it off, Little," someone calls out, flicking a half-smoked cigarette end over end, a flare in the near-darkness. "Can't you see he's not paying attention?"

I don't know whether the fellow is grateful for the curry warming up his stomach, or if he just wants to stir up the irate bantam for some easy entertainment. The remark has a provocative effect, and Gidding is now busy making short, furious rushes at me, his sparsely furnished mustache quivering in anger.

"Think you're hard, do you?" he snarls. "Think you're a big *sterk outjie*? Tarzan? Mr. Universe?"

He pulls hard at my shirt, and a button pops out. I can see it lying near the still-smoldering *stompie*. Ah, well, it will give me something to do tonight and I do find sewing relaxing. I would do it more often if I could get away with it, but how frequently does one want to be called an old woman or be accused of working on my trousseau? I lean toward the button, but Gidding is in my way.

"I'm going to make you eat that *stompie*. That's what I'm going to do." He laughs nastily. He picks up the bent cigarette, a thin wisp of smoke rising from one end, and pokes it into my face.

I wave to shoo him away as I might an importunate fly. My hand floats toward him lazily like an air-filled dirigible. There is plenty of time for him to get out of the way, but he does not move, his brain following a syllogistic line of reasoning: Fatty does not hit back, so that cannot be Fatty's hand moving toward my head with all the weight of Fatty's arm and Fatty's shoulder behind it.

My plump firm palm smacks against his ear and he goes flying head over heels toward the group smoking by the fire. Little Gidding fetches up at an odd angle, his head half tucked under his left shoulder, and for a moment I think I have broken his neck. He lies quite still, and we are all silent, watching. Then he stirs, and there is surprised laughter and someone yells, "Six and out!" the way we did as kids when the cricket ball soared past the playground and over the wood fence into Solly Berman's apricot trees. Little Gidding slowly sits up, shakes his head, and says: "*Die fok!*" Blood trickles from his left nostril and he looks mightily surprised.

Later, he decides to play it for laughs. "Why didn't anyone tell me we were getting revved? That wasn't old Sweetbread, that was a fokken mortar shell." He tells me each morning how his ear is still ringing, seeming genuinely to like me now that I've given him a thumping. And in my secret heart of hearts, I have to admit I enjoyed that moment when my hand struck his head. When I replay the scene, I know that I could have pulled back, I did realize he wasn't going to move away. Instead, I let my shoulder follow through with all the force of old Blackbeard's muscles that lurk vestigially beneath my fat. I cannot turn away from the fact that, after all the torment he had inflicted on me, there was a certain pleasure in knocking the little *stompie* arse over teakettle. Looking around me here, at the likes of Captain Lyddie, at the Special Forces recce Jan Burger, who is no larger than Little Gidding but in whose every movement there is the confident grace of the trained professional killer, I recognize the danger in my state of mind. It would be too easy in this particular world to give in to the joys of violence, to revel in one's own ability to menace those weaker—or even stronger—than oneself.

But I have spent too long being ridiculed for puffing breathlessly on every training run not to enjoy the newfound awareness that I am not only a fat man but a large one, that I can, if I choose, throw my weight around. I have had this feeling before, in training, when we speared straw-filled bags with fixed bayonets . . . all jolly good fun and lots of screaming, *Eeyah! Take that, you fokken bastard*, like we were children in a pillow fight. But those were only dummies, and they had not offered the satisfaction of the carmine trickle from Little Gidding's nostril. "Tapped his claret for him," was Teddy Lester's euphemism after he had delivered a well-deserved straight right to the class bully's nose. But those boy's adventure books had always presented violence as clean and dignified, and, moreover, justifiable. The stirring inside me was from somewhere very deep—the reptilian subcortex, or the atavistic memory of the first australopithecine to brain his fellow hominid.

My brief—and briefly enjoyed—moment of violence has unfortunate results, since it was either witnessed by Captain Lyddie or learned about through the multifarious ways he has of knowing what takes place among the common soldiers. I see him looking at me speculatively at dinner, a new glint in his eyes that suggests some cogitative activity boding me no good.

The morning after the incident, I am on my way back after visiting the latrine, when Captain Lyddie roars through the center of the camp mounted on his personal palfrey, a stripped-down light jeep (a Suzuki or its army clone). He stops inches from me in a cloud of dust. "Hop in, troepie," he calls out jovially. "*Vandag is nog 'n dag* and we're going to have some fun in the sun."

"*Môre is nog 'n dag*," I mutter as I climb on board, and stow my R4 rifle in the back seat (Fynbos insists we carry it with us everywhere we go, even to the toilet . . . *especially* to the toilet). I hope I don't sound insubordinate mentioning my preference for the usual Afrikaans sentiment, bred out of lazy days on the veld with servants to do one's bidding, that tomorrow—not today—is also a day and it will come around in its own good time.

"Ja nee, little troepie. We must make haste while the sun shines."

I am about to correct his misusage when I notice the sardonic gleam of his sidelong glance. I have seen him hit a new recruit—a young tough who was determined not to be impressed by army discipline or fall under Lyddie's charismatic spell—who dared to answer him back. Or rather, there was the stroppy answer, then a twitch of Lyddie's shoulders and the youth's face flew backward, followed by the hard crack of flesh on flesh. The actual movement of his hand was too fast to be seen. So, *It's hay, not haste* stays on the tip of my tongue and I just nod glumly, as the captain pops the clutch and the jeep jinks forward. Soldiers jump out of the way as we go zero to sixty through the camp and out onto the veld.

"You may have noticed," the captain shouts into the wind, his eyes slitted so he momentarily resembles my old red-headed pedagogue, "because I know you, I know you see things even though others may be fooled by your sleepy eyes and your fucking laziness . . . you may have noticed that all the other officers will not go out into the *bundu* unless they're riding in a Hippo or a Rinkhals or some other armor-plated dinosaur. Now, why is that, my clever?"

"Because they don't want to get blown up?" The seemingly deserted wasteland around us is strewn with land mines, some of them ours. Which is why the armored cars have a giant steel plate in the floor and are shaped so they will roll over if there is an explosion underneath them.

"Very good. You see, I knew you were smart. Now, I am willing to sacrifice safety for mobility, but mostly my plan is to move so fast that we will not be there anymore when the mine goes off. I haven't field-tested the plan yet. If you're lucky, we might find out today."

We are indeed moving through the thinly foliated veld at blinding speed, bashing bushes out of the way and bouncing over rocks and potholes. Like many South African males, Captain Lyddie is clearly a speed freak, the type whose idea of a perfect afternoon is trackside at Kyalami watching the stock cars tear by. I used to like playing with my Scalextric Formula One and Lamborghini, stripping down the toy cars so they'd go even faster on their electric tracks, but that was as far as I went in that direction. I try to reassure myself that Lyddie has, after all, survived combat and is not going to get himself killed just to impress a raw conscript.

"You know, what I like is to feel I'm on my commando horse—like a real fighting Boer, *weet jy*?—that I can move around the enemy so fast he doesn't have a clue where I'm going to hit him next. Float like a butterfly, sting like a bee, as that big old kaffir used to say. You ever see a secretary bird catch a cobra? Every time the snake strikes, he hits empty air because that bird is already somewhere else. After a little time the ringhals just lies down and sulks. And that is when the bird walks right up to him and bites off his head."

The captain drives with athletic grace, his constant shifting of gears and manipulation of the steering wheel perfectly synchronized. "Do you know, the same man who invented the clutch built the cupola of Il Duomo. You know, the great cathedral in Florence?" I ask, trying to direct my thoughts anywhere but the ironwood tree growing ever larger in our windshield.

"Thank you, Professor." Lyddie grins. "I'll drive much better just knowing that."

I blush. The one time I was asked to move the transport lorry to the other side of the camp, I ground the gears so loudly everyone winced and then I stalled out. I could not drive like Lyddie if my life depended upon it, no idle phrase out here a hundred kilometers or so from Angola. As he drives, Lyddie speaks out of the side of his mouth, his cigarette wagging up and down and its ash blowing off into the slipstream. His face is fixed forward, his eyes alert for the thorn trees he needs to steer around or for anthills that would not yield to the steel grille mounted to the jeep but would bring us to an abrupt and bone-breaking halt. He informs me of items in the landscape I should take note of, his cigarette bobbing up and down with each word. It is clear he is enjoying himself, Jean-Paul Belmondo transferred to the Kaokoveld: if you don't like the city, if you don't like the sea, if you don't like the mountains, well, go *foudre* yourself.

I finally pluck up the courage to ask him where we're going. "To get some information," he says. "You'll find this interesting: the tribe in this area is the Himba; they're a very primitive people and mostly they don't make trouble. They don't like the Angolans, and they're scared the Owambo will steal their cattle. But lately I hear there's been some infiltration, and I aim to stamp that out."

We hit no land mines and after about two hours we arrive at our destination, a circle of huts surrounded by scraggly thorn bushes and one giant baobab standing sentinel. We pull up the jeep to take advantage of whatever shade the baobab offers. In this backdrop, the jeep is a shimmering illusion of modernity. Its thick rubber tires are near-melting on the baking sand; the engine ticks like something from another world and gives off the mingled odors of isoprene and petrol. Each step away from it feels like a step into the past.

As we walk toward the compound, Lyddie tells me: "You see where the smoke is coming up from that little circle of stones? That's their sacred fire. Behind it is the chief's hut and opposite is the cattle kraal. One thing you must not do, okay, is walk between the sacred fire and the kraal; it's very offensive to these people." He explains to me how the sacred fire is rekindled each morning from an ember kept in a pot in the chief's house, that this fire is carried with them when they change homesteads to follow the rain, it has been passed down the generations and has been burning continuously for hundreds of years. I think of the Roman love of the hearth, how our own word *focus* comes from the fire being the center of ancient lives. On cold Highveld winter nights, I used to build a fire in the stone fireplace in our living room and Mother and I would sit before it drinking tea and dunking rusks or Marie biscuits like a pair of old Boer women. Latin had been her top high school subject, and she liked to repeat this bit of information each time we sat together before the blazing logs, focusing, each in our own way.

Near the chief's hut, a bare-breasted woman is pounding something with an enormous pestle, her body moving rhythmically up and down. She is anointed with a red oil—I later learn that this is a mix of ocher and butterfat—and her skin gleams like polished hardwood. Her hair hangs over her face in braids, but it parts with the motion of her body's efforts and I can see that her features are extraordinarily beautiful. Lyddie nudges me and whispers, "That's the chief's youngest wife. Quite a piece, hey, Sweetbread?"

Francis Galton traveled in these parts 138 years ago, his encounter with the "savages" helping formulate his theory of eugenics. Actually, it's funny that he's called the "father of eugenics"; he might as well be called the father of the fingerprint, or the lottery machine for his delightful contraption, the quincunx, with its little balls falling down different chutes. Galton claimed to have been offered one such Negress beauty by a certain

King Nangoro, but he threw her out of his tent, as he was wearing a linen suit and the woman was "raddled with red ochre and butter, and as capable of leaving a mark on anything she touched as a well-inked printer's roller."

We wait outside the main entrance of the hut, which is the usual wattle-daubed, thatch-roofed affair but neater and better made than the huts of the lesser inhabitants of the compound. Lyddie's patience does not last long, and he soon marches over to the door and calls out loudly: "Hey, Tjihambwa, get out here, man! We don't have all day."

The chief soon appears, looking irritated at being summoned this way. He is a tall, handsome man with a well-trimmed gray-and-black beard, and from beneath a strong forehead shaded by a wide-brimmed hat his dark, inquisitive eyes look at us disapprovingly. He is wearing remarkably fashionable clothes for this rural wasteland: a dark gray sports jacket made of cotton over a formal white shirt, a necklace of beads ending in a gleaming copper shell casing, and a black top hat. He takes a puff from a slim, ornately carved pipe, then pulls back his full lips and spits to the side. I notice that his lower incisors are missing, the upper incisors filed into sharp points. He greets us with a formal, "Good day, Captain. Good day, soldier." Lyddie says that it is good to see him, and I echo the sentiment. All the while, the young beauty pounds in steady rhythm, her lissome body muscular but womanly, her full breasts bobbing with each downward stroke. She keeps her head bowed so we may not see that she is looking at us, observing our behavior toward her lord and master.

Another, older woman emerges from the hut's obscurity and brings a bowl of sour milk to the chief. He drinks, burps loudly, wipes his mustache on the back of his hand, and then gives the bowl back to the woman, who presents it to Lyddie. After Lyddie, it is my turn. The sour milk is not bad, almost a drinkable yogurt. I have seen Africans drinking *amasi* on the pavements of Johannesburg all my life, but it is the first time I've ever tasted it. After I am done, Lyddie takes the empty bowl from my grasp and goes over to a rain barrel, where he helps himself to some water.

I can see from the chief and the older woman's eyes that this is a breach of etiquette, but they say nothing. Lyddie returns, smiling. He squats on his heels and indicates the chief should do the same, then begins to inquire about the movements of terrorist insurgents in the area. The chief waves over the young woman, who stops her pounding and squats a respectful distance from the two men, saying something to the chief in their language. Although Chief Tjihambwa clearly understands some English, the young woman is there to translate.

I feel embarrassed by her half-naked proximity, and I realize I am the only one standing, so I too squat down. This is worse, since the woman is now in the direct line of my vision and it takes an effort for me not to look at her chest. I shift uncomfortably to the side, and now my rifle is pointing at her. *Ai yai yai.* I point it downward and look over to the left, where I can see a young boy of about four shyly making his way toward us. The woman bestows a quick smile on him (but what love there is in that brief look!) and then says in her soft, mellifluous voice: "Our chief says there are no terrorists here."

Lyddie says something insistent about movement having been sighted by a helicopter pilot. The woman translates, the chief waves his hand dismissively and says something, and then the woman tells us: "He says it is just his nephew and some of the young men coming to visit."

"Perhaps his nephew is a terrorist." Lyddie smiles. There is no warmth in the smile.

The chief does not wait for a translation but says, "No, that is not so!" followed by a burst of OwaHimba.

"The chief's nephew came to request a goat. It is for a feast . . . to celebrate."

"A goat, hey? Is he celebrating becoming a terrorist?"

"Hei," says the chief angrily. "He is coming of age. He is the one who will get my cattle someday."

Lyddie stands up abruptly. The little boy starts back nervously, and I smile at him to reassure him. He looks at me as if I am some strange alien trying to act like a human being.

"You'd better tell those young men to be careful," Lyddie says sharply. "They start getting ideas at that age that can get them into big trouble. You send a message to your nephew that he needs to let the territorial forces know before he goes wandering around the bush.

"Where is he now, by the way?"

The woman translates, and the chief responds in her language. I stand up slowly—both so as not to frighten the child and because my calf muscles have contracted stiffly. "He is gone now," the woman says to Lyddie.

"Good. So if we shoot some men out in the bush around here, he won't be one of them." Lyddie notices the small child and waves him over. The child approaches shyly; it is clear he is used to being indulged by adults but nevertheless finds our whiteness strange and frightening. Lyddie reaches in his pocket and pulls out a box of Chiclets, which he pours into his hand and offers to the child. The child stuffs them into his mouth and begins chewing happily. "He's a nice-looking boy," Lyddie remarks to the chief, who has also stood up now. "Your son?"

The chief nods, his eyes skittering to the corners.

"So. Where are those men?" Lyddie asks.

"No men, Captain," the chief says, not bothering with the translation ritual. "I have said this too much times."

"I see." With a single smooth movement, Lyddie grabs the child around the waist and hoists him into the air. The half-chewed gum drops into the dirt, a wad of mastic and white sugar. Lyddie marches over to the rain barrel and dumps the child headfirst into the water. The child's legs kick frantically and we can hear a bubbling rush of air coming out of the barrel. The chief stamps up and down, crying in frustrated horror, aghast, not daring to touch this white man who has so suddenly injected terror into this quiet morning.

"Please, baas," he says. "Please. He is my only son."

Why does he look at me when he says this? It is Lyddie who is pressing the child's body deeper into the rain barrel. Then I realize that it is because I am the one holding the rifle, gripped at the ready in both my hands. I look down at the barrel to make sure it is not pointing at anyone, and when I look up again, Lyddie is pulling a small limp shape out of the rain barrel. But it has not been more than a minute; surely the child could not have drowned in that time? Lyddie wraps his arms around the boy's stomach and squeezes. There is a gush of water from the child's mouth and he begins to cough. Lyddie drops him onto the ground, and the child scurries away like a wounded animal, closely followed by his mother.

"You find out what those terrorists are doing in this area, my good man," Lyddie says calmly. "Unless you want me back tomorrow for another swimming lesson." All dignity is gone from the tribal elder, who looks at us through tear-filled eyes, not daring to let his hatred and anger show. Lyddie glances into the barrel and grins mischievously. "One more thing. You better teach your boy not to *poep* in the drinking water."

Driving back, Lyddie is very cheerful and he whistles "Jan Pierewiet" as he steers. Now and again he will point out a bird, giving both its popular name and its Latin name: There, see, a Bateleur eagle, *Terathopius ecaudatus*, rare to see one in these parts. . . . Bet you he's interested in that dassie we scared into the open. He tells me that the German colonists designated the crimson-breasted shrike South-West Africa's national bird because its colors matched the Imperial German flag,* proof that the country was waiting all along to be occupied by Teutonic civilization. "Very spiritual people, the Germans."

"And if they were Africans, you'd call it witchcraft and superstition," I say sourly.

This makes Lyddie laugh aloud. He might as well be returning from a victorious rugby match, given his air of triumph and merry goodwill. I am glumly silent, and I can tell that my moroseness is getting on his

* Today the national bird is the African fish eagle. The poor shrike—which has undergone a name change to "crimson-breasted boubou"—is out of favor for its imperial leanings.

nerves. He brings the jeep to a screeching halt in the middle of nowhere and jumps out gracefully before the vehicle has stopped juddering. "Piss stop." I sit, obdurate, not feeling the need to go. "Come on, my lad. My pa always said take a leak when you have the opportunity. You never know when the next chance may come. And leave your rifle in the jeep. The way you've been waving that thing around, someone is going to lose a vital part of his anatomy."

I get out and go stand on the opposite side of the jeep from the captain, my back to him. To my surprise, I take a long time to drain my bladder, never having made it to the w.c. that morning. The captain comes up to me just as I am zipping up my trousers. "So," he says, "what do you think of me?"

"It's not for me to say, sir."

"But I'm asking you. Just tell the truth: you disapproved of my actions in that kaffir kraal, nee?"

I nod my head.

"So what did you do about it? If I had waited for you to tell me to stop, that little piccanin would have been drowned long ago. You're a typical English liberal: you think your silent objection means you have no responsibility. All you had to do was say *Stop it!* and that's what I would have done."

Stung, I respond: "Since when is a mere rifleman allowed to tell his senior officer what to do?"

"You telling me that if Sergeant Fynbos was holding Little Gidding's head underwater you'd stand there scratching your arse, dumb as a post?" He does an imitation of me standing around, pretending I'm not really there. I have to admit he's right, I would have said something.

"But it's different . . ." I say, lamely.

"Why? Because Gidding's white? I thought you loved the kaffir like your brother. And you had a rifle with you too. You could have shot me and been a hero to the revolution. No, man, you're a coward. That's the real problem."

I stand silently, hanging my head. All of a sudden, I am slapped hard enough to be sent sprawling headlong. As I start to raise myself, Lyddie kicks me in the ribs and I fall, breathless, trying to contain the pain.

"Never, never let another man call you a coward," Lyddie says. "Look at you, man. Don't tell me you didn't enjoy hitting Little Gidding . . . and that's okay. It was the right thing to do; in fact, you should have smacked him ages ago." Almost gently, he leans down and helps me to my feet. But as he does so, he uses his other hand to whisk the canteen from my belt and throw that into the open jeep too. "Now," he says, blocking my way, "in five minutes I'm going to drive off. If you're in the jeep, you come with me. If you aren't, you can try to walk back to camp. You've made two fatal mistakes here, my boy, getting separated from your rifle and losing your canteen. If you want to see the sun go down tonight, you'd better start thinking like a real soldier."

I stand, looking at him, trying to think of the right words to say to make him relent. We both know that the sun is going to get hotter as it climbs higher in the blue, cloudless sky. Even if I were to trace my way back to the camp by reverse-winding my memory of the drive, I would be comatose from dehydration within an hour or so. I start to say that he's not being fair, but he has the same look on his face as he did when he first noticed that the Himba chief's son had come to sit down with us. The image of that innocent, expectant face enrages me and I launch myself at the captain, bulling him toward the jeep with my sheer weight and fury, and I notice with satisfaction that he bangs the small of his back painfully against the door handle. The next thing I know, I am rolling on the ground, howling in anguish as I clutch the side of my knee where he has deftly kicked me.

"I applaud your enthusiasm, troepie," he chuckles, "but it's a bad idea to forget your combat training. Now up!" He kicks me playfully but hard on the rump, as one might a favorite but obdurate donkey.

I slowly rise to my feet and circle him warily. He has promised that I can stay in the jeep if I'm there when he's ready to leave, so my plan is to make my way into the car and hold on tight until the time is up. When the moment seems right, I dash around the car and am just about to climb in when Lyddie vaults in from the other side and smacks me on the nose with the palm of his hand, sending me sprawling once again.

There is something different about being hit full in the face. Like every South African child, there were times that I got hit in school, since every minor infraction was punished with the cane or ruler. Miss Tompkins was the only one of our teachers not to use corporal violence as punishment, but then she didn't need to. Rooibos Sanders had her own refined methods for dealing with miscreants: she had patriotically purchased a newly minted Krugerrand, which she had her jeweler set above a gold ring. It was an ugly adornment, more knuckle-duster than gem. She would grab the offending boy—usually it was a boy—by the short hair above his ear and give him a quick rap on the temple or top of the skull with her ringed hand. This action forever disabused me of the notion that gold is soft. Of course, she would also give us the usual caning with a ruler, which was less painful but more humiliating. As I mentioned previously, for the rest of the day we were required to wear "stripes" (the number of whacks given represented by red lines drawn on blank paper) pinned to our shirts. But being hit on the nose is different—there is a moment of helplessness, followed by blinding fury and a fathomless desire for revenge.

I rise to my feet again, enraged, ready to use all the knowledge that I have learned so recently about gouging eyes, stamping on insteps, snapping an enemy's neck by grabbing chin and back of head and giving a sudden, precise jerk. Lyddie has started the jeep, and he quickly pops the clutch and drives about thirty meters away. He gets out, smiling, leaving the jeep still running. He knows what is going through my head, is delighted to have stirred awake the assassin in me. I have seen him easily defeat the strongest, most agile private soldier in our practice sessions, and he will probably kill me. I don't care; my one desire is to hurt him, and I go forward to meet his advance. He looks relaxed but alert, his hands held loosely and deceivingly at his sides. There is a moment, though, when I realize that I do not want to play this game, despite the blindly raging animal inside me itching to feel Lyddie's nose crunch beneath my own fist.

He knows he has roused something bestial inside me, but I will not give him the satisfaction of seeing it unfurl into life. I cease my hunched, aggressive momentum, pick my hat up from amidst the dust, and stand at my full height, shaking the tension out of my shoulders.

"The jeep's running, man," he says softly. "If you knock me down you can get to it and leave *me* here. I don't have a water bottle either."

I shake my head. "I'm going back to camp."

He looks disappointed. "You won't make it. It will be forty Celsius in an hour. That sun will dry you out like biltong before you're halfway back."

I ignore him, turn around, and begin walking. I move at a sedate pace, trying to bring my breathing back to normal to conserve energy. I think of a shaded bench near the waterfall in the garden of the restaurant in Heidelberg, the cool quiet of it all—before I tried to eat that bee—the sweet trill of the yellow-eyed canary in the umbrageous willow. There is the smell of flowers and the cooling murmur of water. I tug the brim of my hat as low over my forehead as possible, hoping to shield my eyes from the ferocious sun. My sunglasses must have fallen out of my top pocket during the fray, and I miss them. It is very quiet in the Kaokoveld, the only sound the occasional buzz of a flying insect or gentle stridulation of a cricket. I walk for a long time, the hot bowl of the sun pressing down on my head, my shadow growing tinier in front of me. Then there is the sound of a motor running and the jeep idles next to me.

"Okay, climb in."

I get in and Lyddie hands me my water canteen. I drink gratefully, resisting the urge to drain the whole thing in one gulp. I see my sunglasses on the dashboard, and I wipe the dust off them with my shirt and put them on.

"Sorry," says Lyddie. "But I wanted you to see how much you've got to learn. I hate that look that says, *I don't like this, but I'm not going to get involved.* You're part of this, old son, like it or not. So now you know."

So now I knew.

...

I am up early, as usual, the following morning, emerging from my tent in the gray, cold hour the French call *êntre chien et loup*. A few shapeless figures move around slowly in the chill predawn light, speaking quietly or not at all as we men undergo a metamorphosis from sleeping to waking. The twittering of isolated birds can be heard in the surrounding arid scrub, a testament to nature's astonishing ability to sustain a variety of life amid even the harshest conditions. I have seen the occasional dun-colored and stonelike Burchell's courser in the surrounding desert scrub, and once a magnificent Kori bustard striding majestically away, but I cannot identify this birdsong. As I prime the camp stove, I look up to see the silhouette of a native woman walking away from the general direction of the officers' tents and out toward the open bush. I strain my eyes to get a good look at her as she passes by. Despite the shapeless gray cardigan she had donned against the morning cold, I recognize the handsome Himba mother from the village, both by her bearing and the strands of plaited hair peeping out beneath her double-knotted kerchief. The soldiers lolling around waiting for breakfast or the latrines are too sleepy to do more than gaze listlessly at her as she saunters by, despite the nipples, erect from the cold, visibly pressing against her cardigan. This is hardly the safest place for a woman to be, no matter how somnambulant the troops, and I resist an urge to warn her away.

Captain Lyddie appears a few moments later from his quarters, and his air of being right once again quickly enlightens me.

"That's the child's mother," he tells me unnecessarily, going on to say that she'd come under cover of the dark to let us know where the Swapo terrorists are camped. "I'll bet the old chief sent her. That way, if she gets found out, he can claim he had nothing to do with it.

"We're going to have to hurry up before they get wind of this," Lyddie continues. "What about you, are you going to join the fun? It's time you got a taste of a real firefight, when the target shoots back at you."

He looks disappointed when I say no, that I would rather cook for the hungry warriors than watch them shoot up a band of insurgent guerrillas.

"You're not scared of a bunch of garden boys, are you?" he demands, looking into my eyes.

"No," I tell him. "I'm not scared. I have my duties right here."

The men leave the camp amid clouds of dust from racing tires and much good-natured joshing. They come back a few hours later, dusty and irritable. They had found the remains of the terrorist encampment exactly where the woman said it would be, the ashes of the campfire still warm and the stubs of Russian *papirossi* cigarettes hastily scuffed under the sand. They'd called for light aircraft to scout the area, but they were pretty sure the insurgents would be out of the way and well hidden. As usual, the local civilians were hedging their bets: informing the SADF of the enemy's whereabouts while warning Swapo that they were discovered.

Lyddie is the only one not to seem despondent, telling the others to rest up, that he has a surprise in store for the terrorists. Late that afternoon, a dusty Unimog* arrives ahead of three transport lorries. The four-wheel drive contains an older man, a tough-looking major with laugh lines around his eyes, his batman (a corporal who looks no older than nineteen), and two Bushmen trackers, the first I have seen. They are slight, beautiful men with high cheekbones, brown skin, and short curled hair growing in separate clumps like bushes in the Kaokoveld, the "peppercorn hair" I had read about. They squat on their heels and talk quietly to one another in their stridulating, click-riddled tongue. I can't take my eyes off them. I think of my school days' visit to some caves near Louis Trichardt where there were finely drawn etchings of elands, kudu, and tiny hunters with bows and arrows. The front of the cave was smudged with soot and still

* The preferred four-wheel drive of the SADF, especially in Angola and the Caprivi Strip. Ironically, the Unimog (from UNIversal-MOtorGerät (universal-power-unit) was developed by Daimler-Benz in post–World War II Germany as part of the dismantling of the Nazis' military industries. It was intended to be purely a farm vehicle—a sword beaten into a plowshare, that then got beaten back into an even better sword.

smelled like the inside of a poorly kept fireplace, the scent lightly overlaid by the ammonia of a contemporary visitor's urine. The guide explained in his thick Afrikaans accent how *die Boesman* was hated by the Bantu, who pursued him relentlessly and tried to smoke him out of his hiding place. These two men, small and gracile as human meerkats, were clearly here to exact an ancient revenge. Throughout the evening, I try to find an excuse to come close to them, fascinated by their wildness. They seem to me more like part of the natural kingdom than fellow human beings—though my reason rejects this romantic fantasizing.

"So, how do you like our tame Bushmen?" Lyddie asks, sidling up to me quiet as a cat and seizing my upper arm suddenly in his strong grip. "These little bastards can track a piece of paper blowing across the desert. And before you start worrying that we're exploiting them, you should know that the Owambo and the Herero make slaves out of them. That's when they don't kill them on sight."

"You don't need to defend yourself to me, Captain. I know what we're here to do."

"I'm not *de*-fending myself, you bogger," he growls, a hint of anger straying into his usual expression of ironic amusement. "And I think you know fuck-all about what we're doing here."

...

HIS FIRST LOVE WAS identified for him as an angel. It happened like this.

Anne Greensward and Pamela des Marais had a serious sports rivalry going on. It began when Anne accidentally slashed Pamela's shin during field hockey and became serious when a week later Pamela deliberately tripped her adversary on the muddy field. "I'm going to fix that little *b*——" Anne swore to her friends. The following Monday, at midmorning break, Pamela was walking near the carp pond when a shiny object caught her eye; someone had lost a bracelet. She bent over to pick it up, a shadowy figure detached itself from behind the nearby oak and rushed over, and haughty proper Pamela des Marais and her clean uniform toppled into the algae-filled pond. No one saw or could identify the assailant, but the crowd of students who saw Pamela walking away from the pond, a strand of green slime clinging to her legs, her wet skirt clinging to her muscular buttocks and revealing the outlines of her underwear, spontaneously applauded before a teacher could lead the furious and mortified girl inside.

He was walking by a group of teachers when the female P.T. instructor remarked in the pitch that was so good for calling instructions to girls on the opposite side of the hockey field: "Anne might look like a little angel, but she's a devil, all right. I like my girls spirited, mind you, but that one merits watching."

An angel? He had known Anne since their first days in primary school, when she was a moon-faced girl with freckles and large green eyes. He'd paid her little notice, though they sometimes sat together (he too was a swot). Once she told him a joke: "Why does the queen stand so straight? Because she is a ruler." He looks at her now and sees she has grown up tall, her back very straight, her hair long and shining like flax in autumn light. *Because she is a ruler*. How did he not notice that she is beautiful, her green eyes sparkling with mischief? The skirt of her school uniform is a little small for her—fashion preceding comfort among most of the girls, who want skirts shorter than indicated by school guidelines—and her legs are shapely, if criss-crossed at the knees with small scars . . . this flaw a slight disorder that breeds such wantonness.

He is stunned, astonished, turned topsy-turvy by his discovery. How had he been so blind before? Didn't he sit an aisle-length away from her in history all last term? And what wouldn't he give if the seating arrangements could now be what they were. At morning assembly, he edges closer to where she is, positioning himself at an angle that allows him to watch her. Her head is turned away from him, revealing the hemispherical perfection of a cheek slightly dusted with down. Her ginger eyelashes are transparent in the light that illuminates the headmaster's dais. He has been walking past an ordinary brick building every day of his life, then one day he enters and it is a museum of art, a shock to the eye of one who has never before imagined a painting or a sculpture. Her hand brushes her long hair back from her ear, an intricate whorl of pink, a cutaway nautilus shell. She feels him looking at her and looks in turn at him, smiles, raises her eyebrows in a puzzled question, then turns to look back at the headmaster, who is announcing the schedule of home and away games. It is a blessing that he will be able to replay this moment in every bit of its exquisite detail.

Over the next few weeks he is so perfectly in tune with her that it is as if he can conjure her appearance at will. The bushmen are said to be this way in their hunting, knowing exactly where the eland feeds on the tender leaves in the midst of the thorn tree, the rock behind which the duiker lies still, trusting in its immobility to camouflage it. Their senses are heightened to the point that they can sense the presence of the sought-after animal's spirit by some change in the very ions of the air. Now he goes to the carp pond at break, and she is there with a group of chattering friends! He imagines her waiting at the bus stop he will pass driving home with his mother this afternoon, and there is the beloved head gleaming from amid the crowd. He does not feel the need to get too close, simply reveling in this distant intimacy. Even his nights are filled with abstract thoughts—disembodied legs and breasts and shadowed female faces so remote as not to sully the pure crystal of his love. She has begun to notice that suddenly he is everywhere, although he would rather remain the unobserved observer for a time longer. Her looks are friendly, compassionate. Once she mouths at him in assembly, "*What? what?*" but he quickly glances aside, blushing.

What pleasure he gets from his extraordinary new perception, the sensitivity as if he has grown feathery antennae that quiver when she comes within a few hundred yards of him. For example, he chooses a particular table in the far corner of the lunchroom, where he will sit with his back to everyone, chooses it for no other reason than that he must. And he is rewarded by the signature sound of her walk, a tune he plays in his head to lull himself to sleep at night. He does not need to turn around to know it is her sitting directly behind him at another table, a meter or so of air, as electrically charged as that preceding a Highveld storm, between them. He does not need the confirmation of the male friend's voice addressing her as Anne, though the name tingles in his mouth as if he is the one who has said it, the *A* sharp and tangy as juice from a passion fruit, the double *n*'s woody and fragrant as fresh-picked mushrooms.

Then two things happen. It is the night of the school play; Sedgewick Schwartz is Mercutio, a disappointment to all who would have liked him in the lead—which was performed surprisingly well by Dodger Stone, who'd shucked off his childhood ugly duckling features and emerged darkly handsome. He stays afterward to help put away the props and scenery, in part because he remembers her volunteering to be one of the helpers, but he sees little of her because she is helping Juliet remove her makeup. Then, as he goes into the darkened coatroom, one of the last to leave the theater building that night, there is a rustle of cloth and a penumbral figure hurries up to him. Slender arms slide around his chest and shoulders and embrace him. Warm soft lips press against his own lips and a sweet probing tongue slips into his mouth. His entire self is concentrated on that gentle warm organ that explores his mouth, pushing his tongue playfully aside. The top of his head seems to have been sliced away by a merciful sword and he almost swoons. Then a murmured, "Oh"—or was it "Mmm?"—and she is gone, leaving him trembling at the knees. It was certainly her, he would know her even in his confusion. He stands in the darkness, legs trembling, looking out at the patch of light in the hallway, his mind buffeted by thoughts half born. Was it mistaken identity? Surely not.

"Hey," says Sedgewick, his lanky figure casting a long shadow, "my driver's waiting. You'd better get a move on or I'm leaving you behind."

He almost asks Sedgewick if he'd seen the girl who darted out of the cloakroom, but he does not and knows he doesn't need to. It is too astonishing, too close to his dreams to make any sense, and he hardly sleeps that night. When he arrives at school in the morning, he notices a group of girls—Leslie Gross, Marti Binswanger, and others . . . all friends of hers—nodding their heads in his direction and giggling. So it was just another dare? And yet she had been so close to him, his darling. He had had that kiss; nothing could take it away from him.

He determines that he is not going to let this opportunity slip. If she took on that dare, it was because she wanted to, she is not averse to him. When Sedgewick invites him the following Monday to come see *A Clockwork Orange* at his house, he knows he must ask her. "Bring someone you like," Sedgewick says. His father has access to all kinds of banned or uncensored films, and a few weeks before he had watched the uncut version of *Summer of '42* at Sedgewick's house. Freddie Gluck had seen the same film at the bioscope, and he kept remarking, "They cut that bit out."

"Fine, now shut up," Sedgewick said, his eyes intent on Harry Grimes' heaving naked bottom suspended over Jennifer O'Neill. Would she consider him too bold? There had been other couples at the last showing, Lynn Sonnenschein and Dawie Richgood, two who lost no opportunity to show the world their passion for each other, but he had found as interesting as the film the way Ellie Lipschitz and Trevor Boscoe had slowly drifted toward each other as if drawn by magnets until she was, almost obliviously, lying nestled against his shoulder. The dark room, the flickering screen, created possibilities for romance that had not been there before, which was heightened by the sense of doing something forbidden by the repressive, puritanical regime.

All week he practices asking her. *Hello. Would you like to see* A Clockwork Orange *with me?* No good. It sounds too much like the opening lines of a joke. Can he resist explaining that the "orange" is really the Malay word *orang*, man, as in orang outang or "man of the woods"? He does not want to remind her of his reputation for pedantry. *Want to see that Malcolm McDowell flick with me? It's banned, you know.* Better, but does he need to tell her it's banned? If she knows what film he's talking about, then she'd know damn well it's banned. Perhaps something more neutral: *A bunch of us are getting together at Sedgewick's place. Want to come?* A little bland. *I'd really like it if you came too.* Can he tell her that? Why not?

He is running out of time. It's late Thursday afternoon, the film-viewing is Saturday night, and he hasn't asked her yet. The minute the bell goes, he grabs his already packed satchel and heads for the door, knowing that she would be on her way to the bus right now. "Wait a minute. I have an essay of yours here," Mrs. Svoboda says. She is a young teacher, with a wandering right eye, but nice nonetheless. The boys in the class often sit up front because she wears midlength cotton dresses and has good legs. Now he hates her. "Where did I put it? I'm so absentminded these days. You made some good points about the battle of Delville Woods, but there was a sentence I couldn't read. . . ." He is shifting impatiently back and forth while she shuffles through a pile of blue notebooks. She looks up at him. "Sorry, do you need to go to the toilet?" Behind him, Marti Binswanger giggles. If this should get back to her . . .

The bus is pulling away when he gets there, on its way to take the girls' hockey team to Sandown for another game in the semifinals. *It had two lights on behind, the blue light was my baby, the red light was my mind.* At home, he looks up her telephone number. There are several listings for Greensward, but he remembers that she lives next door to Dawie Richgood—something he doesn't like about that fellow; he is glad his attentions are occupied elsewhere, but what did Lynn see in those flaccid features?—and he has only to cross-reference the listings. He feels a certain satisfactory thrill in knowing her number, like he has just cracked the Enigma code. Now there are just the hours of agonized waiting to get through before his evening call.

He waits until his mother has gone into the living room to watch a rerun of *Dallas*, her favorite American serial, before dialing Anne's number. At dinner, Mother had asked what was agitating him. "You seem very preoccupied," she'd said.

"No, no, Ma. Everything is fine." He spoke brusquely, not wanting to be intruded upon.

"Are you sure, lovie? You'd tell me if something was bothering you, wouldn't you?"

"Mother! I'm not made of glass, you know. School is fine. I'm fine. This dinner is fine, and I'm sure South Fork Ranch and the whole bloody Ewing clan are fine or they will be. End of story! Finished and *klaar*." Rooibos Sanders had liked this tautological phrase, South Africa's "finished and done with," using it to end any argument. As annoying as it had been when applied against him, he can see its usefulness. It gets Mother off his back, for she goes off in a huff to watch her television. Now he can make his call.

Prrr prrr, the phone rings, a far-off black cat sleeping on a side table in a distant room or corridor. It hums for some time, and he has almost hung up in relief, when a white woman's voice answers.

"No, I'm sorry, but Anne's not here at the moment. She's having supper at her boyfriend's house. Would you like the number?"

"N-no, no, definitely not. I mean, it's just about homework."

There is a silence, and then the voice—her mother? an aunt?—says, "I can get you the number. It's no trouble, really."

He hastily tells her that he will get the details from someone else, no need to disturb Anne if she's out. Then he abruptly hangs up, his face burning. How had he known everything about her, but not this? To learn the obvious in this commonplace and tawdry way! He had identified himself at the outset of the conversation, so there was no hiding the fact that he was the idiot who had called. Would Anne share this tidbit of humiliating gossip with her friends, or, worse, quietly pity him?

The following midmorning break he goes to the coppice overlooking what the headmaster rather pretentiously calls the "botanical gardens." His gift has not deserted him, ironically enough, and there she is lying in the grass beside the small pond for showing off water plants. She is looking in the other direction and is far enough away that she would not be able to hear him above the burbling of the motor-driven fountain. She lies in a patch of bright spring sunlight, a profusion of green (some sort of elephant's ear palm) behind her. There are colorful tulips and hostas in the raised flower beds, and a mynah completes the tableau by singing the songs of all the birds it has chased away from its territory. Although he cannot make out the features of her face well, he can tell that she is smiling. Another figure is walking down the gravel path toward Anne, a tall, wide-shouldered, slim-waisted figure. It is Mark Hastings, a rugby-player . . . but not one of the thick-necked loutish "rugger-buggers," he also plays cello in the school orchestra. A nice fellow, with an open expression and large, dark, sensitive eyes; a fitting object of the pretty, spirited girl's affections. Anne springs up and stretches her young body, confirming her new dreams and excellent intentions. The watcher is nothing but a chitinous husk, invertebrate, a dung beetle resting from his toils. He sees her make a happy little leap over the brick border of the headmaster's flower garden, kicking her legs high like a trained dancer or an antelope. Her lover trails behind her, the very set of his back radiating happiness. They pass out of sight and the hidden observer's bleached and desiccated shell wafts away in the playful spring winds.

...

I take the opportunity later that evening to go and sit with the major, who is talking softly to his trackers. It has gotten cold, but rather than putting on a shirt or pullover, the Bushmen have drawn themselves closer to the fire, which illuminates their faces. I see now that one of the child-sized men is not young, his sparse beard and mustache is grizzled at the edges. The two deep wrinkles that run on each side of his face from the corner of his almond-shaped eyes to the chin give him a look of benevolent and shrewd amusement. His neck and shoulders are leathery and wrinkled, and there is no fat beneath the flesh. His life has been hard and effortful, but he has that cheerfulness of countenance that only people who live in close contact with the wild have. I ask the major if he speaks the !Kung language well.

"Oh, ja," he says. "I need to be able to communicate with my guys. And you know what? This is the perfect language for being out in the bush, where the normal human voice carries great distances." He explains that when you are out in the semi-desert, away from the engines and machinery of the urban world, there is a parabolic effect created by surrounding mountains—even the casual tones of ordinary conversation between two people standing quite close to each other carry for many kilometers. But those clicks and *Chock!*s evaporate into the air after twenty or thirty feet, blending into the surrounding bird noise, rustle of leaves, subsidence of gravelly soil, and gentle susurration of the wind. He has seen alert impala lift their heads momentarily and then lower them to graze again at the sparse grasses, taking no special note of a sound that is just part of the ever-changing murmured bustle of open land.

"It sounds like you envy them," I say.

"No, not really. But I appreciate who they are. They are not like us. For the little bushman, every rock, every blade of grass, every tree is its own separate entity. They have no capacity to generalize, that's why they're so unsuited to the civilized world. But it's that way of thinking that makes them great trackers: where we just see stones and sand, they see that this little pebble is not where it was when they last passed this way. It's been pushed aside by a foot. And if that foot was wearing a boot? *Yirrah*, it's like someone has written it all down or put up traffic signs.

"There's another thing that makes them different from you or me," he continues, growing garrulous. "They can eat just about anything. A dead hyena by the side of the road, that's their idea of a feast!" He roars with laughter at the thought, then offers to introduce me to them. Their names are *velar click-alveolar click* and *glottal click-palatal click*. I shake their hands, which are dry-skinned and strong, though slender. The two come up no higher than my armpits, but they are vital and quick and could no doubt dismember a great ox like me in a matter of minutes. The younger one says something to the major, who smiles and says: "He admires your great size and wants to know if you are a chief." I am coming to understand how, for all their bushcraft, the San were an easy slaughter for the nineteenth century settlers. I wonder to myself what will happen to these ardent little men—the subjects of our romantic fantasies—when we lose this war and return to our luxuriant cages in the suburbs, leaving them to face the African soldiers they now help us track.

I'm up extra early the following morning, hours before first light, having been told that if I'm not going to be part of the expedition, the least I can do is make sure those who are taking part are damn well fed before they start out. Breakfast is a special treat, boerewors and fresh eggs brought in along with the corporal and the two trackers. In spite of myself, I am caught up in the excitement, the holiday atmosphere of fresh sausages grilling over a wood fire. Captain Lyddie teases me when I slice open one of the links of boerewors I'm cooking and taste it for doneness. "Come on, troepie. Don't eat it all."

I start to explain myself, moving around the hot chunk of meat and spices with my tongue so as not to burn the inside of my mouth. (Too much fennel, I note.) He guffaws merrily and tells me not to worry, there's plenty to go around. You take things too seriously, he tells me. That's why you should come on a raid with us. Learn to laugh a little, enjoy life. Somewhere out there is a bullet with your name on it, or a *kwela* taxi driven by a drunk, or a little germ. The one thing I would hate, he says, is to die in my bed.

The thin corporal smiles for the first time. "Oh, I don't know," he says. "My *oupa* died in his bed at eighty years old. It was a cold Highveld morning and he'd had the pretty little Hotnot *meid* bring in a pan of hot coals to keep him warm. He must have decided that she would do an even better job of keeping him warm. My ma found them in the bed, with all the windows shut, both stone dead from carbon monoxide."

Your grandfather did not die alone and unanointed, I find myself thinking, imposing Corinthia's features on the poor girl in his story. Horrible, most horrible.

"What state were they in?" Lyddie asks, curious. "I mean . . . "

"Ja," the corporal says, his grin widening. "I was just a *pikkie* at the time, but I heard them talk about the question of separating them. The old man was a magistrate; not a chance they'd bury him together with a little coloured girl. My older brother was furious; he'd had his eye on that *meid* for quite some time."

Lyddie nudged the corporal and pointed at me. "Jo'burg over there doesn't like such talk, but you should have seen him eyeing the tits of the Himba women down at *Droëvlei*."

"*Verbastering is verboten*," the corporal says with a chuckle as I blush at his suggestion that I'm contemplating miscegenation. "But you've got to hand it to that old chief: I remember from when I was stationed out here that he has a good eye for a healthy maiden. Your African believes that's what's going to keep him young forever, you know, and who's to argue? Maybe after we track down these guys you're looking for we can go in for a little R and R."

I move away to watch the bushmen preparing their food over their own little fire somewhere halfway between ours and that of the African troops who've come to reinforce us. The latter are South-West African territorials, our "buddies," recruited from the very villages where Swapo has gotten its forces—this is a war between brothers as well as an occupation by the white man. (There is even a whole division of ex-Swapo soldiers, elsewhere in Namibia, who have been captured and "turned" so they can be used to track and kill their erstwhile comrades.) These men are led by a white South African who could be Lyddie's twin, except his pride and joy are a unit of tough and well-trained African men, far better soldiers than our misfit band. And in turn he sits among them as if they are his closest kin, sharing his coffee cup with his second-in-command, a handsome ebony-skinned induna, and he even goes so far as to reach into one of his men's rations to humorously snag a choice tidbit. (We must not forget how rigorously food apartheid is enforced back in the States; long after the other trappings of 'petty apartheid'—the *Net Vir Blankes* benches—have ceased to exist, white householders will still keep their tin mugs around so the lips of the cook might not meet the lips of the master even by proxy.) The easy camaraderie between this officer and his men, his evident pleasure in them, is not lost on Lyddie, who turns to gaze at me sourly, clearly wondering what offense he had given the gods to wind up in charge of such a sorry excuse for soldiers. I shrug. However much I may want to blend into the background of our army—and, increasingly, I don't—that desire to fit in is as far from chances of fulfillment as the fabled Yossi Greenbaum's.*

Soon, the hunters gather their weapons and supplies and head out in the vague direction of Angola. The two bushmen ride in the back of the Unimog driven by their minder, like a pair of hounds eager to pick up the scent of prey. Later, they will be let out to run in front of the vehicle to examine the seemingly blank, empty desert and scrubland and read the story told there. The world's first libraries were the savannas and deserts of Southern Africa; the first writing, tracks in the sand. Perhaps our love of reading—our ability to spend hours of our precious lives pursuing a

* One of Dad's most beloved jokes, dating back to the Second World War:

Troubled by the division between Afrikaners and English, an army colonel decided to try a little experiment. Going into the mess hall one day, he barked: "All right, I want all the Afrikaners on the left-hand side of the room, all the Englishmen on the right." There was a little shifting of places—most of the splitting up had already been done before he got there—and soon there were two groups of men in the mess . . . except for one lone man still standing in the middle.

"And what are you?" the colonel demanded.

"A South African, sir."

"Very good. That's the answer I've been waiting for. What is your name, soldier?"

"Yossi Greenbaum, sir."

line of inky squiggles—stems from earliest man's discovery that visual tracking gave him the edge over other predators with lesser memories.

The sight of these modest hunter-gatherers riding away in an army vehicle makes me sad. I've seen the anthropological films of how bushmen are *supposed to* live: they should be trailing some giraffe that they've shot with a wooden arrow dipped in a paste made of crushed, poisonous beetles. But the giraffes are all in protected parks now, their hunters forced to tell the ancient Mantis tales behind barbed-wire fences, or to sell their primeval skills to the locust plague of the occupying army. That's still better than being enslaved or shot at by hardscrabble black pastoralists, the Lyddie voice says in my inner ear.

...

It's an excellent thing that I did not go on that raid, as I would probably have been the one blamed for the debacle it turned into. The misadventure was the sole topic of the conversations at mealtimes for days afterward, picked over in minute detail, someone mentioning a particular moment in the unfolding of events and all the other men vying to get in their own anecdote, their chance to point out how someone else had fucked up worse than they had.

The San had quickly picked up the trail of the men presumed to be Swapo, and the posse moved at a fast clip over the dry terrain. Lyddie too impressed everyone with his tracking skills, showing where one of the twelve men they were following had briefly branched off from his group and gone for a smoke and a pee. But the insurgents had a considerable lead on our men, and it was only in the late afternoon that we found any tracks that could be considered fresh. These led to a small cluster of beehive huts; Lyddie stopped the pursuing unit and scanned the area with his binoculars. The tiny village seemed to have been abandoned only a few hours before, as there was still smoke coming from a cooking fire, but there was no other indication of human activity. Swapo had apparently paused in the small community—"Probably wanted to see if there was anything to steal," the captain muttered—then they'd passed on through, as he could see footprints going north. He sent one of the armored cars—a Ratel—to look around. These guys too saw no signs of life and stopped in the middle of the collection of huts, opened the hatch of their armored car, and lit up cigarettes. Lyddie waved on the rest of the troops, who made the mistake of driving into the little village instead of around it. They too were probably looking for something to steal.

Moments later there was a whooshing sound and a hand-fired mortar hit the first Ratel, followed by a cacophony of gunfire. The men inside jumped out and scrambled for cover, one of them firing his automatic rifle at the hut where the shooting had come from. The other vehicles came careening into town, but the driver of the lead Ratel was so shocked by the sight of a gaping, smoking hole in the armored car in front of him that he stalled. The Rinkhals that was only yards behind slammed right into him, and now there were three disabled vehicles providing a perfect target should the terrorist with the handheld mortar choose to pick them off one at a time. The two other jeeps stopped, and their drivers and men jumped down and took cover. Lyddie's vehicle with the trackers in it had meanwhile rushed to the front, and now he found himself *between* his armored cars and the terrorists. He fired a few shots at the hut, which was now strangely silent, then scrambled to get out of the way as the stalled Ratel came to life and began to swivel its machine gun toward him. Before the gunner could fire, the driver jerked the Ratel into gear and drove it straight into the hut, only to stall out again with half the hut collapsed around the armored car.

By this time, Lyddie had managed to round up the other men and had gotten them to behave the way trained soldiers are supposed to: dividing themselves into groups, each of which made a rapid attack on a different hut that might conceal the enemy. Within a minute or so, it became clear that the enemy had fired their bolt and then run, the attack on the first car a delaying ploy to give them time to escape. To all appearances, the village was deserted. However, there was another surprise attack that chased the SADF troepies out of the village: the roof of the hut had housed a large nest of hornets, which now poured out in a furious stream, bent on revenge against the destroyers of their home. The men abandoned all the armored vehicles and tore out of the village crying out in pain and slapping the air around them. They finally regrouped several hundred meters away to count their stings and examine their injuries. One soldier's face had begun to balloon and he was having trouble breathing; the driver of the Rinkhals had whiplash and was sitting on the ground rubbing his neck and groaning; and another man had badly gashed his leg on some sharp object when he scrambled out of the car that had been hit by the mortar. Fortunately, the missile had been fired from too close and had not armed itself, so there was no explosion in the confines of the armored car and no deaths.

Lyddie ordered one of the medics to bundle up and go fetch his supply kit, abandoned in the Ratel. The swollen-faced soldier needed an urgent shot of epinephrine if he was not to go into anaphylactic shock. The captain would have liked to go after the guerrilla band, which now had a good half-hour lead, but knew he had to reorganize his men first and get the injuries attended to. He also knew there was a small Special Forces unit attached to a UNITA* battalion just over the border, two hours away. Reluctantly, he radioed them to expect the guerrillas to cross the river sometime around dusk. He was friendly with the commanding officer of the unit, and he also knew that these guys were quite territorial and had gotten into a firefight with Koevoet† when they strayed into their area of operations. The last thing he needed was for his hopelessly incompetent men to start trading shots with a much better trained group of South Africans.

* Angolan armed forces under Jonas Savimbi. Because they were the main rivals to the socialist MPLA, both we and the U.S. supported them.

† Koevoet—the name means crowbar—was a police counterinsurgency group formed around 1979. Then–Minister of Law and Order Louis le Grange described it as "the crowbar which prises terrorists out of the bushveld like nails from rotting wood." Koevoet claimed a kill rate of twenty-five Swapo to one of themselves and were noted for their disregard of human rights. Ordinary soldiers were mostly not happy about the police doing army work, and disliked the unit intensely.

"Who was driving the Ratel?" he'd then demanded, still steaming. "He almost got the whole lot of us killed. I'm going to rip off the bastard's head and shove it up his arse."

Lyddie found the driver weeping uncontrollably, hunched over a small bundle held protectively in his arms. He prized the soldier's fingers open and removed the parcel, a small body wrapped in a blanket, a perfect and unharmed African baby who examined the captain's face with earnest intensity. He started yelling at the soldier, demanding to know what was going on, but all the infant's rescuer could do was weep. Disgusted, Lyddie handed the baby to a rifleman who was standing nearby, then he and the Bushmen's minder drove into the village. But first they took the precaution of lighting the edge of an army blanket soaked in motor oil so they would be protected from the hornets by dense black smoke. They returned about fifteen minutes later, this time bringing with them a five-year-old boy and his three-year-old sister, shell-shocked and fearful children, both of them as mute as the baby. The machine gun fire had decapitated their mother, and the children had hidden underneath a blanket, protected from the angry wasps, until Lyddie and the major had rescued them.

"And to think I was going to Zippo that hut to get rid of the hornets," Lyddie growled. "Those Swapo bastards shot at us from a hut with a family in it. What did they think? We weren't going to fire back? I wish they were in there right now so I could use the flamethrower on them."

That night, I hear Lyddie telling Fynbos the story. "So I had to radio in how now I've got *four* casualties with this *doos* crying like a teenage girl who's just been jilted, and I've got three little orphaned African piccaninnies who've got to be taken care of. Did the major throw a fit—which is what I would've done if someone had made such a pissing mess of a simple operation? No. He gets very excited and tells me we mustn't move, mustn't touch anything. They're sending out another helicopter with some photographers on it. We've caught Swapo in the act of using civilians as shields in a firefight, which is a big propaganda victory. That's more important than killing rebels, he tells me. So what's the bloody army coming to, hey?"

...

One day I happen to mention to Roelof that I was born on the same day that Bobby Kennedy was shot. He looks at me speculatively. "As he was dying you were being born, hey? Perhaps you are his reincarnation."

I begin to protest, for Roelof's mysticism has its serious side, but I see the slight turning up of the corners of his mouth in an otherwise deadpan expression.

It was a Friday, June, 1968. Almost exactly two years after Kennedy's historic speech at the University of Capetown, when he misdirected his audience into thinking he was talking about South Africa's difficult racial past and present, only to reveal that he was referring to the U.S.A. and not the R.S.A. I've learned the details of the shooting afterward, of course. The late-night walk through the kitchen where the newly announced democratic candidate touches palms with the Chicano busboys, then the surprise explosive shots. While I was entering the world in my own bloody fashion, *inter urinam et faeces*, the senator was leaving it, lying amid spilled sandwiches and finger foods, his lifeblood mingling with the hors d'oeuvres.

Father liked to tell the story of my birth, how he listened to the radio in the waiting room, his sadness at this distant but significant assassination vying with his elation at the arrival of a son. Like many South Africans, Father had been moved and exhilarated by Bobby Kennedy's visit, when the former attorney general had stunned the old Boere by his outspokenness, his refusal to stay on the officially circumscribed routes, his insistence on stopping his chauffeur-driven car to get out and walk among the people of the townships that border the cities' access roads. Dad had gone to Jan Smuts Airport the night Kennedy arrived, accompanying an American representative of a chemical company, a supplier of the latest in toxic dusts and sprays. These were designed to clog up insects' primitive lungs, to be absorbed through their cuticles to dry up the *gogga* from within, or to be eaten and turn the bugs' internal organs into a liquefied mess. The Africans who transferred the contents of the big drums of organophosphates into cans and forced-air sprayers wore neither gloves nor respirator masks, so it must have been presumed they were hardier than the insects.

Dad's American associate had wanted to see the young politician who was making such a name for himself back home, and so they joined the mostly young crowd waiting not so patiently for the visiting politician to emerge from the lighted building. Kennedy had ventured outside and immediately begun shaking hands with everybody, the common touch from a film-star-handsome politician as different from the stolid and unfriendly Nationalist Party crowd as you could find in a book of antonyms. (Imagine forty-six years of governance by the most humorless people on earth!) Just as the glamorous visitor was getting into his limousine a young woman had thrown her arms around his neck and kissed him full on the lips. The crowd had gasped collectively at her audacity, then laughed when Bobby said something about enjoying the warm welcome. And then the police standing at the periphery had formed a line and begun to push everyone out of the way, sjamboking those dumb coeds too slow to move out of their way. Father had managed to lead his supplier to the edge of the crowd, but on the way the American had stumbled into the back of a boy of about twelve who had turned around and socked him hard and accurately in the eye before disappearing into the melee. By the time the fellow got delivered to his hotel, he had a perfect shiner as a souvenir.

"I never believed in Sirhan Sirhan, not for a minute," Roelof muses. "I mean, what do you really think are the chances he was acting alone? Do you know what Vorster said when it looked like Kennedy would be facing off against Nixon? 'God help us if Bobby becomes the next president of the United States.'"

"So what are you trying to say? That we did it?"

Roelof places his index finger on his lips in a gesture of conspiratorial silence. Though he makes fun of the Afrikaners' paranoia, he enjoys arcane conspiracies, a gunpowder plot under every bed, every third man a spy. He even thinks it was the cops who bombed the South African Council of Churches' offices in Khotso House. Crazy, nee? He loves to tell the joke about the South African space program sending a lone black woman to the moon. When she comes back to earth, she is pregnant . . . which proves that the Security Police are everywhere. He has said to me that he knows "the *ou* who did Olaf Palme," and isn't it funny that Mozambique's socialist leader Samora Machel was on his way to meet with South African officials when his plane crashed? The Kennedy connection makes its own odd sort of sense: after all, here was a serious contender for the U.S. presidency who dared ask Bible-quoting students the question: "What if God is black?"

I wonder what Roelof would make of the bizarre recollections of the security agencies' James Bond wannabes. There is Eric Taylor, the cop who murdered Eastern Cape activist Fort Calata, who now claims that watching *Mississippi Burning* made him realize the error of his ways and come forth to testify. I can picture Roelof chuckling over the idea of showing this movie to all former BOSS and CCB* men, to the constabulary in every rural town. Wherever he is now, I hope they appreciate a sense of humor.

...

It is Roelof who effects a grand change in the pattern of my army life. A few weeks after he transfers out from Gemsbok Camp, I get a letter telling me how much he is enjoying the film program in Pretoria. He knows too that there are open spaces in it and he has put in a good word for me with the director of the technical institute. "I know you are wor-

* Bureau of State Security and the Civil Cooperation Board. The euphemisms and acronyms the apartheid administration gave its secret police services managed to be as clumsily sinister as the organizations themselves, which devoted their time to watching—and sometimes assassinating—"soft targets," i.e., professors, union organizers, etc.

ried about not being able to do your part in the battle against our enemies," he writes. "But don't forget 'hearts and minds' and that this is good PR for the army." This is a clever touch on his part. He knows the censor will read this—as every—letter, but only I will know that what he means by PR is not public relations but *propaganda rubbish*. He writes that he is going to film some bushmen trackers at an undisclosed location (security!), and this is another persuasive touch because we shared an interest in social anthropology and he had told me that what he would really like to do someday is make an ethnographic film.

The letter arrives at a difficult juncture in my sojourn at Gemsbok Camp. Lyddie is off somewhere in Owamboland or around the Caprivi Zipfel* ("Control the Caprivi and you control all of Africa," Lyddie had said to me.) The rumor is that he has joined some of his Koevoet buddies on a "baboon shoot." Now that the rainy season is here, the animals are moving south into land that has grown markedly less hostile to daily survival, and with them have come the guerrilla insurgents. For Lyddie, it is like a hunting safari—a chance to sleep in the open and track down his prey. That the prey shoots back and may try to ambush him in turn makes it all the more fun.

Now that Lyddie is not around to placate him, Fynbos resumes his hounding of me. What little leisure time I have is spent raking the hard dirt around the tents and cleaning up the "garden," a patch of dirt with some arranged stones, a scraggly half-dead succulent, and a crude wood carving of our mascot—the civet cat. I have already been pulled off cooking duty a couple of times and sent on foot patrol with some of the worst reprobates in the division, sadistic farm boys who forget that this fat Jew who has such trouble keeping up with them has also improved their daily diet. One large horse-faced individual, in particular, likes to jab me in the back with his rifle anytime I slow to catch my breath, hitting me each time in the fifth lumbar vertebra. Worse, I think they've figured out that the

* Caprivi Strip, a thin spar of land that borders Namibia with Angola, Botswana, and Zambia and touches on Zimbabwe.

debilitating dysentery that struck them a day after they spent patrol mercilessly tormenting me may have been my malicious revenge. (I made sure the double helping of meat they each got had not been fully thawed before being warmed in the stew; gulpers rather than masticators, they had failed to notice the difference. Now I think of them as the Kafka-boeties, for he used to chew each morsel twenty-seven times before swallowing it.)

The only one who is friendly to me these days is Little Gidding, who is strangely fond of me for having clobbered him. I am sitting watching the last ember of the cooking fire glow in the slight evening breeze, when I feel his small pudgy hand on my shoulder. "Homesick, hey?" he says. "It gets me worst in the evening too."

"That which is only living can only die," I say to him. I'm quoting from the wrong Quartet, but I've always preferred the first to the last. Gidding nods sympathetically but with little comprehension. We all say bizarre and random things these days, the vast emptiness punctuated by terror has unhinged the best minds of my division; the rest are just *gesuip* on Klipdrift, a swig of which Gidding now offers me from his military-issue canteen. This is another sign of Lyddie's absence; he didn't mind *die ouen* drinking, but he never allowed liquor in the water canteens, pointing out that was a sure way to die of dehydration if you're suddenly called out on patrol.

Officially, it is only the Permanent Forces who can drink as much as they like. We, the conscripts, are supposed to be content with two beers a day, but that is not how it works out in the bush. There are lucrative opportunities in the army, if you know how to find them. Every time there is a delivery of food supplies by lorry from Oshakati, there will be a couple of cases of Klipdrift or other cheap brandy hidden beneath them. These are quickly unloaded and distributed to the guys, who seem oblivious to the disappearance of their army pay into someone else's pocket. It's funny about "Klippies" being the dop of choice. With a couple of Windhoek lager chasers, it will certainly take you to oblivion as fast as anything else—except maybe Mandies or stolen morphine, which are so far not a problem at Gemsbok. The fact that Lyddie has promised the medics they'll be the victims of a "training accident" if any painkillers are missing from their supplies suggests that we're the exception to the rule.

Before he transferred out, Roelof and I had had a long chat about the origin of the brandy's name. There is, of course, the manufacturer in the Boland, who boasts of following Oom Kosie Marais's high distillation standards. Then there is the eponymous army training camp. "There was the battle of De Klipdrift," I told Roelof, referring to the time the Boers' General Jacobus ("Koos") Hercules De la Rey captured Lord Methuen.

"I'm not sure that counts," he said solemnly, as pedantic as if I had introduced a dubious word into a Scrabble game. "I've always heard of that as Tweebosch."

"De Klipdrift was the name of the farm, Tweebosch was the house where Methuen took refuge."

"Still . . ." He tugged thoughtfully at his spade-shaped beard. "Yes, no, what really interests me is the Independent Republic of Klipdrift, founded in 1870. I bet you've never heard of it, and you an Engelsman."

"Speaking English doesn't make you an Englishman."

"Ja, ja, ja. All you Jews are Englishmen."

Before I could object to the illogic of this statement, he went on: "You might have heard of it as the Diggers' Republic. A bunch of you English guys tried to start your own republic so you could keep the diamonds to yourselves. I've seen the flag; it's even got the Union Jack in it."

"The way I heard it, the Orange Free State Boers decided to grant mining rights to their own crowd exclusively, even though there were lots of people who'd already staked claims in that area. If you take the outlook that everything you see belongs to you, then all the world's a thief." We had touched on the topic in a pre-Brenner history class in high school, but with only the briefest mention and the main purpose being to point out the wisdom of the British colonial government. Lieutenant General Hay had given one in the eye to both the Boer Volksraad, the "people's government," and to the upstart miners by declaring that the Griquas—an independent mixed-race group founded by Adam Kok . . . his name taken from his profession as cook, a name that many of his descendants still proudly sport—had the best claim. It was a typical South African mess, with the same place being given half a dozen different names, each white group claiming to be masters of the land. The British authorities deliberated over the documentary evidence and sided with their duskier citizenry over the Boers, only to annex the territory a few years later. In the end, nature—or, rather, the Vaal River—had brought the squabble to a close by flooding out the diggings and sending everyone scurrying to drier pastures. After their brief—very brief—fifteen minutes of imperial fame, the Griquas found themselves being pushed from pillar to post, scorned as bastards. A major portion of their ethnic group lived in a place called No Man's Land. In a divided land, they suffered from being *neither*.

I relayed much of this to Roelof, who was amused by the extensive schoolroom detail and glad to see I did not solely blame the Boers for everything. He said what an interesting thing it would be to go and explore Klipdrift and Du Toit's pan, where the "ex-president of the Free Diamond Republic," Stafford Parker, had set up shop. Roelof was collecting a list of South African historic sites he would like to visit so he could get to the bottom of the muddy stories of the past, and he has invited me to join him in his quest. Our tour would include such highlights as Bulhoek, where a religious sect called the "Israelites" were massacred by the police after their leader told them their faith would turn bullets into drops of water; Kipling's house in the Cape, curiously named the "Woolsack"; the farm where the great self-taught nineteenth century writer Olive Schreiner really was a governess; and the store William Plomer's family had owned in Zululand. We also argued over whether to include Galpin's Observatory in Grahamstown. This is where a wealthy watchmaker built a giant camera obscura, the moment-to-moment history of his town being recorded on the wall of the room fractions of a second after it happens (if you allow for the time it takes for light to be refracted through a lens and off the giant mirror and thence onto the wall).

"It's a pity the diamond-diggers didn't get to keep their republic," he said, musingly. "We could have had our own English bantustan. What would the capital be? Rain City, instead of Sun City? Dogs would be allowed to walk around freely, while children would be kept on leashes."

We were interrupted by one of our fellow soldiers, who staggered out of a nearby tent to take a remarkably long pee into the dust beside the wheel of one of the Samils. His befuddled expression denoted that he was deep in his own personal Independent Republic of Klipdrift. It was fortunate for him that Fynbos was off on a trek designed to torture a small group of freshly arrived troops: "*roofies,*"who, in his view, needed to be acclimated to our brutal environment.

"What a bunch of fuckups we are," Roelof said to me. "And make no mistake about it: your Captain Lyddie is the biggest fuckup of all or he wouldn't be here, and he certainly wouldn't be hanging around with Koevoet. You know what we called them in Oshakati? FWBs. Fuckups With Beards. They want to look like Voortrekkers and return to some heroic past."

"I thought they're supposed to be pretty tough."

"Well, they're big and they like to kill people," he grumbled. The drunken soldier was still standing around, and Roelof turned his ire on him, calling out: "Sies, man. Pissing on a tire like a dog? Can't you even get yourself over to the w.c?"

The soldier blinked stupidly at him, then a misshapen smile appeared on his face. "Woof," he said. "Woof fucking woof."

Roelof shook his head. "Now you see why I have to get the hell out?"

I understand only too well. Having finished my task of scrubbing out the pots, I have to go and perform another chore that Fynbos likes to reserve for me. We have hit upon a not-so-high-tech but effective early warning system should our camp be raided. I collect all the used cans of beer and cold drinks, then I take them out to the the perimeter and string them off the barbed wire with nylon monofilament. Anyone trying to cut the wire or squeeze through it is likely to make a tremendous racket. Its efficacy had already been proved, sort of, when a few nights back the fence began clanging away late at night, the sound soon obliterated by continuous gunfire from the sentries. In the morning, we discovered the tattered corpse of a hyena. The numerous and poorly healing rips and tears in my hands are surely a small price to pay for saving my countrymen's rubbish from marauding scavengers.

Accompanying the letter from Roelof is an army flier calling for volunteers for the film and video program. I fill it out, worried about the aborted last term of my university studies and that Fynbos may give me a bad report out of sheer nastiness. In the event, he is only too happy to get rid of me. Two weeks after I send in the forms, I am given orders to go with the next day's transport to Opuwo, where I will catch a flight back to the States. I am given only half a day's leave, as the film-training school will have already been in session for one day by the time I reach Pretoria. At least I will be able to have dinner with Mother and spend one night in my own bed, an all-too-brief luxury, as I have to report to the film school by 8:30 A.M. sharp.

This is to be my first leave in ten months and thirteen days. My previous, five-day leave between basic training and my being shipped off to Namibia had not been an unqualified success. I had been looking forward to being pampered by Mother, just as I had previously looked forward to getting away from her smothering attention right before my army service began. But she was the one to be distracted and busy, having recently taken a job as an administrative secretary in the Department of Philosophy at the University of Witwatersrand. This, my first leave, happened to be during the week, so Mother was away from the house for each of my days at home.

"Well, I can't do nothing all the rest of my life, can I, Paul?" she said defensively. "After all, I'm still a young woman."

"I'm glad you've gotten a job, Ma," I replied, but she gave me a look that showed she saw right through me.

At least we would be able to spend time together in the evenings and have some nice dinners. I had expected us to fall into our old pattern of solitary togetherness, with me tantalizing our palates with ever more elaborate and exotic dishes. So I was disappointed when she announced that she had previously invited a new friend to eat with us on what was to be my last night home. "You'll like him," she said. "But I have to warn you that he has gastric ulcers and can't abide spicy food."

Gone were my plans for a fiery vindaloo or even a subtle, apricot-suffused bobotie. My menu then was a consommé Madrilene, roast beef, and a perfectly puffed Yorkshire pudding. It was served to an unappreciative, liquid-slurping, food-gobbling gentleman by the name of Claude Moskowitz, a beetle-browed whoreson with a florid complexion and thick graying hair like an aging German shepherd. I tried hard not to notice the oblivious rapidity with which he was gulping the consommé, a delicate broth that I had watched over and gently heated to achieve the right state of limpidity, a nectar that should be treated with the reverence usually reserved for a fine wine.

He was ten years older than Mother, and half a head shorter, but he was full of a blustery, bullying energy and a confident ignorance. He owned a furniture factory and was acquainted with the Capelands. "A very high class of people," he said, and I had to bite back the question: *How would* you *know?* Claude, it turned out, was the older brother of the lecturer Mother worked for, and Mother was quick to tell me that Claude had truncated his own schooling and taken a job early in life so his brainier brother could complete his education.

"I am so glad you're going to South-West Africa," Mother said to me as we sat down for dinner. I looked at her in astonishment. True, we had just had an awkward moment. Claude had brought Mother a bouquet of half a dozen Stargazer lilies, which she had placed in a vase on the dining table. The overpowering scent of those horrid exotics would have utterly destroyed my carefully prepared dinner, so I bustled them off to the kitchen. "You might have asked, dear," Mother chided. "*I* was enjoying Claude's flowers." But surely this wasn't offense enough for her to wish me *gone*?

"Yes, I was afraid you'd be sent to those horrible, violent townships," Mother said, continuing her thought. "It would have been nice to have you closer to home, but it worried me that you'd be in danger."

"Those places are too terrible," Claude said confidently, breaking a piece off the baguette with his thick fingers and running the chunk of bread along the edges of his empty soup bowl, before cramming the morsel into his mouth. "The Africans have gone quite mad. Burning. Killing. Necklacing. You know what necklacing is, don't you?" I nodded. Yes, I had seen the same pictures on television and in the newspapers. "Mind you," he continued. "I feel sorry for the older blacks. They just want to get on with their lives, but the kids are completely berserk. The Communists have taken over their minds."

"I don't think it helps that the police keep arresting young children," I said mildly.

"They're just doing their job, my boy. Do you imagine those kids give a thought to where they're going to get an education after they burn down their school? You can't get a job doing the *toyi-toyi* dance, you've got to have an education. But that's your African; no memory of yesterday, and not a thought about tomorrow."

I must have made a face, having heard this rubbish about the African's lack of any sense of time before, for he leaned forward and fixed me with his glittering dark eyes and pointed his fork in my direction. "I suppose you think the African is your brother?"

"I don't have any brothers." I delicately sipped the last of my consommé off my soup spoon, trying to focus on the faint tang of sherry beneath the beef stock.

"You know what I'm talking about. You think we're all the same, just the skin is different? I've lived long enough to know that the Bantu are not like us—mind you, they've got their good qualities. But it's a mistake to think everybody is just the same as everyone else. I'll tell you the truth: the African is inferior, and I can prove it."

I looked at Claude with some interest, wondering what his "proof" was going to be. I'd heard plenty of anecdotes during basic training: the foolish maid who put a glass ice-cream bowl into hot water (of course it cracked), the rural laborer's wife who woke her injured husband to give him the sleeping pill prescribed by the doctor. The urban legends and blatantly bigoted comments formed their own "total onslaught," nonsense told often enough that it became believed. "Just replace the word *African* with *Jew*, then see if you still believe that story," Brenner had advised our history class.

"I want you to think about how we've treated the African," Claude said, leaning forward heavily on his elbows and making the knife clink dangerously against Mother's good china soup bowl. "Would any white man let you behave that way toward him? The black man must be inferior, or he would never have allowed us to do the things we've done to him." Claude folded his arms and looked at me, deadpan. *Quod erat demonstrandum*, as we used to write on our arithmetic papers. Thus it has been demonstrated.

After a long journey, I arrive late in the afternoon at our house, but still before Mother returns from her job. She has left me a key and a note describing the leftovers I will find in the fridge, "but I'm sure it won't be as good as your lovely cooking." She is right. There is nothing of note in the refrigerator, and I contemplate bitterly how she might have had the forethought to pick up something savory, perhaps some smoked snoek or mock crayfish, instead of this dried-out lump of corned beef so reminiscent of army fare. Morosely, I eat a little of this compressed-cardboard excuse for meat, trying to provide it with a little flavor by so liberally dosing it with horseradish sauce that tears come to my eyes.

Home is otherwise mostly unchanged, although there are signs here and there that Claude is a frequent visitor: a cigar cutter on the living room coffee table, a photograph from a New Year's party sitting on the mantelpiece above the fireplace: Claude with his plump holothurian's body tightly encased in an expensive dinner jacket, Mother wearing flats to appear shorter and with a shy grin on her face. The four pink worms just visible on the shoulder of her blouse must be Claude's fingers.

I take my army duffel to my old bedroom and lie down for a moment on my own bed. I am awakened by the sound of a car pulling in to the driveway. Mother hurries up the stairs to hug me, clearly delighted. She seems unable to sit still with excitement, telling me stories about her job that she had already included in her letters to the camp. She looks well, slimmer than when I left and evidently paying more attention to her makeup. She informs me that she had some work to bring home in preparation for a big conference in a few days, but she deliberately left it in the office just for this evening so nothing would interfere with our fleeting time together. I even venture to ask—"How is Uncle Claudius?"—and she smiles at my little joke, then tells me he is really very nice and she wishes I would give him a chance.

I am touched to find that she did stop by the grocer's on the way home and has picked up some treats for me—a jar of Peck's anchovette, the fish paste looking pink and fresh, and an accompanying box of Breton crackers; a lamb rib roast, granadilla sorbet—but I have trouble getting past the feeling I am an actor in a play. "You smell different," Mother says, giving me one of many spontaneous hugs.

"I did shower when I got home, Ma," I protest. I'm even wearing my own civvie clothes from the cupboard.

"I'm sure, lovie. It's just something . . . like someone out of the wilderness."

"Where do you think I've been all this time?" I am suddenly cross.

"I know," she soothes me. "I'm just not used to it. Tell me, have you gotten to visit any of the game parks up near you? Mrs. Tremper from my department—you remember, I wrote to you about her . . . of course you do. You remember everything. Well, her son is also in the army and he said he got to take some days off in the Okavango."

"No, Ma. I don't think it's all that far away, but I haven't gone there yet." I wonder how she imagines the life I've been living. I can hardly tell her about Sergeant Fynbos offering to suck out my eyeball or Skattie DuPlessis smashing his forehead over and over against his metal locker after his sweetie sent him a Dear John letter.

"Claude was just saying that if I can get some time off we could make a trip up," she continues. "Maybe we could meet you in Windhoek, he knows some of the businesspeople there. We could go to the game park or the coast, whichever you prefer."

"Mother! I'm not there as a tourist. I carry a gun every minute of every effing day. I mean, you don't have a clue—"

"Well, at least you do look like you're getting plenty of exercise."

We sit in awkward silence for some duration, and I finally say softly: "You look good too, Ma."

We stick mostly to neutral subjects at dinner: the personalities in Mother's office, how much she enjoyed Harrison Ford in *Working Girl*, Mrs. Wissle's heroic battle with breast cancer. "Poor woman," Mother says. "She's never had much luck in her life."

The lamb has turned out perfectly, the fatty skin crisp and the inner flesh still moist and pink. Mother annoys me by dousing her portion with mint sauce from an ornate glass cruet, then topping it with unnaturally green mint jelly, but I hold back from complaint. She registers my disapproval anyway, and says with an uncharacteristically girlish laugh: "I know it's not the most gourmet way to eat this, but I've always thought of lamb as an excuse to eat mint jelly."

I give a half-smile in acknowledgment. "Whatever makes it taste good to you, that's what's important," I lie.

"Yes. You know, Paul, I'm so pleased you're learning a new skill, something that will be useful when you return to ordinary life. And the nice thing is, I'm sure you're much safer carrying a camera than a gun."

"The photo units go everywhere the regular units do," I murmur morosely.

"Well, nowhere is safe anymore, is it?" she says, a little too brightly. "You know, they had a bomb in downtown Johannesburg a few months ago. It rattled my office windows."

"I heard about it on Forces Radio, Mom. I'm sorry I didn't think to ask you about it."

"You have plenty to worry about on your own, I'm sure. We just do the best we can, don't we? I mean, there's no point fretting over things you can't control."

After dinner Mother asks if I want to bring a book into the living room and sit with her. I decline, saying I'm to be picked up at 5:30 the next morning and had better get an early night.

"Are you sure you should be traveling that early? It's a dangerous time of day. They like to bump your car, and when you stop to see the damage they shoot you and take off with the car. Promise me you won't stop for any reason."

I laugh. "I'm being picked up by some army guys. Anyone who tries to hijack our car would have to be bloody stupid." To my own ears I sound like someone else, someone crass and boastful, someone a lot tougher than Paul Sweetbread.

"Okay, dear. It's just I know you've never liked getting up early."

She reaches up to touch my cheek, but I move aside. "What I like doesn't seem to matter very much anymore," I say bitterly. Seeing the hurt in her expression, I add: "The army, Ma. I'm talking about the army."

...

I have never liked Pretoria, a city as determinedly Afrikaner as Johannesburg was English, filled with sour-faced government men and buildings whose main architectural impulse is to belittle the onlooker. The Africans on the streets look more fearful and harried than in the city's more liberal neighbor, as if any moment someone is going to shout at them and demand what business they have being there. Yet it is almost with relief that I disembark outside the SADF College for Educational Technology, although the first thing I notice when I run in to leave my duffel in the barracks is a gigantic portable stereo complete with lights. I know that this will mean my head is to be battered with bad music for the next several weeks.*

We are taught the handling of Hi-8 cameras by Corporal Kleynhans,

* I am shown to be all too prescient when the owner of the boombox plays in an endless loop an awful song—"Live Is Life"—by the German band Opus.

a malodorous man in his mid-forties with a severe strabismus and the red-veined cheeks of a hard drinker. He had briefly worked for S.A.'s top commercial studio, Ster-Kinekor, and his greatest claim to fame is that he lent technical assistance to Mimosa Films for *The Gods Must Be Crazy*.*

"I can't believe I just heard a grown man say 'lent technical assistance,'" mutters Deon McBride, a sharp-witted ironic fellow with a far greater knowledge of cameras and the history of film than our earnest teacher. Deon observes sotto voce to me that Kleynhans must have been first grip on the tea trolley at Ster-Kinekor.

I am jumpy at first at being away from the vast emptiness of Namibia and instead surrounded by traffic and pedestrians hurrying who knows where with great intent. However, I am happy to be back in a classroom—even one run by the SADF and located, not insignificantly, in the same building as the army counterintelligence operation Komops. Making films proves to be simply fun, like stepping back into a child's world of gadgets and play: there is a visceral pleasure at the whirring motor held close to one's head, the sense of making a permanent record (mind you, a selective one) of the world around you. Most enjoyable for me are the still cameras. Since we are vaguely connected with army intelligence, the authorities have not stinted on supplies. We have several state-of-the-art large-format view cameras—two beautifully calibrated Sinar F2s, the expensive Swiss 4 × 5 as precise as any watch, and a Linhof Master Technika with a range of different lenses. There are also plenty of Hasselblads, chosen, Deon says, so our army photographers can blend in with the press at demonstrations. I am initially claustrophobic about the darkrooms deep in the bowels of this brick building in Pretoria, but soon find the developing process to be not unlike cooking. There is that wonderful moment of alchemy amid the smells of sulfur and hydrochloric acid as the image reverse-fades into reality beneath its chemical bath.

* The enormous international success of this movie suggests South Africans are not the only ones to feel a nostalgic love for the noble savage. Did those Owambos relentlessly pursued by bushmen trackers also call them the "harmless people"?

What is harder to take is how seriously the army treats the hearts and minds campaign. Daily, we are exposed to hours of film of patriotic content: smiling, handsome soldiers waving from astride Hippos; heart-rending military funerals . . . usually filmed with the sun behind the sorrowful comrade standing with his hand over his own heart in silent memory of his brave friend. The calm, manly tones of the voice-over do not tell us what killed the soldier lying in the flag-covered bier, for that would be too awkward. We are officially not in Angola, so he couldn't have died there. The recce Jan Burger had stopped by Gemsbok Camp on his way back from an operation deep in Angola. He told us how Foreign Minister Roelof "Pik"* Botha had paid a special visit by helicopter to their commando base. Two days later, they heard his voice on the radio saying he could assure the world that there were no South African troops whatsoever in Angola. "Man, we cracked up over that. All night long, guys kept falling over laughing: 'We don't exist. We don't fucking exist.'"

They might have said that the soldier was killed by terrorists crossing the border, but we were supposed to be doing a great job containing all border crossings. Deaths were usually attributed to "training accidents," which made us the world's most accident-prone army. Just as well that the press was not allowed to write anything about the army without prior approval.

Other films show in gruesome detail what the enemy is capable of: a farmer and his family strewn around their kitchen floor in pools of blood. The camera pans across the Afrikaans cookbooks—and a Bible!—atop the homemade shelf on the kitchen wall, the pot of *mielie* meal congealed on the stove, the old lady's panties around the ankle of her blood-smeared leg. Several of my fellows weep at this film, and even I feel a fierce stirring desire for revenge. There is the bizarrely contorted, burnt body of an African man—caught buying milk for his children during a shopping boycott staged by the local Communist youth organization, the

* This key figure in the Nationalist Party government was known by the Afrikaans abbreviation for penguin (pikkewyn).

announcer tells us with dripping sarcasm. There are also happy shots of "natives" running after our transport lorries with joyous faces, or playing soccer with soldiers in the townships. I juxtapose these images in my mind with Lyddie's clinical expression at the bubbles rising in the rain barrel . . . but there are so many of these short films and army photographs, their message enhanced by careful attention to lighting and by tricks in the developing process. Crude as these might be—the young, pretty *meisie* waving goodbye to her boyfriend/husband as he heads out to do his duty is always soft-focused and grainy; the atrocities always starkly lit and luridly colored or heavily shadowed in black and white—they stir one's emotions and the tear rises unbidden to the eye.

"Never forget," Corporal Kleynhans says, "we are facing Total Onslaught and have to make a Total Response. Every photograph you take is a weapon."

"I thought it was illegal to quote the ANC," Deon McBride murmurs just loudly enough so that only I can hear. I ran into him at the Golden Spur in a deep tête-a-tête over the restaurant's famed American-style hamburgers with a slight, angular *borselkop* who was obviously his boyfriend. That I waved in a friendly way and then went about my business has endeared me to him, and our friendship was sealed by his learning that I know Sedgewick. ("Gorgeous Sedgewick," he calls my friend.) His knowledge runs deep, and his cynical assessments of our propaganda films is like rain at the end of a molten summer day. His first short is a work of genius; it opens with General Jannie Geldenhuys reading one of his poems at a funeral, then splices to recruits firing at human-shaped silhouettes, and a Rinkhals armored vehicle tearing over the top of a hill. The corporal loved it, and missed the point of the jump-cut juxtapositions, the embedded images of other recruits going on leave with their golf bags and boomboxes, the scared bloat-bellied African toddler staring at a vehicle as incomprehensible to him as the sudden appearance of a live apatosaurus. All the corporal sees are the patriotic images of our *weermag* in action. (How it sounds like Wehrmacht, the shock troops of another master race!)

"Brecht is my master," Deon tells me, lending me a dog-eared, much-underlined copy of *The Good Soldier Schweik*, one of the master's influences. I am able to read Jaroslav Hašek's World War I satire of army incompetence in another dying empire, the Austro-Hungarian, quite openly, even earning a friendly nod from Corporal Kleynhans who is happy to see any title with the words *good* and *soldier* in it. He senses that those two words are precisely what I am not. Still, he is impressed by how quickly I learn to match apertures and f-stops, the correct proportions of mixes and temperature for color development, and to recognize the signature use of light and camera angles of particular SADF cameramen. And when I am looking through the lens of the cine-camera, my single cyclops eye recording the world, I am transformed. "Your rifle is the most important part of your body," the staff sergeant at basic training had bellowed at us. (Like Fynbos, he was another screamer, seeking to force his philosophy into our recalcitrant bodies through sheer force of decibels.) For me, my R4 had always been an attached and dangerous nuisance, inclined to bump into objects and people, to point its deadly nose at whomever was nearby. The camera is different. It is as if I were born with it growing out of my head.

Which is not to say that it does not betray me. After tedious repetition of how to load film, focus, compose our shots; after we have filmed each other walking around the streets of Pretoria or drinking coffee in the basement lounge at KomOps; we are told that we will be going to do some real work. We will accompany a unit of reserves going into Mamelodi, the township just outside Pretoria, one apprentice photographer to a Casspir. We will save our film for the moment when the soldiers will spontaneously begin a game of soccer with local youths. We are shown one of the soccer balls, a nicely stitched leather ball with the words "We Protect and Serve" and "*Servamus*" indelibly printed on opposite sides. "I bet it cost the army a couple of hundred rand for each of these, when you could just pick one up for twelve rand at the OK Bazaars," Deon whispers to me.

"I heard that, Deon, and it is simply not true," Corporal Kleynhans says, squinting angrily. "This a good example of the rubbishy lies you like to tell."

"How much did the ball cost, sir?" Deon asks innocently.

"Much less than you said, my boy. But I cannot reveal the exact amount, as that is classified information."

"Isn't that the police motto anyway? Ours should say "*Uit die Volk, Vir die Volk*,"* I interject.

"Yes, that's true. The police must have given them to us, so it didn't cost anything. Satisfied, McBride?"

"Thank you, *meneer*. I understand much better now and I do apologize for my earlier remark."

Kleynhans looks mollified, having little ear for subtleties of tone. He continues to tell us our expected duties, warning us to make sure we capture the moment when the commanding officer donates the ball to the township kids as a gesture of friendship. Of course, we have already seen films showing these exact scenes; our spontaneity too is fully preplanned.

Our orders are to present ourselves at the Reserves Camp at 5:30 the next morning, and are given the evening off. I am grateful for this, as Roelof is on leave between photography training and being sent back to South-West Africa, and he has invited me to his house in Observatory for dinner. Deon is going to join me, which I am grateful for, as he has a car, and anyway I do not feel comfortable driving in the dark—I hate driving at the best of times, since I am constantly distracted by the vise of my own thoughts and memories, and my reaction times are slow. Overall, I drive too sluggishly for my frenetic countrymen and often I will find myself with some angry BMW driver or overloaded township taxi pressing up against my bumper, trying to get me to go faster or pull to the side. Deon is amused when I tell him this, and he informs me that I was born in the wrong century.

* "From the People, For the People." In translation, Afrikaans ideology often sounds like the U.S. Declaration of Independence or the Communist Manifesto, but one has to remember that *people* here means only the Afrikaner, *die Volk*.

We are greeted at the door by Roelof's "woman friend," Riana—he no more believes in marriage than he does in God. Strange humming, vibrating noises come from the upper rooms of the small house. "That's just Roelof practicing the mouth-bow. He doesn't quite have the hang of it yet." Roelof has often complained to me that we are surrounded by African music, by "brilliant musicians" working as gardeners and dustbin boys, and yet we know nothing about it. This strumming sounds oddly familiar to me, and I realize that it is much like the background noise to Sedgewick's production of *The Cherry Orchard*. The noise abruptly stops, followed by the loud clumping of Roelof's army boots on the wooden stairs. He appears before us, flanked on either side by flat wooden carvings in ebony of a man with a spear—these are affixed to the wall and are silhouetted against its white paint, each spear-brandisher mirroring the other. "How do you like my civvie uniform?" Roelof jokes, pretending to model his clothes, which consist of a pair of cutoff jean shorts and a colorful shirt sporting various kinds of birds so outlandish they appear imaginary but in fact are all found in the Okavango Delta.

Roelof grips the banister and swings himself down past the last five steps and lands with a loud thump on the wooden floor. "What is this, my brothers? You have been here ten minutes already and you don't have any drinks. What must you think of Afrikaner hospitality?" He is brighter-eyed than any time I have seen him, and he smells distinctly of eau-de-cologne. He has always been jocular, but this is the first time I have known him to be cheerful—a sign of how good it is for him to be away from the army, with its narrow and demanding view of life.

Our drinklessness is soon remedied with enormous gin rickeys, and Roelof escorts us to the outside veranda, where some hardwood coals are glowing in a built-in brick *braai*. Riana talks to us about her job with a liberal-minded advertising company, which has just made a commercial showing a female Afrikaans pop star dancing with a black petrol attendant.

"The old *tannies* in the heartland sent in stacks of complaints, but sales have soared because the black van drivers love it," she says happily, her eyes following Roelof's busy, energetic motions as he stokes the embers, oils the sliced aubergines and courgettes, and places these vegetables and four stuffed trout on the grill bars. There is soon the enticing smell of sizzling fish merging with the odor of the herbs—thyme, sage, and French tarragon.

"I am glad you're out of that camp for fuckups," Roelof calls over to me. "I'm telling you, Riana, it's like Tara* out there, only run by the inmates. It's ruddy marvelous that we're both away from that place. So tonight we'll eat food you don't get in the army, and get drunk on good liquor you won't get there either. No pig fat, no chunks of cow, no geriatric sheep. I often think it's our diet that makes whites in this country so aggressive—meat and beer, beer and meat. You know, when a cow is hauled into the abattoir, its muscles fill with fear and an urge to fight. That's what goes into your body when you eat a steak—the chemicals of fear."

"Monkey gland fear," murmurs Deon.

"Rolled tournedos of fear," I respond.

"Golden Spur's charbroiled fearburgers," says Roelof, not to be outdone in his own house. "Filet of fear. Fear tartare."

We eat and drink well, the gins being followed by a very cold Sancerre. Roelof tells us that this is a special occasion, not only because we are all together. He gently places his hand on Riana's arm, who says shyly: "We're working on a baby."

"Ja," adds Roelof. "I have decided to be an optimist about this country. It's something we've been wanting to do for ages, but I didn't think it fair to bring a child into this mess. But things are changing fast; the talks with the U.N. and Swapo are only the first step. With the collapse of the Russians, we won't be the "bulwark against communism" anymore and all those clandestine dollars will dry up. Henry Kissinger *gaan kak*. Namibia is going to be independent before you know it, and then it's our turn. But let's forget about politics and have a proper old *jol*."

This we do, along with congratulating Roelof and his lover on their

* Lunatic asylum outside Johannesburg, not the home from *Gone With the Wind*. Rooibos used to threaten that I would wind up in Tara someday.

news. The trout is done to perfection, the skin crispy, the white flesh moist, with a subtle aroma of herbs. We get caught up in making more and more absurd toasts—to Ektachrome! to Carl Zeiss and his Jena optical company, to Sam Nujoma's kindergarten teacher, and may she see the day when she can vote for him to be Namibia's next president. Deon and I wind up playing *tching, tching, tcha*! to see who gets the couch, who the sleeping bag on the dusty carpet, and before I know it, I am being shaken awake by Riana, who has kindly woken early so that we might get to our rendezvous with the soccer brigade on time. Even so, it is close to six when we pull up at the camps, trying to think of an excuse for being late that our disheveled states and alcohol-tainted breath won't belie. The officer in command seems sufficiently distracted that he hardly pays attention to our excuses. "Ja, ja, never mind, let's just get going."

Deon and I fetch the net bag of soccer balls from the trunk of his car, and give one to each of the Casspir drivers. One of these drivers, an angular fellow as dark as an Indian, begins to pass the ball skillfully from foot to knee to head, keeping it in continual motion as he makes his way to the armored vehicle. "*Maak gou*, now. Don't mess around," the C.O. yells at him. I follow this driver to his Casspir, and he tells me not to worry, the C.O. is usually much more relaxed. "He's a pretty good *ou* mostly," he says. "Maybe he's got stage fright or something." I ride in the top section of the Casspir, the hatch open so that I can observe the world without an interfering screen of bullet-resistant clear plastic. Our convoy roars and rumbles along the road to the township, and I can feel a heady sense of power brought on by being up above the traffic in a machine that could ride right over an ordinary car. The wind rushes by my ears, and I wave foolishly at a bus filled with Africans going in the opposite direction; they look back at me with stony, indifferent faces.

We arrive a half hour later at the entrance to the township, which is already flanked by armed and nervous police. I have put on the radio headphones to communicate with the driver, and he says that something must have happened. There had been talk yesterday of a general stay-away. "I'll bet the bloody comrades are out to keep decent people from going to work. That's because they're all too lazy to hold down a fokken job."

"Do you think so?" I murmur into the microphone.

"I bloody well know so. I rescued one woman the other day from a gang of them who were going to beat her up for trying to get on a bus. Do you know what her job was? Nurse-midwife. She doesn't get to the hospital, some poor blerry woman is going to have to take care of her breech birth by herself."

I film the C.O. earnestly discussing things with the policemen, who hold their shotguns at the ready. One of them looks up at me angrily, starts to shout something, then turns back to his conversation with our commanding officer. It has been illegal under the State of Emergency Act to take pictures of the police or the army performing their duties, but I *am* the army—surely no one can object to my filming what is going on around me? The lead driver revs up his engine, and then we are all waved through and are heading into the township.

It is the first time I have been inside a township, I'm ashamed to say. I have not had any reason to go before, and now here I am riding in like the cavalry from the Wild West. There are some Spaza* shops, an open-air barber's, a lot of matchbox houses. Washing hangs from makeshift lines in the dusty yards between jumbled-together houses, and over everything hangs the smell of rotting food, burning rubbish, and coal fires. The crowdedness of the place is its other most salient feature; there are people walking in all directions, and children play in the streets and alleyways, darting between cars, trucks, bicycles, and the legs of pedestrians.

I notice some men and women in work clothes walking with downcast heads and nervous expressions toward a bus stop, where several policemen are standing with their guns held loosely at their waists. The workers do not look at us, they just head dutifully toward the waiting bus. Everywhere, though, are young men; some are of schoolboy age, a few are

* There are no supermarkets in or near the townships, so local entrepreneurs set up their own unlicensed businesses selling sundry goods.

older. They stare boldly at us, and these are not the smiling countenances of our training films. The faces are set and rigid, the eyes hard with anger. The message in those eyes is clear and unlike any I have seen, even in the towns of Namibia: *We want you dead, white boy!* Miss Tompkins had told us that African children are taught to cast their eyes down as a sign of respect for their elders, and how white missionaries had taken this shifting of the eyes to mean African children are dishonest, forever hiding guilt at some misdeed. There is no looking down, no fear, no docility in the faces of these youths. For all that I am high above them and can quickly disappear into a casing of thick, bulletproof metal, I feel more vulnerable than the young men standing unprotected on the street.

I start filming, and my camera eye focuses on a small boy about eight years old. He gives me the same just-let-me-get-you-alone-for-one-minute look, then bends down and fumbles with something—a rag doll? a homemade ball? The rag toy begins to emit a dark, oily smoke. The child pulls back his arm and throws it at me. He has a good arm, a junior cricket player in the making, and the oily burning bundle lands on top of the Casspir, a mere foot away from me. "That little bastard," the driver yells, turning the vehicle and beginning to drive after the child, who now runs in terror. I keep filming as we gain on him, though he is pelting as fast as his legs can carry him down a narrow side street. Stones begin to bounce off the metal sides of the Casspir, and I am suddenly pulled back inside by one of the other soldiers, who yells in my face: "The next Molotov cocktail's going to come right down the effing hatch, you cretin."

I scramble to look through the Plexiglas observation port but I can't see the small boy any longer. Perhaps he ducked into a doorway. There is now a small knot of teenagers standing in the middle of the street and the Casspir comes to a stop in front of them, maneuvering so that the machine gun is facing them. "You guys, you've got to clear out of here," the driver says through the loudspeaker. The youths, four boys and a tough-looking girl with cropped hair and a grim, angry face, stand obdurately, looking directly at us. Their faces are deliberately expressionless. I am impressed at their courage, confronting a multiton armored vehicle bristling with weaponry as if it were no more dangerous than a cow. They stand this way for several minutes, then, at some invisible signal, they turn and saunter off without bothering to look back at us. "What a bloody cheek," says the soldier who had yelled at me, admiration involuntarily mixed with his annoyance.

We patrol the street for another hundred meters or so, then find a place to turn around and rejoin our convoy. Near the entrance of the street there is some rubbish burning on the side of the road, emitting an oily smoke. The weapons of these kids seem to be stones and burning petrol-soaked rags. It is only when we get close to the bundle that we realize what it is, as a blackened flaming arm lifts toward us in horrible imitation of a jaunty wave. We stop near this burning human being, aghast, hardly able to admit what we are seeing. One of the soldiers opens the hatch and climbs out, shotgun first, his boot catching me a hard blow on the shoulder as he scrambles past. I'm next, ignoring someone's shouts that I am stepping on their fucking fingers, and the rest of the soldiers follow. Ignoring the horrible smell of burning petroleum and charred meat, I film the smoldering body, which still seems to writhe in agony, though I tell myself that is just involuntary movement, like the settling of logs in a fire. No one could still be alive in this state. I film the men standing around gazing at this sacrificial pyre, tears running down their faces. "Fucking kaffirs," one murmurs, and though it is meant in sympathy I hope that these are not the last words heard by whatever remnant of a human being suffers through this awful fate. There are no more stones falling among us, the street has emptied out, and that is just as well, as our men would be inclined to take their revenge on the first person to cross our path.

"We'd better get back to the rest of the unit," says the driver, and we all slowly climb back into the armored car. The driver carefully maneuvers past the oily, smoky, unrecognizable patch and we drive back at high speed. The other Casspirs have moved on and we race to catch them, causing pedestrians to jump out of our way and curse us as we pass. We find the rest of the unit about a kilometer deeper into the township, the armored vehicles set up in a half circle with a group of soldiers standing around on the dirty street. A thickset, overmuscled sergeant, his brutal face red with some inner fury, has tight hold of a small boy of about eleven, the sergeant's large hand engulfing the boy's thin upper arm. The child's face is swollen on one side, and as we walk over, the sergeant slaps him hard on his swollen cheek.

"Hey, man, don't do that," says our driver. The sergeant looks surprised, objecting that his captive was part of the gang beating up this woman. There is a woman talking to our C.O., her nylon top has been torn and there are buttons missing, her *doek* has come undone revealing curly hair with a sprinkling of gray. Surprisingly, she is asking the C.O. to let the child go.

"But lady, he was trying to beat you up!"

"No," she says, fearful but adamant. "The children are just angry. They h-h-hit me because I'm going to my work, but the madam she will fire me if I don't show up. She knows nothing what is going on here in this place."

"We saw him and his friends trying to beat you up, lady. Who knows what they would have done if we hadn't come along?"

"Nothing." Her voice grows firm. "They would have done nothing. It is because of you that they're angry. You do not belong here."

"A lot of thanks we get," the driver mutters. There is a sudden shout of pain and we turn to see the sergeant clutching his hand in surprise, the small boy sprinting away. The sergeant suddenly turns and brings up his shotgun so it points at the child and the crowd of people he is running toward. Fortunately, a soldier next to him pushes the barrel down and yells: "There's a lot of people over there, *jou doos*. You can't just go shooting in all directions."

"The bloody kaffir bit me. He fucking bit me," the sergeant says, holding up his hand, which now bears a perfect impression of a small mouth. The teeth marks are blue and red, and the skin has been broken in one or two places.

"This *is* bad," says the driver sympathetically, shaking his head. "You're going to need rabies shots."

"Rabies?" inquires the sergeant, turning pale.

"Ja, you know you gotta be careful with them. Once a week for a couple of months, a big needle right in the stomach."

"No, man!"

"'Strue's God. It happened to my cousin. But don't worry, after that you'll be fine."

The sergeant looks around in anguish as we try to hide our grins. "It's not bloody funny," he says. "I hate needles."

"I must go to work now," the woman says, collecting herself and marching toward the bus stop.

"Can you believe these people?" the driver says, motioning us back onto the Casspir. We pile in and drive for another fifteen minutes until we get to a school. It is quiet in this part of the township, and the children press against the classroom windows to look at us. One of them yells something about *amaBhunu*, Boers, but he and the other kids are soon moved away from the window by their teachers. We get out of the armored vehicles again, bringing the soccer balls with us. "We were supposed to be here half an hour ago, during their break," the C.O. says.

One of the soldiers begins to juggle a soccer ball from foot to foot, then responds to someone's request to pass it. Soon we have a game going between ourselves on the empty schoolyard. I film it at first, but join in shortly afterward, feeling the relief of tension that running after a ball provides. The ball goes back and forth as we form unspoken teams, dribble each other fiercely, try to score a goal. After a while, the C.O. starts shouting at us to stop. Next to him is a middle-aged African man in a dark jacket and a tie, sweat running down his plump face. He is a teacher, or more likely the headmaster from the school.

"I don't want to offend," he says nervously, "but you must go play your game somewhere else, please. The children are upset to see soldiers playing in their field. We don't want trouble."

Now we can hear a rhythmic chanting coming from the school building, a protest song of some sort. The C.O. looks fed up, and I wonder whether we are going to form up a laager, Casspirs standing in for ox-wagons, and have our own Battle of Blood River with these schoolkids.

There is a moment of tension, then the C.O. lets out a breath and says, "Okay. *Klaar uit.*" He hands a soccer ball to the headmaster and says he should give it to the kids when they calm down. The man holds it gingerly, as if it might explode, and watches us going back once more to our vehicles. His face looks as if he is engaged in some deep internal struggle, that there are words trying to come out but he is making great efforts to keep them inside himself.

"What *kak*!" the driver says into the microphone, revving the engine, then abruptly driving off so a cloud of dust envelops the headmaster. One of the soldiers, who was introduced to me as Rifleman Cronje, has brought a small tape player with him, which he now turns on. The sounds of Bob Marley singing about Exodus fills the inside of the armored vehicle. Several of the other soldiers sing along, happy that we are on our way out of this mad place.

We arrive back at the township entrance, where the police have been joined by one of their dog units with enormous German shepherds that growl ferociously at our ungainly vehicle. One of them breaks free of his handler's hold on the leash and launches itself straight at me. I manage to jump back in and pull the hatch down millimeters away from its snapping teeth. The police rein in the dog and wave us on with their shotguns, their fingers on the trigger guards. Soon we are in the comparative normalcy of Pretoria traffic on a Wednesday morning: gleaming Mercedes and BMWs containing lacquered ladies going shopping, clean-shaven businessmen in suits imported from Hong Kong on their way to a late breakfast meeting, complacent civil servants driving to some bureaucratic appointment.

At the Reserves Camp we are met by a major from Military Intelligence and his female assistant, a one-pip lieutenant. She has a full figure, but any womanly attractiveness is neutralized by her uniform and her tight-lipped intractable expression. The major has a bristling, well-tended blond mustache and a cheerful countenance. He joshes with us about seeing a bit of action, then lets us know that he is there to collect our cameras and give us the rest of the day off. Obviously, KomOps does not want us to see what is on our own film, as if we don't know what footage we shot.

Corporal Kleynhans is surprisingly happy with the film we took, and he tells us that we will be shown our work in a few days, after it has been "processed." When we do get to view it, it has been judiciously cropped: There are the policemen protecting the township, the innocent men and women trying to go to work. There is the boy throwing a Molotov cocktail at us, the zoom making him look older and more menacing, and no doubt there will eventually be a voice-over to say what restraint our forces show in the face of extreme provocation, for the record of us—full-grown, armed men in a combat vehicle—trying to chase down a terrified child has been erased in the editing room. Next, there is the burning body and our weeping men, a soldier handing a torn shopping bag to the woman who had been attacked, a quick view of the driver heading the ball, with the school name—"Mofolo High School"—visible behind him, the C.O. handing the ball to the headmaster. It makes a nice fairy tale, visual proof of our protecting the ordinary, law-abiding African during a violent, troubled time.

This rubbish brings me good fortune. I am promoted to second lieutenant, and Corporal Kleynhans remarks on my bravery under attack (the child with the rags). Perhaps I will even get a combat medal. Deon too is promoted . . . which he tells me is a sign that the army is softening us up in preparation for something really nasty. He had been in the townships before, gone there with friends from work, but he too was shaken up by what we'd seen. "It was different going in with guys from work, ANC guys mostly. I mean, those kids really hate us." I see the eyes again, hatred deep as a vein of ore in stone. It bothers me that, in spite of myself, I feel a touch of pride in my promotion. No matter how much I would like to deny it, I am closer to the men in the Casspir than to those people in the township. So now I know where I get my marks.

And Deon is right. A week after our promotion, we are matriculated from the video training program, given a certificate to prove our competence as cameramen. The same morning, I am handed orders giving me six hours to report in for transfer back to Namibia. Deon is given orders too, sending him to the Northern Transvaal, near the Mozambique border. "We're lucky," he says. "Anything is better than township duty."

"It is always dangerous to remark on your luck," I say, half jokingly. I am feeling more superstitious these days. It is as if my invisible chitinous protective shell has been dusted with carbamate and is breaking down. Soon my soft interior will dry up, the life-sustaining liquids evaporating into the harsh and poisonous air.

...

I HAVE JUST ENOUGH time to drive home in a borrowed army jeep and have tea, chicken mayonnaise sandwiches, and a lachrymose parting with Mother. As I am gathering a few items in my room that I want to take with me to Namibia—the bird guide, swimming goggles to protect my tender eyes from the chlorine in the officers' pool at Ondangwa—I am conscious of Mother's own tear-filled, brimming eyes watching me. I find myself thinking of *Etaion Shrdlu or "It Must Be True, It Was in the Newspapers,"* a slim book about printers' errors. One of these was a line from a serialized novel: "she raised her tea-stained face to his." I kiss mother's wet, flaccid cheek and throw my duffel into the jeep, then make the drive back to Pretoria. It is a scene out of one of the many clips we have watched: soldier-boy has a brief, tender reunion with his family before soldier-boy drives off jauntily, if a little heartsore, to do his unshirking duty. Roll the credits, Messrs. Botha and Geldenhuys.

The major who greets me and processes my moving orders at Waterkloof, the military air base outside Pretoria, is an agreeable man in his mid-forties, with smiling eyes, a bristly graying mustache, and a weak chin. His name is Ben Hirschmann, and he says I should just call him Major Ben. He emanates a genuine warmth, telling me that he is sorry I did not get more leave between my training and my return to the field . . . "although then you would just have more time to feel sad, hey?" It is all strangely normal and human. Away from Gemsbok Camp and Sergeant Fynbos, away from the basic training that is acknowledged to be brutal the world over, the South African Army gives the illusion of being a fairly ordinary way to spend one's time, no worse than many jobs.

The transport plane is late, and I spend the afternoon and early evening reading old copies of *Paratus*, the army's own news chronicle, and the Afrikaans daily, *Die Burger.* As in most army locales, the only other reading material consists of evangelical Christian tracts, which are hardly part of my normal literary diet. A private asks if I would like something to eat. I am so surprised by his salute that I almost fail to return it, and I nod dumbly at his offer. I am not yet used to my new status as an officer, however junior. He brings me a cup of tea and sandwiches for dinner—one is chicken mayonnaise, the other a pork pâté that is mostly fat. I eat them in the office, which smells faintly of the major's flatulence, and then of my own.

I'm starting to think that I will wind up spending the night, when a plane is revved up, its lights blazing, and there is the noise of considerable human activity outside. The major comes back in to tell me that the "Flossie" is ready to take off and I should go get my things. His face is grim, and I ask him if something is the matter. He at first fobs me off, then changes his mind and tells me I might as well know. He has just learned that a camera crew up in Northern Owamboland had gone behind a termite mound to get a little away from their unit, relax, and smoke a *zol.* A sniper had introduced them to Swapo's own hearts and minds campaign, shooting one of them in the chest and the other in the head. "He was a bloody good shot," the major says. "Must've been a Cuban. The bastard just melted away into the bush and even the trackers couldn't find him."

"They were just sitting there unarmed and he shot them?" I ask, feeling a chill of fear for myself. Although I knew better, I had still harbored an unspoken hope that carrying a camera would put me into a special category, *hors de combat.*

"Ag, ja. Swapo prefers it if you're unarmed," the major replies dryly. "Most of the camera guys buy a sidearm while they're stateside. I know a bunch of places in Pretoria where you could pick a revolver very reasonably. You'll still be able to buy one in the South-West, but you're going to be paying through the nose for anything decent. I've heard you can get anything on the black market there—ivory, diamonds, you name it—as long as you've got the dosh."

I had envisioned my role as a sort of bar mitzvah photographer for the SADF, taking pictures of the C.O.s and of soldiers relaxing in camp, but now I have to contemplate the fact that I'd been in far less danger as a cook in remote Gemsbok Camp. Another thought intrudes on me, one I have been trying my best to ignore, and I ask Major Ben if he knew the two guys who got shot.

"One of them I met a bunch of times, Dawie Viljoen. He's been in the field for some time. A very nice fellow, you know, always ready with a joke. You must have seen some of his footage during your training, I would think. The other guy just came through here a couple of weeks ago, as a matter of fact. A tall fellow, a little too wound up, but he seemed pretty excited about his assignment. What was his name now, damn it? I just heard it too. De Villiers. Ja, that's it, I think. De Villiers."

Not De Villiers. I think of the plans Roelof and Riana had for their future, and how Africa is soon to produce yet another fatherless child. I cannot absorb the notion that that restless life has been stilled. My friend, my Enkidu, who has now crossed the border into the land from whence no man returns. Roelof, who liked to talk about our lives being governed by what he called the "Laughing Chance," the lines of fate and misfortune having an inexorable bias toward the ridiculous.

...

Six hours later I am back in the Nam. It is dark when I disembark in Ondangwa, a desolate place with a bunch of wooden huts surrounding the landing strip. I hang around the pilots' hut for several hours waiting to catch a ride to the officers' quarters. One of the mechanics offers me a cup of coffee, which I accept gratefully, although it proves to be of the sort Brillat-Savarin described as "bursting with oils and bitterness, good at its best for scraping out the gullet of a Cossack." Finally, a lorry loaded with barrels of petroleum is ready to give me a lift, and I climb into the passenger seat of the cab. Although it's quite cool, I roll down my window, so that I can look out at the early morning dark of Namibia. The wind brings with it the fragrances of this largely uninhabited country, overladen with the tang of petrol exhaust and wood smoke from the occasional fire. This particular smell of South-West Africa, perhaps whatever it was that Mother had detected on me, is one I had missed in Pretoria, a subtle muskiness that had nevertheless permanently seared itself onto my olfactory bulbs.

I wind up spending several mostly idle weeks in Ondangwa, where I do get to swim in the pool and go out for chilled Windhoek lagers at the local *dhukas* with the other NCOs. One of them keeps trying to get me to go jogging with him, the idiot. We mostly talk about the impending peace agreement, whether UNTAG* will be able to enforce the cease-fire, and how nice it is that the camp hasn't been attacked for a couple of weeks. "We were getting revved every other night," one of the medics tells me. "We had a shuttlecock net up in that field behind the huts until a mortar round blew right through it and left a bloody great hole in the ground. For weeks, I slept with my rifle in my arms like she was my favorite mistress."

Just when I am getting used to this, thinking I will see the war out like a stay in some dull holiday camp, I'm told to muster out with a lorry that is leaving that afternoon. I'm not worried, because that same morning the radio has announced that the March 31 cease-fire is still on and all sides are expected to adhere to it. The lorry is full of food supplies and arma-

* United Nations Transition Assistance Group, the multinational military and civilian advisors, headed by the euphonious Martti Ahtisaari, sent to oversee the end of armed hostilities and ensuing elections in Namibia.

ments, and I sit up front with the driver, a taciturn *plaasjapie*, a country boy with the missing teeth of so many rural Afrikaners, whose response to my questions about our destination is that I'll find out soon enough. He is quietly and cynically amused by the attention I pay to the ball compass on the dashboard. "Ja," he chuckles. "There's nothing wrong with it. We *are* going due north."

I keep coming back to the thought that this must have been the kind of last ride that Roelof took, that he had been able to revel in the sight of the parched countryside as it swept by him, now that he was no longer an enforcer of the occupation but an objective recorder of it, a witness. He must have felt at peace with the landscape, free to enjoy the Africa he loved before the abrupt cessation of his life. In my mind I see his face with a hole in the temple, the skin peeling off the skull, the witty intelligent visage transforming into a ghoulish, laughing skull. I try to make out features of the geography slipping by us—the solitary acacia, the unidentified, isolated bush, a sentinellike termite mound—but grains of sand sting my eyes, and I lean out and look backward at the dust trailing behind our passage like the trail of a comet soon to burn out.

Several hours later, long after we leave the tarmac and have been driving for hours on a dirt track, we stop at a makeshift camp occupied by motley, tough-looking Koevoet guys, whose attention is stirred at my arrival as might a pride of lions should a wandering fawn stumble into their midst. And there, smiling in greeting, more rangy and wired up than ever, is Captain Lyddie.

BOOK THREE

Time Gone Awry

1990 – 2000

I came here because of my deep interest and affection for a land settled by the Dutch in the mid-seventeenth century, then taken over by the British, and at last independent; a land in which the native inhabitants were at first subdued, but relations with whom remain a problem to this day; a land which defined itself on a hostile frontier; a land which has tamed rich natural resources through the energetic application of modern technology; a land which once imported slaves, and now must struggle to wipe out the last traces of that former bondage. I refer, of course, to the United States of America.

Robert F. Kennedy
University of Capetown
Capetown, South Africa
June 6, 1966

"*I feel fuck-all.*"

There are a baker's dozen of us sitting in a circle in this large, white-walled room. We are sitting cross-legged, like some misbegotten Buddhist sect, and there, playing piggy-in-the-middle, is the dunderhead who has just asked me what emotions I have experienced today.

"*I feel fuck-all,*" I repeat, much to his consternation. He is a pastor and a medic, who is getting his training in clinical psychology through the army, and we are in the old hospital for soldiers at Pretoria's 1 Mil. This is our third session of "group." Dominee Jakobus Venter gives me a disappointed look; he clearly thinks I am not really trying . . . and I am certainly not helping him to get this group of blank-faced men with thousand-meter stares into any better focus. He waits patiently for another minute, perhaps thinking this will elicit some further response, but I just gaze through his wraithlike figure into the distant hills of Kaokoland.

"What about you, Conradie?" Venter asks in a gentle voice. "What did you notice today? What feelings, even ever so slight, did you register?"

"*Ek voel fokol,*" Conradie says in a Haldol monotone.

The next fellow in the circle says the same thing, and the next, but the patient after him, an immense, hulking chap who has been convulsively squeezing his fingers into fists while otherwise sitting dead still, glares at Venter balefully. "I feel like giving you a fucking good punch on the nose," he says, looking down at his enormous fists.

"Oh, ja, well, anger is an important emotion," the therapist says, turning pale. "But we must try to harness it into something useful. Okay, let's see what Williamson here has to say. Now, how do you feel today, Williamson?"

"I feel fuck-all . . . and I feel like giving you a fucking good *klap* on the nose," Williamson says, deadpan.

Dominee Venter glances around nervously, feeling the heat rising in the room. Emptiness and bottomless rage are twin emotions for we men in the circle; such is our paradoxical non-Buddhist void, it can be filled with fury and remain empty. He looks over at the two attendants leaning against the wall, but they feign interest in a smudgy pastel drawing of a flower pot, the patients' art that is the sole decoration for our meeting room. These attendants are Quakers, conscientious objectors, whom the army has allowed to serve their conscription period as workers in the psych ward, while dressing them in the same pajama-and-dressing-gown uniforms as their charges. They have even more reason to fear ex-combatants with war-blasted minds than does Venter.

"Let's call it a day, and we'll try again next week, men," Venter says bravely. And for once he has hit the right note, as one by one we rise and shuffle to the door to go back to our wards. This session has at least given me something to think about, the word *punch*. There is the physical act (Gidding hurtling backward); there is the etymology, *panch*, the Hindu word for five. The drink, punch, served in the Officers' Club in India's Hill Stations, had five ingredients in it. The fingers you fold into a clubbing instrument are five in number. There is the Arabic numeral, looking like a pregnant woman with a peaked cap, or an overweight railroad conductor. I can look at the wall now and contemplate *five*, a fixed point and not just the emptiness of a flat surface.

...

My thoughts are interrupted later that afternoon by the arrival of a new psychologist, who introduces himself as Lieutenant Peter McLaughlin. "I'm finishing up my National Service, just like you," he tells me. "I did my postgraduate work in clinical psychology at Wits, and then the Defence Force got hold of me."

He is tall and well built, with an affable, guileless face and an almost cartoonish widow's peak. His dark eyes are kindly and perceptive, and he is astonishingly open about himself, blurting out his personal history while other interns and doctors here have perfected a clinical detachment. "I looked up your medical history," he says casually, "and I see that you were in the care of Dr. Vishinski for a while when you were younger. I attended some lectures of his at the university, and thought he was rather good. Did you find him helpful?"

Steepled hands, pointy beard, red armchair. "I suppose so."

"Now, there's a ringing endorsement!" McLaughlin chortles, settling himself onto my bunk bed. Can you recall one of his sessions for me?"

Recalling is no problem for me, no matter what state I am in. I settle back and look at the whitewashed wall and begin talking.

"Your thoughts are too scattered," Dr. Vish tells me. "Every time you think of your childhood, a score of images rushes to your mind. No wonder you have trouble getting a handle on it." He recommends to me that I try to keep my memories of Father restricted to a handful of iconic images, that I should go through my memory as if sorting through a shoe box of photographs and throw out those whose associations might be too painful or that are too obsessive in their detailed minutiae. Fine to think of his flannel pajamas, not fine to picture the threading on each of its six shirt buttons and the way the zigzag pattern was different on the sleeves than on the breast front, how it all made him look like an elongated, taffy-pulled zebra, a white-African Buster Keaton with an imaginary yarmulke topping.

To myself I call these canned recollections "Pieces of Papa," a label I did not share back then with my good doctor—yes, I was sometimes resistant, withholding—since he seemed always to read so much into jokes, a habit that destroys the pleasure of them. That the unexamined life isn't worth living doesn't mean the examined life is worth living either.

Dad, being pre-post-Freudian, was not aware that jokes were a symptom of *Minderwertigkeitsgefühl*—trust the Germans to make "feelings of inadequacy" into a single word, bulky and ponderous as a tank, intimidating enough to inspire the very condition it describes. He had not come across the notion that all humor was about disparagement and therefore a form of bigotry; self-directed humor, in this light, is projected disparagement. And so he was free of distrust for wit and its by-products, and was unwilling to leave any bon mot unpunned or joke unsaid. He was an equal opportunity humorist—Van der Merwe was as likely to be mocked for his Low Country dim-wittedness as Sixpence or other domestics were for theirs—but most of his jokes would have fit into a compendium of self-mocking Jewish humor.

"I do like jokes," Dr. Vish once assured me, when I accused him, not for the first time, of being humorless. "I even tell them at the dinner table sometimes." Of course, I could not resist parading my collection of funny phrases and lengthily set-up punch lines like the (good) bad boy in class who *has to* let the teacher see the frog in his jacket pocket, the poopoo cushion in his school satchel. "What worries me are the excesses," the good doctor continues. "The humor that acts to block out the world like another brick in a wall."

Hey! Teacher! Leave us kids alone.

Vish helps me cull the memories in my "father file" by suggesting that I close my eyes, then walk through my parents' bedroom in my mind, open the closet, and select a single item. I do this, and see in the far right corner, leaning against the wall, Father's set of golf clubs. Since this was one of the few items I had managed as a child to rescue from Mother's urge to divest us of any object that loudly proclaimed the existence of a former husband, and it was resting in my own cupboard at the time of our session, I knew that I was entering into my parents' bedroom at an earlier time, when he was still alive. The clubs are contained in a marvelously well stitched blue leather bag as tall as I am; they have been used exactly once.

The day that Dad goes out to play on the golf course in Melrose, he takes me with him, telling me that we might run into Gary Player on the first tee. I have no experience of golf, yet even I can see that Dad's stance is not what it should be. We are followed around by several African caddies my own age, although Dad insists on carrying the clubs himself. They giggle behind the palms of their hands at the way he crunches and misaligns his body, his head bobbing up and down as he looks at the white ball sitting like a mushroom cap on its white tee in the brown earth, then over at the distant flag in its green toupee, then down at the tee again. Strangely, his spidery, bandy-legged stance and thin shoulders produce a surprisingly powerful drive and the ball sails all the way to the green, resting on its outer lip. Father is a poor putter, though, unable to capitalize on his early success. I try a shot or two, but the clubs are too long and too heavy for me, twisting in my hands as I strike at the ball, which shoots sideways, practically hitting the annoyed businessman on the next green.

We stay on the golf course for a long time, almost until the sun is going down. I amuse myself by drawing an invisible line through one of many teeming ant routes and watching them scurry around in confusion before they form a seamless stream again. When we return to our car, first turning in the scorecard and extra balls, the place is closing up and we see half a dozen ragged and dusty children walking toward the road. Uncharacteristically, Dad asks if they would like a lift. The children look astonished, hardly believing their luck, and they pile into our car before we can change our minds. One gives a shrill whistle with his lower lip curled beneath his front teeth, and several more of the caddies come pelting out of a shed and get into the car with us. I have somehow wound up in the back, pressed between a six-year-old with a green plug of mucus in either nostril and his older brother, who smiles encouragingly at me. There are three others in the back and three more in the front, all of us squeezed into the Chevy like Smarties in a tin. I am wearing shorts and try not to let my bare legs touch the dusty, streaked black legs of the boys next to me . . . then I grow self-conscious and ashamed of what I am doing and let my legs relax against the warm and companionable familiarity of my fellow children. The oldest and boldest of them gives directions. He is a very dark ten-year-old in a hole-filled green pullover, his thoughtful expression rendered ferocious by a crooked left canine jutting sideways into the space where a missing bicuspid should be. He gives directions with the precision and assurance of a master surgeon, solemn, aware that lives depend on him. The other children gasp and giggle at every bump, lurch, or turn and it gradually dawns on me that this may be the first time any of them has been in a passenger car. This ride is a rare luxury for them; though I can't wait until they are all out again and I can stretch and breathe freely once more. After about five miles, the child leader indicates a corner where there is a bus stop surrounded by adult Africans waiting to go back to the township. The children tumble out of three open doors, shouting "Goodbye, baas. Thank you, baas." The leader is the last to go, nodding briefly at first Dad, then me, before disappearing into the crowd to find his charges. He is the only one not to use that word. It is clear that he is pleased at what we have done—it has saved them a long and wearying walk—but he is not grateful, nor need he be.

I think it is this ride, so generously and unthinkingly given, that keeps Dad from returning to play golf again. The set of clubs stays in the back of the spare cupboard, behind an old coat and a rattan carpet beater.

I lie back on my obstinate bed in Ward 24 at the end of this narration, utterly exhausted by the outpouring of my own words, affectless though the tone might have been. McLaughlin tells me he's very pleased with my progress.

"I want you to hold on to that idea of the shoe box with a finite set of memories in it. Dr. Vishinski suggested a handful, so let's make it five," he tells me, smiling benevolently. "Most people with PTSD . . . Oh, shoot. I know I'm not supposed to tell the patients my diagnosis, but what the hell!" he laughs before continuing, and I realize I am paying enough attention to find his digressiveness endearing. "Well, they have trouble remembering *anything*, except for flashbacks and so on. You dissociate by remembering everything, but it's much easier to pare down than to gain access to stuff you are blocking. So, remember, five objects in the box. You've given me the first, and I look forward to hearing more tomorrow."

In the state of *voel fokal*, you do not so much sleep as lie with a constant hum in your mind, as if you are listening to heavy machinery on a nearby motorway amplified to the exclusion of all else. This night, I do sleep somewhat, passing in and out of that semi-waking state when light seems to press on my eyelids and formless chatter drowns my inner thoughts. I rise at 7 A.M.—the crazies get to sleep late by army standards—make my bed, eat my sodden cornflakes, and watch the wall until McLaughlin comes by again.

"Okay, since I've already made the gross error of diagnosing you to your face, I'm going to try to explain post-traumatic stress disorder to you, which is funny because you're the one living it. What's happened is, you have undergone events in an environment utterly unlike the normal experience of reality, and these have produced emotions of such intensity and force that they appear impossible to assimilate into the daily experience of living. The result is you feel literally blasted out of time, dislocated from life. Is that about right? No, don't answer. We're not going to dwell on it, we're going to put time back together."

He pauses, takes a breath, cracks his knuckles, and then focuses on me again. "Close your eyes," he says firmly. "I'm handing you your mental shoe box. Got it?"

I can feel its sharp edges of frayed cardboard, smell the trace of rubber and canvas whitener from the Bata *tackies* it once contained. I reach inside and grope around, although I know already what I am going to find: Father's blue wool dressing gown with its red brocaded sleeves. This garment would have been considered a treasure by the university's theater, so suited is it for an Edwardian drama. Did Father really wear it when he toddled to the bathroom for a matutinal pee or foamed his mouth with toothpaste before and after a night's sleep? I see him marching to my room in the middle of a night when I have been awakened by bad dreams, draped in his gown with a torch in his hand, Wee Willie Winkie in drag. The robe now hangs in my cupboard, but it is there more for admiration than use. I was swamped by it when I first tried it on, a year and a week after Father's death . . . which was one day before Mother had arranged to give his clothes to an African charity. Jewish tradition holds that the departed's spirit lingers on earth for one year after death before vanishing forever, or at least until the Messiah shows up. Mother has never been formally religious, but some atavistic side of her remained in shock until the passing of a full year, at which point she began furiously to dispose of anything that bore a trace of Father. So intent was she on expunging his memory that she sold the extermination business to Piet Erasmus for far less than its worth. He revamped it along military lines, and became wealthy as his legion of insect-slayers branched out into the whole Vaal triangle.

A month before I went into the army, I had again attempted to wear the dressing gown, but my arm fit in its sleeve like a stuffed sausage and I would have burst the seams if I'd attempted to put the whole garment around my shoulders. Today, with some adjustment it might fit me, but I haven't made an attempt again and it stays in the back of my cupboard along with other clothes I don't wear—Mother's forlorn attempt to pretend I will one day come home again. It hangs there, empty, Father himself all but for his corporeal body. Unfortunately, it does not even smell of him anymore, for while I was away on my little holiday in the SADF training camp, Mother sent it home with the washerwoman, who used too much blue soap and dried it on a clothesline exposed to the wind and sun and the occasional drifting coal smoke of her township until it was stiff as a board.

Time drags along as usual the next day, but I can feel somewhere in me a sense of anticipation as if I am looking forward to McLaughlin's questions. However, a different doctor arrives at my bedside, McLaughlin's senior, judging by his insignia of rank. The name on the breast tag reads "Major Koekemoer."

"You're making good progress, I'm glad to see. So I'm discharging you. Get something to eat, pack up your things, and report to me in one hour," he says brusquely.

"Discharging me?" *Canst thou not minister to a mind diseased, Pluck from the memory a rooted sorrow?*

"Ja. You can thank Lieutenant McLaughlin that you'll be G.T., and not a medical discharge on psychiatric grounds. He said that would be a nasty thing to do when you're so close to *klaaring* out."

G.T. is the term for a temporary discharge, and I find myself asking: "Does this mean the army can call me back anytime it wants?"

"Theoretically, that's true." The doctor gives a dry laugh, and adds, "But it's so improbable that I'd wager my favorite dog against it happening . . . and I'm not about to give up Fang."

I spent my first three months home from my National Service just sitting on the bed in my room, sleeping late, eating only those meals most easily prepared, and bathing when my own smell became annoying even to my muted senses. Mother was patient much of this time—after all, Mrs. Tremper's son, he of the sojourn in Okavango, had returned from the Nam seemingly normal, then one sunny afternoon he discharged his 9mm Parabellum directly under his chin . . . a "cleaning accident." But one morning, instead of going to work, she marched into my room, whipped the covers off me as if I were a child late for school, and said: "Come on, go and shower and get dressed."

"What?"

"I'm tired of seeing you sit like a lump of fat congealing on a plate. You're coming with me to the university, and I'm going to see to it that you register for classes you *want* to take."

There was no arguing with Mother when she was in this kind of mood. Resistance requiring more effort than acquiescence, I dutifully, if dully, went along with her. She had somehow contrived a special arrangement with the registrar, and I was soon enrolled in an English literature course, two anthropology classes (one in methodology, the other in general background), and introduction to psychology. When we returned home that afternoon, there was a strange car in our driveway: an old but lovingly kept Volkswagen Beetle.

"Someone's here, Ma." I was a little concerned that I could see no one around; although old Volksies were hardly the getaway car of choice for Johannesburg's ever-growing population of housebreakers.

"I know, dear," she replied, just the hint of irritation in her voice. "That's Claude's car . . . or rather, it used to be his late wife's. He's inside."

Why didn't I know he had a key to our house and the security code? Had I been that oblivious to the goings-on around me?

Inside our kitchen, Claude was sitting at the table with a cup of coffee, his jacket on the chair behind him. I wondered how Mother could bear the round alopecic monk's tonsure on the top of his head. There was a small scab there where he'd scratched at sunburn or an insect bite. He was very relaxed and at home, but he quickly jumped up, being ever gallant toward my mother, rethreaded the belt he had loosened for the comfort of his bulging stomach, and came over to hug her and say hello to me.

"How does he like our little surprise?" he asked Mother, with a heavy wink in my direction.

"I'm not sure I get it," I started to say, and then I put two and two together and looked at him in astonishment.

"It was just sitting around, taking up space and pushing memories onto me. Good ones, but I don't want to be reminded all the time. You see, it was Beryl's car, and she treated it like a pampered child. It's yours now. I got it all fixed up and running at my garage—not much to it, the mechanic said, just a matter of shaking out the cobwebs."

"Claude cooked up the idea himself," Mother said.

"Thank you." I was genuinely touched by this gesture.

"That's alright, my boy." He clapped me heavily on the shoulder. "A young man needs his independence. I'm just sorry it's not a sports car, Paul, so you can make a splash with the girls."

"Now you won't have any excuse to miss your classes," Mother added, obviously relieved that I had accepted the gift.

In the months that followed, I did indeed start to come back to myself . . . albeit with the occasional day of being moored in the doldrums, my own personally created intertropic convergence zone. I weathered these days by giving in utterly to them, and Mother learned to let me alone when my door stayed shut and there was no answering greeting to her greeting, no goodbye to her cheery goodbye. It was as if I had been one of those flies on a winter windowsill, the desiccated hulk seeming dead to all outward appearances but the cold-blooded creature slowly stirring to life and its gross appetites as the sun warms it up again. And so the gaps between my dull days grew longer every time.

Claude was an increasingly tangible presence in our lives, taking Mother out on weekend nights, telephoning in worried whether she had made it home when she'd had to stay late for a faculty event. Mother took to accompanying him to synagogue on Friday nights—*shabbos,* she now called it—a major change for her, as religion had scarcely been part of our lives after Father died. I did not even have a bar mitzvah . . . not that Mother discouraged me from doing so. I did take Hebrew lessons; two, to be exact. These were taught by a thin, balding man with an unusually long neck and prominent Adam's apple, Dr. Simchah. He came to our house, and when he drank tea, his Adam's apple would journey up and down like one of those external elevators in an ultramodern hotel. He showed me the Hebrew alphabet at our first lesson, giving me a tape of my *Haftorah* portion to familiarize myself with it. At the next lesson, I sang my Haftorah to him without mistake (not that I have much of a voice, mind you). "Very impressive," said Dr. Simchah, unimpressed. "You have your portion memorized. But what does it mean to you?"

This was not a question I could answer then, or even now, so I told Mother it would be hypocritical of me to have a bar mitzvah I didn't believe in. She did not press me on the point . . . although Nigel Capeland expressed shock when I informed a group of my school friends about my decision. "But then you'll never be a man!" he said. "Not in the Jewish sense." After his own bar mitzvah—a lavish affair just short of apotheosis—he informed me in great detail as to the presents he'd gotten: the fat cheques from his uncles, the stocks in mining companies, the fancy pens, books, and gift certificates. I felt a moment of passing regret, although I knew *I* would not have earned such bounty.

Although Claude spent long evenings with Mother, he was too old-fashioned to stay the night . . . especially with me still in the house. One of the other anthropology students, Jack Cronje, was leaving the country to continue his studies in Texas, and he asked if I'd like to take over the cheap lease on his Hillbrow flat. I had some money from my army pay and I was fairly sure I could get a research-assistant job, so I said yes. The neighborhood still bore signs of its early glamour, with ornately carved leaves of stone decorating the mock Corinthian columns at the entranceways of now-dilapidated blocks of flats, the floors lined with grimy tiles suitable for a Roman bath. Elysium Court, my new home, included a row of balconies on each story that were attractive to the eye but likely to crumble if stood upon, but the building had the advantage of being close to the university. Although the area was becoming increasingly crime-ridden, Jack said he had never had any trouble and I should just be on the alert if I came home at night. When I told Mother I was moving out, she said that was not such a bad idea. She and Claude had talked about getting married and selling the house, but she did not want to leave me in the lurch. This way, I could use some of the money she would get for the house to help me get established.

...

Mother became the second Mrs. Moskowitz in a well-attended ceremony at the Oxford Street Shul two months later. Claude smashed the marriage glass with unseemly vigor, raising a foot shod in expensive and neatly stitched Italian leather, and bringing it down hard on the velvet pillow placed in front of him and Mother. His rubicund face beamed like a blood moon over his midnight-black dinner suit, while he shook every hand in the house and clapped every shoulder in a fit of crimson joy. Mother, I have to admit, looked younger and happier than I had seen her in years. Although I was in a tenebrous mood that I could not shake off, I finally let Claude cajole me into dancing with a young niece of his, an apple-cheeked, dark-haired young woman with a shy and fleeting smile.

"Come on, Paul. You don't have to marry her, just ask her to dance."

The poor girl spent the rest of the evening in physical pain after I accidentally trod on her instep.

...

My flat in Hillbrow is the kind known as a "batch," a small abode with limited space for furnishings, suitable for a modest bachelor, some spinsterish old chap with his hair parted behind. The living area consists of a recessed kitchen, a living room slightly larger than my bedroom at home, and a bedroom not much bigger than a walk-in cupboard, with a small w.c. and shower leading off from it. There is a sizable clawfoot bathtub next to the kitchen, which is covered with a large, square board so it serves primarily as a dining table. There had once been an ornate fireplace at the far end of the living room, but this had been boarded up, the wood covering it painted a shade of white slightly paler than the color of the walls, or perhaps only of newer vintage. The mantel around the fireplace still shows signs of its original scrollwork—an attempt at elegance from a previous era—skulking beneath generations of clumsily added paint, and I spend hours just tracing the scroll lines with my eyes. It may not be an atelier in Paris, but this is the first time in my life that I've had a place of my own, my own Independent Republic of Sweetbread, and though I am still going through my days by rote, I can feel things quietly knitting together in my interior.

I brought little enough here from my childhood home—there is, after all, not much room, and Claude kindly offered some storage space for Father's books until I can house them myself—and for months, the items that are not furniture sit in cardboard boxes in the corner of my living room. I have no desire to handle them, and do not unpack them, as I know what each box contains; the recording device has not switched off, no matter how glazed my eyes. I am sitting deep in my armchair, gazing morosely at the ziggurat of homely brown boxes, when I become aware of myself reviewing each item in the box that is second from the top. There is a cigar box just below a rolled-up map and a painting of the old Polana Hotel in Lourenço Marques; in this box, with its Dominican stamps, are the three remaining objects that are my *pieces of Papa*, my fetishes of memory, that I was going to disinter for Lieutenant McLaughlin.

I choose to rise and fetch a paring knife from the kitchen drawer, move the top box to the floor, then remove the one with the cigar case and slice open the packing tape that seals it. The map, which shows the Cape in the seventeenth century, concentrates on the achievements of Simon van der Stel, the first governor of the Cape—the founding of the town of Stellenbosch, the search for copper in Namaqualand, his estate at Constantia—but does not mention that given the origins of his mother, Maria Lievens, he would have been classified as "coloured" during the height of Afrikaner nationalism. This document goes on the floor; the Polana Hotel goes on the wall opposite, where there is already a slightly bent but serviceable picture hook; and then I carry the cigar case lovingly over to my writing desk to review its contents. Although I know what it contains, there is something about the physical feel of objects held in one's hands, as if touch itself has its own memory that can only be awakened by handling that which you want to review. I move aside the slim Parker pen, which was a thirteenth-birthday in-lieu-of-bar-mitvah present—it's the old-fashioned kind, with a ribbed bladder that you squeeze three times to draw up the ink—and pick up Father's antique magnifying glass, which had been given to him as a boy by his own father. It has a beautifully made German lens that is still sharp and clear despite scratches on its surface, and is lined with a fine filigree of silver as well as a silver swivel that allows it to be concealed in a folding case of black leather. Father confessed to using it to fry ants when he was a small boy. He would begin at some distance, then narrow the glowing white orb until the luckless myrmid began to flee, after which he would bring the sun closer and closer until a puff of foul-smelling smoke spiraled up from a body in the process of metamorphosing. His father lent him this precious object to keep him entertained while he negotiated with African headmen or straightened forks for the *boerevroue*.

"He probably didn't know—or care—that I used it to play God with the *goggas*, like Aristophanes' boys did with the frogs," Dad said. "Of course, I also used it to observe the beauty of small things." He liked to go on to tell me the story of Van Leeuwenhoek, the Dutch lens-grinder who invented the microscope, another brilliant amateur who changed the way we regard the world. This was a message I heard from him often—like the time he gave me a chemistry set for my birthday, a gift I am ashamed to say still sits unopened. He would reiterate in tautological phrases how the greatest scientific discoveries were the provenance of gifted amateurs. "It's important to learn stuff at school," he said, "but don't forget how much knowledge you can pick up just by paying attention to what's around you."

Funny, the one adjective I've heard most often applied to him by those who knew him is "distracted."

...

In my distractable school days I did not get past the three aforementioned objects with Dr. Vish before moving on to other issues—Sanders' persecutory jokes at my expense, my mother's melancholic presence at home. Now, there is something meditative in the discipline of holding to a handy set of memories, keeping the magic number *five*—McLaughlin's knockout *panch* for my nightmares—at the fore of my consciousness. The two objects that had sat just below the cigar box provide the perfect foci for my meditation.

The first sits in its own casket, a white cardboard box marked "Paul Reads Poetry" in my father's spindly handwriting (like bugs on a white page). It is a spool of magnetic tape, looking more like an anachronistic cine-reel than like its closer relatives, the cassettes we so cheerily pop into the car tape player so we can shut out the clamor of Africa while listening to Johnny and Sipho croon about these selfsame sounds. The blue, amazingly heavy National Panasonic tape recorder has long since been given away with the rest of Dad's things, but this tape remains. Mother must have kept it only because *my* name is on the outside of the box, not his.

I remember, of course, the day I read to the machine. I was nine years old, one of the finalists trying out to represent our school at a national poetry reciting competition. The previous winners had always been from one of the Afrikaans schools, but our headmaster hoped to change that. None of us were allowed to recite in English—there would be no inferior Wordsworth, Blake, or Shakespeare. We would compete on their terms, reciting a sophisticated poem in Afrikaans. ("My dad says there's no such thing," Danny Mainzer had whispered into my ear.) Miss Tompkins, who was usually at odds with Mr. Burnside, took on this task wholeheartedly. She told us how pleased she was that we would have this opportunity.

"I would have liked to introduce you to the works of Ingrid Jonker or Antjie Krog, such marvelous young Afrikaans women writers. They started when they were not much older than you. But there are some people—ignorant, loutish souls—who complain their work is too critical, unpatriotic. So you won't be reading 'Of a Child Dead at Sharpeville,' or *My Mooi Land*, beautiful and evocative though those works might be." She had no problem speaking of things she knew would never be part of our curriculum, going on the assumption that some good would come of our being aware of the existence of works and ideas outside the confines of Christian National Education. I found out much later that the works of both these poets were taught at the Afrikaans schools . . . minus the offending texts, of course. Still, she was probably right: if children from the Barney Barnato Primary School* read even the most innocuous works by these authors, the panel of somber Afrikaans judges would surely consider this an act of sedition.

In the event, I was given a long section of "Oom Gert Vertel," Miss Tompkins' serendipity showing up in her selection long before the poet became my favorite food writer as well. Memorizing my selected reading for oral recitation was no problem; however, Miss Tompkins felt there was room for much improvement in how I projected my voice or conveyed the feelings beneath Leipoldt's words. "This is *poetry*, Paul," she said to me with unusual severity. "Not the *Rand Daily Mail.*" She advised me to find some way to record my words, so I might hear where I went wrong and listen to myself improve. I knew Dad owned a tape recorder, an expensive toy that he rarely used as he had a general dislike of mechanical things, resenting their mulish recalcitrance at his hands, no doubt a source of conflict with his own father, who could take the most mangled machine and get it whirring and humming seemingly just by looking at it. I asked him to tape me as I practiced, and, after much fiddling with the plug and controls, and twice threading the tape backward, he did so.

One of the horrors of death, its very permanence, is that you will never again hear the beloved parent, friend, or lover's voice again. My recall may be perfect, but I am non-musical and my memory translates heard speech into words on the page. I can remember exactly which words Dad spoke, but the aural feel of it, that immediacy of sonic vibration, is lost to me. I know that he said almost nothing during and after my recitation, just, "Yes, okay," when I asked him if I could listen to what I had just recited. But I feel an intense longing to hear the sound of those few words in his own voice.

* Barney Barnato was a Jew from London's East End, a boxer and vaudeville entertainer. He cofounded DeBeers Consolidated Mines, was an M.P. for the Cape, and, at the height of his considerable wealth in 1897, committed suicide by jumping off a ship in the mid-Atlantic.

The problem is that the tape-recording machine has long ago gone the way of all Dad's things. I could scour the pawnshops, I suppose, but the thought of the effort involved exhausts me. One afternoon, as I am leaving my Methods in Anthropology class at the university, I realize that there must be trained people in the audiovisual laboratory who could easily enough transfer the reel to a cassette that I could listen to whenever I choose. And that is what I do.

"I need this urgently for my research," I nervously tell the assistant in the media lab, a lackluster young man with a bent pixieish nose and acne-scarred skin, who nods casually.

A few days later, when I pick up the cassette and the old reel, profuse thanks about to spill forth, he grins conspiratorially at me and says: "If you'd like to research children reading poems, I can find you plenty more where that came from."

"No, it's all right," I begin, before realizing he is making fun of me. I blush and stammer out my thanks before rushing out of there, almost knocking over the diminutive and pretty teaching assistant from my other anthro class as she is coming in, earning me a ferocious scowl.

I am sitting in the comfy armchair in my living room, a glass of Johnny Walker Black (Dad's favorite brand) on the coffee table in front of me. Next to my drink is the tape player that I have not yet dared to turn on. Finally, I do so. I take a sip of my scotch, wondering for a moment whether I should have chosen a distillation with a more assertive character . . . or to have been born with a more assertive character. Then I close my eyes and listen.

God, what a high-pitched voice I had! To my own ears, filtered through the bones of my skull, that voice had been agreeable and mellifluous. I listen all the way through, and throughout it is only me but for that final, "Yes, okay." Yet I am transported, and I immediately rewind the tape and play it again. Dad was sitting on the rocking chair slightly to the right and behind me where I was standing to recite my verses. That chair too has been sold, although Mother kept far less interesting or well-made furniture. The chair was put together by my grandfather, his hands rubbing it smooth, his sweat absorbed by its dark wood, the *riempies** of leather that formed its seat lovingly stretched by his strong arms, dexterously tied by his powerful but arthritic fingers. Mother appreciates the magic life of objects, their latent energy, so she gets rid of those that seem to her to preserve the wrong spirits.

Now and then, Father pushes back with his feet and the chair creaks back and forth for a few seconds, clearly audible at first, then slowing to diminuendo. *Tick! Tock!* A rhythm like a heart starting and stopping. I close my eyes and listen intently to that gentle creaking of floorboards, the audible silence of Dad's listening, and here he is, though dead these past eleven years seven months and fourteen days, as vivid a presence as ever he was in life. My reasoning mind tediously notes that these are sounds made by a pattern of negatively and positively charged ions on a metal-impregnated celluloid tape, but my own heart tells me that he is here with me in my Hillbrow flat . . . a visitation helped along by technology. I am physically stunned by how palpable he is, though so quiet. If I had instruments sensitive enough, no doubt I could hear his breathing, the pulse of blood in his veins. There is a space the size of his body in the room with me, a space created by the slightest of sounds and the absence of sound, the silent presence that absorbs my words. The chair, his own father's spirit trapped in the lovingly worked wood, holds his body in time and rocks back and forth with his living weight: *tramp*, *tramp*, *tramp*.

What was the result of the poetry competition? Karen Stegman, Lynnie Davis, and Lyndall George—three Standard IV girls—beat me out with a group recitation of N. P. Van Wyk Louw's famous poem about our wide and woeful land alone under the great southern stars—*O wye en*

* I wonder now where Grandfather learned his art. You'll find a footstool or rocking chair made with strips of cured leather in many Afrikaner households, but not in Jewish ones. It is possible, then, that Grandfather was on better terms with the Boerevolk than he let on . . . or did he learn to make these chairs by eye alone?

droewe land, alleen/onder die groot suidersterre—which they mournfully iterated in unison like some witches' threnody. This most beloved of Afrikaner poets should have been a safe choice—after all, he was one of the inspirations for the language monument at Paarl, where Europe and Africa bow at the feet of *die Taal,** and years later F. W. de Klerk accepted his shared Nobel Prize quoting from this very poem . . . although he did leave out its final stanza with the ambiguous reference to *wit gevaar*, the poet's canny reversal of the "black peril" fears that were the justification behind so much of Afrikanerdom's actions. The three Jewish girls did not even get past the first round of the national semifinals.

The final image-object—on my hand it would be the "pinkie," or what the French call "*l'auriculaire*," the ear-cleaner—is of recent derivation while having been with me all my life. I'm referring to the square of white cardboard with my name written across it in block capitals, a memento from my days in Ward 24. "PAUL N.M.I. SWEETBREAD." The army does not allow any deviation from the norm, so the middle three letters of this name tag are not really mine but a monogram for the condition of having no middle initial.

Father wanted me to be like Jean-Henri Fabre's son Paul, who helped him in his insect studies "with his good sight and his undivided attention." He tells me about how Fabre's little child would accompany the great entomologist on delightful nights hunting wasps' nests, full of questions, eager to learn. I, on the other hand, am obtuse, more like the yellow-jacketed wasps who, after Fabre had blocked off their exit tunnel with a bell jar, lost sight of the fact that they were expert diggers. These creatures are in

* Afrikaners long recognized only two languages: theirs and (out of necessity) English—as opposed to the eleven official languages in S.A. today. The story goes that a hotel manager asked a visiting German businessman whether he spoke any other languages. "Well, altogether I speak German, English, French, Spanish, and Russian."

"Oh, so you're not bilingual," said the hotelier.

love with light, and so they would beat themselves to death against the bell glass while trying to follow the luminous pathway that flowed through its transparency. A mere minute or so of digging beneath its rim would have provided an escape, but over and over they flew upward until they hit their invisible obstruction with stunning force. I can parrot back everything that Father tells me about insects, but when we go into the garden it is *his* quick eyes that spot the lurking stick insect on the peach tree, the drone flies protected from predators by their resemblance to bees.

"Those were drone flies that Sampson found in the lion's carcass, not bees, so there's no surprise he did not get stung. The honey he's supposed to have found there must have all been in his imagination. The Bible gets a lot of entomological details wrong, you know."

I am sure that Father named me after the great insect expert's son, and Mother confirms that there was an argument over my name. She wanted me to be *Saul*, and for a change she and my old grandfather were in agreement, although for different reasons. My mother's best friend as a child had kept two budgerigars, one blue and yellow, one yellow and green. These little parakeets were so tame they would fly to her friend's finger when she whistled. As in the children's song about the two little dickeybirds, one was named Peter, one was named Paul. Mother did not want me to have a budgie's name. Grandfather, on the other hand, wanted me to be called after the first Jewish king, a monarch who successfully defeated the desert people, the Amalekites, and fought against the Philistines, not after the Christian convert. In the end, Father won out and my road to Damascus occurred without any input from me as I bobbed cheerfully around inside my amniotic sac.

I've thought of changing my name, returning to my roots—it's all the rage among my coevals to Hebraicize—and Saul Schwartzbart has a nice dignified sound to it. I could be my own great-grandfather, without having to prove it by mathematics, whose name this was. Grandfather was Isidore, reminding me of the conundrums Dad liked to tease me with: when Isidore not a door? When it is *ajar*. Now, when I eat the Malaysian-style preserved mango or lemon pickle known as *atjar*, I invariably find myself thinking of my late forebear Isidore. And yes, all this stress is making me bad again.

This being the new New South Africa, perhaps I would be best off with a real African name: Jabulani, to celebrate the joy of our pristine freedoms. Or I could choose one of the great chiefs—but one has to be careful here, Dingaan has the wrong associations (the Battle of Blood River, his assassination of his own brother, Chaka), mPande was a sell-out, one of the first of the *impimpi** (on our school tour of the Voortrekker Monument, the guide told us: "Panda was a good sort of Native. He wanted to be the white man's friend.") Perhaps Makhana . . . or would it be seen as arrogance to claim resemblance to a hero of the Xhosa wars of liberation, a man betrayed by enemies who promised to treat him honorably, an undefeatable fighter who drowned trying to escape from captivity on Robben Island? I like him the most as a source for a new self, for he went through several instars in his own life: from Christian convert to liberation prophet. Makhana wasn't his real name, though,† but a description of his left-handedness (another strike against me).

Some of my buddies at the university have "gone Af," taken to speaking their own versions of *tsotsitaal* and to wearing Madiba shirts,** even changing their names to the nearest Nguni or Sotho equivalent, from John to Jabu, Benjamin to Bongani. *(No, reeeaally, my bra. Ken jy nie Bongani Goldstein nie, mfo? Hy's 'n !twa outjie, unnerstan'?)* I could come full circle and call myself Sipho, the Zulu for "gift," but I already know a Stephen who has laid claim to that name. I might just ask Professor Koopman, the great expert on Zulu names, what the correct term would be for one who remembers. Anything but Elephant, although

* During the Apartheid years, any township dweller who worked for the government ran the risk of being called a pimp or informer and risked being murdered or burned out of his or her house.

† It was Nxele.

** After Mandela's clan name. Our beloved Living Legend likes to wear these shirts to denote his continued roots in Africa: ironically, they are based on an Indonesian design.

Ndlovu is a popular surname; I was tormented enough with that association as a teenager. I know, I know, I am babbling on, a most annoying habit. But who is Paul Sweetbread? A nice Jewish Christian boy, a liberal soldier in the army, a lousy good South African, a *ware Zuid–Afrikaner* Englishman? Can such a person even exist?

I have drifted quite far from what I started to say about my own naming after the forgotten son of that early fond observer of wasps. So. Fabre. Thinking about it now, I have to wonder if Father did not fancy himself less a scourge of insect life than a naturalist like the nineteenth-century Frenchman, his beloved author whose *Souvenirs Entomologiques* Dad owned copies of in several languages, including the original. He especially liked the Stawell retellings of the Alexander Teixeira de Matto translation, a translation of a translation like some etiolated play inside a play inside a Russian doll. Dad did complain that Fabre anthropomorphized his insects, that given half the chance he would have tricked them out in pretty costumes from the reign of the Sun King. But that did not stop my father from quoting Fabre's more felicitous phrases: "The Mantis, I fear, has no heart. She eats her husband, and deserts her children."

...

LET'S GO BACK TO the question of what makes a man a man, what specific attribute or skill distinguishes him from the rest of the animal kingdom. Language has the strongest case, chimpanzees' ability to learn a vocabulary of signing notwithstanding. Our use of metaphors, including the monarchic one I just used for the animals, is, I think, what makes us most human. No other organism seeks to define its world through the use of analogy. While metaphor is a remarkable tool (*metaphor! metaphor!* blinks the meter), it reflects both the current state of technology and our hidden assumptions. When we lived closer to nature, we compared ourselves—favorably, of course—with animals: strong as a bull, brave as a lion (a notable coward in the animal world), fierce as an eagle. Later the metaphor became the machine; and now we understand our brains in terms of computers—this is "hard-wired" into our brains, we don't have the "software" to understand man's relationship with God (the *Meister-programmer*, no longer an old man with a long white beard but Bill Gates with his smeared glasses).

What I'm getting around to here, taking my usual meandering pathways of thought, is that we still haven't found the right metaphor for how memory works. We're not like cameras, creating a giant carton of images that we can shuffle through until we find the right one; we're not even like computers that have to call up folder and file. The process is more like acquaintanceship: each memory is akin to one of those discussions when you try to establish contiguity with a stranger. You went to St. Trinian's? Did you know Marty Molesworth? He was in the same class as your brother? Ah, then I met your brother, Cyril Crockett-Smythe, a tall hairy fellow with bushy eyebrows who liked to collect stamps. And then you are able to build up the whole dinosaur from a few bone fragments; you know exactly whom you are dealing with and have established them in their correct phylum, family, genus, and species. And the more people you know, the more of these links you are able to form. And therein lies my downfall, for I go on and on obsessively spinning out ever more attenuated filaments of connection.

I'm thinking about metaphor because of a conversation in the canteen here at Wits, where I am now a graduate student in social anthropology (my specialties: food, film, and culture). There is a visiting lecturer from America, a teacher of philosophy, who likes to use the phrase "the bottom line." The bottom line is that Nietzsche brought into question the rationality of believing in a deity. The bottom line is that there are not enough dormitories for the students. The bottom line is that the high crime rate has permanently driven away foreign investment. One of the others at the lunch table is an Afrikaans history teacher, Kobus Koos Kannemeyer—an old-style conservative whose days are surely numbered in the New South Africa, even if he does have tenure. "What exactly is this 'bottom line?'" he asks the American. "I assume you are not referring to bikinis."

"You know, it's a metaphor for the final result, the way things turn out."

"Ja, ja. I know, but what does it really refer to? What are its origins?"

"It's an accounting term," the lecturer in business administration interjects. "When you look at a column of numbers, the bottom line is where your results are. That's when you know whether you're in the black or in the red."

"These days you really can't tell the difference," says the history professor. He makes no secret of the fact that he clings to the notion the ANC is a Communist organization. The graduate students refer to him either as the KKK or as Kortbroek after his predilection for wearing khaki bush shorts as if he were a farm Boer inspecting the *mielies* and making sure the workers behave themselves, not a university professor.

Dr. Snyman is here, enjoying lunch with his colleagues despite his formal retirement. "Analogies are always interesting, aren't they? The Latin and Greek terms for the bones are primarily descriptive metaphors," he remarks. He holds up a diminutive white hand decorated with age spots but still remarkably steady. "Take the navicular and the hamate, for example. Both are wrist bones; one is in the shape of a boat, and the other is very like a hammer, hence the names."

He beams around at each of us. With his snowy beard and hair, his shrunken figure and wry, intelligent face, he looks like a clever gnome. In honor of the conversation we'd had years ago in the Adler Museum, I took his introductory medical anthropology course at one point, but found myself less interested in the forensic science that was his main topic than in his sardonic asides about the culture–bound conduct of various branches of the medical profession. Miss Tompkins had awoken in me an appreciation of just such peripatetic and divagatory thinking.

I eat a little of the Caesar salad; it should be a side dish, not a lunch. "You know," I muse to the philosopher, "South Africans use a different term than bottom line: we would say 'at the end of the day.' At the end of the day we need to have created jobs for the unemployed or there will be chaos." How different are the underlying assumptions in our two countries! Americans think in terms of the accumulation of wealth; we still think like farmers—even now a *boerenasie* at heart, a farm nation. The sun drops so fast below the horizon here that there is no ignoring the inexorable cycle of African reality.

"At the end of the day night falls . . . and the void is filled with darkness," Kannemeyer says glumly. He is a lugubrious, cynical chap in his daily university persona, not particularly friendly, so I am surprised that he joins me on my walk back to my office to invite me to his house that weekend. We can play a nice game of croquet, he tells me. I accept the invitation, only to be told that I should come in the early afternoon, at 2 P.M. to be exact. This puts me in a foul mood, as I take it that I am being asked neither to lunch nor dinner. There will surely be a pot of badly made tea, some Marie biscuits, perhaps a soggy cream cheese sandwich, the seminar lecture poorly disguised as conversation. I know these academics, bachelors even when married.

In any event, I am happily surprised. His house on the southern edge of the Northern Suburbs is small but beautifully landscaped. When I arrive, he is busy setting up the bent-wire hoops for croquet. "You do play, nee?" Yes, I affirm by contradiction. It is one of the few competitive sports I enjoy, and I am quite good at it. Old KKK is an expert, however. He contrives on several occasions to get through the hoop and leave his ball just touching mine. He then places one foot on his own ball, whacks the ball with a resounding *thock!*, and sends my own poor spherical proxy into the surrounding shrubbery. "Going to be a little more exercise than you expected, my *kleintjie*," he cackles. He laughs just as uproariously when I reciprocate later in the game and it is his ball that goes flying into a thicket of imported cacti gleaming with barbs like a Zulu regiment. I would never have succeeded in even this small revenge if we hadn't been drinking Windhoek lagers all afternoon, the German-style beer kept deliriously cold in a tub of dry ice.

At the end of the day, we sit on the stone porch overlooking the gorgeous rocky jumble of his garden and drink brandy sours while his wife smiles radiantly in our direction. She is a plump, weathered lady with thick bifocals and an old person's out-of-date clothes—had I passed her doing her market shopping, I would not have looked twice: just another nondescript *mevrou*—but there is an odd spark of sexuality anytime she and Kannemeyer exchange glances. Our talk comes around to the Truth Commission, the magnet for all social discussions these days. With a negotiated settlement between two powers in a Mexican standoff, there could be no witch hunt of the police and army, no jail time for ex-Minister of Justice and Prisons Police Jimmy Kruger or the police spy and assassin Craig Williamson. Instead, there is a daily performance of Jerzy Grotowski's live theater presided over by Archbishop Tutu beaming his tough and beneficent love on us all. And this theater is recorded in the papers, on radio, video, and television, seared into the very souls of South Africans so no future generation can disbelieve in apartheid or the wars that have riven this land.

"We talked about metaphors the other day," Kannemeyer remarks. "What kind of metaphor does the Commission have in mind with its proprietary use of the word *truth*? Revenge, perhaps? Or for some fairy-tale history in which all the whites are bad and all the blacks are saints?"

Kannemeyer is of the opinion that the Commission does more harm than good, and I am not sure that he is wholly wrong . . . especially about the Commission's assumption that the revelation of horrors is "healing." On the other hand, I am only too glad that the white South African should be forced to recognize what was done on his behalf, to see the human suffering that kept his swimming pool blue and provided his game-viewing holidays. That the neighbor seen leaving for his office job with the police was spending his day torturing some seventeen-year-old African about his connection to black youth organizations, that the sociology professor shot in front of his toddler on his own doorstep was a "soft target" of the people sworn to protect and serve, were, in fact, aspects of the white South African dream not to be swept under the rug and permanently forgotten. Anything is preferable to the old amnesia that led to Rooibos Sanders telling us sincerely that the Voortrekkers found the country's interior empty of people, not that masses of the

Bantu had moved away after being devastated by white people's diseases. But do I really believe the uncovering of these events and memories would change the hearts and minds of apartheid's beneficiaries and cure the wounds of the black majority through the miracle of the *truth*? This I cannot say.

I prefer not to share my own qualms with such as Kannemeyer, and choose instead to annoy him by pointing out that black policemen confessing their sins far outnumber the government ministers willing to admit that they might ever have been complicit in some wrongdoing. So right there we have a distortion of the past. A Martian or Betelguesian reading the hearings' transcripts would be justified in believing that apartheid was something enforced by a few rogue policemen and that blacks did to each other, while the honorable ministers shuffled their papers and picked their noses in Pretoria. ("No, no. When we said someone 'should be permanently removed from society,' we just meant they should be encouraged to change their ways, not that they should be killed.")

"But it's the truth," he says angrily. "It takes a special sort of person to kill in cold blood, and Adriaan Vlok's* biggest mistake was letting guys like that keep their jobs. But the African has been killing his brother since time began. Just look at Rwanda or Uganda. What about right next door in Zimbabwe? The first thing Mugabe did when he got in power is massacre his own tribe's neighbors, the Ndebele. There's not a single African country whose people weren't in better shape before independence than they are now. But South Africa is going to be different, of course; just get the white man to leave and everyone will be happy and healthy, and they'll all have jobs as lawyers and scientists."

I look away in irritation with the staleness of this argument, but Kannemeyer seems to take my lack of response for agreement. When his wife goes inside to tell their faithful servant—Dora, who has been with them

* Minister of Police, 1986–92. He did eventually turn on former Prime Minister P. W. Botha and told the Truth Commission that Botha ordered bombings and the murder of political activists.

"since time immemorial"—that dinner can be served, he leans toward me and says in conspiratorial tones: "You don't have to go. Just tell them it would be too much for you. No one's going to force you to testify."

I look around his white man's paradise for a moment before answering. There are the sounds of birds settling down for the evening, the ubiquitous rasp of the hadedah, the cloying sweetness of apricots rotting beneath a tree gifted with overabundance, the rival smell of jasmine from a nearby bush. It gives the impression of the Africa that has always been, a wild Garden of Eden now tamed for our consumption . . . but is it an illusion soon to disappear beneath the dark waters of history?

"I never told you I was testifying," I say quietly.

"Of course you are. Isn't everybody? This whole damn country is turning into one giant Apartheids Anonymous meeting, with everybody falling over themselves to confess their sins and parade their victimhood. Don't take it wrong, I want what's best for you."

I am too furious to answer, and we go on to other subjects. He has done his job, made his pitch, and if I don't wish to pick up the ball we might as well enjoy a fine dinner. It is a fine dinner, in fact. Roast shoulder of springbok from his son's game farm, served with a wine and mushroom reduction and new potatoes baked in a rock salt and rosemary crust. There is a Bellingham Shiraz to wash it all down, and the finale is a pudding made with ladyfingers and homemade strawberry jam, topped with whipped cream and Cape gooseberries. While my tongue and palate enjoy the traditional meal, there is a small bilious stirring inside me that objects. Every bite is intended to be a lesson: this is the world—serene and civilized—being ground into Africa's red dust by the heel of the Commission in its headlong pursuit of the ultimate vanity they dare to call Truth.

At the midpoint in our dinner, Kannemeyer touches me on the arm and says, "Look, I didn't mean to offend you. That's not why I invited you here. I simply thought we could have a nice time and get to know each other."

Yes, we are, I say. And you don't have to apologize . . . not to me.

"Do you think there is somebody else I should apologize to?" He is angry now, his face suffused with blood that is more than the flush of meat and wine consumed in quantity. He points his fork toward the servant, who has just brought in another plate of roasted potatoes. "Just ask her, Paul, who paid for her son's education. Who bailed him out and defended him to the magistrate when he got in trouble for breaking windows? Whose money bought the pondokkie she's going to retire to, the sewing machine that will be her livelihood when she retires? Do you think your Lower Houghton Jewish liberals do that? No, they dismiss their maids with a handshake and then feel sorry that the poor Africans have nothing in their old age."

"No, my love," his wife says. "Our guest has not accused you of anything." She turns to me. "Kobie likes to growl like a lion, but he's got a kind heart."

"I'm sure of it," I say . . . sincerely, for there is something touching about their mutual devotion.

I smile now at Mrs. K. "I can see your husband is a decent man."

"Thanks," he says, laughing. "That's the nicest thing anyone's said about me in years."

...

I AM SITTING AT the bathtub kitchen table finishing my dinner—a truncated paella of my own devising, really a risotto with prawns and spicy Portuguese chourico sausage—and watching the news on the small portable color set that Mother gave me as a present for obtaining my bachelor's with honors two years ago. The news does not help my anxiousness, for there has been the usual, harrowing brief clip from one of the Commission hearings, this time from P.E. The Port Elizabeth police had been the worst; somehow the old animosities from the early frontier days on the Eastern Cape had erupted in the 1980s like seventeen-year locusts rising from the bitter ground. I am due to talk to the Truth Commission tomorrow, and the strain tells on me, returning me to a state I have not been in since shortly after Father's demise. What will happen at that meeting house tomorrow? Is someone going to rub my shoulders while I blubber, tormented by my memories? Will I be hauled off keening and wailing like those poor Xhosa mothers whose sons were shot? Will I sit *stumm*, cutting my eyes in anger at the commissioners while they accuse me of crimes I had not known I'd committed? I try to hold on to my reflections and ideas, but they keep streaming away in the wake of my lumbering thoughts like the star-spangled tail of the comet Tempel-Tuttle.

I have just fixed myself a cup of strong filtered coffee—paradoxically, the caffeine helps me calm down—when my telephone rings. I gulp my coffee, scalding my mouth, but I am sure it will be the advisor assigned to me by the Commission, and she has a tendency to keep me on the phone as we review yet again the questions I'm likely to be asked. I hate cold coffee.

"Hello," I croak, trying to breathe through my open mouth to cool my scorched palate.

"Howzit, troepie?" The cheerful voice is instantly familiar despite not having been heard for almost seven years.

"Captain Lyddie. I mean Major Lyddie." I had heard he had been promoted shortly after we withdrew from South-West Africa.

"Ja, my bra. Have you missed me?"

"Major, you know you're not supposed to be calling me. And how did you get my telephone number anyway?"

"The operator, of course. I just wanted to dial an old friend and so I asked the operator to put me through. Nothing wrong with that."

I take a deep breath. "My number is not supposed to be listed, nor given out."

"Why are you so full of fear, troepie? I could have waited until tomorrow to say hello, but you know how busy and crowded the hearings are and I get shy around so many people. Besides, your assister doesn't like me. So I just wanted to talk to you as a friend, you know, like old times. A friendly conversation, not about the Commission or any of that nonsense, anything; we can talk about the weather if you like. I hope it stays sunny for the Boks on Saturday."

There is a rugby match between our national team and the New Zealand All Blacks that is the chief topic on every white South African male's lips. I have never enjoyed watching organized sports, and the word *rugby* calls to mind my fumbling attempts to drop and kick the ball and of being shoved forward into a smelly urinal while out on the field my teammates are being elbowed and punched, intimidated, and roundly defeated. And since when are Lyddie and I supposed to be friends?

"It's good the international teams are coming back, hey? That was one of the worst things the Commies did to us, denying the common man his little pleasures. It didn't hurt the rich industrialists or the military-industrial complex, did it? Just your ordinary bloke who only wanted to come home after work, drink his dop on his *eie stoep* and watch the broadcast. What about you? When are you going to open a restaurant? Maybe one with a big-screen telly in the bar, Paulie. Now, that would be *lekker*. I wouldn't mind investing in that; we could be partners. You cook, I meet and greet."

This is a vision of such preposterous unlikelihood that I gather the courage to say, "I really can't talk to you anymore, Major. I'm going to be testifying against you tomorrow."

His tone changes from its contrived jollity to one of wounded feelings. "I thought this was supposed to be about *truth*. You tell the truth; I tell the truth. What's this nonsense: *testifying against*, hey? Who said anything about that?"

"Yes, Major. I will just tell what happened. Now I really must—"

"As you remember it, you mean? You'll be saying what you remember, I say what I remember, and then we all go home and live happily ever after. That's what this is about, is it? Did you ever notice how in their public commentaries the Commission only ever mentions the 'oppressor' and the 'oppressed?' You're a student of humankind; do you really think that you can separate us so simply into two different species? Man the victim goes into *Box A;* Man the victimizer goes into *Box B*. Is that the sort of rubbish you've stuffed your mind with at the university?"

"Come on, Major Lyddie—"

"No, man. I'd hoped you'd learned something. Remember what I told you: never complain, never explain? That's part of being a man . . . but you, you've always been weak. So you'll let your Communist friends put their words in your mouth, just as long as they pat you on the head and say they like you."

"I'm going to put the phone down now. I shouldn't be talking to you."

"Hey, I'm sorry, Sweetbread. Really, I'm not trying to intimidate you. Just think of this as one friend calling another; that's allowed, even in the New South Africa. I just wanted to tell you to be careful tomorrow, not for my sake but for yours. Things are not always what they seem, you know. Don't let yourself be used."

"Don't worry, I won't."

"I'm worried, I'm worried."

"Goodbye, Major."

"Good night, troepie. Have a good life, as they say. *Lekker bly.*"

I hang up, my hands shaking. I'm not really concerned that Lyddie or his colleagues will try to do something to me—despite all the stories about the Civil Cooperation Board and the secret hit squads manned by guys with names like "Slang" Van Zyl and "Peaches" Slabbert. I'm not frightened, because they have bigger problems than me. Lyddie had been with the 32 Battalion when they did much worse things than anything I might have to talk about. I'm disturbed that he has gotten hold of my "secure" phone number so easily, but I think what really throws me off is the awareness that I will be looking at him, that we will be in the same room together, while I talk about what happened in the Himba village and later during the false cease-fire. I have tried to set aside the two chronological realities—my life in the army then, my life as a university student now—to put them in two different plastic containers like those the university shop sells for school files, to follow the advice Dr. Vish had given me years ago about what he called "compartmentalizing." You can't live in all time zones simultaneously, he had told me. He had recommended that I create different mental cubbyholes for the different phases of my life. It's an orderly progression through time, he had told me, not a stew.

I drink some chamomile tea and take the prescribed Lorazepam before going to bed, as Dini van Vuuren, my advisor, had suggested I do to cut down on my anxiety. I don't bother to play the meditation tape she has given to me, though; it sounds too much like a long, dull conversation in a ward for adenoidal patients, and I keep hearing the slight variations in each chant—*sa-ray-sa-sa*, *sa-ray-sa-sa*, *ha-re-re*, *ha-re-re*, and so forth. But still, I cannot sleep. I find myself standing in the broiling sun with a shovel, Sergeant Fynbos is shouting at me, and I try to imagine that his spittle is a cooling, moisturizing mist like at the veranda of the Skukuza Restaurant in Kruger Park. He grows increasingly exacerbated at my obtuseness, finally grabbing a tuning fork and dinging it, then holding it up against my ear.

I hate when the alarm clock becomes part of my dream. That's why I had to get rid of the radio alarm that Mother gave me, because I would invariably incorporate the morning news or ads into some half fantasy of my own. (The traffic report was the worst: there is still a stalled car blocking traffic on Louis Botha Avenue forever lodged in my mind.) I feel groggy and hung-over, though I have drunk nothing stronger than chamomile, but I am hopeful that a shower will help get me ready for my testimony. The phone rings just as I am about to get into the shower, and I run over naked to the stand where it sits. It is Dini, calling to make sure I am up. She'll fetch me in half an hour, with a thermos of coffee, she promises. I almost tell her about Lyddie's call, but I feel embarrassed standing without any clothes while I talk to her, my penis a sluggish thermometer that registers my interest in her—she is buxom, pretty, a spray of freckles on her nose and cheeks, and when she talks she emphasizes her words by touching my hand—so I just say I'll meet her downstairs at eight.

I leave the building and walk down to the curb around the same time Dini pulls up in her sporty green Karmann Ghia. The car had originally been the yellow of police cars, and she bought it cheap from an American photojournalist who couldn't understand why his windows were always being smashed, or why he immediately became the focus of wrath of every rioting crowd, narrowly escaping with his life on several occasions. She had promptly had it spray-painted blue, and then green—following the advice of an ex-boyfriend who worked in a chop shop. "It pays to have friends in low places," she jokingly told me, and now she ran little danger of her car being mistaken for one belonging to the much-hated police.

We leave the car in a nearby parking area that has a special rate for TRC officials and its own official car-watchers (more reliable than those who've made it their unlicensed business on the street), and walk to the municipal hall where the hearings take place. Dini clutches her purse tightly underneath her arm while scanning the pavement for potential muggers. There has been an increased police presence here after it was noted that journalists and Commission officials had become favorite targets of downtown Jo'burg's entrepreneurial robbers.

I am a little disappointed to see no gaggle of reporters or spectators when we get to the municipal building, a picture that had formed in my mind from the coverage of such celebrity witnesses as Winnie Mandela. I am a little saddened that Major Lyddie is viewed as a small fish; no comparing him with the infamous policemen Colonel Swanepoel or Captain Benzien, men who have made a name for themselves as particularly brutal torturers. Or perhaps it is that we've all become a little too accustomed to the bombardment of revelations, the tales of persecution and violence, of husbands and lovers murdered by their captors, the children vaporized by land mines. One of the techniques for getting rid of phobias is "flooding," a method I learned of from *Our Useless Fears* by Joseph Wolpe (yes, the brother of the Rivonia trialist and dramatic escapee). The trick is to overexpose the sufferer to the very stimuli that create anxiety so he will simply shut down that mechanism and not feel the symptoms. Perhaps white South Africans' dysmnesia is a kind of phobia—a horror at the thought of remembering—and the ultimate effect of all the daily broadcasts on radio and television and the newspaper stories of the Commission's hearings has been to flood that phobic response, to shut down memory once and for all in promise of a cure.

Inside, the hearing room is more crowded, and there are a few sleepy-looking journalists in the section reserved for the press. I see Lyddie come in, conferring as he walks with a round, red-faced man with the little Voortrekker beard popularized (or unpopularized?) by Eugene Terre-blanche and his neo-Nazi militia, the AWB. You know the look, like those drawings you turn upside down and there's still a face. Once, I got off the plane in Port Elizabeth, on the way to visit a friend at the university, only to be horrified by a receiving line of about twenty of these guys, uniformly dressed in bush suits with a malformed Hakenkreutz on the armband, uniformly bearded, uniformly muscular and chunky, uniformly saluting *me*? No, when I turned to look back, there immediately behind me was Terré Blanche, old White-Earth himself, carrying his round bum-face on his thick neck while he radiated benevolence upon the small phalanx of the gathered faithful.

"That's De Kok, Major Lyddie's advocate," Dini whispers, her warm breath tickling in my ear. "Watch out for him. He looks like a country *magistraat*, but he's got a sting like a scorpion."

Lyddie catches us looking their way, and he waves cheerfully at me. He is dressed crisply in his major's uniform, but I can see he has put on some weight and his face is jowlier; his hair has thinned in the seven years' interim, and he now sports a pair of wire-rimmed eyeglasses. I murmur a timid hello, impossible to hear from this distance, and Dini glares ferociously first at him, then at me. I see Lyddie mutter something into De Kok's ear—just making out the one word, *poes*—and they both laugh. Dini elbows me hard in the ribs. "Don't be taken in, okay? *They* are not your friends."

There is a lengthy preamble while the chairperson, translators, legal representatives, and commissioners are each introduced by name. The assembly represents the rainbow nation we have always been but have only recently grown into, although the chairperson is a severe-looking middle-aged white man with a neatly trimmed beard. Tables and chairs line the room in a circular pattern, with name cards in front of each of the commissioners, and behind the chairperson there is a large TRC flag, with the word "Reconciliation" prominent. Some of the audience and commissioners are wearing earphones, which protrude from the sides of their heads like dragonfly eyes, and if I half close my own eyes it looks as if I'm attending a tribunal judged by insects.

The chairman thanks all of us for being here, and makes a special point of thanking the three translators, and then he explains the program for the day's business, the expectations and obligations for those testifying, the scope of the Commission's mandate.

De Kok immediately raises the objection that any testimony regarding events in South-West Africa is surely the provenance of the Republic of Namibia. He sounds just a trifle bored, as if this is territory that has been traversed before, but Dini mutters to me: "Clever of him. There's no way the Swapo government is going to want to reopen old wounds, or be investigated themselves over the thousands of alleged South African spies who died in the rebel camps."

The head of the Commission responds somberly that this is an investigation into the role of the SADF, its treatment of soldiers and citizens, and as such the occupation of Namibia is an integral and inseparable element. "We are also examining the amnesty application by Major John Lyddie, in reference to the Acts, Offenses, and Omissions detailed on the paginated pages 176 to 178 in the document supplied by his legal representative." There is a pause while the chairperson confirms that each of the five commissioners and the legal representatives have copies of said document. "The Commission is aware that it is in no way a court and these are not judicial proceedings. Should there be call for any criminal sanctions, the Commission would make a recommendation, at that time, as to the question of where proceedings ought to be filed and adjudicated. In the meanwhile, this is simply a public hearing and an exploration into Major Lyddie's own request for immunity."

"Don't look so glum," Dini whispers to me. "This will be a piece of cake. Just do your thing when they call on you. I'm here to support you in every way." She smiles reassuringly, regarding me intently and sympathetically. I feel a flutter of happiness at her attentiveness; she has been solicitous since we first met to discuss my legal representation, but I have become aware of her increasing warmth toward me.

"I'm going to do my thing," I respond quietly. Dini spent a year in university in the States, and another two working for an international nonprofit over there. I had been surprised, the first time she drove me to a coffee shop in Yeoville to discuss my testimony, that this young Afrikaans woman should be blasting James Brown on her car stereo.

She gives me an encouraging wink as I'm called to the front as a witness, giving me a friendly little push in the commissioners' direction. Before I sit down, I am asked whether I wish to take the oath or to make an affirmation. I agree to take the oath, and I swear that "the evidence I will give before this commission will be the truth, the whole truth, and nothing but the truth, so help me God." Dini begins the proceedings by discussing why I have been asked to testify, out of all the soldiers who served under Lyddie in Namibia. She points out Lyddie's special interest in me, characterizing it as a desire to show off (a term at which De Kok immediately objects). Then she offers to demonstrate my remarkable memory, and, having gained the Commission's permission, asks one of the commissioners to take a telephone directory from the stack on the table that had been dropped off that morning by a government clerk and choose a page at random. She then reads to me from the Ventersdorp phone directory from two years previously.

Dini begins with Steenbras, Johannes. Soon she is in the *T*'s and there is a titter of laughter when she reads the name Treurnicht—the same as that of the late politician known as "Dr. No." There are several more Treurnichts—I had not realized it was such a popular name—a Terblanche, Trano Industrial Supplies, and so on. I picture the capital *T*'s standing like so many crosses—some are for burning, others memorials for the hastily buried dead—as they march down the page and over to the other side. *U*'s are more pleasant, a plumber's pipe to catch the excess dirt and remove it before the entire system gets stopped up. The numbers are lovely, grouped in couplets like lines from Milton or "The Rape of the Lock."

Dini reads rapidly without inflection for perhaps ten minutes—I know this because the head commissioner taps his watch meaningfully and I become aware of impatient coughs and foot-shufflings. Dini stops and hands the book to the head commissioner, then gestures to me. I take a sip of my coffee and scroll back to where she began: the Asculepius snakes slithering, the crosses, the shepherd's-crook sevens, the rolling noughts and spiky fours. Upinshaw, L. M., has a number ending in two fives, and I linger momentarily over the delectability of this closing spondee—*punch, punch*. As I reach the final name and number, I inadvertently cause another laugh by imitating the chairman's wrist-tapping gesture and his impatient frown. He looks at me ironically. "You got Van der Bijl, Johannes's number wrong. It is four seven, not seven four. How do you explain that?"

"I'm sure that is how Dini . . . Miss Van Vuuren read it. I particularly noticed that one because it made me think of a delectable fish, the seventy-four, and how we began the list with another member of the bream family. . . ." *Polysteganus* is, indeed, fine eating and the thought of it makes my mouth water. The fish gets its peculiar name from its resemblance to the hull of a seventy-four-gun warship.

"You can check the tape," Dini cuts in.

The chairman smiles. "I don't think that's necessary. This is not a fishing expedition, despite Mr. Sweetbread's interesting associative leaps. I think the commission can accept that he has rather, um, unusual powers of recall and move on." He taps his watch again, hamming it up for the audience, who laugh dutifully.

Dini, I'm glad to see, stays serious, focused. She carefully leads me through my testimony—the exact amount of time I spent in South-West Africa, Lyddie's heavy-handed befriending of me, what happened in Kaokoland. The audience stirs a little when I describe the immersion of the chief's son in the rain barrel, although I am sure they have all heard far worse.

"You later transferred out of the infantry, is that correct?" Dini asks. I answer in the affirmative and tell her a little about my photography training in Pretoria.

"You see, the army gave this boy an education. Is that so bad?" De Kok says to no one in particular, earning him an annoyed glance from the chairman.

"But even though you'd transferred, this was not the last time you saw Captain Lyddie—"

"He's become a major since then," I interject nervously.

"Correct. And I understand Major Lyddie personally requested you be sent to join the unit of disbanded Koevoet members and Special Forces personnel at the time of the April cease-fire?"

"Oh, come off it," De Kok explodes angrily. "There's no evidence Lyddie put in a request for this fellow. If they saw each other again, it was a coincidence."

"Not a coincidence," Dini replies smoothly. "There was another and more experienced video unit closer to his base of operations than Ondangwa, where Mr. Sweetbread was stationed. We don't have a copy of the orders, but we know someone made the request."

"You *know* this? My learned friend here has no right to blame Major Lyddie, though . . . unless you're offering some sort of proof?" De Kok grumbles, tilting his torso back and grabbing his jacket lapels in each hand like an attorney in an old-fashioned Hollywood film.

"This really seems irrelevant, an argument over trivialities," the chairman interrupts. "Let's move along and allow Mr. Sweetbread to tell his story."

"If my learned friend is quite finished, I will be happy to continue . . ."

Dini says acidly. Turning to me, she changes her tone. "We will be getting into some detail about an event that I know was traumatic for you, but before we do, I just want to confirm some facts. After this traumatic event you had a nervous breakdown, is that correct?"

We have gone over this territory numerous times during our prehearing discussions. Dini wants to preempt any attempt to portray me as mentally unsound.

"Yes, that is so."

"You were not given a medical discharge from the army, though?"

"No. They sent me to hospital, but since my time was almost up and I was getting better, they just gave me a G.T., a normal discharge but with the option to call me back."

"And can you be a bit more specific about your breakdown, what do you think caused it to happen . . . ?"

Although I have known this question would be coming, the lead-in for me to open up a box and pull out the stacked bodies of murdered black men Lyddie is responsible for, I am not ready despite all my preparation. I begin to sweat, to shuffle from foot to foot, to wring my hands. Finally I blurt out: "I couldn't get rid of the feel of those dead people. I just couldn't. I couldn't sleep. I smelled them on my hands and I couldn't eat."

I am crying now, my words barely audible, and Dini requests a short break. Which the Commission chair grants.

An hour later, I return to the hall and tell the Commission what happened on that day in Owamboland, near the Angolan border.

...

"YOU KNOW ABOUT THE cease-fire, don't you?" the taciturn driver says, jumping to the ground and stretching his bandy legs. The presence of all these tough armed men must have awakened in him a hitherto unknown garrulity. "It's been on the radio all day."

"What cease-fire?" Lyddie says. "We don't have a radio here, do we?" he says to a huge muscular fellow, who looks to be at least seven feet tall, and whose hand almost completely covers the portable wireless held to his ear.

"No, of course not. We're too far north," says the giant. "Now be quiet and let me listen to *Forces' Favourites*. I like it when they read the girls' letters to their boyfriends."

The driver looks at them in puzzlement, then grins. "I bet Swapo don't have radios either," he says. "I bet they don't know about the cease-fire."

"There is no cease-fire," Lyddie says coldly. "Now let's get that stuff unloaded and you can bugger off back to where you came from."

I take my duffel and my camera equipment to the tent Lyddie points out, then I am snookered into helping unload the lorry. The driver and I struggle with large cases of ammo, fearful of dropping them. The giant, who could carry with ease twice what the two of us can barely lift, sits nearby with a blissful smile on his large round face, radio glued to his ear.

The atmosphere at this base in the bush is fairly relaxed. Lyddie introduces me around as a rifleman from Gemsbok Camp who managed to make parole and became a trained cameraman instead. Most of the *ouens* respond to me in a friendly way, now that I have been acknowledged as a *blougat*, a "blue-arse."* The men in this unit are an irregular bunch: a lot of decommissioned Koevoet guys who fit the FWB model.† There are also a number of battle-hardened Permanent Force soldiers, with the thousand-meter stare of men who have seen a lot of death. They appear to be both jubilant and apprehensive at the impending end of a war that seemed as if it would go on indefinitely.

* Seasoned soldier. When male chacma baboons attain sexual maturity, their rear ends turn blue.

† Koevoet members—like other right-wing groups—modeled themselves on the early Dutch Voortrekkers in manner and dress. The average soldier didn't like or respect Koevoet, and referred to them as FWBs or "Fuckups With Beards."

A jeep drives up in the late afternoon with two dead impalas tied onto the back. "Did you pull out the bolts yet?" asks the Koevoet giant.

"No, man, just cut around them. And try not to mess up the feathers," a recce who has just gotten out of the jeep responds. I peer closely at the impalas, one of which has a barely visible feathered bolt embedded behind its left shoulder. In the front seat of the jeep are two high-powered crossbows.

"Why the crossbows?" I ask Lyddie.

"Ag, use your *kop*. That's how we kill when we don't want to advertise our presence. We've been living off the land for months, not just here but . . . " He gestures toward the north with his chin.

"It was great," says the hunter. "This bow is so silent, you can drop a buck and the rest of the herd just look around and then go on grazing."

"That's *one* of the ways we kill," the giant interrupts. He has hung an impala from a winch off the front of the Casspir and is rapidly stripping off its hide, separating skin from flesh with a razor-sharp Swedish elk knife about eleven inches long.

"He's our cook and our game dresser," Lyddie says of the giant. "You should watch him. You might learn something."

I film the giant, who has obviously had considerable practice separating an animal into different cuts and portions. I ask him why they're still bothering to hunt with crossbows when it doesn't matter anymore if their presence is known to the insurgents, not with the cease-fire and UNTAG on its way. He doesn't bother answering. After a while he tells me I should make myself useful and gather some firewood for the *braai*. I say that a fire will surely advertise our presence, and he tells me that I am beginning to seriously annoy him. This doesn't seem like a very smart thing to do, so I wander around the camp picking up small twigs for kindling until one of the Owambo trackers takes pity on me and points out a good-sized stack of wood behind one of the tents. I had noticed a fire ring when I first drove in, and I soon have a crackling fire going. With the smell of wood smoke, the call of birds in the brush, and the drone of passing flies attracted to the antelope carcass, we could be in a holiday camp somewhere, enjoying the good life that is the due of every South African. The afternoon passes tranquilly, dully.

The radio is now lying on its side, its volume turned up. "This next song is for Lance-Corporal Kotze of Fifth SAI Battalion," the tinny voice declares. "Your wife has a message for you. 'Hello, darling. I love you stacks. Can't wait until you come home.' Well, he can't wait either, Mrs. Kotze. And here's your request—'Just the Two of Us. . . .'" The Koevoet giant nods happily at this announcement. He has been steadily downing beers from a large ice chest covered in camouflage cloth. He tells me that just because he's not going to bloody well offer a lager to me, it doesn't mean I can't have one. I am so thirsty that I knock off the can of beer in a couple of gulps and go back for another. The giant grunts approvingly. The first thing I've managed to do right.

Dinner is jovial: a group of men sitting around a campfire, eating venison, telling jokes, drinking more beer followed by swigs of Klipdrift. There is nothing for me to learn about the art of *veldkos* here, though; the impala is partly burnt, partly raw, and greasy with smoke—caveman cuisine. For a while we listen to the radio, mostly popular music of the *Forces' Favourites* kind, with a periodic broadcast of news when we hear South Africa's administrator-general for Namibia, Louis Pienaar's voice telling us that he has confirmed information that a major invasion is under way. "Confirmed, hey?" a ginger-haired lieutenant with several combat medals on his shirt snorts, exchanging grins with Lyddie and the cheerfully *poeg*-eyed giant.

Captain Lyddie fetches out a guitar, and in the glow of the embers he sits picking at it soulfully. He sings "Norwegian Wood," and "No Reply," his reedy tenor as much a surprise as the choice of Beatles songs. "This one's for you," he tells me, and sings "Where Have All the Flowers Gone." We all join in, and he follows up with the popular Bee Gees hit "Don't Forget to Remember." When he stops singing, the sounds of the surrounding bush rush in to fill the vacuum: a jackal yips, a hyena calls with its mournful giggling howl and is answered by a distant companion, a nightjar swoops by in pursuit of the moths attracted to our firelight. As if responding to an announcement, we all clamber to our feet and stagger toward our tents at the same time.

I wake up in the morning to realize that everyone else has arisen before me and are going about their purposeful business in the light rain that is falling steadily on this far corner of Namibia. "Happy April Fool's day, you lazy bastard," says Lyddie, his tone friendly as he gestures toward the welcomingly bubbling coffeepot over a kerosene camp stove. I have a bit of a *babbelas,* and the coffee helps to reduce my headache. Because my senses are loosely wired this morning, it takes me a while to recognize that there is a special intensity of focus to the men's activities. Lyddie has a hunter's look of alert awareness, and he talks quietly every few minutes into a walkie-talkie. "Eat something fast," he says, tossing a heel of bread in my direction. "We're going to want you to have a steady hand with the camera."

"What's up?"

"Swapo's on the move. There's a big force just a few klicks north of us. They crossed the border in the middle of the night, and they're heading this way as fast as their little legs can carry them. Right where we want them."

This makes sense to me. April first is the day the guerrillas are supposed to start demobilizing and turn their arms in to UNTAG. These guys will be returning from Angola, glad to finally be home after years of hanging around in the bush being harassed by both us and Savimbi's army. Lyddie tells me that we're planning to meet them a few miles from our camp, and that there is a good ridge there for me to observe and get everything on film. I double-check my cameras, and bring along extra film and batteries, ignoring Lyddie's good-natured chiding that I am cluttering his jeep with my equipment like some auntie going on holiday. All the vehicles in the camp are taking off, loaded with armed men. Lyddie gives some orders on the walkie-talkie, then starts the jeep's engine, pausing to let the Casspir pull out in front of us. The sight of this armored behemoth makes me realize that something is wrong.

"Shouldn't the U.N. guys be here to take care of the disarmament?" I ask. I know that things have been a little confused; most of the People's Liberation Army troops who've returned have simply rejoined the villages from which they were recruited instead of going through any formal process.

"If you say so. Those guys are always getting lost, though. The last I heard, UNTAG's observers were wandering around the bush forty kilometers south of here. Maybe they found something to observe over there."

"And nobody told them where to go?"

"That's not my job, *my broer*. They don't even recognize our existence, so who are we to tell them anything? You know something? I'd love to tell the U.N. where to go, but I'd get in a hell of a lot of trouble if I did."

I sit quietly in the passenger seat the rest of the way, a sinking feeling in my stomach. We pull up at the base of a rise of land that terminates in a rocky outcropping. Lyddie jumps out and tells me to get a move on and take whatever I can carry. I grab the cine-camera and one of the heavy cases with extra film and telephoto lenses, and follow him as fast as I can, the case banging painfully against my shins as I try to climb the rise. The rain has stopped by this time, but it's still cool. When I finally catch up to him behind a large kopje, Lyddie motions me to stay down while he carefully makes his way to the top, his field glasses in his right hand. He gazes over the top for a few minutes, then motions me up. As I climb, I can hear singing, and when I look over the top of the rock outcropping (Lyddie pressing my head down with his hand so I don't create too obvious a silhouette) I can see where it is coming from. Half a kilometer away, where the land forms a natural basin, is a band of men, about eighty of them, walking in a casual, spread-out line toward us. They are singing in unison, doing a much better job than we did the previous night, and occasionally pausing to wave a rifle in the air or perform an exuberant dance. After years of hiding in the bush or living in distant villages in Angola, the Owambo fighters are coming home.

"Magnificent, aren't they?" Lyddie says, in put-on clipped British tones. "It reminds me of that film, *Zulu*, the one with Buthelezi, not the other one."

"They sound happy," I remark, already having my camera raised to eyelevel as I try to get some panoramic shots before switching to the telephoto.

"Why not? They think we're just going to turn this whole bloody country over to them." Lyddie then murmurs something into the walkie-talkie, something in Afrikaans about wildebeests coming into the kraal and it being time to shut the gate. "No, man," he says, as if to himself. "When you play with the big boys, you play by big boys' rules."

I switch to the 175mm lens and focus on a man near the front whose bright red shirt caught my eye. As I look at him, I am vaguely aware of a sharp crackling sound. The man looks bewildered, and I zoom in on his expression of surprise. There is a loud pop and the *crump*! of a mortar shell exploding, and I zoom out again to get a wider view. Red Shirt has dropped to his knees anyway, and is now pointing his rifle in our direction. There is a high-pitched pinging as a bullet careens off one of the rocks a few meters away. Lyddie gives another order into the walkie-talkie, then tells me to shade the bloody camera lens, as we're attracting attention.

I keep filming and watching the band of soldiers as they fall to the ground or dart around in confusion. At first it is simply a massacre, the ragtag soldiers falling where they stand like sheafs to a scythe. But these are battle-hardened men, who quickly find whatever slight rises and dips in the uneven land will give them protection and begin to get into small groups and fight back, firing the rifles and grenade launchers they had been earlier waving in the air like flagpoles. This is the fiercest fighting I have yet seen, and I had thought the war was over! For a while it seems as if the guerrillas will break out of the cordon around them—they do, after all, outnumber us considerably—but then the Casspir appears behind them, roaring along at high speed, machine guns chattering in deadly conversation. The newly regrouped bands break up in panic, some dropping their guns to flee faster. The Casspir completes one sortie, turns, and is starting on another when there is a very loud bang and smoke begins to pour out from the armored vehicle. The top opens, and the Koevoet giant jumps out and begins to run in our direction. He suddenly does a little jump and a spurt of red appears on the front of his jacket. Then he staggers and pitches headlong on the ground. I hear Lyddie swearing, demanding to know where the fucking helicopters are.

Below us is the rapid prattle of light machine guns, the staccato reports of rifles and occasional explosion of mortars. The guerrillas have again formed into fighting groups and are now retreating from the ambush but advancing toward Lyddie and me. He hands me an R4 rifle and tells me to wait until he tells me, then pick off the leaders as I've been trained to do. And I should put the fucking camera down. With the camera lens no longer between me and the death that is everywhere below, I am terrified, *kak*-scared, ready to jump up and run away screaming for my mother. I fumble at the rifle's safety catch, knowing that fighting back is my only chance of survival. The stray thought of what Miss Tompkins liked to say about how the Blitz failed to soften the will of the British public intrudes into my consciousness. "It brought the best out in us," she had proclaimed. "Adversity often does that." *What utter rubbish*, I think, as another barrage of machine gun fire makes me twitch and jump. I am suddenly infuriated into calm by the thought of Roelof's senseless death, and I become aware of Lyddie holding me back, his face tense, while he counts aloud.

"Let's go," he yells, rising over the rock and beginning to fire the Uzi, his personal weapon. I stand up, aim carefully at a broad-chested man with his shirt unbuttoned who is running toward us, and I then squeeze the trigger. His torso jerks backward while his legs keep moving forward, and he topples over. I see with terrible clarity the figures running up the hill toward me, and I turn, sight on another man, and watch as his right cheek disappears in a spray of blood. He does not fall immediately, but stands, screaming and clutching at his face, then slowly crumples to his knees as Lyddie turns the Uzi on him. I suddenly become aware of what an attractive target I must present with my broad body outlined against the kopje, and I slip back down again, refusing to budge. Lyddie is slightly sheltered at the side of a rock, firing the submachine gun in short bursts. He talks steadily to himself, saying over again, "Shit. Shit. Fuck. Fuck." The shell casings clatter around me like brass rain accompanied by his song.

I can see a large group of black faces running up the hill toward me from our side of the hill, and the thought passes calmly through me that we are about to die. Then it registers that they're wearing our uniforms, as the Territorial unit breaks up around the kopje in an ox-head formation, a central front and two flanking pincers, just like Chaka's army 150 years earlier. (When the famous chief's unwed mother's belly began to swell, she told everyone she had a bug inside—*uTshaka*, an intestinal parasite.) Around us the men swarm like soldier ants from a disturbed nest, and from the other side of the hill comes a loud and prolonged burst of firing, which gradually subsides, then tapers off into silence.

Lyddie takes a long drink from his canteen; afterward, he playfully pours a little water over my head. "Have a drink, lightie," he says. "It's cleanup time." I take a grateful swig, then stand up. I feel exhilarated, but shaky in the legs. I hand him back the rifle, pick up my camera, which has a slight dent in the casing, and follow him down the hill. Our men are turning over the dead and wounded soldiers, bandaging each other where they've been wounded or simply cut from banging against rocks. I focus the lens on a tall, olive-skinned man with a lean face slightly longer than it should be—he had made us all laugh the night before when he sang the refrain "No reply-y-y-y" in a sweet, high tenor, chiming in at the wrong moment. He is standing over a Swapo soldier who sits with his legs outstretched, his left hand covering his right shoulder and a look of shocked pain on his face. Our man asks him something, listens to the dull response, then calmly points the barrel of his rifle at the injured soldier's chest and shoots him. He prods the inert body with his foot, and walks off.

Lyddie takes me by the arm, his strong fingers digging into my biceps, and leads me a few meters up the hill. He indicates a man lying on his back, a stitching of holes in his shirt, his cheek and eye missing. "You bagged this one," he says cheerfully. "I just finished him off for you, but you put him out of the fight." He leans down, dips his fingers into the blood pooling beneath the man's head, then rubs it across my cheek. "That's what my *oupa* did for me when I shot my first buck," he said. "It was a klipspringer, hardly any meat on it, but I made a band for my hat with its hide and wore it until it rotted away. Now you can go back to Johannesburg and say you're really one of the *ou manne*, that you didn't sit out the whole war with your thumb up your arse."

There is nervous laughter in the spectator's gallery when I relate this, and I see some of the reporters busily scratching in their notebooks. They will replace the major's actual words with some innocuous euphemism, perhaps calling it a colorful phrase. There is more I have to tell, though. After Lyddie has radioed in the results of our "contact," we will have to bury the bodies. We do this ostensibly because dead flesh rots rapidly out here, if the scavengers don't get it first. Already there are vultures overhead, a wheeling mass of them. They're still afraid to land because some of the two-legged creatures below them walk upright among the many that lie in odd, still positions on the ground.

We went back to our camp then—I tell the commissioners. The usual procedure to evacuate casualties, I'd always understood, was to try to land the helicopters with the doctors and medical equipment as close to the field as possible, but we moved our own dead and wounded back to camp in jeeps and armored vehicles—the two new Casspirs and a Rinkhals that had come belatedly to the battle site. Back at camp, we drink brandy and beer while the men guffaw, slap each other on the back, and repeat their stories of how they took out this guy who was aiming right at them or blasted ten terrorists with a single grenade. There is little mention of the black cavalry who saved our white behinds. Lyddie keeps talking about what a good shot I turned out to be: "He can cook and he can shoot. If he was a woman, why, I'd marry him." Me, I feel ill as I relive that instant when the Owambo man's face split apart nanoseconds after I pulled my rifle trigger. My sole distractions are the helicopters that fly off with first our injured, then our dead, like great birds with their bellies full of flesh.

Most of the next day we do nothing. I eat a desultory breakfast of cold scrambled eggs, accept the bottle of Klippies passed to me. It helps the headache I brewed in a night of hard drinking, but it does not get me drunk. There is no relieving my burden of consciousness.* The soldiers who had spent the night in the battlefield on hyena watch—and perhaps to make sure no more PLAN† fighters pass through this natural corridor—return around ten, relieved from duty by a group who had delayed to have breakfast and nurse their hangovers. Lyddie spends most of his time in the radio tent talking and occasionally shouting at someone at some central command unit. Finally he storms out, obviously furious, grabs a beer from a surprised warrant officer who has just opened it for himself, and growls: "The bloody graders aren't going to get here until tomorrow or the next day."

"Well, I hope nobody else gets here first," the Koevoet lieutenant says. "It could get embarrassing."

"The number of vultures circling around, even those blind bastards from the U.N. are going to figure something is up. Maybe we can tell them there's been a lion kill."

"No joke. We caught a hyena today trying to sneak past us with a guy's arm in its mouth," Ginger-hair says with a laugh. "Hannie started shooting at it and nearly killed Smit and Pisang, he's such a lousy shot. The hyena got away, but he dropped the arm and this is what I found on it." He fishes into his pocket, then holds up a watch on a silver band.

"Does that dingus work? It looks like a pretty nice watch for a fucking garden boy."

"Ja, but it keeps Cuban time. . . . I'll have to turn it ahead twenty years."

* A favorite Roelof phrase, his rationale for the soldiers who were drinking themselves blind (or, to use the expressive Afrikaans/English term, *poeg*-eyed).

† People's Liberation Army.

There is more laughter. All the *ou manne* have been cracking jokes ferociously since the firefight; the way to blot out the memory of singing, celebrating men getting shot to pieces, I suppose. The Koevoet guys are pretty proud of the fact that they've officially been disbanded, that they're just ghosts, not really here . . . so the massacred bodies represent a particularly bad case of suicide. They've started to talk about the killing ground as "Jonestown."

Another night and day of waiting. The men take turns sitting guard at Jonestown, but I am fortunately spared this task. Lyddie has a small traveling chess set in a faded blue velvet case, and he and I play several games. I've read Pandolfi and a smart little English book called *The Chess Mind*, and for a short time I was on the high school chess team. I usually win but find it mentally exhausting; it's only with great difficulty that I can focus on the game at hand and not get lost in all the possible past games it will lead up to. Ginger-hair turns out to be a smart but erratic player, getting the only win off me with a series of creative knight-and-bishop combinations. Around four, we see a large cloud of dust moving slowly toward us, and at dinner the armored vehicles with attached earth-moving plow blades arrive. The sergeant in charge, a short man with thinning straw-colored hair and a remarkably creased face (as if laugh lines have been cut into his cheeks, then the artist changed his mind and scored in the buccal and maxillary crease lines a second time), says they could fit up lights and get to work that night, but Lyddie says we've waited this long it can hold until morning.

He rouses me at first light and we drive to Jonestown, mugs of steaming porridge in our laps. Although we're jouncing around, I try to eat breakfast before we get to our destination. I have all of my film equipment in the back of the jeep, and yesterday I gave Lyddie some pointers on using the camera, so he jokes now about being my assistant. It turns out that there was not much need to hurry. I film the earth-movers digging a deep trench in the place Lyddie has directed them, but it's obvious that it is going to take a while. The air is filled with the sweet, deeply nauseating scent of bodies turning ripe, and the fallen figures are stiff with rigor mortis, lying around in peculiar attitudes like badly handcrafted sculptures. Around midday we break for lunch, driving around to the far side of the kopje where we can get away from the smell. I think that there is no possibility I'm going to eat, but I turn out to be quite hungry, as usual, and the sandwiches contain fresh roast chicken brought by the grading crew.

"When you're finished *vressing* that *sarmie*, you might as well have a rest," Lyddie says, rolling up his bush jacket for a pillow. "It'll be at least a couple of hours before there's anything for us to do."

I too lie back against the sun-baked rock, warm and inviting as a woman's body, and shield my eyes from the glare with my hat. I can't sleep, as before my eyes lie the sculpted, twisted dead, the arid plain that is their last rest. I can hear the whine of the machinery over the hill, the grinding of the loader's toothed shovels against intransigent compressed earth. I sit up once to change my position, and in doing so I startle a slim brown snake that glides away effortlessly over the rock, its head an arrow, its body a slim line of moving fluid. Amid all the harshness and death, beauty. I lie down and close my eyes, try to see the liquid arrow of the escaping snake, not the cruel rigor of murdered bodies. It comes as a relief, then, when Lyddie says it's time to go back.

The machines are idle now, the soldiers who manned them having a quiet smoke in whatever shade their vehicles offer. They have managed to create a trench about ten feet wide and eight feet deep, and fifteen to eighteen feet long. It does not look large enough to hold the sixty-eight bodies that lie on the ground at various distances from their burial site. "Fok," Lyddie mutters. "I'm not hiring these guys to build a swimming pool for me. I'd be at the other end in two strokes."

"The ground here is packed hard as bloody rock, man," one of the nearby soldiers answers.

"It'll have to do, I suppose," Lyddie replies. He shouts orders to our own men, and they begin to pick up bodies in a businesslike fashion, dividing into pairs with one taking an arm and the other a leg to haul the corpse unceremoniously to the pit's edge. "Pack them in tight, like sardines," our captain says. "We need a couple of feet of earth near the top or the hyenas will just dig them up again."

I follow the men around, filming their actions, trying to keep my rebellious stomach in control. One of the soldiers looks at my green face and drops the dead man's leg that he is holding, his fingers clearly imprinted on the bare flesh, to toss me a pack of cigarettes. "This'll help blot out the smell, man," he says. I don't normally smoke, but looking around me I can see all the men are puffing away like the engines of a coal train, chain-lighting one cigarette after another. I light up a Lucky, and the acrid smoke stings my nostrils but it is a relief.

I am some distance from the trench, filming the pair who shared their cigarettes with me, when I notice Lyddie standing behind me. "Here, let me take a turn with the camera, Sweetbread. You go relieve Verster there," he orders, standing very close to me. I look at his face, aghast, and shake my head. "I'm not *asking* you, my boy," he hisses. "Or do you want me to fuck you up?" I look over at the two soldiers. Verster bends and rubs his hands in the dirt, then straightens up to stand washing his palms with the red dirt of Namibia. His companion, a burly man almost my height, is still holding the dead guerrilla's wrists and is staring at me balefully, his large head rigid with anger, his eyes red. Shaken, I go over and take the corpse's feet.

"No virgins in this army," Lyddie comments jovially. I can hear the whirring of the cine-camera as he follows us. We carry the body as you would a beach chair, trying to keep it level so no body fluids run down onto our hands. "How's about a smile, Sweetbread?" Lyddie calls. I give him a dirty look. "That's not going to do anything for the girls back home," he jokes. The burly fellow begins to cackle with laughter, a high snorting sound, and soon I can't help myself and a silly grin spreads across my face. We reach the edge of the trench and, still giggling, toss the body into the heap below. The bodies lie like bundles of sticks in higgledy-piggledy combinations, not neatly stacked as Lyddie would have had it. Here and there, a black arm or leg pokes up out of the pile, the most recognizable sign that these were once humans . . . and how tempting it is to forget that very fact.

"One more and you're done," Lyddie tells me. "Come on. You bagged two, you tidy up two. Don't always expect others to do your dirty work for you. Come on, just think of it as stacking firewood."

I stand glumly, trying hard to resist the temptation to rub my hands on my pants. The next corpse we come to is of a large, fat man, his stomach grotesquely bloated. The burly soldier goes over to him, pulls out his knife, and pierces the stomach as if he were vandalizing a car tire. "We don't want that exploding all over us when we haul him. He's so bloody big, we better each grab a foot." We do this and drag the corpse over to the trench, trying not to listen to the sickening sounds of the head bumping against the rocky ground. We stop at the edge of the trench, and have to get behind the body and push to make it roll in. I turn my head suddenly and spew vomit to the side, almost splashing Lyddie's boots in the process.

"Christ," he exclaims. "Show some consideration."

I go over to the pile of dirt waiting to be shoveled back into the ground and plunge both hands into it, frantically rubbing it all over my hands to try to get the awful feeling of dead flesh out of my fingers and palms. I keep rubbing my hands together until the palms are raw and thoroughly scoured. "Stop that nonsense, Lady MacBeth," Lyddie's voice comes from behind me. "I need you to film this last bit, then we can go back to camp and relax with some cold beers."

I follow him numbly, take the movie camera up again, and film the heavy machinery pushing dirt into the trench. I try to focus on the technicalities of filming amid dust and bright sunlight, to ignore the lurking sensory memory beneath the pain of abraded fingers and raw palms. After all the dirt has been bulldozed into the trench and the bodies are hidden from sight, Lyddie orders the drivers to go back and forth to spread any remaining soil as widely as possible. He has also sent out some of our own guys to gather up whatever scraggly bushes and shrubs they can find to replant over this mound after it has been pressed down flat by repeated driving over it with the Casspirs. "I don't want this place to be too obvious from the air," he says.

Finally we are back in the camp, and like everyone else I drink the cold Castles and slugs of Klipdrift until my face feels as numb as my soul. Drunk as I am, I cannot sleep, the events of the day recurring over and over again with all their smells, feel, and images. I spend much of the night in the far corner of the camp, away from everybody else, retching over and over again until there is nothing left but a dry, painful rasping. One of the soldiers on watch comes over and gives me a fistful of boiled sweets, which help a little until I throw them up too.

In the morning, Lyddie looks at my face and tells me that I'll be going back with the crease-faced captain. He goes to the radio tent for a while, then comes back and tells me I'll be glad to hear I'm going to Oshakati for some R and R. . . .

"We can see from the medical record how successful that was," Dini cuts in, standing up and striding toward the commissioners with a folder full of papers in her hand. "It took another six months before Paul could sleep without having to be shot full of tranquilizers. And even now he has constant nightmares."

"Not only tranquilizers, Miss Van Vuuren," says De Kok in his bass growl. "I've also looked at the medical papers, and I believe our friend here was on a major antipsychotic drug, Thorazine, for a while. This medication is used to treat schizophrenia, I believe."

"It's the most common treatment for PTSD— " Dini blurts out, then loses her temper. "And don't you try to pretend the witness is schizophrenic, you understand me. You lot have done enough damage to him already."

"We have testimony in the Cape sessions about the pharmaceuticals used for traumatic stress," the chairperson says mildly, "and I believe that Miss Van Vuuren is quite correct concerning the widespread use of this medication."

"I haven't done anything to hurt your witness, so you owe me an apology. I'm just pointing out one of the illnesses this drug is often used for." De Kok is true to his pattern of trying to get in the last word. And here he drags out his usual guttural pronunciation of the word *drug* to maximum effect. I catch a grin on one or two of the Commission members' faces when he does this; like me, they cannot help admiring the skilled bluster of the old goat.

...

Now Advocate De Kok has moved to a seat in my direct line of vision so as to ask me some questions. (We try to avoid the term *cross-examination*, to maintain the illusion this is all just a friendly fact-finding inquiry.) He is silent at first, beaming at me in an avuncular way. In spite of myself, I smile back.

"Are you feeling better now?" His tone is kind, genuinely solicitous.

"There is nothing wrong with the witness," Dini leaps in, tag-teaming him too soon. De Kok handles the interruption superbly, raising one thick eyebrow to show he is tolerant of the ill-mannered interruption.

"Of course not. But these testimonials are hard on all of us. Even the advocates, who have a little tendency to fly off at the handle now and then, Miss Van Vuuren. Yes, these times—these times of change—are difficult and confusing times for all of us. It becomes hard to know what is up and what is down, what is fantasy and what is real, what is true and what is imaginary. Everything is *deurmekaar* these days, all mixed up. So, I hope you will give me a little time to ask my questions in my old-fashioned way, as I have not quite caught up with all the changes." He winks at Dini in a friendly manner, grins at the chairman, basks his sunny visage on me. Dini smooths her skirt and reluctantly sits back down.

"I must start by saying how much I admired the little memory show you put on"—he smiles again at me. "I'm sure my grandchildren would enjoy it. Do you ever perform at children's parties? It could make you a nice income, you know. I am reminded of the hypnotist I once saw: he told a fellow an onion was an apple, and that good chap ate the raw onion like it was the most delicious Granny Smith he'd ever encountered."

"I don't see how this is relevant," Dini says, but is motioned into silence by the chairman.

De Kok goes on, hardly missing a beat. "That hypnotist also got people to perform amazing feats of memory with random numbers and words, a lot like you did. You know, you could take me outside right now and ask me to describe everybody in this room, I would only remember a few—the lovely Miss Van Vuuren, our witness, Major Lyddie, one or two of the commission members. But I'm told that if I were hypnotized, I would remember every face and even what people were wearing!"

"Are you saying Mr. Sweetbread has been hypnotized?" Dini interjects, pronouncing the last word with as much contempt as she can muster.

"Not at all, not at all. But . . ." He holds his hand up to emphasize the pause, spacing out each of the words in his next sentence. "He could be wrong! It has not been established—truly been established—that his memory of events that have happened in the real world is any more accurate than yours or mine. Or Major Lyddie's."

Having unwrapped my gift of total recall and demolished it as rapidly and carelessly as a child with a fragile birthday present, he proceeds to run through much of my earlier testimony. He has brought with him some paperwork from the army—orders that had sent my division somewhere else than where I had claimed to have been at the time. "Those orders must have never reached us, or been changed," I said. "Orders from Pretoria went astray all the time." When asked for proof, I had to admit that I wouldn't have been privy to the orders anyway, not being an officer, but I was certain the army files were not all totally accurate and that surely orders did get changed and rescinded. I had run into Jan Burger in a café in Johannesburg about a year after my National Service ended, and he told me that he kept getting first-time call-up notices, and when he complained was told that there was no record of his ever being in the army. He figured that the army had expunged documents relating to the recces and other SADF soldiers involved in secret operations so that this information wouldn't fall into the hands of the ANC government after the elections. "When I asked what I should do with the call-up notice, the *ou* said, 'Just tear it up, that's what most people do,'" he remarked, smiling at the irony of an army spokesperson advocating draft resistance, but with something else on his face akin to shame or regret.

Finally, De Kok is through with me and I get to step down . . . feeling that I have had my flesh stripped off ream by ream, but in the kindest way possible. When I sit down beside her, Dini grasps my hand and murmurs that it has gone pretty well, all considering.

Then it is Lyddie's turn. He looks reduced, seated in public view with earphones clamped to his head as he tries to speak into a thin microphone that protrudes from the table before him. He now appears as a humble soldier, often searching for the right word. He admits to giving the orders to shoot the soldiers descending on his base. But Swapo were the ones who'd violated the truce by crossing the border before a cease-fire was in effect. "Sam Nujoma wanted to get a jump-start on intimidating the voters," he says. "This is a well-established fact."

When he had seen a large contingent of the enemy approaching, he had done what any professional soldier would have done. It was his responsibility, and he would have to live with the consequences. "Don't forget, I lost six of my men in that firefight, and had nearly a dozen wounded. I don't take these things lightly." But, he insisted, he had performed his duty and he felt to this day that the insurgents were trying to take advantage, even the U.N. findings backed him up on that! Yes, it's true what Trooper Sweetbread said: orders do go astray. Sometimes the air force even bombed our own servicemen because someone got the coordinates wrong. As for the story about the Kaokoland village, he did not make war on children. "I like children," he says in injured tones.

Now it is De Kok who interrupts from where he has been busily and noisily rummaging through his papers: "Yes, this is the absolute truth. Major Lyddie received a commendation for rescuing three African kids while under fire. I have a photograph here verifying that fact." He passes around a five-by-eight glossy showing an intent-looking Lyddie and the corporal running from a smoldering half-destroyed hut with children in their arms. I have to admit it's quite impressive, even knowing that the photographers couldn't have gotten there until hours later, and that the Swapo terrorists were miles away at the time, getting their heads blown off by a very effective ambush on the part of the Permanent Forces.

My version of events is the product of a fevered imagination, Lyddie continues. "Trooper Sweetbread tried his best, don't get me wrong, but he was weak; he was often sick. He even gave himself sunstroke by going without his hat. I tried to take an interest in him and show him what it means to be a real soldier, but he really wasn't cut out for that line of work." He points out that this was the problem with conscription, especially in the later years, when men who should have been G4K4* were assigned to combat units.

"Sweetbread really wasn't any good at any of the things the army called upon him to do, not even the photography," Lyddie concludes. "I'm not saying he's deliberately telling lies, but the story of one's martyrdom is much more compelling than the story of one's own incompetence. He's not a bad fellow, and I mean him well. I just think he's confused and he takes life a bit too hard."

Dini questions him rigorously, not tripping him up but forcing him more and more often into stock answers. War is war. It is not a picnic. When elephants fight, the grass and trees suffer. He regrets any loss of life but his job was to defend his country and his people. "We all believed in what we were doing," he says pointedly. "That's why we gave the best years of our lives to the army."

When Lyddie steps down, I find it hard to say which side would call the questioning a success. It seems about equal. De Kok asks if there is time for one more witness, and, after a short break for tea, we are back in the hearing room to see Dr. Vishinski take the stand. He is a tall, thin figure, his hair and pointed beard slightly more grizzled than the last time I

* A rating for someone whose disabilities would constrain them to a job with minimal physical responsibility. G1K1 would be for an individual able to handle any military requirements of physical or mental toughness.

saw him some ten years ago, but it's the same Dr. Vish I conjure up when my demons get bad, the guide who helped pull me through when my own gifts threatened to engulf me.

"That's my old shrink, Dr. Vish," I murmur to Dini, amazed to see him in this place. "Has Major Lyddie been going to him too?"

She gives me a pitying look.

"Not Lyddie, Paul," she says. "He's here to talk about you."

Seeing my horror, she quickly grasps my hand. "Don't worry. He's limited in what he can reveal, and if he tries to cross that line, *I'll* sit on his head." Her face hardens, the steel showing beneath her symmetrical exterior. Dini has tied her soft light brown hair tightly back, but a single fawn-colored tendril has escaped to dangle over her round cheek. I fix my eyes on this strand of hair, a lifeline of some sort.

"What's he doing here?" I cry out in my anguish. "I mean, that's the doctor my mother sent me to as a kid."

"Hush, Paul. Try not to get upset. I'm sure his treatment of you was in line with the standards of his profession, but, you know, your doctor friend has some skeletons in his cupboard. I've been researching him for another case I'm working on."

I picture Dr. Vish as a bony relic grinning at me, the yellowing jawbone propped up on steeple-making fleshless fingers. I quickly snap down the magic slate to dispel the image. But when I look up again, Dr. Vishinski is still there, swearing to tell the Commission the whole truth. De Kok spends some time establishing the good doctor's credentials—the papers he has given, the conferences he has attended, his degrees, his awards and citations. He asks if Dr. Vish knows me, and my friend says yes, of course, I came for treatment with him as a child and saw him regularly up until the time I went into the army.

"And what was your reaction when Mr. Sweetbread said he would be performing his National Service?"

"I tried to recommend gently that he get a deferral while he went to university."

"And why is that?"

Dr. Vish looks uncomfortable. "I felt he was still rather fragile. He had had some difficult times emotionally. Sorry, Paul."

"You didn't suggest a psychiatric deferment? You were in a position to help him get one, no?"

"I'm afraid I've always been very wary of *that* means of getting out of the army. It labels the young person in a most destructive way. It's a hard diagnosis to recover from, and I've seen people whose doctors thought they were doing them a favor deteriorate when they have been so labeled. You will never get a government job, there are a lot of doors closed to you. And then there are the personal doubts, the fear that you really are mentally unstable. I hope we have come a long way from the days when we called emotionally troubled patients crazy and put them out of sight, but, you know, the stigma is still there. I also wanted Paul—Mr. Sweetbread, I mean—to make his own decisions . . . even if they were not the ones I would have chosen for him. That would be the only way to achieve some independence and mental toughness of the sort you need in order to survive in this country. In that, if not much else, I am in agreement with Major Lyddie." He rests his hands in that steeple-making gesture, but briefly. I can see that this is not a place he wants to be.

De Kok asks about my relationship to authority figures, but Dr. Vish says he would never, given his professional adherence to confidentiality, ever go into details of my treatment without my permission. De Kok then asks if I mind this line of questioning, and I shake my head no. Dini interjects that any specific details of our patient-doctor conversations will need to be vetted carefully first, and De Kok promises to keep his questions general. "Dr. Vishinski is an honorable and well-respected member of the medical establishment. He will know how to answer *professionally*, I'm very sure," he says. He repeats his earlier question, and Dr. Vish says that the sudden and tragic loss of my father at an early age was the source of much of my pain, that I both needed and rebelled against any substitute father figures.

There ensues some further wrangling over whether it is okay to have Dr. Vish give his diagnosis of my condition, and Dini and De Kok approach the chairman to present their arguments less publicly. I hear De Kok reprove Dini for condescending toward me—"he's a grown-up, for God's sake, so let him hear the truth like anyone else." Finally, the chairman calls me over and asks if I am all right with having my therapist give some details of his diagnosis—nothing too personal or embarrassing, just the outlines. I am curious to hear what he has to say, so I make no protest.

"Perhaps my diagnosis is a trifle unconventional," Dr. Vish says with an affectionate glance in my direction. "What I came to conclude was that Mr. Sweetbread suffers from delusions of memory. The human mind does funny things in response to overwhelming trauma—sometimes we blot the bad event out completely, so it never happened. Other times, we re-create it over and over in our minds, adding new details each time. Paul was one of the haunted ones, replaying his father's suicide continually; remember, he witnessed the discovery of his father's body. He essentially split his psyche into two entities: one, the everyday 'normal' person; the other, a hypertrophied, prodigious recording device that was beyond his control, what he so eloquently called his 'poisoned gift.' I felt that any empowerment in his tenuous and fragile situation would help him survive, so, perhaps mistakenly, I did not disillusion him but helped instead to suggest mechanisms that might give him a sense of agency. This way his novel defense would not in itself become an illness worse than what it had sprung up to cure. This dissociation is a form of PTSD, albeit an unusual one, and I have to say that it did predate his military service. I think that covers it."

"Thank you, Mr. Vishinski—I mean, Doctor," Dini says sarcastically. "It's nice to see you know when to stop. Now I have some questions about *you*. How would you characterize your relationship with military intelligence and the National Security Management Services?"

"I have no such relationship."

"Let me rephrase that. When SADF intelligence called you to ask about former patients of yours who were seeking exemption on psychiatric grounds, how did you respond?"

"With discretion. Miss Van Vuuren, I would never betray a patient's confidences."

"You're quite sure of that? Did you not tell the army some of your former patients were mentally fit for armed service, although their current psychologists had come to the opposite conclusion?"

"I've already explained my opposition to that practice. We can't be sure of the long-term effects of labeling an individual mentally unfit for National Service, and that diagnosis should certainly not be made on the basis of politics, as I am afraid some of my colleagues did. If the SADF wanted to know whether *my* diagnosis would provide grounds for a patient to be absolved of their legally mandated National Service, I felt it was quite within my rights and professional responsibilities to tell them the truth. It is the specifics of a patient's revelations during therapy that it is wrong to reveal, as you pointed out."

"One last question, Doctor. Did you warn your patients beforehand that this was your policy? Did you inform them that the SADF was in the habit of checking in with you when your patients went elsewhere?"

"No. I didn't see the need. And I think you're presenting a false sense of a pattern here."

"You didn't see the need? You were aware of the unusually high rate of suicide among army conscripts, but you didn't see the need to keep your patients informed of a policy that certainly affected them?"

"If I thought a patient was potentially suicidal, certainly I would have done everything in my powers to help him! Those were stressful times, especially for the young men on whose shoulders the defense of South Africa rested. And you know, there were often no clear indicators just who might break down when they were out in the field—"

"Not only that, Miss Van Vuuren," De Kok interrupts, "there's a lot of evidence that anti-army propaganda caused the confusion in young men's minds, and that's what led to nervous breakdowns and even suicides. They're still treating ex-soldiers in America for psychiatric disturbances, thanks to all the anti-Vietnam propaganda."

"How interesting. And I thought it was the pointless killing of Vietnamese peasants that led to those breakdowns. That and Agent Orange."

"Ja, well those are the lies *you*'ve chosen to believe. Nobody has cornered the market on truth, Dini van Vuuren. You believe your propaganda and I'll believe mine."

Seeking to avoid a catfight among the advocates, the Commission chair calls it a day. Dr. Vish steps down with dignity, giving me a last look that is at once sorrowful and seeking to convey reassurance. I want to tell him not to worry about me, though I'm not at all sure he shouldn't. Dini is breathing heavily after her tiff with De Kok, but her flushed face shows satisfaction too. She thinks she has helped me by undercutting Dr. Vish's testimony. Yet I need only look at him and I am back in his office, a small child attentive to the only adult who seems aware of the enormous burden that child's memory imposes, the only one to offer relief without ridicule. I fear that Dini has well-meaningly sliced through one more guyline that holds my unruly zeppelin still tethered to the ground. I hope I am not called back tomorrow. It would not take much to send me soaring into the upper reaches of the already oxygen-thin Highveld atmosphere. "Let's go fly a kike . . ." Dad sang, after he had taken me to the bioscope to see *Mary Poppins*. "Up to the highest hike." I would not be surprised to see our two ardent Afrikaans advocates—aardvarks, *aasvoëls*—go singing and dancing together arm-in-arm out of this hearing room before launching themselves into the air.

"Step in time, Dini," I murmur.

"Sorry?"

". . ."

"You feel like having a nosh, or are you utterly exhausted?" she asks, patting me solicitously on the shoulder.

...

For once I am not hungry, but I let myself be talked into going anyway. I try to beg off at first, claiming truthfully that I need to have a shower before I go anywhere. I want to wash off the stink of all this truth-telling, to let the image of Dr. Vish's bowed head slip down the drain with the soapy water, to rinse away that momentarily grasped contemptuous sneer of Major Lyddie at the end of the day, when he thought only his advocate was looking his way. Dini chuckles and says that she doesn't mind my being a little sweaty, so I shouldn't be the one to complain. Besides, it will be good for the foreign tourists to be near some genuine South African perspiration, the real thing, and so when they go back to their sterile international hotel in Sandton they will wonder what is missing there.

Dini starts her car, but before she pulls out she turns and gazes intently into my face, a mere foot of airspace separating us. "I know you have a soft spot for Major Lyddie," she breathes. "I don't know why, although it's not uncommon for people to identify with their persecutors, especially when you're stuck with them for long periods of time. But listen, I intend to *get* him." Determination crosses her even features, making her for a moment not pretty. "He hurt you, you know?" she says softly. "And I don't like that. I don't like bullies, especially if they pick on someone like you."

"And what am I like?" I smile at her.

"You're good," she says simply. "You don't have to beat people up and shoot things to be a man. I like that you're someone who thinks, and is sensitive."

For some reason, this brings tears to my eyes and I look away. She grabs my hand and gives it a warm squeeze.

"Hey," she says. "We're celebrating now. We're gonna have a good time tonight."

"That sounds like an order."

"It is if I say so, troepie."

We go to a restaurant named after one of my true heroes: our country's greatest food writer, the author of *Bushveld Doctor*, the poet, botanist, and roving gourmand Christian Louis Leipoldt. (As a child, I had secretly wished that our public education system—Christian National Education—had been named after him instead of being a descriptive term. Might we not then have beaten our swords into frying pans, our rifles into ladles?) When I moved to my flat in Hillbrow, I did not bother bringing the more fanciful *First Catch Your Camel*, Laurens van der Post's contribution to African cookery. But I kept my Leipoldts. The eponymous restaurant serves not only our national dishes—*bobotie*, *geelrys*, *sosaties*—but also the very fauna the tourists have come here to photograph: crocodile, bushpig bacon, saddle of springbok, python. All is served in large aluminum vats (shades of the army's *varkpanne*!), and the shoulders you nudge while ladling your food belong to speakers of French, German, Swedish, American English, and Japanese. It becomes hard to know what you've put on your plate: is this pallid meat bathed in a cream sauce crocodile or python or plain old chicken? Was the bushpig wild or raised on a game farm? And was the ostrich overcooked to start, or did it turn into leather on the warming pan?

We have been placed at a corner table, with a tall tapering candle in the center. "After the ordeal, a romantic dinner," I blurt.

"Why not?" Dini says. She places her hand on my arm. It is an interesting, contradictory hand—from the knuckles to the styloid processes it is childishly foreshortened, but the fingers themselves are long and graceful. Her palm is soft and warm, her finger pads callused from the reins of the horses she likes to ride on her days off. "I know this has been hard on you, but what you've done today is important."

"You sure?"

She nods emphatically. "Ja, I'm sure. You see, people forget bloody fast. A year from now, we'd be hearing the stories of how Lyddie was a protector of the innocent, a kindly paternal gent trying to bring progress and order to the primitive savages of Namibia as they march into the twenty-first century. Now there is no hiding what sort of killer he really is."

"And it does the world good to know that?"

"The truth shall set you free. It's the Commission's motto, but I believe in it. Don't you?"

"I don't know. I'm not being cynical, but I'm wary of mottos that offer to make you free. I don't want to see '*Wahrheit macht frei*' emblazoned on the walls of this country. Sure, lies trap you into more lies, into doing things you wouldn't believe of yourself, but I'm not at all sure the reverse is true."

"You have the right instincts, but you think too much. That can become paralyzing, and we don't want that." Dini grins at me when she says this, her hand still resting on my arm, her pupils enlarged as they peer into my face.

"I'm a Zeno's paradox in the flesh," I murmur.

"Well, maybe you can get more than halfway tonight." She grins, lifting up her wine glass in a silent toast. "Have some more of this lovely Shiraz. Maybe it'll help turn off that brain of yours for a while." We clink glasses. It is Friday night, and while this may not be a traditional *brochah*,* it is a blessing all the same. Perhaps by consuming the fruit of the vine brought over to Africa by this lovely woman's Huguenot ancestors, by eating my native fauna, I will return to myself. Perhaps this is a coming-of-age story after all.

...

After dinner, and after a long, lingering intimate conversation over Cape brandy and Zimbabwean coffee, Dini and I decide to walk off the effects of our large meal. Once outside, I hesitate, crooking my arm toward her as I had seen Claude do with Mother. Dini chortles affectionately and says, "Ag, what a gentleman!" But she does reach up and embrace my arm in hers, and we stroll in this slightly awkward way along the empty street. My mind tells me we should fear mugging, but my attention is fixed on the warmth and softness of the narrow strip of her flesh that so lightly touches mine. All my senses focus on this tiny contiguous border holding us together, and the Johannesburg night seems to

* Claude had performed the Kiddush at his wedding to Mother—*Baruch atah adonai, elohenu melech ha-olam, borei pri hagofen*—words I had not heard spoken since last my father said them at Passover, one of the few holidays we celebrated. (We celebrated none after his passing.) Had spoken with the same Litvak intonation: *bowruch ataw adonnoy* as his successor.

fade from my awareness. I am conscious of breathing very hard, as if I have been made to do a lengthy uphill run with full kit, and I start to worry that Dini will notice my stertorous respiration.

There is light coming from one building, a neon sign, to be exact, that reads "No. 12 Bomb Squadron." The windows are dark, though, and we try to peep in through the glass door to see whether there is really anything here, imagining men with leather caps and flyers' goggles exchanging droll tales of night flights over Tobruk, Mersa Matruh, and El Wak. We linger there long enough to attract attention, for the door swings open and a very drunken bartender beckons us in with an overelaborate bow. "Come on in," he says in thickly accented slurred tones, "this is a *lekker* bar with *lekker* people in it."

How can anyone resist such a welcome? Inside, there are mostly empty tables with small glass pots of light on them, candles in a vase meshed with nylon netting. A few thick-bodied men sit on barstools, swiveling their heads to look at us with dull eyes. These are Brueghel's tipplers, but with all the jollity removed and only the drunkenness remaining. Behind them, barely visible on the ill-lit walls, are photographs of flying men, and dangling here and there from fishing line attached to hooks in the ceiling are incongruously precise models of Junker 86 Bombers and Hurricane and Hartebees biplanes.

Dini likes the place, enough at least that she asks me to get her a drink while she visits the w.c. I go to the bar and try to think what to order for her, the bartender swaying gently in front of me to the rhythm of his own bibulousness. He is tall and lank, with a scraggly beard and a mouth shrunken with missing teeth, his T-shirt rolled up at the biceps to hold a pack of cigarettes and reveal a vivid tattoo of a naked woman riding a B-52 like a bronco. He seems to read my mind, though, or at least to recognize my uncertainty. "How 'bout a nahss exotic drink for the lady? I make a helluva daiquiri." I order a helluva daiquiri for Dini and a Windhoek lager for myself, then go to sit at one of the booths in the corner, where I am soon joined by Dini, who slides onto the pillowed seat beside me. The barkeep brings us our drinks on unsteady legs, yet managing not to spill a drop from glasses filled to the rim. Dini laughs with delight when she sees the brimming glass with a wedge of pineapple on its edge accompanied by a silly umbrella toothpick. "How did you know just what I wanted?" she chuckles. She sips her drink, grimaces. "A heavy hand with the rum, our bartender friend."

I boldly reach over and take a sip, noticing the perfect red imprint of her lips on the far rim. "Hmmm. A delicate floral body with overtones of diesel and treacle pudding."

"Northern Suburb snob," she says, smiling with her eyes.

"Funny. That's what Captain Lyddie was trying to cure me of, something he never missed the opportunity to remind me about. I don't know why he bothered."

"You know, I thought about it too. I read all the records, obviously, and after a while I could see he wanted to convert you somehow. I think he could see you weren't like the others, that you wouldn't just go home and remember some rose-colored dream of '*lekker* days in the army.' He wanted your approval. Sort of pathetic, isn't it?"

As I contemplate Dini's features—her pale soft skin, unblemished except for that spray of sun-freckles on the nose, is delightfully free of the impasto makeup favored by so many young women from the suburbs; her eyes are large and luminous and lightly washed with cobalt blue; her expression gentle and placid, except when she is angry over some injustice—I think of how much she bears the best traits of her Huguenot ancestry. All I have learned would lead to the idea that she should have remained within her Afrikaner enclave, her paramour someone much more like Lyddie than like me.

"How did you escape the laager?" I ask her. "Shouldn't you be surrounded by almond-hedge thorns to keep Africa out?"

"Some of us Afrikaners have made a little progress since Van Riebeeck's day. But I suppose you're right, we do have to find our own way out of our circle of thorns. I think it was going abroad that made me realize how restricted my life had been, how what protects you keeps you stuck inside a small place. I decided that I want to live a larger life."

I tell her the story of Sedgewick's father: He had always been an adventurer, a wealthy filmmaker and bottle-store owner who had his youthful contacts in the ANC and had stayed friends with them through the years of banning, even visiting their headquarters in Lusaka. However, as he got richer and Johannesburg more violent—or rather, violent crime moved north and east from Soweto to the sheltered lands—he became more security-conscious. His large Houghton house, whose capacious garden filled with fruit trees had once been visible from the street, disappeared behind a tasteful hedge of oleander not so tastefully topped with razor wire. A few days after he had installed a new, high-tech security gate, he tried to leave his house and go to work, but the gate wouldn't let him out. He walked over to it to see what was wrong and discovered that it had been locked from the outside with an enormous padlock and thick-linked chain. He had needed to call in a locksmith to cut it with an oxyacetylene torch. He knew it must have been his friends who had decided to teach him the lesson that what shuts others out also shuts you in, but he never found out who had done it. Perhaps that was because the jokesters also started to enclose their goods and loved ones behind razor wire and electronic gates.

"It's exactly like that. You feel safe and protected, but you can't move, you can't breathe." She tells me of her early life, how everything was planned out for her. She was supposed to get married when she graduated from Potch*—"the poor man's Stellenbosch, you know"—to a Potgieter,† no less. A nice guy, she'd known him all her life, and she still regretted it in a way, her running off to find herself. He was married now, to someone else, and they had two beautiful children. "I could have been teaching my *kindertjies* to read, instead of tilting at the windmills of jus-

* University of Potchefstroom.

† Another illustrious name in Afrikaans history: Andries Potgieter (1792–1852) was one of the Voortrekker leaders, who crossed the Vaal River, helped found the city of Potchefstroom, and who achieved victories over the Matabele; his son Pieter was commandant-general of the South African Republic.

tice. Would the world be any worse off for it? I don't know." She had just woken up one day and realized that she couldn't live out a life someone else had mapped out for her.

"I had to do my own thing, my own *thang*. Like them." She indicates the couple who have gotten up to dance, or rather to lean into each other while they stumble around the room. He is box-shaped and burly, his short hair obviously kept trimmed with an electric razor; she is a blonde with dark roots, her sunken mouth where the molars are missing giving a poor imitation of a model's cheekbones. The jukebox is playing an old Marvin Gardens tune, Jimmy Buffett singing, "Why don't we get drunk and screw?" Sedgewick's father had the record in his extensive collection, the title of the song being listed for propriety's sake as "Love song from another point of view."

"Romantic, isn't it?" I smile. "I'm glad, though. I mean, I'm glad you're not sitting in some red-tiled house with a bunch of sprogs crawling all over you. You wouldn't be here with me then." I realize that this somber bar with its underworld inhabitants slipping beneath the surface of their barstools or clinging to each other on the dance floor must seem like a poor consolation prize for the middlebrow paradise her parents had envisioned for her, but I hope she will take the sentiment for its intent rather than its worth.

"You're sweet. I couldn't have lived that other life, which doesn't mean I don't miss it."

She tells me about her parents, who had both come as children to the city when their families lost their farms in one drought or another. City outskirts, really. Her grandfather had worked as a mine foreman; her father had done his Matric and then become a policeman. It was funny to be interrogating these cops on the witness stand, trying to find the holes in their amnesty applications. Pa had been one of them; though she could not believe he would have been party to torture and assassination . . . she has to admit that's exactly the thinking of the families of the men who calmly narrated how they had eaten their sandwiches while some murdered activist's body burned nearby. (This hideous caricature of the Sunday afternoon *braaivleis*!) Not that she could ever ask him. Like so many Afrikaans men, he had eaten boerewors and fatty mutton for lunch and dinner, eggs and bacon for breakfast, smoked three packs a day, and liked his brandy at night, and in his mid-forties he had keeled over on his way from the dining room to the parlor to watch television. It was only a few months after she had precipitously gone abroad, and her mother had long blamed her. "I come from a long line of people with bad hearts," she says, smiling wryly.

"Hold that thought," I tell her. "I'm going to powder my nose and then get us more drinks."

As I am heading toward the gents', I notice that the male half of the dancing couple has peeled himself away and is staggering toward a booth where sit two couples whose arrival I had not noticed, so intent had I been on Dini. The newcomers are well dressed, the men wearing pin-striped jackets and matching trousers, the women in fifties-style fashionable dresses that cling tightly to their plumply curved bodies. They are probably no wealthier than the other patrons of the bar, but black South Africans dress up to go out on the town while their white counterparts go to equal lengths to look shabby and down-at-the-heel. *Trouble*, I think. It's not that I'm surprised to see them in the bar. Integration in this country has long been like Schroedinger's cat: it's always been there, but if you try to look at it directly it disappears without a trace. Now, suddenly, it is in plain sight and we are all trying to avoid being seen to stare in astonishment at this feline—no domestic cat, he, but a full-grown, black-maned lion grooming his lethal paws in the living room.

I ask the bartender for the same again, but he has anticipated me and already prepared the drinks. The Windhoek bottle says prominently on the lable that it is brewed according to the German Purity Laws, the *Reinheitsgebot*. I carry my sixteen fluid ounces of purity and Dini's miscegenated rum drink over to our table, not quite able to avoid some of the sticky liquid spilling over my knuckles. I lick it off after passing Dini her glass. She promptly spills quite a bit lifting it to her mouth and laughs merrily. "I'll use a serviette for now," she says, dabbing at her neck and chin. She purses her lips and looks at me shrewdly, and I blush. I *had* been thinking, just for an instant, of what it would be like to lap the viscous liquid off that dimpled chin. I look away in embarrassment and see the drunken dancer carrying a half dozen beers in his large fists over to the booth where the African couples sit.

They thank him and he pulls up a chair and launches back into the diatribe he had obviously broken off to get some more liquid refreshment. "You know, I don't understand you people," he says loudly. "I like to hunt, so I go to Botswana with some of my friends, right? This African *ou* at the border, he searches my car from top to bottom, giving me dirty looks the whole time from behind his dark glasses. 'Where'd you get the car?' he wants to know. Then it's the permits that have got to be checked and rechecked a hundred times, though there's nothing wrong with them in the first place. Then he has to go through our duffel bags. I say to him, 'what's it about? You've got your independence. You want bloody tourists. What's the point in giving me a hard time?'"

The younger of the black men nods in sage agreement, revealing his own tipsiness. "Policemen, heyyy! I don't like policemen. They always give me trouble too."

"Ja. The hell with the police. Let's drink to that." The Afrikaner raises his beer aloft, then downs half of it, leaving a whitish froth on his burnt umber mustache.

"What are you really saying?" one of the women asks. "We need the police. Not those Boers who liked to shoot us for doing nothing, but somebody to get the kids to listen. The kids are getting wild; they don't listen to their parents, they don't listen to their teachers. Never! They need *Role Models*, yes. How are they going to get a job if they don't go to school?"

"Ag, these days youngsters only expect someone else to pay for them. Black or white, it doesn't matter, they're spoiled," Leather Jacket says disgustedly. "I had to go to work when I was sixteen, but my son—he lives with his mother—he always wants me to buy him records, only now they're called CDs. He wants basketball shoes, as if I can afford to buy Air Jordans."

"They seem to have found common cause," I whisper to Dini.

"Consumer goods and the peace to enjoy them in, that's the great leveler. We're moving into a whole new set of distinctions: who has Nikes, who doesn't; who's well enough dressed to come into your shop or restaurant, who is not. It's going to be the color of your money that really counts."

"A cheering thought," I respond. "Especially for someone who is getting a degree in the lucrative field of cultural anthropology. Perhaps I should follow De Kok's advice and perform at children's parties."

"You'll be all right," Dini says, smiling. "I have faith in you."

The barman is back at our table with two new drinks. "On the house," he slurs. "A nice young couple like you should be having fun." He wanders back to the bar and puts on Jimmy Buffett again.

"A nice young couple of what?" I mutter, and Dini elbows me hard in the ribs. Everyone is having fun now. The older African man is collecting more cold Castles at the bar, his bald head shining in the rays of an overhead globe lamp; the younger one is talking earnestly to the toothless blonde, his own wife laughing loudly at something Leather Jacket has said.

"Don't get sour on me now," says Dini, motioning me to my feet. We dance, holding each other close until the music stops. Then we go over to the jukebox, where Dini is pleasantly surprised to find Kerkorrel's "Somer." "I love this song," she says. "It reminds me of happier times in the Cape." We dance while Ralph Rabie sings in his mellifluous Afrikaans, first about the clouds of the Cape and the sun sinking into the sea, then another song about how eternal is our Africa. Afterwards, we wander toward the door, calling out good night to the bar at large. A chorus of voices bids us good night, good night, *lekker bly*.

Outside, the African night is eternal, the Southern Cross gleaming through the orange light of Johannesburg's polluted skies. Dini has a firm grasp of my elbow and it is clear, without the words being spoken, that we are going back to her small, shared house in Yeoville. She sings softly the refrain of the song still echoing in our heads: Halala, halala. God bless. God bless. A nice young couple of what? But I am not, at this moment, nervous or cynical and I know in my heart that nothing will spoil this moment. Later, perhaps, but not now . . . and I will always have this now.

...

So, yes, mine is a *bildungsroman* after all. It's taken time to get here, but what is time when you think about it? For me it is ever-present . . . nothing that has happened is gone, though it might be changed. (Whether into the ghosts of tortured beings howling through the galleries where the Commission sits or, as the scientists have it, transformed into an information-bearing protein in the brain, I cannot say.) We have all become experts on the past, here in the New South Africa. Among all that is new here, the past is the newest thing yet. A fresh set of ancient bones belonging to some early hominid has been unearthed in Swartkrans, furthering the claim that all of mankind started in the southern tip of Africa, the true Garden of Eden. A paleontologist has shown through the patterned scratchings on ancient bone tools that our long-lost ancestor, *A. robustus*, supplemented his diet by digging for termites, much like the gorillas of today.

That which was covered is being unearthed. Our busy archaeologists are brushing away the accumulated dust on Iron Age settlements in the Kruger Park, formerly kept hidden from sight by a government holding tightly on to the myth that whites came up from the South at the same moment as the pastoral Bantu came down from the North. I have become involved in "cultural archaeology" in my own small way. I have gotten my students to go out and record the stories of the elders still living in the former Bantustans—gnarled, ancient human libraries dwelling in one-roomed, asbestos-roofed houses in Mmabatho—that their lives may not be lost to future generations. Now that the university that was so proud of being integrated is finally *integrated*, oral history means different things to different students. For some, it is leaving their comfortable suburban nests to venture for the first time into a world hitherto unimagined, but which was created in their name; for others, it's a long-overdue visit to Grandma or Great-Grandma, an "endorsement" to the countryside for educational purposes. There is even a museum of apartheid opening up; those days already relegated to Time Past, the midden of a failed and dead culture. And all around us Johannesburg's landmarks—the mine dumps, monuments in sand of the industry that built Ferreira's Camp into the Republic's major city—are disappearing. At night, lorry loads of the finely crushed rock mounds are stolen and hauled away, so the tailings can be leached with toxic chemicals of their last traces of gold.

It is only the future that has become more opaque, harder than ever to foretell. I have been looking at the ads in the *Weekly Mail* and the *Sowetan* for *Dial-a-Sangomas*—pay-per-call witch doctors. You call up the diviner and he or she will throw the bones while you are on the line and ask the ancestors what is causing your fatigue, love sickness, or bad luck. I've been considering giving one of these *inyangas* or *sangomas* a ring because I've been sleeping so poorly, although I otherwise feel better than I have in years. I can't say my luck has been bad, as I have a lecturing fellowship at Wits, although I did have to move out of my Hillbrow flat and am now occupying a smaller and more expensive place in Killarney. (I didn't want to move and had grown fond of the neighborhood, but Hillbrow is now a war zone, run by Nigerian drug lords. Most of the flats are horribly overcrowded, and after the second mugging, I felt that if I valued my life at all, I had to move.) I've lost weight, and I have joined a gym, where I have gotten vastly more fit with the help of Mr. Procrustes, one of the trainers. Still, I lie in bed at night and a host of images comes to me, a second-by-second replay of my army days, which were quite long enough in the original, thank you. My doctor, a dashingly handsome Cuban by the name of Hernandez—the adenoidal G.P. long ago emigrated to Toronto—has prescribed Nembutal, which does make me sleep but I awake unrested and with the feeling of a dark black hole where the night's hours should have been.

I suppose some of this is loneliness. I miss Dini—our being a "nice young couple" was never destined to last?—though I can briefly fill my solitary moments by consciously remembering our time together (Dini, face flushed, generous strands of her thick hair dangling over her face, laughing hysterically as I clumsily row us in circles at Zoo Lake . . . other, more amorous times when she is flushed of face and laughing). It's funny, but she got annoyed with me for the same reason that Lyddie did: that she could not reform me. When I told her, only half joking, that memory is itself a subversive act, she replied in all seriousness: "The time for subversion is over. You've got to stop living in the past, Paul. You're like an old rabbi endlessly studying the same passage in your Jewish Bible. Now it's time to *build up* the New South Africa."

On one of our last evenings together, Dini came to my old flat where I had prepared a fully vegetarian meal for her. (She described herself as a reformed carnivore, with occasional lapses.) I had set out two large blue wine glasses and lovingly cooked a cashew-nut *bobotie*—not a speck of minced meat in sight—and a *chole dal* with chickpeas, *garam masala*, and dried mango powder. She had been gloomy and furrowed of brow, hardly touched the food but treated the expensive Klein Constantia Riesling like fruit juice. When I asked about her day, she said she didn't want to talk about it, then glowered at me and said: "You always want everything to be nice, don't you?"

Now that I am living in Killarney, not too far from my old primary school, I make a different kind of venture into the past. I have gotten in the custom of taking long walks, partly to keep up the habit of exercise that the army had introduced to me, and partly because it was something Dini and I had enjoyed doing together. I find the rhythm of walking, particularly when you settle into the even stride necessary for a march of some duration, to be soothing and conducive to thought. One morning, my footsteps take me to the entrance of Barney Barnato Primary School, and I use the intercom at the security gate (something unheard of in my time) to ask the principal if I might not visit. He kindly invites me to come in and see him. This is not Mr. Burnside but his successor, a gray-haired, elegant gentleman, Mr. Nkosi, who has held the position since shortly after the general election six years ago.

The school that was once all-white and funded entirely by the government is now a Section 21 school, largely paid for by parents, Mr. Nkosi tells me. Students learn both English and Zulu, and admission is highly competitive. Mr. Nkosi is justifiably proud, and he takes me around to see the new buildings, which extend into what used to be our playing field. Our route takes us past flower beds as lush with mimosas, geraniums, and roses as they were in Burnside's day. While we walk, Mr. Nkosi tells me about Miss Tompkins, who died during apartheid's final gasp at the end of the 1980s. I was not surprised when he told me what she had been up to before her death. He had known her in another context, her extracurricular teaching of domestic workers in one of the volunteer programs run in defiance of the Bantu Education Act. "We used to have to move from house to house, just to teach people how to read." He chortles, as if this were one of the funnier things he had experienced. "Miss Tompkins was a great lady, very generous, and a fine teacher. She had a *big* funeral."

I am saddened that I had not known about her passing . . . and angry that Mother had not informed me of it. Though I suppose Mother had plenty to worry about concerning me without bringing in the death of my beloved schoolmistress. I asked about some of the other instructors. Mr. Coetzee? Retired. Mr. Duncan? The new principal knew the name but had not met him and did not know what had become of him. "I think he has gone somewhere up north. Maybe even Zambia." Mrs. Sanders? Nkosi smiles. "Now, here you are in luck, for she is due to retire this very year. Her class is just returning from midmorning break. Let's go and see if she has time to say hello."

We knock at the classroom door, and Rooibos Sanders opens it. But she is a much diminished Rooibos, a small, elderly, and clearly harmless lady. When the headmaster presents me, she gives me a quick hug, the top of her dyed red hair barely reaching my sternum. She seizes my hand and leads me inside. It could be my own childhood class, the children looking spruce and orderly in their uniforms, except for the computers in a row on one side of the room and the fact that the children come in many hues.

"Boys and girls, I want you to meet someone," she announces. She pauses to get their attention, looking at me with genuine fondness. "This is one of my favorite 'old boys,' Paul Sweetbread. I am so happy that he has come back to visit us. We had some great times in those days, back when Paul was my pupil."

Surprising me, the children applaud.

"Do you know, I used to call him Gogga?" Rooibos says affectionately.

Mother too is gone, having left me for the more salubrious climes of Australia only a few months after Dini's abandonment. Claude's daughter and grandchildren live in Sydney, and he wanted to be closer to them. "You know a country is in trouble when its Jews start leaving," Claude said, in one of his many pronouncements. "We are like the miner's parakeet, and we *are* all going . . . to Australia, Canada, Israel, you name it."

Not all of us. Although Mother encouraged me to emigrate as well, I told her no. "I would be happy to visit, though," I said. "I've never seen Australia, so I have trouble believing in it."

Now I try to focus on my work, but the thought constantly intrudes: What will become of us all? It is not just me I worry about. Johannesburg seems to have become a city out of control. It is no longer the place I know, but one of those vast African cities, chaotic and inexplicable. The money and the whites have moved out to Sandton, where settler life goes on with mere cosmetic alteration and a smattering of black people in business suits. The proliferation of ads for *sangomas, inyangas*, and "Genuine First-rate Zulu Witchdoctors" suggests I am hardly alone in the search for spiritual succor. A couple of times, I actually dial the number of one of the advertised *inyangas*, but lose courage and hang up. Then it occurs to me to ask my colleague, Jock Botha (a Scottish Boer, talk about strange amalgams), if there's anyone he'd recommend. His specialty is African divination systems, and he recently was honored at a Medical Association dinner for his help in teaching traditional healers to sterilize the razors they use for cutting therapeutic cicatrices in their patients. Since a lot of the healers' clients have "slim" disease—named after the wasting that accompanies the HIV plague sweeping our country—Jock is deserving of all honor.

He is a tall, well-built, intense man, a chain smoker, with dark skin and jet-black hair worn long. Once, Mother and I met him coming out of the cinema—it was *Shakespeare in Love*, with Gwyneth Paltrow and Joseph Fiennes—and Mother referred to him later as "that coloured guy." I pointed out that he came from a long and distinguished line of Afrikaners, but she sniffed and said: "Nevertheless, he's got a touch of the tarbrush."

Jock is in a pissed-off mood, as he'd just looked at a copy of a *Houston Chronicle* feature on "White Witch Doctors." He'd spent hours with the reporter, an eye-catching young woman with an accent out of a western movie, who'd wanted to include him as one of the new white shamans despite all his efforts to deflect her. "I tried to explain to her that there's a lot of this kind of stuff all of a sudden, and it's all too often just another way for whites to be *reeeal* Africans. As if we're not already." He's upset because none of his scholarly and gently dissuasive comments have made it into the news article, which is instead a gushing profile of a suburban woman in Durban whose cook turned out to be a "famous Sangoma" and now they happily sniff out witches together and cure people's stomach ailments and high blood pressure. "I bet her domestic has made a lot more money out of this lark than she ever did washing dishes and changing nappies."

"You've been complaining about the lack of funding lately," I tease, falling into our usual pattern of joshing with each other, as I sense this would be a bad time to ask him for a referral. I don't want to be put into the wannabe category too. "Maybe you could advertise courses for visiting students to train to be witch doctors. You know, after they've done the bungee-jumping and game park trips, give them a week in the bush gathering herbs, throwing the knucklebones. 'Amaze your friends and family. Consult the ancestors about the past and the future.' You could have a thriving cottage industry."

"As if I'm not in enough trouble with the ancestors already. Actually, I kind of like the idea. We can send those kids back to their parents in America with a nice set of initiation scars," Jock responds sardonically.

"How about those wash-off scars like the tattoos kids are wearing these days?"

Jock himself has a line of faint marks on his left wrist, though he refrained from the cheek scarification that many Sangomas favor. He gives me a piercing look. "You know, if you want a consult, I've got an old friend visiting me for a few days later this week. She's coming to talk to my classes on Thursday, and you could meet her then."

"Is she the real thing, then?" I ask, embarrassed at how transparent I must have appeared.

"MaRathebe is real, all right. She's one of the best divines I've ever met, if that's what you're asking. But I try to tell my students not to think of these guys as charlatans versus the genuine article. You won't get a grip on this stuff with Western binary thinking. I know some real charlatans who are also great witch doctors, guys who might give you stupid cures with poisonous enemas and who also know more about native herbs than anyone else around."

Jock is very big on African nondualist philosophy and contradictory thinking. He often argues with Tiny Shabalala, a lecturer in economics, who teases him that he's been just as taken in by romanticism as those he complains about, and that Africans are as rational as anyone. Tiny studied at the London School of Economics, has a fruity English voice in contrast with his dark skin and robust frame. Jock responds in kind, saying that for an economist to believe in rationality is a clear indicator of delusional thinking.

Come Thursday I meet Jock and MaRathebe at a nearby hole-in-the-wall run by a former Mozambiquan banker who makes the best piri-piri quail south of the equator. ("Be careful of the little *bawns*," he tells his customers as they voraciously take apart the tiny birds.) Ma is a short but big woman. She arrives wrapped in layers of bright blue cloth that flow in many directions; on her head is a mauve scarf, once the favorite color of the Princess Eugenie. "My goodness," I blurt out, "you look like a tropical flower garden."

MaRathebe cackles loudly, while Jock turns his head aside in disgust at my gaucheness. "This one I like too much," she says. She gazes at me with her small bright eyes, her mouth puckered in amusement. "If you were a bit fatter, I would marry you. You could be a big chief, but that white woman of yours made you go on a diet, hey? Stupid. What you need is an African woman."

"What about you, Ma?" I ask. I am drawn to this lady, whose ample flesh jiggles with each chuckle and who is so clearly confident of her enormous powers of sexual attraction.

"Hih-hih. I have so much boyfriends already. You would be *jealous*! You would just to stay home and cry while I am out having fun with all my boyfriends. No. You will find a nice woman soon, but you must keep your eyes open and forget about the Immorality Act. We are done with that rubbish!"

It is one of the most enjoyable meals I have had in a very long time. MaRathebe eats an enormous bowl of spicy lamb stew and makes fun of us for eating quail, which she calls chickens on a diet. She and Jock talk partly in Zulu—as far as I can make out, they are gossiping about their faith-healer colleagues. Then Jock finishes up and says he is going to his office to meet students. Ma orders filter coffee, which she dilutes with milk and five spoons of sugar, drinking the treacly mix with her eyes squeezed tightly shut in pleasure. Then she takes the small aluminium mini-percolator and empties the fine grounds onto the melamine table, stirring them with her spoon and looking at the results with interest. She does this for some time, humming to herself and swaying side to side, the joints of her wooden chair cracking threateningly beneath her.

"What advice do you have for me, Ma?"

"Oh, I already gave you *my* advice. Now you must be patient while I talk to *maKhosi*, the ancestors." She closes her eyes and hums again.

"Okay," she says. "Here is what you must do. There are bones of two men, they are not happy for you. They can forgive you for killing their bodies, because they were warriors. But just to leave their bones out in the bundu, *haaiyi*, that is bad. Those bones have been crying, crying. Even now their spirits are restless, complaining, and that's what you hear when you try to sleep."

"I thought the Namibian government had disinterred everybody, given the bodies to the families."

"Yesss. But what did *you* do? And how long were they lying there all jumbled up until the government came and got them?" She looks at me accusingly. "You can't rely on the government to do things for you, my son. You have to make amends yourself."

That is good counsel, for sure. I refrain from telling her what she already knows: that every white South African needs to hear that advice. "How can I do that now?" I ask.

"I am telling you. Okay. You must be giving me five hundred rands. And you must buy two white chickens—live, fat ones, not like those sparrows you were eating. Then I will come your side and we will make a feast for those guys."

I think of the delight with which my landlady, Mrs. Fogarty, a pinch-faced Englishwoman in her mid-forties, will greet the sight of me and MaRathebe slaughtering poultry in the back garden behind our flats, and I try to smile my enthusiasm. It is time to go, and I help MaRathebe into my little Volkswagen. Even with the passenger seat pushed back as far as it will go, she still spills over onto my side and each time I shift I bump her and she giggles. After I park, we walk slowly over to the building where Jock's office is.

"I will come next week this time. Jock will have to pick me up."

I tell her that he usually has office hours and tutorials at this time, but she makes a waving gesture as if shooing away a fly. Once in his office, we tell Jock about the agreement and, as she indicated he would, he accepts with equanimity that he will accompany her. "I am going to exorcise your friend," she says. She pronounces the word, exercise.

"Yes," Jock says dryly. "I'm sure he could do with it."

I say goodbye to Ma, feeling already a certain amount of relief. She gives me a warm hug, her *doekied* head coming just to my midriff, and tells me that I must not forget what she has said about how to cure my love troubles.

In the evening I phone Jock at home. We've gone out for beers a few times, but I've never called him after hours before. When he answers, I hear the clatter of dishes and a woman's high voice in the background—a girlfriend, I guess. "Hey, Sweetbread," he says cheerfully. "To what do I owe the pleasure? You're not getting cold feet, are you?"

No, I tell him. I'm just wondering where the hell one buys a pair of live white chickens in Johannesburg. He laughs at this, then gives me the phone number of a farmer friend who supplies some of the city's restaurants. "He's used to this kind of thing. Just tell him what you want. Of course, you could save some money by going downtown on Saturday and checking out the street vendors, but you'll probably get mugged and you'll definitely get cheated. It's pretty clear you wouldn't know a healthy chicken from a sick one, and these have to be healthy if you want the ceremony to work."

"What do you think of this . . . ummm, exercise?" I ask, hoping not to offend him.

"Well, Ma is very good. So if anyone can cure you, she can. You know, I had a verruca on my hand that none of the doctors could help me with. She gave me some mashed-up herbs mixed with vaseline and it was gone overnight. So I'm sure she can help you. And she told me she liked you; it's important to make a good impression with someone like her, hey."

Yes, I liked her too. And I am sleeping better, as if the bones can divine my good intentions. There's also a young woman at the university, a junior lecturer in African Languages, that I find myself talking to. She is daintily made, with ears like tiny, whorled shells and skin the color of Dutch chocolate. I'd met her a while ago, and she told me that her name, Thabile (pronounced *Tuh-bee-lay*) means Thankfulness. Her parents had been trying for a long time to have a baby, so they were extra thankful when she came along. Yes, I had noticed her before, but I had worried that my attention might be unwelcome. Now I find the courage to ask her if she will have dinner with me, or, better, we could go and hear Louis Mahlanga at the Bassline on Friday. She accepts, hesitates, then says: "I thought maybe you did not like me."

"Oh, sorry. I'm just a bit shy. I hope you will forgive me."

"Of course," she replies, smiling at me. "You are very polite. It is nice to meet a man who is not beating his chest all the time."

"I could beat my chest for you, if that would make you happy."

"No need just now," she says with a laugh. "We'll talk about it." She clasps the outside of my hand in saying goodbye, and I am awed by how soft the skin of her small palm is, how delicate the bones of her hand.

Wednesday morning I pick up the sacrificial fowl, two mid-sized cockerels. I meet Jock's farmer friend Henk outside the rear entrance of L'Épicerie, one of my favorite restaurants . . . a good sign for the quality of his product. He is a brawny, thickset fellow, his floppy bush hat too small for his large head, but his light blue eyes are clear and intelligent. He gives me a large wooden shipping case with holes in it, saying he doesn't want me to get into an accident because the roosters are flapping about in my car. He advises me to put the birds in the box just at bedtime, but let them wander around my flat in the meantime, and he also gives me a bagful of dried corn to feed them. The fowl flutter around hysterically when I release them in the apartment, but they soon settle down and wander around curiously. After a while, they act quite tame, as if this is the kind of domestic life they are used to. While I am eating dinner, the larger of the two birds hops onto the table and pecks at the slice of bread on my plate. "Shoo," I tell him. He gives me a skeptical look with his small bright red eye, then turns his head so the other eye can gaze at me quizzically too. I give up and let him share my dinner, feeling sorry for the part I will play in his fate.

The next day, Ma and Jock show up an hour later than I'd expected them. It is Jock's fault, and Ma complains about how he keeps "white people's time." You can never rely on him, she says. Jock gets his own digs in, telling me how they had had an argument in the foyer. The small lift obviously wouldn't hold the two of them and he had offered to walk up the stairs. Ma took umbrage at this and had insisted they both squeeze in. "Ja, I think I broke a couple of ribs," he grins. Then neither of them had been able to reach properly to pull the gate closed, and they'd had to get out again and rearrange themselves.

"This lady came out of her flat on the ground floor, and she just looked at me. Just looked!" Ma made her face as devoid of expression as possible, her eyes flat and hard. She guffawed merrily. "She doesn't say anything. Just give me that *look*. I want to say to her: *What is the matter with you? You have never seen a black person in your flats before?* Don't you know the president of this country, he is black now?"

"I think he's always been black," Jock says.

"Ah, *suka*!" She slaps him on the shoulder, then flops down on my armchair and fans herself. "You must get me something to drink, Paul. This mad Boer makes me tired."

I fix the three of us granadilla and sodas, and when I bring them in Jock has already caught one of the roosters and tied its feet with twine. The other cockerel has retreated to safety in the bathroom and is cowering in its box, occasionally poking its head out to see what's going on. Jock glides over swift as a mongoose and throws a towel over its head, then grabs it and binds its feet. With the towel covering its eyes, the bird stays calm and he carries it in and sits down with it on his lap. Ma sends me scurrying around to get a deep bowl (I can only find a casserole dish), a large towel, and some newspaper to cover the floor. I realize with some relief that we will not be performing the ceremony outside in full view of the neighbors, but I wonder how we will be able to kill chickens in my small flat without the place looking like a crime scene.

Ma asks me for a clean saucer, pours some herbs from a leather sack into it, and lights them with a butane lighter. The room fills with a sweet, not unpleasant smoke. She bids me take off my shirt and kneel before the casserole dish, then she squats opposite me and begins to murmur indecipherable words and sway from side to side. Her eyes roll upward and she talks faster and faster in a low murmurous rumble, then her arms extend with the jerky movements of the hypnotized and Jock holds out the first cockerel beneath her hands. She strokes its head gently, quietly murmuring, until the bird relaxes. Jock slips an open clasp knife into her hand and she swiftly beheads it. The headless creature jerks spasmodically, while Ma directs its neck downward so its crimson blood spurts into the bowl. After a minute or two, its juddering diminishes and Jock lays the corpse down on the folded towel. The second rooster is treated in the same manner. Ma utters some more unintelligible words and Jock motions me to lean forward. She grabs the first cockerel, dips its foot in the blood-filled bowl, and scratches me on both cheeks with its sharp claw, dips it again, and makes three horizontal scratches on my chest. She chews an herb that she has pulled out of a sachet nestled in her ample bosom, spits the wad into her hand, and rubs the mixture into the cuts on my face and chest. Then she seems to come slowly back to herself, looking around at us with a faint smile of bemusement on her face.

"Now comes the really hard part," Jock says.

"What's that?" I ask with some trepidation.

"We have to get Ma back to her feet. I'll take her left arm, you get the right."

We both lean to our task, with Ma giggling and doing her best to rise herself. With some exertion on all our parts, we get her to stand up again. She tells me that the bones are much happier now, but the dead men's relatives are still suffering and it would improve my position with the ancestors if I sent them a present, something for funeral expenses or school fees for their kids. It is the first time I think of the possibility that the men I killed would very likely have had children. I don't know the men's names, of course, but I determine to look into it, to send something to the school or medical center that serves the villages in the area. I give Ma an envelope with the five hundred rand in it, and we put the chickens' bodies and heads into a Pic 'n Pay bag for her to take home. Jock then leaves to bring the car around to the front. Ma and I sit in companionable silence while he is out, she with her eyes shut and a faint smile on her face. I think about what has just transpired and whether my feeling better is just an illusion. Still, I have a date with Thankfulness on Friday night, thanks to Ma's suggestion. I don't share her faith that miscegenation will solve my problems, but it is just nice to have a date with a pretty girl, someone who is soft-spoken and gentle-hearted and not annealed by years of being a madam, of ignoring the evils of colonialism. There is a ring at the intercom, and I buzz Jock in downstairs. I realize that his brief remaining absence gives me the opportunity to ask a few questions of my helpful prophet while she is still here.

"Ma," I venture. "Did you really speak to *my* ancestors when you were in that . . . umm . . . trance?"

"Sure. Your dad says hello." She gives an amused chortle, and I can't tell if she's joking or not. "He is still too much thinking about those *goggas*. But he is very caring for you."

I have not told her anything about my parents, so her words are eerie. They are also comforting; perhaps Father is happier now.

"And me?" I demand. "What does the future hold for me?"

A deep chuckle. "Everybody wants to know that, my son, though some just want to know the winner of the next July Handicap or the right numbers for the Lotto. That is not what the ancestors do. They can say who is jealous of you at work, who is trying to make trouble for you. Me? I can help to quiet down restless spirits when they get up to mischief. But that other business: you will just have to wait and see. You and everybody else."

Author's Afterword

The Persistence of Memory is a work of the imagination, and none of the characters are based on real persons, living or dead. My portrait of military life has more in common with such satires as *The Good Soldier Schweik* and *Catch-22* than it does with any actual battalion of the SADF.

The mostly secret war in Angola and Namibia did happen, however. As a proxy war between the Soviet bloc and the U.S., it deserves to be better known and understood in the United States. All told, around a million and a half people died in a conflict that was kept largely hidden from the public, and countless others bear emotional and physical scars from these events. I include here the many courageous South African soldiers who were misled into taking part in a futile and unnecessary war by cynical politicians. The indigenous inhabitants of Namibia and Angola bore the brunt of the suffering, and continue to be deeply affected to this day.

I wish to give here a very broad background to the war for Namibian independence, in which my fictional character, Paul Sweetbread, finds himself an unwitting participant:

Although Portuguese sailors landed in South-West Africa in the fifteenth century, it was one of the last parts of Africa to be colonized. The Germans established a colony there in 1884, expanding their territorial control over a vast area. (Present-day Namibia is some 318,000 square miles.) Even by the standards of the day, the colonial authorities of German South-West Africa were particularly brutal, massacring close to eighty percent of the Herero people and declaring much of the sizable territory to be a police zone. South Africa took over control of South-West Africa in the First World War, and was granted a League of Nations mandate over the territory, promising to "promote to the utmost the material and moral well-being and the social progress of the inhabitants of the territory."

South Africa sought to incorporate South-West Africa in 1945, but was turned down by the U.N. General Assembly, who declared that it should come under U.N. trusteeship with a view to eventual independence. South Africa continued to administer control over the area, and also to apply a number of Apartheid-era laws—including the Prohibition of Mixed Marriages Act—to South-West Africa. In 1960, the South-West African People's Organization became the leading opposition group under Sam Nujoma, who went into exile in Botswana to avoid arrest. Swapo's military wing, the People's Liberation Army of Namibia (PLAN), was formed in 1962 in response to crackdowns on the independence movement by the South African authorities. The first battles between the South African Defence Force and PLAN (Swapo) fighters occurred in 1966, and the conflict did not end until 1990, when Swapo won a majority in the country's first true general elections.

Namibia was to be affected by events in another part of the world in 1974, when young Portuguese officers, tired of being sent to fight in the Portuguese colonies of Mozambique and Angola, overthrew the dictatorship of Marcello Caetano. The new Portuguese government declared its intentions to withdraw from Angola by November 1975, and South Africa now found itself faced with the prospect of socialist governments in two more of its northern neighbors. A complex struggle, involving shifting alliances, now ensued between the strongest of the Angolan liberation groups, the Soviet-backed MPLA (People's Liberation Army), and two others. The MPLA defeated an attempt by one of these, FLEC, backed by France, to take over the oil fields at Cabinda. However, when it was clear that the MPLA would have power over most of oil- and mineral-rich Angola, the South African military, along with the CIA, entered into the skirmishes on the side of UNITA, led by Jonas Savimbi. (Ironically, the SADF had helped the Portuguese attack UNITA in previous years.) In thirty-three days beginning in October 1975, the SADF, UNITA, and the CIA pushed from a small enclave in southern Angola to just outside Luanda, the capital, where they were stopped by MPLA fighters assisted by a small number of East German and Cuban advisors. (Another liberation group, the FNLA, now backed by the U.S. and China, was also threatening Luanda). At this point, the U.S. Congress learned of America's unauthorized involvement and ordered it to stop—one South African veteran of the time told me that he knew they were in trouble when American fighter planes flew overhead, waggled their wings in greeting, and turned around again . . . a possibly apocryphal story, but there is no doubting that South African soldiers felt betrayed by the U.S., which had encouraged them to go into the conflict. Readers can find an excellent first-person account of this period in noted journalist Ryszard Kapuscinski's *Another Day of Life*. The MPLA requested help from the Soviet bloc, and Cuba immediately airlifted a large contingent of forces into Luanda, and the South African and UNITA forces were pushed back to southern Angola. The Cuban forces stayed in Angola for the ensuing fifteen years and—while estimates vary—may have come to number as many as fifty thousand troops.

Swapo's use of Angola as a base, and the presence of Cuban forces there, led to a greatly enlarged South African military presence in Namibia. This in spite of numerous calls by the U.N. in the late 1970s—notably U.N. Resolution 435—for the end to the "illegal occupation" of Namibia and the implementing of free elections. The SADF staged several very effective military operations and preemptive strikes against Swapo/MPLA forces in Angola, while seeking to keep these attacks secret from both the world and the South African public. These incursions culminated in the battle of Cuito Cuanavale in 1987, in which both sides suffered heavy losses and both sides claimed victory. Following talks between South Africa, Cuba, and Angola in 1988, the various combatants established guidelines for peace and elections under the supervision of the U.N. Ironically, some of the fiercest fighting during the entire low-level war took place over nine days in April 1989, when there was an official cease-fire and Namibia was ostensibly under the aegis of U.N. peacekeeping forces. As with most South African history, different sides have differing opinions as to who was at fault. What is clear, however, is that the SADF had intelligence about the movements of returning Swapo troops, still bearing their arms, and used supposedly disbanded forces to confront the homecoming guerrillas.

Readers may learn more about this period and about South African history through several excellent books, notably Leonard Thompson's *A History of South Africa*, and the *Reader's Digest Illustrated History of South Africa*. The five-volume report of the Truth and Reconciliation Commission provides an invaluable record of the accounts of those who lived through the worst of the Apartheid era, as does the TRC's Web site. Antjie Krog's remarkable *Country of My Skull* is must reading for anyone interested in the TRC. The full story of the Namibia/Angola conflict is yet to be told, but there has been considerable progress in recent years. Accounts by and about the SADF soldiers who fought in Angola and Namibia are beginning to emerge in books and on the Internet, notably from Sentinel Publications. Angola was to be Cuba's own Vietnam, and autobiographical histories and novels by Cuban veterans are also starting to appear. I understand that the Namibian government now has an effort under way to collect the oral histories of its own Swapo fighters. The Namibian government has, however, rejected any attempts to set up its own Truth Commission.

I have done my best to make this fictional work of my own devising bear some relation to the facts, although Paul Sweetbread is not intended to represent a typical SADF soldier of the time. South Africa's is a slippery and disputed history, and I apologize for any unintentional errors of fact in this novel.

Glossary

AASVÖEL—vulture

ASSEGAI—a short, stabbing spear possibly invented by Chaka.

BABBELAS—hangover.

BAKKIE—pickup truck.

BANTUSTAN—area designated by Apartheid government as African homeland.

BILTONG—dried meat, jerky.

BOEREVROU(E)—rural Afrikaans woman, farmer's wife.

BOEREWORS—literally, farmer's sausage.

'N BOER MAAK 'N PLAN—"A farmer makes a plan." Traditional saying that reflects Afrikaners' ingenuity in hard times.

BOESMAN—bushman, savage.

BOETIE—brother.

BORSELKOP—"brush-head." Person (usually Afrikaans) with cropped hair.

BOSBEFOK—driven crazy by being out in the bush too long.

BRAAI—barbecue.

BREDIE—traditional South African stew.

BUNDU—wild, open country; the middle of nowhere.

CASEVACCED—evacuation of injured person, from casualty evacuation.

DAGGA—marijuana, a particularly potent form going by the name of "Durban poison."

DASSIE—the rock hyrax, an animal resembling the prairie dog.

DHUKA—small general stores in Namibia and Angola.

DIE OUEN—the guys.

DIE TAAL—literally, "the language"; i.e., Afrikaans.

DOEK, DOEKIE—a scarf that covers the head, once a standard item of clothing for many African women.

DOMINEE—reverend (as term of address), church minister.

DONGA—a gulley, ravine.

DOOS—jerk (obscene).

DOP—alcoholic drinks.

DORP—small town.

EIE STOEP—"own porch," home.

FLOSSIE—military transport plane.

GAAN KAK—"Go to hell" (obscene).

GESUIP—drunk.

GET—(Hebrew) marriage annulment, divorce.

GOGGA—bug, insect (of Nama—bushman—origin).

IMPIMPI—police informer, sellout (Africanized from "pimp").

INDUNA—captain, headman (Zulu). Used condescendingly for foreman of work crews as well.

JOL—party, have fun.

KAFFIR—derogatory term for black, nigger.

KAFFIRBOETIE—literally, "kaffir brother." Pejorative term equivalent to "nigger-lover."

KAFFIR BOOM—flowering tree (*Erythrina caffra*).

KLAAR—clear, done with.

KLAAR UIT—muster out of army.

KLEINTJIE—little one.

Klipdrift, Klippies—popular brandy.

KOMBI—minivan (e.g., V.W. van).

KOPJE (KOPPIE)—hill, peak.

KORTBROEK—literally, "short pants." Used as a noun for Afrikaner males, who stereotypically wear bush shorts.

KRAAL—African homestead, animal enclosure.

KREG—(Yiddish) complain.

LEKKER—great, delicious, excellent.

LEKKER BLY—stay well, take care (as in goodbye).

MAAK GOU—hurry up.

MEID— black or coloured woman (derogatory).

MEISIE—young woman.

MENEER—Mr., sir.

MEVROU—madam, mistress.

MIELIE—maize, African corn.

MOFFIES—derogatory term for homosexuals. Originally, *moffies* were men in the mines who dressed up as women for the entertainment of the all-male barracks.

MOHEL—(Yiddish) person who performs ritual circumcision.

MÔRE IS NOG 'N DAG—literally, "Tomorrow is another day." The Afrikaans version of *mañana.*

MOSSIE—sparrow.

MUTI—African medicines, herbs (Zulu, *umuthi*).

MY BROER—my brother (often a self-mocking or camp expression).

OU—guy (noun), old (adjective).

OU MANNE— veteran, seasoned soldier (army slang).

OUPA—grandfather.

OUSIE—term used by whites for an African woman, intended to be polite.

PANGA—machete.

PAP—(pronounced "pup") maize-meal porridge, a staple food.

PASOP!—watch out, be careful.

PIESANG—banana.

PIKKIE—kid, youngster (from piccaninny, but less derogatory).

PLAASJAPIE—farmboy (derogatory).

POEG-EYED—drunk (Anglicized misrendering of Malay *poegaai*).

POENSKOP—baldie.

POES—obscene word for a woman, cunt.

PONDOKKIE—hut.

POTJIEKOS—food cooked in iron pots over a fire, the way the Voortrekkers did.

PREDIKANT—Dutch Reformed Church minister.

ROCK—nickname for Afrikaners.

ROOMYS—ice cream.

SARMIE—sandwich.

SCHTUMM—(Yiddish) stubbornly mute.

SJAMBOK—rhino-hide whip, to whip.

SKRIK—fright.

SLASTO—slate and stone mix, originally trade name.

SMOUS—itinerant peddler.

SOUTIE, SOUTPIEL—English-speaking South African (obscene).

STEENBRAS—popular South African line fish, a bream.

STERK OUTJIE—strong man, tough guy.

STOEP—veranda (has emotional resonance of home for Afrikaners).

STOEPDORP—small town (somewhat derogatory).

STOMPIE—cigarette stub, short person (derogatory).

STRANDLOPER—literally, "beach walker." Beachcomber, vagrant. Also, a now extinct group of San bushmen from the coast of South-West Africa.

SUKA!—get lost, go away.

TACKIES—sneakers, tennis shoes.

TANNIES, TANTES—aunties.

TREKBOER—Afrikaner who went on the Great Trek.

TREYF—(Yiddish) nonkosher food.

TROEPIE—soldier.

TSOTSI—gangster, thief (from the habit of wearing zoot suits).

TSOTSITAAL—an idiolect from the townships, combining multiple languages and homegrown slang.

VAT JOU GOED EN TREK—Take your things and go.

VELDKOS—bush cuisine.

VERBASTERING IS VERBOTEN—miscegenation is illegal.

WEERMAG—army.

WEET JY?—you know?

ZOL—a thick, hand-rolled marijuana cigarette—usually a mix of *dagga* (pot) and tobacco.

Acknowledgments

I owe a debt of gratitude to the many veterans of the SADF who generously shared their experiences with me, and to the participants in the End Conscription Campaign—veterans and nonveterans alike—who struggled bravely to end the militarization of South Africa and who openly responded to my questions. To properly thank the friends who have supported me in my writing would take more pages than this novel, but I am thinking of you. Worth special mention is Michael Anderson, who continued to believe and encourage unstintingly. Howard Norman offered advice and encouragement at a crucial stage. Locally, I have been inspired by the independent-mindedness and kindness of Vermonters, with special mention of Joe Madison.

A portion of Book III appeared in slightly different form ("Pieces of Papa") in the online journal *Tarpaulin Sky* in Winter '03. I also wish to express my grateful thanks to the National Endowment for the Arts and to the Dorland Mountain Arts Colony for their support.

Boundless thanks are owed my family for their love of stories; to my mother, Liesel, for her courage, warmth, and wit; and to my in-laws, Polly and Alvin Schwartz, for their patient support and encouragement.

I have been remarkably fortunate in having Robert Weil as an editor, who has been lavish with praise and brilliant in his meticulous and ever-thoughtful criticism. Brendan Curry, Bob's *very* able assistant, and the staff at W. W. Norton have made the publishing process a rare pleasure. Faith Childs never fails to impress me with her insight, integrity, and advocacy.

Mega-thanks to my son, Brendan, for his humor, intelligence, and loving nature. And to Judy, for everything!

About the Author

Tony Eprile is the author of *Temporary Sojourner & Other South African Stories*, a *New York Times* Notable Book of the Year. He grew up in South Africa, where his father edited the first mass-circulation multiracial newspaper. Tony has received grants from the National Endowment for the Arts and the Ingram Merrill Foundation. He has taught writing and literature at Williams, Skidmore, Northwestern, and Wesleyan and is Writer-in-Residence at the New York State Summer Writers Institute. He lives in Bennington, Vermont, with his family.

THE PERSISTENCE OF MEMORY

Tony Eprile

READING GROUP GUIDE

A CONVERSATION WITH TONY EPRILE, AUTHOR OF THE PERSISTENCE OF MEMORY

The narrator of The Persistence of Memory *describes himself as having "a poisoned gift, a picture-perfect memory." What led you to choose a protagonist with a perfect memory, and how did this help you write about the complexities of South Africa?*

I can trace my narrative decision to a specific occasion. It was my first visit back to my birthplace after a prolonged absence, and I was continually struck by how white South Africans had recast their memories to fit in with a changing political climate. The year was 1990 and I was listening to my former upstairs neighbor wax nostalgically about the time my parents were arrested and she had sheltered my brother and me for several days. On the day the police simultaneously raided our apartment and the office where my father edited a black newspaper, my mother asked this neighbor to . . . drive us to school. (We each carried briefcases filled with my father's sensitive papers.) In the intervening years, this modest change in our neighbor's car-pool routine had grown into something nobler, her gesture of support for those in opposition to Apartheid.

The larger distortions of memory were evident everywhere. Take the former mixed-race area of Sophiatown, which had been razed to the ground and rebuilt as the Afrikaans suburb of Triomf, *Triumph.* Even the beautiful murals celebrating the people of Sophiatown had been whitewashed over, so white churchgoers would not be disturbed by images of the people they had displaced.

Shortly after this visit, I read *The Mind of a Mnemonist* by the Russian psychiatrist A. R. Luria, an account of a man tormented by a perfect memory. It got me thinking about the limitations of memory, the ways we distort our recollections, the difficulties of knowing what *really* happened. In a repressive society that constantly sought to impose its own mythology on the past, what would happen to someone who could not stop himself from remembering *everything*? And so my narrator was born.

But you put the book aside for ten years; why is that?

The main reason is that events in South Africa were moving a lot faster than my own imagination. Instead of the political crimes of the past being hidden or swept under the rug (as in Argentina, for example), throughout the nineties they were presented almost as a theatrical spectacle before the Truth and Reconciliation Commission, one of the most interesting and unusual attempts by a society to record the "truth" of the past. The Truth Commission has its detractors, but, overall, it was a remarkable and important social experiment. I felt I had to grapple with the Truth Commission in my own way within the novel, hence my protagonist, Paul Sweetbread's appearance before the TRC.

Do you have a perfect memory?

Not at all. But exiles tend to hold on to their memories very tenaciously, fixing a place, time, and people into memory the way you might "fix" a photograph. The people who stay wind up rearranging their memories, rather the way one might rearrange the furniture in a lived-in house and then think the bed was always in that corner, the picture always on the wall.

In the novel I try to explore different ways that we store—and, invariably, distort—our memories: photography, film, tape-recording, the "official histories," the stories and jokes we tell, the very words we use. Our words and expressions are another form of collective memory—in fact, every month or so friends will send me nostalgic lists of South African slang that are doing the rounds of the Internet. Food, too, is another form of memory that is an important element in the story I tell.

The Persistence of Memory *is written in a very intimate, first-person voice. Is the novel autobiographical?*

The short answer is: no. I was fortunate in having a family who were strongly anti-Apartheid, and my parents constantly pointed out the inequities of the racially stratified society we lived in. My father edited a black newspaper—his friends and colleagues included some of the top black editors and reporters, and Nelson Mandela even showed up at our home when he was in hiding from the police. So, I had the usual privileges associated with being a white South African but also the unusual privilege of seeing the other side at an early age. I wanted to explore what it was like for an ordinary, decent South African Jew who grew up without that background, who had to figure out what was wrong with his society for himself, his only tools being memory and the willingness to pay attention. I also wanted to show that it is impossible to live in a position of privilege in an oppressive society without becoming implicated yourself.

How is your novel different from other post-Apartheid novels?

Americans are most familiar with the works of J. M. Coetzee and Nadine Gordimer, two writers I admire tremendously and whose works have influenced me, but whose literary approaches are different from mine. My real influences, though, are the eastern European writers—Hasek, the author of *The Good Soldier Schweik*, and the humorous side of Kafka. (Some readers have likened *Persistence* to Gunter Grass's *The Tin Drum*, a comic novel about dark and serious subjects.) I've tried to respond to Apartheid with satirical humor—to undercut the pieties of racism by showing its absurdities.

Also, the formative experience for men of my generation and a little younger was the secret war in Angola and the occupation of Namibia. There have been a fair number of books on the topic in South Africa, but mine is the first novel dealing with this issue to appear on this side of the Atlantic. The story of soldiers trying to act as peacekeepers while being resented as occupiers is all too timely, given the current situation in Iraq.

It was eerie writing the Namibia scenes while the United States was gearing up to invade Iraq. Here, my character was suffering heat, extreme cold at night, attacks by insects, and the hostility of the local population of an arid country. When South Africa invaded Angola in 1974 (with U.S. help), the army was predicting victory in less than two weeks. The conflict continued for fifteen years and hugely damaged all the countries involved, which should certainly give us something to think about today.

DISCUSSION QUESTIONS

1. Compare the way food is associated with recollection and reflection in *The Persistence of Memory* to other books and movies that have used similar techniques, such as *Like Water for Chocolate*. It is clear that Paul is culturally sensitive when it comes to his choice of cuisines, but does his culinary diversity mean he is unprejudiced? How does Paul interact with nonwhite South Africans on a social and economic level?

2. Discuss the effects of Paul's sudden suspension of memory after witnessing the Owamboland atrocities. Do you begin to lose faith in the accuracy of Paul's memory in the wake of this gap in the narrative, or is our faith in his powers of photographic recall actually strengthened by these events?

3. Of all the books and movies about Apartheid and South Africa, *The Persistence of Memory* is unabashedly written from the point of view of a white man of British descent. Compare this to Richard Attenborough's *Cry Freedom*, in which the story of anti-Apartheid agitator Steve Biko (played by Denzel Washington) is told through the lens of a white journalist (played by Kevin Kline). What does it mean in this book to have the "memory" of South Africa come from a British source, rather than a white Afrikaner or a black South African?

4. How does Paul cope with the many ethnicities (white, British, Jewish) to which he belongs? How does his religion complicate his experience and our interpretation of the book?

5. How does the literary technique of memoir writing form our perception of Paul and his fellow characters? How does Eprile's narrator compare to other famous fictional memoirists such as Lionel

Essrog, the detective afflicted with Tourette's syndrome in Jonathan Lethem's *Motherless Brooklyn*, or Salman Rushdie's protagonist in *Midnight's Children*?

6. Even though Apartheid only ended in the early 1990s, this novel describes a world that seems ages apart from our own. Did the book explain the pressures and motivations at that time for white people to accept Apartheid?

7. Looking back on Paul's testimony before the Truth and Reconciliation Commission, discuss the implications of a perfect memory for disciplines that require documented evidence, such as history and court proceedings. In what way does personal perception shape what we consider to be the truth? Could the testimony of a perfect memory be considered an accurate historical record?

8. Can we read anything into Paul's close relationship with his mother and her two marriages? Is it symbolic that Paul's father was an exterminator?

9. Discuss the death of the father and its impact on Paul. The details of the scene are surprisingly vague given Paul's remarkable memory, and they stand in stark contrast to the gruesome details of Lyddie's massacre in Owamboland. Was his father's death a suicide? What role did the father's affair with Corinthia, the maid, play in his death and Paul's memories of the event?

10. How does anti-Semitism enter into the story? How does Paul handle anti-Jewish sentiment? Is he discriminated against because of his faith?

11. Paul begins the remembrance of his father by harking back to his grandfather. In what sense is Paul's character defined by the memory of his family?

12. Do you think Major Lyddie and Paul will have any further interaction? How do you think they might react to one another if they were to meet by chance outside of the Truth and Reconciliation Commission's chambers?

13. How do you respond to Paul's conclusions about the state of South Africa at the end of the book? Do you think Paul has made an accurate assessment of the political situation?

[illegible]

[illegible]

[illegible]

[illegible]

[illegible]

[illegible]

[illegible]

[illegible]

[illegible]

[illegible]

[illegible]